The
Kafir
Project

LEE BURVINE

PRAISE FOR THE KAFIR PROJECT

"A thrilling roller coaster ride. Fast paced and riveting. I couldn't put it down."
Lawrence Krauss—award winning astrophysicist, and author of *A Universe From Nothing*

"Grips you from the first page ... seamlessly intertwines sci-fi, applied physics, and a healthy dose of archaeology."
Natalia Reagan—anthropologist, writer, TV animal expert (National Geographic Channel)

"A compelling read that weds scientific accuracy with an anti-scriptural plot."
Peter Boghossian—philosopher and author of *Street Epistemology*

"With strong male and female characters. Everything a nerdy faithless feminist could want."
Karen L. Garst—author of *Women Beyond Belief: Discovering Life without Religion*

"Burvine gives the world a new kind of hero, an intelligent science communicator in the mold of a Richard Dawkins or Neil deGrasse Tyson."
Andrew L. Seidel—Constitutional and civil rights attorney for the Freedom From Religion Foundation

"Blends the breakneck pace of the best page-turning mysteries with genuine religious history."
Emery Emery—film editor (Aristocrats), and host of the award winning podcast *Ardent Atheist*

"Historians and scientists have long known the Abrahamic religions are fiction. Who would have thought those findings could be turned into such an entertaining science fiction thriller?"
Dan Barker—author of *GOD: The Most Unpleasant Character in All Fiction*

"Endless fun."
Alexander Rosenberg—philosopher, novelist, and author of *The Girl from Krakow*

"Of note, Burvine forges two villains who are truly frightening in their drive, competence, and unpredictability. An impressive first novel."
Ross Blocher—Co-host of the popular podcast *Oh no, Ross and Carrie!*

Author's Note

I have made some leaps of imagination with the physics, as required by the narrative. I apologize to those scientists whose work I've mangled for the sake of story.

The archaeological research and textual criticism referenced in The Kafir Project are real and based on peer reviewed science. I invite skeptical readers to explore further for themselves.

Nullius in verba.

Lee Burvine
February 2016

DEDICATED TO

Asif Mohiuddin, Ahmed Rajib Haider, Sunnyur Rahaman, Shafiul Islam, Avijit Roy, Oyasiqur Rhaman, Ananta Bijoy Das, Niloy Neel, Faisal Abedin Deepan

The truth cannot be silenced with steel.

And to M.T.L. For all the times you saved my life and for all the ways you make it worth saving.

Foreword
by
Lawrence M. Krauss

I have to admit that when Lee Burvine came up to me after a lecture I gave in Pasadena and asked if I would look at his book, *The Kafir Project*, I agreed to do that expecting to glance at it later and send a polite note encouraging him to keep working. Then, a day after the meeting, he sent me an electronic copy of the book and it got buried in my inbox. A few weeks later I received a hard copy, but I departed almost immediately on a trip and left it in my office. Two months later he kindly asked me if I might write a blurb for the book, and I told him I would try to do that in the coming weeks.

Unfortunately I was close to finishing my new book, putting everything aside to complete it including outside travel and all other commitments. And once again Lee's book got short shrift. Showing remarkable patience, two months after that Lee wrote to ask if I might consider composing a foreword for the book, and took time to describe its contents.

By this point my new book was done, and I had time to respond to a backlog of requests. Something in Lee's description of his book struck a chord. I finally managed to download a copy of the draft onto my computer and started reading it on a plane. The problem then became that I couldn't put it down (because I had other pressing work to do before landing). In my spare time the next week I would open my computer and read. Eventually I wrote back to communicate with Lee with some thoughts about the book, in particular the main character, Gevin Rees, and the way he interacted with other scientists. Lee responded with thanks and asked for additional suggestions in order to make these interactions more realistic. It was particularly embarrassing when he then informed me that I had served as one of the models for that character.

Although flattered, I was initially skeptical about getting involved in contributing to what might be called science fiction, because I have a kind of love-hate relationship with sci-fi books. Clearly I have enjoyed the genre, but ever since *The Physics of Star Trek* I have been called on to comment on almost every new major sci-fi book or movie. And in fact while I read a lot of sci-fi as a young person, I quickly found as I got older that actual science interested me far more. In addition, most science fiction requires one to suspend disbelief, and the more one knows about science, the more suspension is required.

Ultimately what makes such suspension possible is not the plausibility of the imagined science, or lack thereof, it is the quality of the story. As a famous sci-fi writer once told me when we were on a TV panel together, the operative word in science fiction is not science, but *fiction*. A good story allows one to forgive the speculative or even the impossible science that one might encounter in the story, either because one wants to find out what is going to happen next, or because the characters are particularly gripping. This latter aspect is what usually grates on me the strongest in sci-fi, because the representation of scientists and their interactions with one another is often stereotypical or stilted. Too often they simply don't sound like the people I have worked with throughout my professional career.

Happily, reading the Kafir Project I had no problem suspending any disbelief. The story is fast paced and riveting with unexpected plot twists at every turn. The characters are likable and believable—even the scientists and engineers! And the science touches on subjects, like quantum computing, which while very speculative nevertheless build on legitimate, current research.

But the most fascinating thing about this exciting story is the premise on which it is based. Anyone who has read even lightly about the history of the world's religions knows that the sacred books, as usually represented, are essentially fraudulent. The New Testament, written by various authors at best decades after any actual events took place, helped to deify someone who at the time made no such claims. The Qur'an is highly derivative of earlier myths, and Mohammed never visited a Mosque in Jerusalem on a winged horse because (for one thing) there were no Mosques there at the time. And the Old Testament refers to the use of camels in a period when camels had not yet been domesticated in that region of the world. All of this, of course, is independent of the numerous miracles described in all three books which undoubtedly never happened.

While modern scholarship has already largely dispensed with the myths on which all three of the world's major religions are based, wouldn't it be nice to have more direct evidence contradicting them? Of course, I suspect that even if such evidence did exist, the guardians of theology would find ways for the doctrines based on the myths to persevere. Too much money and power rides on the institutions created to propagate them.

Ah, but *The Kafir Project* is a work of fiction, and in the fictional world we can sometimes live out our fantasies. While I would certainly not relish living through any of Gevin Rees's experiences in the book, it was a thrilling roller coaster ride to read them. For those of you who just bought a ticket for the ride, enjoy the trip, and I hope you come out the other end thinking a little differently about the real world.

Lawrence M. Krauss, 2016

The Qur'an which We sent down to you is the fountainhead of divine knowledge and the chief source of divine information. It elucidates every aspect of every thought and it is a guide into all truth.
— Surah An-Nahl 16:89

"I am afraid that the schools will prove the very gates of hell, unless they diligently labor in explaining the Holy Scriptures and engraving them in the hearts of the youth."
— Martin Luther

"Science is what we have learned about how to keep from fooling ourselves."
— Richard Feynman

CHAPTER 1

THE FACE TO face meeting came as a huge surprise to Gevin Rees. To begin with, Edward Fischer was notoriously reclusive. The world's most celebrated physicist never granted personal interviews to a science communicator like Rees, let alone asked for one.

Additionally, he was dead.

Or he was supposed to be anyway. Rees leaned into the salt mist blowing cold off San Francisco Bay and watched as Fischer—looking very much alive in dark sunglasses and a red and gold '49ers hoodie—continued to scour the waterfront.

"Are we expecting someone else?" Rees asked.

"Our muscle."

"Muscle?"

"Yes, but we can't wait any longer. Gevin, you're in serious danger. You weren't directly involved in the research, so I wasn't as discreet with your identity as I was with the others. That was a mistake."

"Others? Wait, what kind of danger?"

"You didn't tell anyone you were coming out here to meet me?"

"No. I did exactly as you asked." Rees was trying his best to look calm. Given how he really felt, that amounted to lying with his face. "Can you just tell me what the ... what's going on here, please? Everyone thinks you died in the explosion at Fermilab. They're saying they found you. Pieces of you."

"And that's good. I want them to believe they succeeded in killing me. They think they've destroyed all my data too, but it's still right here in my DNA. Oddly enough we owe that one to church. Herodotus will have it all soon if not already. Five hundred exabytes. He'll be contacting you."

"Herodotus?"

"An alias. For his protection. Another man we're calling Anaximander is bringing the artifacts. The science I'm entrusting to you." Fischer dug into a beaten up leather pouch he had slung over one shoulder and mumbled to himself. "It's all coming together. The end of their authority."

Artifacts? Jesus, he's lost his mind. Rees wondered if the shock of the explosion had thrown the man into some kind of psychotic episode. By reputation he wasn't all that mentally stable to begin with.

At thirty-three, Fischer was ten years younger than Rees. But right now, shaky and slump-shouldered, he actually looked the older of the two men.

He began to pull a notebook of some kind out of the pouch, but stopped in mid-motion. He was looking over Rees's right shoulder, eyes tracking something back there.

Rees turned and looked too.

A middle-aged Japanese couple—tourists, judging by the guidebook they were consulting—strolled close by. Apart from them, this stretch of Fisherman's Wharf near Pier 35 was mostly deserted. Swept clear by dark skies and the imminent threat of a chilling December rainstorm.

Behind the two tourists, a white van pulled up to the curb nearby and stopped.

As Rees turned back toward Fischer, the scientist jerked the pouch off his shoulder. "No! They can't have it." He heaved it over a nearby railing, into the bay. Then he turned back to Rees. "Run!"

Before Rees could even move, he heard a loud *pop*. Fischer dropped in place like someone had just flipped off his master power switch.

A man in sunglasses and billed cap, wearing a Jimmy Buffett T-shirt, stood outside the van now, maybe a hundred feet away. He held a gun in front of him in a two-handed grip. A fat, black cylinder stuck out from the end of the barrel.

Rees tried to run and couldn't. His feet seemed bolted to the walkway.

The two Japanese tourists didn't have the same problem, apparently. They turned and fled up the waterfront.

The gun popped again. Once, twice.

As Rees watched, the man and woman both dropped. The man lay there quietly. The woman screamed as she tried to crawl away.

A third shot silenced her.

Rees, meanwhile, had finally come unstuck.

Survival instinct kicked in and the rest was automatic. Without looking back he took a single long step and launched himself headfirst over the railing.

Another *pop* behind him.

Gray sky and green water rotated, trading places while he tumbled.

Cold shock as he plunged into the bay. The taste of salt water in his mouth.

Rees reopened his eyes underwater, fighting the sting after shutting them reflexively. Disoriented, twisting this way and that, he hunted for the surface, having already formed the intention to swim the hell away from it.

There...

He spotted the green glow of daylight filtering through the murky waters. Above and below suddenly fell into place again in this weightless and featureless expanse.

Making his best guess, Rees swam downward and in the direction that he fervently hoped would take him back under the walkway. He couldn't see much farther than the tips of his fingers, though. For all he knew he would be forced to resurface in full view of the gunman.

He swam using breaststroke and frog kick. On and on. The green emptiness all around killed any sense of forward progress. His lungs felt about to burst.

This had to be too far. If he were going the right way, he'd have reached—

Something materialized out of the haze in front of him. A pylon encrusted with barnacles and marine algae.

His lungs burned as he let himself float upward alongside it. It looked dark above him, so he was coming up under some kind of structure, thank God.

Rees broke the surface, purged his lungs explosively, gulped briny air, and dove right back down. He held his breath as long as he could, and then floated up again for another quick lungful of air.

He repeated this process maybe twenty times.

Eventually, Rees reasoned that if the man with the gun were coming for him, he would probably have been discovered by now. The next time he came up for air, he stayed on the surface and looked around.

He was under the walkway from which he'd jumped. No sign of the shooter.

After another five minutes or so of waiting, he decided to risk a move. The situation merited an abundance of caution, so he planned to swim from pylon to pylon, staying under the walkway wherever possible, and to head for Pier 39. There was a marina over there. And people. He could call for help.

Rees had just started out when his hand bumped something floating half-submerged in the water.

Fischer's leather pouch.

He pulled the strap over his shoulder and began to swim.

Making good on its threat, the sky finally let loose torrents of frigid rain. The splashes of thousands of heavy drops hissed loudly around him as Rees slogged toward Pier 39 and that marina. The swim seemed to take forever.

When they pulled him from the water, his teeth chattered so violently he couldn't make himself understood.

Finally, he managed to get out two words.

Police and *murder.*

CHAPTER 2

"SOMETIMES REGULAR PEOPLE look a lot like famous people," the officer whose nametag identified him as Honeycutt explained. "We have an ID kit that works on exactly that principle. Some guy's got Brad Pitt's eyes, John Travolta's chin, or what have you."

Within minutes of Rees being hauled out of the bay, Honeycutt and his partner had arrived at the marina in a patrol car, siren wailing and lights flashing. A rescue vehicle followed another minute later, repeating the noisy show.

"No, it wasn't a lookalike," Rees said. "Okay? Edward Fischer asked me to meet him here. I flew out here to meet him. He said someone was trying to kill him. He wanted them to *think* he was dead. But he isn't. I mean, he may be now, but..."

It sounded insane even to Rees. And that was without the bit about the ancient Greek code names he'd intentionally left out. Nevertheless, the officers called it in. From what he could make out, a police unit was dispatched to the scene near Pier 35.

Honeycutt rode in the back of the ambulance with him for the short trip to San Francisco General.

Hospital staff in the ER stripped off Rees's wet clothes and buried him under layers of warm blankets.

Shortly after that, Officer Honeycutt took the full report. Lanky and bug-eyed, Honeycutt actually looked a lot like a young Christopher Walken—though Rees certainly wasn't going to mention it.

"So you got a phone call last night from Edward Fischer?" Honeycutt asked.

"He called me in New York."

"This is after he was killed in the explosion?"

"Yes. No. Obviously he hadn't been killed. He wanted me to meet him here in San Francisco. And no, he didn't say why. Just that no one could know. I grabbed the first flight out of La Guardia this morning."

"And were you friends? Had you worked together?"

"No. We'd spoken before, just once. I'm a science communicator."

"Uh huh. And what is that exactly?"

"Well, you've heard of Carl Sagan, Neil deGrasse Tyson? I'm basically in the same line of business."

Honeycutt jabbed a finger at Rees. "Ah, yeah. On TV, right?"

This was good. At least the officer might be less inclined to think he was just some random lunatic. "You recognize me now."

Honeycutt shook his head. "No, sorry. I've seen those other two guys."

"Oh. Anyway, the point is that's why Fischer wanted to speak with me. There was some science he needed to make clear to the public, to non-scientists. Something that he was working on."

"Right, okay." Honeycutt wrote something in a spiral notepad.

In Rees's imagination the officer was drawing a caricature of him in a straightjacket, running away while men in white suits with giant butterfly nets chased after him.

Honeycutt asked for a description of the gunman. Rees couldn't give him much. Only that the shooter had been a white male of average height and weight, who might have had blond hair. He apologized for not being able to offer more.

"No, that's good. It's a good start." Honeycutt put away his pad and pen, and excused himself to check in with his superior.

Rees lay back under the mound of blankets in the busy ER, amid the beeps and pings of medical monitors, and the sharp smell of disinfectant. Pins and needles sensations pricked his hands and feet as the restored blood flow woke up the peripheral nerves there.

He closed his eyes and tried to put it all together.

Six months ago, when he got that first call from Edward Fischer, he thought a colleague was pranking him. The famous physicist's Brooklyn accent and staccato cadence were easy enough to imitate. Rees humored the caller, working in a few wisecracks about Fischer's well-known eccentricity, which was said to border on outright insanity.

When he realized it really *was* the great scientist on the phone, he felt simultaneously thrilled and mortified. "Dr. Fischer, I'm so sorry. I really thought someone was pulling my leg."

"Not to worry. It was a reasonable hypothesis. Also, I'm well aware people think I'm half-crazy. They're right. It's fortunate for me the other half of my mind functions pretty well."

Fischer informed Rees that his current research, when completed, would be *impactful*—as he put it. He wanted to know if he could call on Rees when the time came to help make it all more comprehensible to the general public.

"Yes, of course," Rees told him. "That's what I do, and I'd be honored. But I have to ask—when did *you* become concerned with what the public understands?"

The popular press loved to compare Fischer to Albert Einstein. In temperament, however, Fischer was more like the solitary and obsessive young Isaac Newton. He made Rees, who also tended to keep people at a distance, look positively gregarious.

Fischer replied, "I'm concerned with the public's understanding because their confidence in the accuracy of this work affects its larger purpose. Beyond that, I can't say anything right now."

Rees wondered if perhaps all this was about some breakthrough in climate change modeling. The credibility of science and the course of public policy did intersect there. But before he could say anything, Fischer spoke again.

"Gevin, I understand you're not a religious man."

"I ... no, not in the traditional sense.

"You were raised Mormon, though."

Where the hell did that come from? Rees knew the information was out there on the internet. But it was hard to picture the twenty-first century's most famous genius seated at his desk, Googling your name.

"Yes, I was a Mormon," Rees said. "Can I—"

"How did you lose your faith?"

And it gets even weirder. "Okay. Well, as you yourself are fond of saying, the theory didn't fit the evidence. Israelites in the Americas. The 'reformed Egyptian' and the Anthon transcript. It just doesn't stand up to scientific scrutiny."

"And did it stop there?"

Rees wasn't sure exactly what Fischer meant, but the conversation was making him increasingly uncomfortable. "Can I ask what all this has to do with the work you want me to help popularize?"

"Thank you for your time, Dr. Rees."

Fischer disconnected then without even giving him a chance to say goodbye. Was he offended by something Rees had just said? The whole call had been exceedingly strange. He remembered it had left him wondering for days whether there was something he missed.

He opened his eyes at the sound of approaching footsteps in the ER.

Officer Honeycutt was returning. Something in his demeanor had shifted. It was subtle, but Rees picked up on it right away.

Honeycutt reached Rees's bedside and stood looking down at him, eyes probing. "Sir, are you currently under the care of any physician or institution we should notify?"

Tactfully put, but the meaning was clear enough. Rees sat up in the hospital bed. "I know how crazy this sounds. But one of those poor people back by Pier 35 really is Edward Fischer. *The* Edward Fischer. Was anybody still alive there?"

Honeycutt paused a moment. "I just spoke with my supervisor, sir. The units that responded to your report didn't find anything at that location."

"What do you mean, 'anything'? No bodies?"

"No bodies. No blood. No bullet holes or shell casings. On the chance that you may have misremembered or been confused about which part of the wharf you ... jumped from, officers checked the nearby piers. Nothing there either."

The rainstorm.

It had poured down buckets as Rees swam for the marina. The rain must have washed away any blood. As for bodies and shell casings, well, obviously the gunman didn't want to leave any evidence behind. And apparently he did not.

"So what now?" Rees asked. "Someone killed three people today. And tried to kill me too. Dr. Fischer said I was in danger. And that gunman is still out there."

Officer Honeycutt nodded along, as if he agreed completely. "What we'll do, sir, is we'll file a suspicious incident report. My supervisor will be looking into this thoroughly."

"A suspicious incident report?"

"Yes, sir. That's really about all we can do at this point. Would you like us to contact your family?"

"No, thank you."

Officer Honeycutt finished by asking if Rees was staying in town and if so where? Rees gave him the name of the hotel Fischer had instructed him to use. He was too tired and mixed up to attempt to fly back to New York right now anyway.

Honeycutt produced a business card and handed it to Rees. "You can reach me at this number if you have any questions."

Rees read the card and looked up again. "I'm not crazy, Officer Honeycutt."

"I didn't say you were, sir."

"I know how this sounds. If I were you, I don't guess I'd buy it either. But just ... please. Just take this seriously. Because something very strange and terrible has happened here. And someone needs to get to the bottom of it."

Honeycutt nodded with a solemn expression. "We'll do everything we can, sir."

And that was it. Officer Honeycutt left.

Rees looked around at the controlled chaos of the ER.

Nearby, hospital staff cut the bloody clothes off the victim of a car accident and prepped her for emergency surgery. It brought back an unwelcome memory from Rees's teens, images of his late sister. He felt a pang of sadness mixed with resentment, and turned away.

The room was buzzing with life and death crises. And as was the case with many big city ER's, the resources here appeared to be strained to their limits. If someone walked in off the street, claiming to suffer from a severe allergy to leprechauns, not a lot of staff time and energy would be assigned to him.

The San Francisco Police Department was in exactly the same boat. Rees didn't think they were really going to investigate the shooting of a man who had already died the day before.

The two Japanese tourists, the only other eyewitnesses, had to be dead now too. If they were foreign nationals here on vacation, it could be days or maybe even weeks before the SFPD received any formal inquiries regarding their disappearances. Would someone then connect two missing tourists back to Rees's "suspicious incident" report? He didn't know, but it didn't seem very promising.

You're in serious danger, Fischer had told him.

Three thousand miles away from home, in a city where he knew virtually no one except a colleague or two he might see at a scientific conference, he felt completely alone. Ordinarily, that was a condition Rees immensely enjoyed, even cultivated.

Today, he would happily make an exception.

He lay back down in the bed and tried to think productively. Somebody wanted him dead. It might help to know more precisely...

Why?

He needed to plan his next move. But it was no use theorizing without any real data to work with. Somehow, on his own, he would just have to generate it.

How he'd do that, he didn't have a clue.

An orderly appeared then, carrying Rees's wet clothes in a clear plastic sack. And something else.

Fischer's waterlogged leather pouch.

CHAPTER 3

TERRY SABEL DIDN'T have to wait long to move the bodies. Night fell early in Northern California this time of year. Even earlier than usual with the day's overcast sky.

Not that Sabel minded waiting. He didn't mind anything, really. It was part of his special talent.

You gotta find your special talent, and when you do, that's what you do. And nothing else. That's what Sabel's old man always said.

He piloted the rented boat on a heading due west. The Point Bonita lighthouse beacon drifted back lazily on the starboard side, as a chill wind tousled his light blond hair.

Sabel thought about his own special talent. It had taken him thirty three years and four tours of duty to find and fully engage it. But he had. Just a matter of applying his unique assets where they produced the most results.

He learned that you got some leverage when you could do things other people can't. Turns out you got even more when you could do things other people *won't*.

The boat's engines thrummed steadily as the Golden Gate Bridge and the lights of San Francisco receded behind him. The smell of diesel smoke mixed in with the living scent of the sea brought back pleasant memories. Fishing in the Gulf of Mexico with his father.

Sabel's old man was a shrimper with a small, two-man operation out of Carrabelle, a pissant town in the Florida panhandle. When Sabel was old enough, he started helping out with the family business. By the time he was seventeen, he'd learned all there was to know about the ship itself and the fishing end of the whole deal. He replaced the second crew member permanently.

Sabel was out at sea with his old man on the day he died.

They got caught in a furious rain squall. His father was out on deck, hauling the nets when he lost his footing and fell overboard.

Sabel grabbed a life preserver and ran to the rail.

His father looked up and spotted him there. "Terry. Throw it!"

That's when it happened.

Sabel's father was a violent drunk. And though he hit his son pretty regularly after getting sauced, the old man saved the real beatings for Sabel's mother. He wasn't mad at his father for any of that stuff—at least he didn't think so. He wasn't sure what anger felt like, but he knew what it looked like and he'd never behaved that way.

But Sabel's father had got to be a real problem for their family and its little shrimping business. His drinking reached the point where he missed good fishing days. The beatings were getting worse too. Sabel's mother feared for her life, and with good reason.

And Sabel didn't understand the business end of shrimping at all. That was entirely her thing. For that reason, he needed her to stay well and functioning.

What they both didn't require any longer was Sabel's alcoholic dad.

As his father sputtered and thrashed in the rough seas, Sabel stopped there at the rail and set the life preserver down on the deck.

"What are you doing, Terry? Throw me the damn thing!"

The rain hammered down thick and heavy—a gray curtain, cutting the two of them off from the eyes of the world.

Sabel could barely even see his dad out there in the water. But it looked like he'd managed to catch hold of a section of the net. Yes, he was pulling himself in toward the boat now.

Sabel ran aft, found what he needed, and returned to the rail.

By then his father had made his way to the side of the boat. He was using the shrimp net like a rope ladder. Almost halfway back up already.

Sabel extended the gaffing hook down to his father.

His father stretched his hand out for the pole. It was just beyond his reach. "Lower. Hold it lower. I can't—"

Sabel lunged down and gaffed the side of his father's neck. Then he heaved back hard with both arms and squatted down, levering the pole off the gunwale.

His father's full body weight now held him dangling on the hook, which ran behind his trachea and exited his neck under the right ear.

Sabel's father gurgled horribly and grabbed for the pole. He tried to free himself, but it was no use. The gaffing hook did exactly what it was designed to do. Keep a flopping catch from working itself loose.

When his father finally stopped struggling, Sabel lowered him back into the water until he floated there on the surface. With the weight off the hook the gaff slid out easily, like it should. That's why you don't ever want to use a barbed gaff.

It was something the old man had taught him.

As the rains continued to drench him, he silently thanked his father for being a good instructor, and always providing the right tools.

SABEL HAD REACHED his destination and cut the engine. This was far enough off the coast for the corpses to sink deep and to rot in peace and privacy.

He dropped the bodies into the dark waters one by one, in no special order. Whatever rank they'd reached in life, they were all on equal footing now. The fish and crabs certainly weren't going to taste any difference.

Sabel restarted the engine and steered the boat back toward the mouth of the bay. As the lights of the city grew brighter, he considered his next objective.

The ambulance had taken Gevin Rees to San Francisco General. The hospital itself would not do as a working location. Too many witnesses. Security cameras to boot. You could go in disguise, but that sort of Mission Impossible shit worked better in movies.

Rees's background information indicated no close contacts in the Bay Area, so the man was likely to end up in a hotel somewhere. That would do just fine.

The boat's engine thrummed on. The smell of the ocean and the diesel smoke once again returned Sabel's mind to those teenage days back on the shrimp boat with his father.

Fond memories, all.

CHAPTER 4

WHILE THE HOTEL desk clerk processed his credit card, Rees watched CNN on the lobby's TV monitor. No sound, but the chyron beneath the picture displayed the headline: *BREAKING NEWS.*

The scroll beneath that summed up the story. DNA analysis of body parts confirmed it, and federal investigators had made the official announcement.

Edward Fischer died in yesterday's blast at Fermilab.

Yesterday.

At Fermilab.

Federal investigators.

Rees didn't want to follow the line of thinking this news story suggested, but he couldn't stop himself. Whatever was going on here, it reached into the US government. Those DNA tests had obviously been faked.

What the hell have I gotten myself into here?

A decidedly upper class clientele passed through the lobby, paying no attention to the TV monitor. The Mark Hopkins on Nob Hill provided by no means the most affordable hotel rooms in the City. But Fischer had absolutely insisted Rees should go there and nowhere else.

Rees finished checking in, grateful that he still had his wallet. The cell phone was a goner, though. And he'd abandoned his overnight bag out by the pier. If the killer didn't take it, someone else certainly would have by now.

San Francisco General Hospital had dipped into its clothes bank—items left behind and laundered along with the hospital's linens—to provide Rees with shirt, pants, jacket, and a pair of very new looking Nike running shoes that actually fit reasonably well.

He politely passed on the proffered secondhand underwear and socks. Thanks, but no thanks.

Once he'd finished checking in and making some quick arrangements with the concierge, he headed up to his suite.

The first thing he did there after he dead-bolted the door and attached the security chain (did those little brass links really stop a determined intruder?) was to take a long, hot bath.

He did his best thinking in the tub. A personal quirk that left him feeling let down whenever business travel landed him in a hotel room with only a shower.

As condensation fogged the bathroom's gilded mirrors, Rees soaked the remaining chill out of his bones and debated with himself on whether he ought to call someone back in New York and explain what was going on out here.

But who? And what exactly would he tell them?

That Edward Fischer wasn't really dead, except now he was? That a dark conspiracy was underway at the level of the US government, by persons unknown, for reasons unknowable?

"Yeah," he said to the bathroom ceiling. "That would go over great."

His assistant was aware of the impromptu trip to San Francisco and would hold down the fort as usual. Per Edward Fischer's instructions, Rees had made up a vague story about a relative's medical emergency. He'd given no timetable for return.

As luck would have it, there were no interviews or TV appearances scheduled for the next several days. Rees had a deadline for a Scientific American article coming up at the end of the week, but he'd finished the first two drafts. It only needed a polish. He could get to it later.

For the moment, Rees could do what he wanted. And he wanted to find some goddamn answers.

If he went public now with what he'd seen and nothing to back it up, it would only damage his reputation. He might be safe confiding it all to a close friend, but for the small matter of his not really having any. Warm acquaintances both professional and personal, sure. Closer than that and the risk/reward ratio just didn't work. Not for him.

People ultimately disappoint. He'd learned that long ago.

So, no phone calls. No statements to the press.

For better or for worse, you're in this thing alone.

The bath water had gone tepid. Rees climbed out of the tub, toweled dry, and wrapped himself up in one of the hotel's luxurious, terrycloth robes. Thinking next, as he always did, that there was no good reason to wear anything but one of these things. Ever.

He carried a dry, white towel with him out of the bathroom and spread it out across the hotel room's mahogany writing desk. Then he removed Fischer's wet leather pouch from the clear plastic bag in which the hospital had returned it to him.

The police and hospital staff had just assumed the pouch belonged to Rees. At first he thought the bag's contents might connect it to Fischer, and support his story. Then he realized he couldn't establish a timeline to prove he hadn't just possessed the pouch since before Fischer was supposedly blown up.

So, on the chance that something in there could throw some light on all of this, he decided not to inform the police of their mistake. He kept the pouch and its contents for himself.

Rees carefully removed those contents again, one item at a time, and laid them out on the towel.

"All right, let's take another look at all this stuff."

Green, spiral notebook thoroughly waterlogged. He set that aside.

Bus schedule from Greyhound. That didn't look very promising.

Next, he gently pulled out several soggy, loose sheets of paper, covered in mathematical expressions and the occasional brief note. Most of them were badly smeared.

One loose sheet stood apart, inasmuch as it had not been authored by Fischer—a printout of a published paper on DNA synthesis. Something about the author byline drew Rees's attention. Upon closer inspection, he didn't recognize any of the scientists listed there. He moved on.

Toothbrush. Cheap reading glasses, and...

"Hey, hey, hey. Where'd *you* come from?"

Something there at the bottom of the pouch he hadn't noticed back in the ER. A black, plastic flash drive.

Unsurprisingly, the drive was as wet as the rest of the pouch's contents. It might be waterproof, many were these days, but if not, borrowing a laptop and plugging the flash drive in with any moisture present would fry it.

He set the drive on the towel to dry out thoroughly. Then he returned to the green notebook. Fischer had written #127 on the cover. Maybe this was part of a series?

Rees opened it. As with the loose sheets the ink here had smeared, though not quite as badly. Large portions were perfectly legible.

The entries were dated. Turning to the very last page showed the notes there had been made about five years ago. Why had Fischer been carrying around *this* particular old notebook?

The notebook's contents looked familiar to Rees, as they would to any astrophysicist with the requisite mathematical training.

The first section contained explorations of the Einstein Field Equations for General Relativity. These ideas alternated back and forth with novel formulations of the Dirac and Yang-

Mills equations, which suggested thinking more along Quantum Mechanical lines.

"What are you up to here, Dr. Fischer?"

Further along, Rees found formulae representing higher dimensional structures called D-Branes. Some form of String Theory there. An angry hand had viciously crossed out several pages of those expressions, rewritten them somewhat differently, and crossed them all out again.

"Well, that didn't quite work for you, did it?"

The ideas in the notebook seemed at war with each other. And no surprise there, really. Relativity *was* in a sense at war with Quantum Mechanics. Or if not war, then at least hostile estrangement.

Relativity described gravity and the universe on a vast, cosmic scale. Quantum Mechanics operated mainly at the sub-atomic level and described the other three fundamental forces. Each theory required the other for completeness, but no one had succeeded in marrying them together into a workable theory of Quantum Gravity.

Rees turned another page and stared at it for a full minute in wonder.

"What in the world?"

Something bizarre and elegant, to be sure. Still mathematical expressions of some kind here, but the symbols and diagrams were entirely unknown to him.

Fischer had written out something like a key at the bottom of the page and on the next few pages, along with a note.

not workable, nothing for it
but the Newtonian approach

"The Newtonian approach? Calculus? This thing is already filled with calculus."

Rees flipped forward through the notebook.

The strange notations decorated the pages like some kind of fantastic alien artwork. He could sense something here of enormous power and beauty, and the effects of it were almost hypnotic. He felt his mind relaxing open.

And as he flipped back to Fischer's key, it came to him.

Nothing for it but Newton's approach.

"Jesus. He's invented a whole new mathematical discipline."

When Newton developed his laws of motion and optics, the mathematics available to him at the time were inadequate to the task. So he simply invented the calculus.

Apparently Fischer had done the same sort of thing here.

Rees studied Fischer's key, applying it to the complex expressions that filled the rest of the notebook. He flipped back and forth, slowly but steadily teasing out the ideas expressed in this glorious new language that he was reading.

And as he did, Fischer's math completely transported him. He no longer sat in a hotel room in San Francisco. He was soaring above a landscape of pure idea.

This was the world Rees had longed to live in since his teens, a world beyond human cares and woes. An eternal place, shining and true, that revealed itself only to the pure of mind. This was the very reason he had turned to science as his passion. To live and work *here*, among the forces that shaped the universe and ignited the stars.

SABEL PARKED THE van at the bottom of Nob Hill and walked up Mason Street toward the Mark Hopkins.

The wet, black asphalt shone like volcanic glass, reflecting the rubies and diamonds of car taillights and headlights as they passed.

Finding this target had been a routine matter. Gevin Rees left a local address with San Francisco General as part of their standard patient processing protocol. The government ID Sabel had flashed at hospital staff gained him easy access to their records.

Through his shoes, Sabel felt the faint vibration of the twisted steel cable whirring beneath the street. The power that drove the city's cable cars flowed underground, out of sight.

Where all real power dwelled.

A tingle arose deep inside him. A city at night, even cold and damp like this, always excited Sabel. Darkness invited those who didn't fear it. And fear was another emotion that Sabel only knew from witnessing it.

But he had done that many, many times.

CHAPTER 5

A SOUND INTRUDED into Rees's awareness. Rhythmic. Thumping. Someone knocking on the hotel room door.

Slowly he realized that the knocking had repeated itself several times already. So deeply had Fischer's notebook engrossed him, that his mind hadn't fully processed these interruptions.

Even now he resisted breaking off from the mathematical highwire act before him. Especially since he'd just begun to see that this was more than pure theory.

It had a purpose.

The knocking persisted.

Rees sighed and rose from the desk. He quickly checked that he'd properly closed and tied his bathrobe, and walked over to the door.

As he began unhooking the security chain, he flashed back on the awful events of the day. He paused to look through the peephole.

Hotel staff. He recognized the navy blue blazer and the hotel's cursive MH insignia in gold thread.

He un-slotted the chain, turned the bolt, and opened the door.

"Dr. Gevin Rees?" the young woman standing there asked.

"Yes, and that's for me?"

"Yes, sir." With a service professional's perky smile, she held up a small bundle wrapped in brown paper and string.

Socks and underwear, he assumed. New this time, not used.

He'd felt a bit like some spoiled aristocrat, asking the concierge's assistance with something like that. But then, high-end hotels like the Mark Hopkins were always happy to pamper quasi-famous guests. Like Gevin Rees, the TV science dude (as he'd heard himself called once by a younger fan).

He accepted the package and thanked the young woman.

And just as the door clicked closed it dawned on him. While he was ruminating on the oddity of his underwear request, he'd forgotten all about tipping her.

He dashed over and grabbed his wallet off the desk, then yanked the door back open. Three steps down the hall he realized he didn't have a room key in his bathrobe.

Yikes.

He spun on his heels and made it back the instant before the door latched itself shut. Close one there.

He stooped and grabbed the clothes package off the floor where he'd dropped it, then stepped outside and wedged a corner of it into the crack on the hinge side of the door. That froze the door in mid-close, freeing him to race off again down the hall.

He hustled to the elevator lobby taking long strides, and made the corner just in time to watch a pair of elevator doors meeting in the middle.

"Ah, son of a ... sorry, miss."

He made a mental note to leave the tip in an envelope for the young lady tomorrow morning, then turned and started back for his room.

He stopped the instant he rounded the corner.

A man was walking down the hall ahead of him. Street clothes. Not a hotel employee. Another guest, perhaps?

Some motion to the right caught Rees's eye. The fire exit door closing.

Rees backed up quietly around the corner. He took a deep breath and leaned out again to look.

The man had reached Rees's room. He stopped in front of the open door. Reached inside his coat...

And pulled out a gun.

Rees jerked back, heart already pounding. He rushed to the elevator call button and jabbed the down arrow three or four times, watching it light up green as he did. A moment later he hit the up arrow too. What the hell, right now he just had to get off this damn floor. Up or down didn't really matter.

_ Indicator lights over each elevator showed its location. Four cars, three of them descending. None of them this high up. The elevator directly in front of him had just begun the trip up from the lobby.

Second floor... third floor... fourth floor.

He was on the sixteenth.

C'mon, c'mon, c'mon...

Rees heard footsteps approaching down the hall from the direction of his room.

Eighth floor. Nine floor.

The car stopped there.

Footsteps still growing louder.

Damnit! I gotta get out of here.

He spotted a window. Newer hotels rarely had windows that opened on the upper floors, but this one didn't look to be retrofitted. It appeared to have the original moving parts.

He unlatched it and gave it a good shove. It didn't budge.

He crouched down and eyed the top of the lower frame. Taking aim as best he could, he sprung up and caught the topmost part of the frame with his right shoulder. He heard a sharp crack and hoped like hell that was the window and not his collar bone.

Cool air licked his cheek. The window had gapped open.

He hit the frame again—an upward shot with the heels of both hands. It flew open the rest of the way. Surprisingly well-oiled mechanism, really. He gave silent thanks for the maintenance staffs of Four Star hotels.

He stole another glance back at the elevator indicator light.

Tenth floor... eleventh... twelfth.

The footsteps sounded like they'd reached the corner.

Out of time.

It had to be heights, didn't it?

Acrophobia. Rees suffered from a crippling fear of heights.

As a child, he'd been deeply affected by a clip of the Tacoma Narrows Bridge tearing itself apart. Images of torsional waves galloping along its expanse as huge, dark chunks of the roadbed fell away haunted his dreams. But they also fascinated him, and he grew obsessed with understanding the physics there.

Many years later he realized the incident had formed the start of his life's main efforts. Learning was his personal weapon against fear. Unfortunately, the whole episode had also left him handicapped at times. He had on more than one occasion—and to his secret shame—driven hours out of his way just to avoid crossing a high bridge.

Right now, he didn't have that luxury.

He side-stepped across the window stool, humped over and eased himself through the opening.

Cold outside. There was a narrow ledge out here. Well, maybe three feet wide, but it looked damned narrow to him. And wet. And slippery.

He climbed all the way out.

Shit. Shit. Shit...

Out of the corner of his eye he saw the man entering the elevator lobby, moving fast.

Rees stood up there on the ledge. Instantly a wave of vertigo overwhelmed him and he involuntarily stiffened. He felt his body arcing away from the building and reached out to catch hold of the receding window frame. But it was already out of reach. He was going to fall.

All his nightmares coming true.

From inside the hotel a hand shot out and grabbed his.

CHAPTER 6

Ten months earlier—San Francisco

IN AN EMPTY lecture hall, in the science department of San Francisco State University, Edward Fischer played the recording for the man who would henceforth be called only Herodotus.

If he agreed to come along. But if he didn't, if he decided instead to blow the whistle...

Fischer comforted himself with the thought that he wouldn't even see the bullet coming.

He had viewed the video clip and the ceremony in it many times by then, but he was looking forward to this moment. He kept his attention mostly on the other man's full, round face.

Herodotus watched the images on Fischer's tablet computer with a childlike awe, frequently shaking his balding head. At one point, teary and overcome with emotion, he had to pause the playback.

When the short clip ended, he sat back in his seat, blinking rapidly. "How can you even play this for me, Edward? Here on this, I mean," he tapped the tablet. "I thought the data sets were impossibly large."

"They are. These are just superficial images abstracted from the complete data. But they're accurate. They're real."

Herodotus was a heavy man. When he shook his head, his cheeks and the dark flesh on his neck jiggled. "I just can't ... I know what I'm seeing here, but I just can't believe it."

"Well, your coordinates were very close to exactly right," Fischer said. "And so I have to ask you, have we succeeded?"

The other man looked again like he might burst into tears. He drew in a couple of deep slow breaths. "I'm sorry. Sorry."

"It's all right. It really is overwhelming."

Herodotus took a moment to compose himself. "All my adult life, I've been listening to ghosts. Ghosts whispering in broken sentences. Trying to put together their stories. And now this..."

"I understand. And I think I have my answer there."

"Yes, you do," Herodotus said, smiling. "We have succeeded. The rest is up to Amsel. I'm assuming the trace showed sufficient continuity for recovery. And enough material has survived?"

"As you predicted, yes. Very recoverable. And very nearly intact, we think." Fischer let a few moments pass in silence while he held Herodotus's gaze.

"And there's more, isn't there? It's why you're meeting me out here away from oversight back at Livermore."

"Yes, there's more. But I will require your help, and our sponsors must remain in the dark. I need more coordinates. For a new target. Amsel has agreed already to what I'm going to propose. I'm not saying that should influence you, just that the path ahead is open if you should choose to join us."

There it was. Fischer had let out enough rope to be hanged with. And the man sitting next to him held the trap door lever.

Herodotus looked down at the tablet still in his hands, the screen now dark. Seconds ticked by in silence. "I can guess what it is you want to try for, because I believe I know you well enough by now. So I will just ask this one question. Can you keep my part ... underground? I have a family. Can we do that?"

"Yes, of course we can. And should." Fischer rose from his seat. "I will require just one other thing from you. The complete data sets—we're going to need a copy on the outside.

Beyond the reach of Fermilab and Livermore. Eventually I'll ask you to hold on to that for me."

Herodotus frowned up at him. "Why don't you just encrypt it? Hide it online in the cloud somewhere."

"It could be found and deleted. Physical storage is the way to go. Forget the internet. No emails either. Ink and paper. That's how we beat them."

"Ink and paper. All right. So long as it can't be traced to me."

"Yes, absolutely. That's the whole point there."

A look of deep sadness came over Herodotus. "They will kill you for this, Edward. If they can. It was dangerous enough to begin with. You'll have no side to turn to now. You know that, right?"

Fischer gave just the slightest nod. Herodotus stood up then and ceremoniously offered his hand. Fischer took it.

He had weighed all the risks, and they were acceptable to him. He had already begun preparations to ensure that his own death wouldn't stop them reaching their final goal.

The truth.

It was all he'd ever really wanted.

CHAPTER 7

A STRONG ARM pulled Rees back in through the hotel window. He rolled awkwardly over the sill and flopped down to the carpet.

"Mr. Reese, are you all right?"

He was looking up at a woman's face. An attractive face.

Short brown hair. She was wearing a weatherproof, blue winter coat and khaki pants. A uniform of some kind.

"Yes, I'm ... I think I am. Yes. Are you with the police department?"

She pulled a wallet out of her coat and flipped it open, revealing a shiny badge in there. "No, sir. I'm with the Defense Criminal Investigative Service. We're a federal agency."

Rees nodded up at the badge.

As she put that away she glanced over him at the open window. "What the hell were you doing out there?"

"Oh. I thought you were a man."

That drew a head tilt and a hard squint.

"No, no," Rees added quickly. "I mean ... I saw your gun. And there was a man this afternoon. He tried to kill me."

She looked back toward the hallway. "We should probably talk in your room. I have some questions I need to ask you."

That was fine with Rees. He had a few questions of his own.

REES WAS FEELING even more than the usual painful awkwardness he experienced in the company of strangers, and wrote it off to the odd circumstances. He was, after all, standing in the foyer of a very nice hotel suite, with a rather good-looking woman, and wearing nothing but a bathrobe.

It felt a little ... breezy.

The woman introduced herself as Special Agent Kerry Morgan and got right down to business. "I understand you witnessed a shooting this afternoon on Fisherman's Wharf, Mr. Rees."

"Yes, I did."

It was *Dr. Rees*, technically. But he never made that correction and always disliked it when another academic did.

He watched as Agent Morgan pulled out a notebook. She stood about his height: five eleven. Younger though, late twenties. She had a tough look about her and a certain athleticism.

In his mind it all added to her appeal.

"I apologize in advance for asking a lot of the same questions you probably already answered for the San Francisco police," she said.

He dismissed her concern with a head shake. "Not a problem. But I'd like to know ... you do understand who was shot out there today along with those two tourists. Who it is that I saw."

"Yes, sir."

"Edward Fischer."

"Yes."

Rees paused. Then said very clearly, "*Professor* Edward Fischer. The man who was blown to bits at Fermilab yesterday."

"Yes, sir. I understand."

Finally. Finally, someone believed him. And what followed immediately on the heels of that was a question.

Why the hell should she?

He could think of only one reason.

He invited her into the dining area and offered her a bottled water. She politely declined. He put it on the table anyway.

When they were both seated across from each other Rees said, "You already knew Edward Fischer wasn't killed in that explosion at Fermilab. Or you wouldn't be talking with me."

Morgan took a moment. He got the impression she was weighing how much she needed or wanted to reveal to him.

"Fischer called me last night," she said.

"He called you too? So, you knew him."

"He was involved in a project for the DOD and we met there. Just once, about a year ago. Last night he verified his identity for me and said to come out and meet him here. Over by Pier 35."

"Wait, you were supposed to be there today?"

"My flight from D.C. was delayed two hours. By the time I made it to Pier 35, SFPD was already there responding to a report of a shooting. Your report."

"You're the muscle!"

That drew the hard squint again.

Rees hurriedly continued, saying, "Fischer mentioned you. Not specifically, but he was talking about you. It had to be you. The muscle."

"I've been called worse, I guess."

A hundred questions swirled in Rees's head like autumn leaves in a whirlwind. He mentally snatched one as it flew past.

"Your flight was delayed? So you took a *commercial* flight? The Department of Defense doesn't have transport jets at its disposal these days?"

Morgan paused again. "The DOD didn't know that Fischer was still alive or that I was going to meet him."

"Why?"

"Because I didn't tell them."

The whirlwind had turned into a tornado. He waited for her to continue and was thankful that she did without any prodding from him.

"Fischer asked me not to tell them he was alive as a condition for our meeting. He said the explosion wasn't an accident. I figured he was just rattled by the blast. Then ... well, you know what happened then." She looked over at the suite's giant, flat screen TV. "Have you seen the news about Fischer's DNA? The body parts?"

"Yes, but that can't be right. This sounds nuts, I know, but they have to be in on it. 'They' the investigators, I mean."

"*They* are DCIS. That's our investigation out there."

Rees felt his stomach fluttering. "Someone in your own agency faked the data."

"Yes. We took over this case because Fischer was engaged in DARPA research."

DARPA. Defense Advanced Research Projects Agency. Even the name sounded spooky. "So what do we do now?" Rees asked. "Do we call the local police again?"

"And report what? What you already told them?"

"Well, if *you* tell them—"

"No. My agency's involved. You understand what that means, right? No one can even know I'm out here."

Rees suddenly remembered how Morgan had arrived at his floor. Via the fire exit. Avoiding cameras wherever she could it seemed.

"Also," she said, "I don't think these people are done with you yet."

"What?" Rees's heart didn't exactly skip a beat, but it did launch into some kind of funky, off-rhythm dance.

"They thought they killed Fischer back at Fermilab, right? So who'd they follow to San Francisco? Who was the target here today?"

It hit Rees like a slap on the back of the neck. "Me. Ah, shit, they were after me."

"Yeah. Finding Fischer too was just a bit of good luck."

"Good luck?"

"From their perspective, sure. And if *you're* the target? Airports, bus terminals, and yes, police stations too—all fine spots to reacquire you once I get you out of here. So ... no cops."

A new species of fear crouched in the dark recesses of Rees's mind. Not the swift panic he'd felt several times today. Something heavier and more enduring. Dread.

"But why?" Rees asked. "I didn't do anything goddamnit!"

Morgan rose from her chair and stepped over to a window facing the bay. She stood there awhile with her back to Rees, looking out into the darkness. He was about to ask her what she was thinking when she finally turned around.

"Okay." Morgan said. "Out by the pier today. You're talking with Fischer, and this guy shows up and just starts shooting."

"Yes."

"What did Fischer tell you?"

Rees shrugged. "Not much. There was no time. He said ... everything was coming together here. Data and some artifacts. Herodotus and Anaximander would do that."

"Who are they?"

"Aliases for people that are, I don't know, involved. Fischer said he was entrusting me with the science."

"His DARPA research?"

"Maybe. I don't know. It was just the one phone call back in June before all this."

"And what did he tell you then?"

Rees laid his hands flat on the heavy table in front of him. Dark hardwood. Myrtle maybe. It felt solid and reassuring. "He was doing some kind of work that he needed the public to understand. That was a big part of it. Public perception. He wanted my help in making that all layman friendly."

"Because you're a science popularizer."

"You've seen my work."

She shook her head. "I looked at your Wikipedia page."

"Oh. I ... well the last special on exoplanets did pretty good numbers, actually." Rees felt oddly defensive.

"Listen, Mr. Rees—"

He interrupted. "You can call me Gevin if you like."

"Fine. You can call me Special Agent Morgan."

"Seriously?"

"Look, here's how it is: they're aware you've had contact with Fischer, the people behind all this. Whatever Fischer was working on, it was a threat to someone. *We* know he didn't tell you much. But *they* don't. Ergo, you're a threat."

Rees didn't like that idea at all, but he couldn't argue with the logic. "All right. I get that. But where does that leave me?"

"In a bad spot. But not without options." Morgan returned to the table and sat down again across from him. She took the bottle of water he'd offered earlier and cracked it open. "Who have you spoken to other than the police?"

"No one."

"Not even your closest friends?"

"I ... don't do close."

"You *don't do close*. What does that even mean?"

"It means no one else knows about this. Okay?"

Morgan took a long and thoughtful swig off the water bottle, and seemed to let that all go. Thankfully. Because he really didn't want to get into his social life right now. Or lack thereof.

"All right," she said, "here's what I think. If we knew what Fischer was working on, the best thing would be for you to use all your media resources and make it public. Get it out there as widely as possible, as quickly as possible."

Rees immediately saw the strategic sense of it. "There'd be no point in killing me anymore."

"Apart from spite, and I don't think that's the kind of game that's being played here."

"Well that all sounds great, Special Agent Morgan, except Fischer never told me what the project was about. He just said explicating the science would be my part."

"Then that's what we need to hunt down." Morgan said. "What it was all about."

Rees sighed. "Well, I can show you where we start." He got up and walked over to the desk. "Right here. With this."

Morgan came over to stand next to him. "What is it?"

He pointed down at the soggy green notebook. "That's Fischer's. He ditched it and I ... recovered it. Also this." He picked up the flash drive. "It's wet. I haven't tried to access it."

Morgan gazed at the open notebook with a puzzled expression. "And you understand all this stuff?"

Rees shook his head. "The only man who understood this fully is dead. But I have a vague idea what he was working on."

"And what do you think it is?"

He tried to find some way to put it that didn't sound like science fiction or an insane man's fantasy. And then gave up. It was what it was.

"Time travel," he said.

CHAPTER 8

AS REES AND Morgan crossed the lobby on their way out of the Mark Hopkins, someone called after them.

"Dr. Rees."

Rees started at the sound of his own name and involuntarily squeezed Fischer's pouch tighter under his arm. He and Morgan stopped just a few steps from the glass front doors.

Rees turned toward the voice. "Yes?"

One of the front desk clerks, a young Asian man with a severely styled side-buzz haircut, stepped out from behind the front desk. Something in his hand. He was rocking a slim, hip-looking black suit that succeeded in making Rees feel even more self-conscious in his hand-me-down clothes from San Francisco General.

"Uh, there's a phone message for you, sir." He held out a slip of paper for Rees. "The caller didn't want to be put through to your room. He insisted on leaving a written message. I'm sorry if we didn't get that all quite right for you."

Rees reassured the clerk that everything was just fine and accepted the note with a quick thank you.

— —   From: Herodotus

   To: Dr. Gevin Rees

   If you know my history, you know
   where to find me at work. Look for me
   in the JPL library tomorrow afternoon.

Rees handed the note over to Morgan, who seemed to read it through more than once.

She looked back up at him. "Herodotus. That's one of the men Fischer told you about. An alias, right?"

"Yes. Unless of course this is the *real* Herodotus we're talking about. That would fit the pattern at least."

"What pattern's that?"

"Well, counting Edward Fischer, this would be the second time inside of two days I've been contacted by people who were already dead."

SABEL WATCHED AS the two targets exited the hotel together. The mission had changed in mid-flight. The Office wanted Rees taken in alive now.

The higher-ups definitely caught a little break there. Sabel had been riding a hotel elevator up to kill Rees in his room when he received his new marching orders. He could easily have missed that call for want of a decent cell signal.

Can you hear me now?

Damn lucky for them that he could.

Some folks flat out insisted that everything happens for a reason. More because they need it to be that way—in his own opinion—than because anything proves it. Well, maybe shit all goes according to some great Plan and maybe shit doesn't. Sabel sure as hell wasn't gonna lose any sleep over that.

He did know one thing. If there was something like luck playing in Gevin Rees's life, it was about to run out. 'Cause as soon as they got solid intelligence on this woman ... Sabel was taking him, or them, in.

To see the Specialist.

And that wasn't no lucky thing, baby. A grotesque but funny image popped into his mind then. Blood. Bone. Ruptured innards. That glasses guy from the commercial, in blue coveralls and massive agony going...

Can you hear me screaming now?

CHAPTER 9

New York City

"WE DIDN'T KNOW a backup cache existed until now. We're still going through Fischer's private belongings."

"I'm no longer surprised by the shit you don't know. You didn't know he got out of Fermilab alive either."

The only name Carl Truby had for the operative walking beside him was Mr. Doubleman. Together they were making their way past waist high mounds of dirty snow that banked a well-lit street in Gramercy Park.

"Fischer has been taken care of," Doubleman said.

Truby shook his head in disgust. "Yeah, terrific timing on that one. Now he can't tell us where he stashed the backup. What about The TV Science guy? The one you were *supposed* to be targeting out there in the first place."

"Gevin Rees is still alive."

Truby stopped in his tracks. "What the hell?"

"That's actually good thing."

They had paused beneath a street light, and Truby searched Doubleman's face in the unnatural blue-white glare. The man was tall and quite thin, with a large nose and pronounced Adam's apple. He reminded Truby of an animated version of Ichabod Crane he'd once seen.

The outfit that Doubleman worked for was mainly populated by people who were once either military intelligence or elite combat troops. Now they were just shadows. Search as much as you like, you'd find no trace of them, even as a brass plate front company. They referred to the organization as the Office, and they fielded contracts through a network of personal contacts. Among people who knew, they were considered the best.

Truby was beginning to wonder about that.

"You screwed up again?" Truby said. "How's that good?

"When we learned about the data cache we gave our man in San Francisco new instructions. Rees may know exactly where it is. We have eyes on him now, and he's just met up with someone who might be another one of the conspirators. We're bringing them both in alive, to a man who's very good at extracting information."

"You assured me this all stopped with Fischer and the Israeli archeologist."

"Amsel. A British Jew, actually. The dig's in Jerusalem."

"Like I give a rat's ass. Then this science guy turns up. And now these other two, the Greeks."

"Herodotus and Anaximander. Obviously not their real name. Did I explain the references?"

"I don't give a shit about the references. Is it one of those men? The guy Rees just connected with?"

"As I said, we don't know yet. We have a strong idea who Herodotus might be and it's certainly not him. Because Rees just rendezvoused with a woman."

Ruby could feel the bile rising in his throat. "Jesus Christ."

"Look, part of the trouble is whatever planning or communications went down between Fischer and the others, it wasn't done via email or phone."

That part had already been explained to Truby and it made sense. Face to face communications were generally the most secure. That's why he was meeting Doubleman here in New York in person like this. But there were practical limitations to it.

"All right," Truby said, "so they were all part of the original project. But these guys, and girls," he added sarcastically, "weren't all in the same place. Communications couldn't have been done entirely in person."

Doubleman shook his head. "No. We found a rented mailbox in Chicago under a phony name, and we have video surveillance of Fischer using it."

"Mail? You're talking about physical mail?"

"Low-tech communication has its advantages," Doubleman explained. "You can't eavesdrop on a physical letter if you don't know where it's sent from, or who it's sent to. We're checking that PO box daily for incoming mail. Most likely that will come from another rented mailbox on the other end, though. But you never know. We could catch a break."

Truby coughed out a short laugh. "The US Mail. He beat the best signal intelligence technology in the world with stamps and envelopes. It's funny really."

"Yes, hysterical."

The two men had reached a red light. They stopped and waited for the signal to change.

Truby noted the Korean Christian church on the corner and its blue neon cross as a signpost for the walk back. "What now?" he asked.

"As I said, we grab Rees and this woman and find out what they know. Then we terminate them both, and move on to the others in Fischer's little cabal."

Truby thought he heard optimism in Doubleman's voice and he didn't like it. Now wasn't the time for it. "And what happens if these two are a dead end? What if someone else has access to the backup, wherever the hell it is? What if all the artifacts turn up at the goddamn Smithsonian?"

"The artifacts themselves are worthless without the corroborating data, and vice versa. It's all or nothing there. That's good for us, because if we knock down either half of the equation, we're done. And in any case, we're being paid to stop this, and we will. You needn't be concerned about the details."

The signal turned to *walk*, and the two men headed across the intersection.

"How? How will you stop them, if you don't get the names from Rees and whoever the hell he's with?" Truby looked over at Doubleman. He wanted to read the man's face when he answered.

"The Office will take broader action." Businesslike. Almost nonchalant.

As they reached the other side of the street and continued along, Truby's guts tightened up. He stayed silent for almost a half block.

Finally he said, "'*Broader* action.' Really? All of them then. Everyone who worked on the project."

"It's the surest approach. We're reasonably confident that only two more scientists were involved, beyond Fischer, but we can't be absolutely certain. On the other hand, if we eliminate them all..."

Doubleman was looking at him, waiting. Truby knew enough of the project details to understand exactly how many lives they were talking about here.

He gave a single nod.

They set the time and place for the next meet and Truby walked away, back in the direction of that little Korean church. He could still see the blue neon cross off in the distance.

Truby marveled, as he often did, at the near endless variety of religious belief. Such a strange force. It could simultaneously pull people together while at the same time pushing them away from other groups, even within the same faith.

An amazingly useful property.

You just condoned the murder of fourteen people.

The thought had arisen unbidden, and Truby forced it back down. Some things were easier done than considered.

Where do you draw the line when everything you ever accomplished or cared about or fought for is at stake?

At whatever it takes.

He and the very powerful people he represented would do or sanction whatever it takes.

There was no goddamn line.

CHAPTER 10

AS SHE DROVE south on Hyde Street keeping a wary eye out for anyone who might be tailing them, Kerry Morgan struggled to get some kind of handle on this whole thing.

Despite everything she knew about Edward Fischer and the stratospheric level of genius he possessed, it just seemed too fantastic to take seriously.

Time travel. Really?

It was hard to imagine. But then up until now, Morgan couldn't have imagined her own agency would ever be involved in the assassination of a US citizen and the related cover-up. You can't deny the evidence, though.

And Morgan was taking it as a personal betrayal.

She glanced over at the passenger seat. Gevin Rees was lost in Fischer's notebook again. She was pretty sure that if Bigfoot lumbered by in a crosswalk wearing white vinyl go-go boots and spinning a flaming baton, Rees wouldn't notice it.

Whatever Edward Fischer had written in there, it was apparently quite engaging.

She'd only known the famous scientist briefly. They met during her investigation of a security breach at Fermilab the year before. He was leading a small team of particle physicists in some DARPA sponsored research. So top secret, Morgan wasn't even allowed to have its code name. Maybe they called it *Project Time Tunnel*. In which case, yeah, that would've been a bit of a giveaway.

At any rate, someone had tried to smuggle out project-related data on an advanced type of storage device. Hidden within containers of food scraps intended for composting.

Morgan never did determine who'd done it. It might have helped if she were permitted to examine the contents of the drives. Not a chance.

Nevertheless, she had some idea who could be behind the breach. Mainly through the process of elimination, and various factors involving access and timing.

Fischer himself.

She confronted him during lunch one day in Fermilab's cafeteria. They sat together at their own table in a corner, away from other scientists and staff. As she'd planned.

"This is where you did it, right?" Morgan said over a so-so chicken salad sandwich and some pretty good coffee.

Fischer had just finished jotting in a diary he nearly always had with him. Something he did rather obsessively. *For posterity,* he once explained.

He closed the diary and looked up at Morgan. "That's your theory then?"

"That's my theory."

He gave her a challenging look that must have withered many a physics grad student. "Since you didn't witness the primary event, I'm assuming your theory explains all the observed secondary effects."

"I didn't, and it does."

Fischer sipped a spoonful of his tomato soup, then wiped his mouth with a paper napkin. "Then it's a good theory, Special Agent Morgan. But it hasn't helped you. Because you still don't have the answer you're really after."

He regarded her openly, calmly. His dark brown eyes, which Morgan knew well from photos and a couple of very popular posters, looked even larger and more penetrating in person. A hint of humor sparkled in there. It would be very easy to get lost looking into those brilliant eyes.

"What answer am I *really* after, Dr. Fischer?"

Fischer tented his fingers in front of his chest. "Let's say, hypothetically, that I did this. Why? You'd want to know why. Given that I'm apolitical, care nothing for money, and already have the best research tools in the world available to me, why would I expose myself and my work to so much risk by smuggling out classified data? Why would I turn traitor, so to speak?"

Morgan waited to see if Fischer would continue on his own. But apparently he wanted to be prompted. She obliged him. "All right. Hypothetically then. Why?"

Fischer leaned back in his chair and smiled. "You know the funny thing is, that's the one question science ultimately can't answer. *Why?* The fine structure constant—I can measure its value to the nth decimal place. But I can't tell you why it is that particular number and not something else. Same with the other dimensionless physical constants. And if just one of them were a smidge different in one direction, there's no carbon. Just a tic in the other direction, no stars. Either way, no life in the universe. At least not human life. Now *why* should that be? Some people believe this is the hand of God at work."

"Are you going to suggest now that God told you to leak classified information?"

Fischer's smile broadened. "It would be exceptionally difficult to prove that He did not."

"And what if I don't believe in that sort of God? Who whispers directions and fiddles around with the numbers."

Fischer nodded awhile and seemed to be considering the question. "Well, if you did, at least you'd have an answer to the so-called 'fine-tuned universe' question."

Morgan could see Fischer intentionally leading her away from the investigation here. But the opportunity to talk about God with one of the greatest minds in the world, maybe even in all of history—that was just too valuable to pass up.

"I don't need answers that desperately, Dr. Fischer. I'm not afraid of a little mystery. How does the quote go? 'I would rather have questions that can't be answered than answers that can't be questioned.'"

Something shifted in Fischer's expression then. "Special Agent Morgan, I am engaged in a kind of war, fighting a most dangerous enemy. It's an idea. The idea of truth by authority. The arrogant notion that some revered book or prophet or head of state represents the final word on what is or isn't so. Throughout history no single concept has generated more human misery. As a scientist I have spent my entire life opposing that kind of authoritarian epistemology. So no, I'm not a traitor. My alliances remain unchanged and will till the day I die." His eyes softened and he smiled again. "That might not even be that far off, eh? God only knows."

Morgan's investigation never progressed any farther than that. She suggested a few places to tighten up security at Fermilab, and moved on.

She didn't give the episode another thought. Not until the explosion and the phone call from Fischer.

"Impossible," Rees said from the passenger seat.

Morgan glanced over. Rees still had his head buried in the notebook. "What's impossible?" she asked.

Rees looked up and seemed to notice the world around him again, which had literally and figuratively declined quite a bit from Nob Hill. At that moment they were passing a homeless man sleeping on the sidewalk outside an adult book store.

Rees scowled at his new surroundings. "Nice neighborhood. Where are you taking me?"

They were cruising the heart of the Tenderloin District, one of San Francisco's sketchiest neighborhoods. Morgan had her eyes peeled for a dive hotel that would take cash and not worry about foregoing any ID. The Tenderloin was as likely a place to find one as anywhere in the city.

"Someplace safe," Morgan told him. "And what's impossible?"

"Oh, the method Fischer is proposing for handling the infinities that arise out of Quantum Gravity."

"I'll play. What's Quantum Gravity?"

"Ah. Quantum Gravity can be, and in this case it is, an attempt to reconcile Relativity with Quantum Mechanics into a Theory of Everything. But renormalizing is a problem."

"And without the jargon that means...?"

"Sorry. The problem is that the math gives rise to infinities. It's like trying to divide numbers by zero. You don't get meaningful answers. Fischer found a brilliant mathematical trick for dealing with the infinities, what we call renormalizing. But the resulting complexity is hellish. The best supercomputer in the world, running for thousands of years, might grind out approximate solutions to these equations."

Suddenly Morgan knew why Fischer had made his way to San Francisco. Why he absolutely needed to be here. "What about a quantum computer? Could you do it with that?"

Rees raised his eyebrows. "Oh, well, yes, theoretically. A quantum computer with enough qubits might do the job. But that's decades away."

Morgan made a quick right turn at the corner. "Actually, it's more like an hour at this time of night."

CHAPTER 11

Six months earlier—Syrian Desert

ADNAN TOTAH SQUINTED against a dusty gust of hot wind, and looked out over the dig. He felt a twinge deep in his gut, as he had for days now. His crew was excavating in the desert about eight kilometers southwest of Busra, and something was not right.

It wasn't just that the dig was probably illegal. In Syria, particularly in wartime, the difference between legal and illegal was just a matter of opinion. Opinions could be bought, in any case.

No, it was the whole approach here. On the face of it, very amateurish looking. Too narrow a field, and no test digs at all. The grid system they used was also entirely unorthodox.

And yet, nothing about Joshua Amsel, the American archaeologist they worked for, bespoke amateur. He knew the desert. He was well financed and equipped. His security team was shockingly well armed and trained. And the old man's face—Totah prided himself on his ability to read faces—it was wily, not stupid.

And then there were the finds.

Everywhere Amsel directed them to dig, they struck pay dirt. Not most spots. *Every one.* And not just the usual potshards either, but tools, and foundations. At first it looked like wild good luck. Then like magic. And while Amsel certainly seemed pleased, he did not appear at all surprised.

He uses a jinni, one of Totah's men had told him with eyes narrowed. Others thought the same.

Totah's crew foreman was hurrying toward him now, kicking up more dust as he came. "We have found more artifacts," he said, in the Levantine dialect they all spoke at home and amongst each other.

When Totah reached the active site, Amsel was already there. Totah's men had begun uncovering this particular structure three days earlier.

The day before, Totah had overheard the old man speaking to someone on the sat phone in English. He used the word *repository*, which Totah looked up with his smartphone.

A place where things are stored.

Gold. Let it be gold.

They might be seeking caches of ancient coins, possibly Roman. It would be dangerous if they succeeded. And difficult. To hide and export such a treasure out from under the nose of Assad and the rebels—that would be no mean feat. But Totah's agreed upon cut could make him a very rich man.

Amsel stood near the center of the dig, taking measurements with something like a GPS unit. Very bulky though, this handheld device of his. And custom made by the looks of it. Certainly not any piece of archaeological equipment Totah had ever worked with.

The old archaeologist seemed to find the spot he wanted, and got to work with hand tools.

Mere minutes later he appeared to have what he sought. He held his prize aloft. "Yes! By God, yes. We have it."

Not gold. A codex. Vellum pages bound between two covers. Metal covers, it looked like. Very unusual, that.

The old man reached up for a hand to climb out of the dig. "Someone help me here! Let's go!"

In his blue rubber-gloved hands, Amsel carried the codex back to one of the trucks. Totah and some of his men followed to watch.

Amsel removed some kind of high tech scanner from an AV case in the back of a truck. He passed it over the codex, several times front and back. This appeared to be yet another custom piece of equipment. A standard USB cable connected the scanner to a laptop computer.

Then Amsel spoke to the man who Totah had decided was his lead researcher. A frail man with one leg shorter than the other. That man hooked a satellite phone to the computer, and undertook some kind of uploading or downloading procedure.

Amsel lit a cigarette and sat, and waited. Totah waited too. The tension in the air made clear something of great import was set in motion.

Before Amsel finished the cigarette, his man looked up from the computer with eyes shining.

"The signature matches," the frail man said.

Totah knew the English word *signature,* but this only confused him. They hadn't even tried to open the codex yet. And certainly nothing like a legible signature could be read on the oxidized metal covers.

Amsel spoke quickly after hearing that, and used an English word Totah was most definitely not familiar with.

Lectionary.

He would look it up, later.

Something about the codex held great meaning for the grizzled old archaeologist. That much Totah could be absolutely sure of. Amsel had just broken out a bottle of whiskey in celebration.

And he was laughing now. Laughing and smiling broadly.

But with malice in his hooded eyes.

CHAPTER 12

THE NSA HAD a fully functioning quantum computer. Well, all right then. Just when Rees thought the day couldn't possibly get any stranger, Special Agent Morgan had laid that on him.

Morgan drove them along the 80 East in light traffic, toward the Bay Bridge. They were heading to Lawrence Livermore National Laboratory, which housed the quantum computer.

"They use it for cryptography, right?" Rees said. "With a quantum computer running Shor's algorithm, you could crack any public key cryptosystems based on integer factorization. You could read your enemies' encrypted files."

"You could," Morgan confirmed.

"Yes. I knew it."

"Which is why the US and every other government in the world switched over to security based on, uh, symmetric ciphers and hash functions. Post-quantum cryptography, they call it."

"Oh," Rees said, feeling a bit sheepish now.

Morgan glanced over. "You thought we were the only country that had one of these things, or was trying to get one?"

"No. I thought they didn't exist. Apparently I'm a little behind the times on my super-secret government programs."

Morgan changed lanes. "Don't feel bad. They were thinking cryptography when they funded it. So you're more or less right there."

Rees let out a little laugh. "Well, that's why they pay me the big bucks. To be more or less right."

"Any more thoughts on that message back at the hotel?"

"Not really. It said if I knew the history, I'd know where to find him, or her. It's like a riddle, or a code. Herodotus's main work is called The History or The Histories. So okay, I get the reference. I've even read it. That doesn't give me a location. And the bit about the library at JPL? It sounds pretty straightforward. But then, what would be the point of the riddle? It just doesn't make any sense."

"JPL, the Jet Propulsion Laboratory. Isn't that near LA?"

"Between Glendale and Pasadena. So what, are we supposed to meet in a library there tomorrow?"

"If that's the message, we have a choice to make. Lawrence Livermore will be there the day after tomorrow. The meeting with this Herodotus person may not. We can shoot straight down the I-5 and be in Los Angeles in about six hours."

Something about it didn't feel right to Rees. "The message said if I knew the work I'd *know* where to find this person. And I don't know."

"Sometimes you can't know. You make your best guess."

"Normally I'm fine with guesses," Rees said. "That's how most hypotheses start. But if Herodotus was working with Fischer, then he or she is very likely a scientist. The message said I'd *know*, not guess. A good scientist wouldn't conflate the two terms."

"The message was specific. The JPL library."

"Yes, but I still don't think—"

"Dr. Rees, I apologize if I didn't make this clear before. I want to hear your input, but I'll be making the decisions."

Rees sat there a second before he realized his mouth was hanging open. He shut it, and reminded himself that Morgan was a federal law officer going to extraordinary lengths here to help him. He wondered if he'd lost sight of that because of her gender and felt a hot stab of embarrassment.

After an uncomfortable length of silence, Morgan said, "By the way, I agree with you. We're going to Livermore."

Rees got the point. "You just wanted me to know who's in charge."

Morgan didn't reply, which in this case worked as good as a *yes*.

He remembered a question he had for her. "How do you know about this quantum computer program? You're not with the NSA too, are you?"

"I know for the same reason I knew Edward Fischer was working for DARPA. There were security leaks and I was called in. One of the quantum computer scientists had a gambling addiction, owed the wrong people. He needed money, and the Chinese wanted the technology."

"What happened to him?"

"We disappeared him. It's like he never existed now." Morgan's face looked cold, emotionless.

"Jesus, really?"

"No. But I was curious to see how far you thought we'd go."

Rees shook his head. An interesting character, Morgan. He liked her. Under other circumstances he might ... what? See her a few times, and then let her know that he didn't really do the whole *intimacy* thing? Yes. Most likely, that's what he'd do.

Or maybe not this time.

"So then, you've seen the quantum computer?" Rees asked.

"Not the hardware, no. I signed off on the new security system. Got to know some people there. We'll ask around about Fischer. You think he worked with them at least once already?"

"I'm thinking he had to. If his research at Fermilab was built on this," Rees lifted the green notebook, "he would've needed solutions to these equations only a quantum computer could generate."

"So you think he wasn't finished? That's why he was coming back?"

"I don't know. At our meeting out there by the pier, he mentioned data. Massive amounts of it. Maybe an ordinary supercomputer couldn't process it. With any luck, someone at Livermore can tell us the details."

A bump-bump of the front and back tires across an expansion joint told him they had just finished crossing the Bay Bridge. Rees had crossed a lot of bridges today and wondered how many more were yet to come.

About forty minutes later they pulled off the freeway in Pleasanton. Livermore was still one town away.

Morgan steered them through a residential neighborhood that, at least at night, looked just like a thousand other neighborhoods to Rees.

Mostly one story homes. Not big, not small. The parked cars they passed weren't Beemers and Mercedes, but there weren't a lot of old beaters around either. Middle America. Welcome to the burbs.

Rees had grown up in a neighborhood like this one. About eleven hours northeast of there, near Salt Lake City. Reminders of that part of his life always evoked mixed emotions. And thoughts of his sister, Anna. Thoughts he had no time for right now.

"This is it," Morgan said as they slowed. She had apparently kept the address of one of the quantum computer scientists from her investigation at Livermore.

They pulled into the driveway of a house near the end of a cul-de-sac, behind a Honda Civic already parked there. Lights were on inside.

"Shouldn't you have called first?" Rees asked, as they climbed out of the rent-a-car.

Morgan frowned. "What, and ruin the surprise?"

He followed her as she walked to the door and rang the bell.

The sound of something breaking came from inside, followed by a muffled *Goddamnit* spoken in a higher register. Then footsteps.

The door opened.

A young woman, mid-twenties, stood there in sweats and a T-shirt. A shocked expression on her face.

"Kerry! What the hey?" She smiled broadly. "Why didn't you call?"

Morgan smiled right back. "Wanted to surprise you."

The two women hugged.

"I freakin' hate surprises," the other woman said. "Like you didn't know."

Rees watched as the hug lingered. The women separated, still making eye contact.

Morgan gestured to Rees. "Danni, this is—"

"Gevin Rees!" The woman's eyes popped. "Holy shit! Dr. Gevin Rees. Wow. So nice to meet you."

She offered her hand and Rees shook it. She had dark skin and Asian features. And despite the rather exotic effect, something about her seemed instantly familiar. Some people were just like that. Rees found himself automatically returning her huge smile.

Morgan made the formal introductions. "Dr. Gevin Rees, this is Dr. Danielle Harris, who will insist that you call her Danni. She's one of the world's leading experts in Quantum Computation Language, QCL. She actually studied under its inventor, Bernhard Omer."

Danni was still beaming. "Man, I watch all your specials. I saw the spot you did on the new Cosmos. That was radical."

"Thank you," Rees felt disoriented and flattered at the same time.

After a moment of quiet, Morgan said, "Can we come in?"

"Whoa, yeah, sorry. Come in. It's a mess, but, yeah." Danni stepped aside to let them by.

Rees saw something flash again between the two women as Morgan passed Danni in the doorway.

He made a mental note. Whatever level he'd thought his ability to guess someone's sexual orientation was at, he needed to downgrade it a notch or three.

CHAPTER 13

"**THIS WILL ONLY** take a second," Danni said.

Morgan watched her scoop up shards from a white glass vase off the white linoleum tile with a whisk broom and dustpan. Apparently Danni had been washing the vase when the doorbell rang, and tried to set it aside too quickly.

Danni tended to rush things.

Morgan hadn't seen her since the Livermore investigation and their brief but mostly satisfying entanglement. About a year and a half had passed since then. And even under these bizarre circumstances, she felt happy to see Danni again. Surprisingly happy.

Not that it had ended badly. But Danni wanted children one day. One day soon in fact.

Morgan had very different ideas about parenthood. She thought it would be like having extra sets of little arms and legs growing out of you that you couldn't control, but through which you could still feel every single painful injury. Everything from a scratch to an amputation without anesthesia.

Gee, what fun, and no thanks.

And so they called it a fling and went on along their separate, unconnected paths. Until now.

"Sorry about that." Danni emptied the dustpan into her garbage and stowed it under the sink. "Let's go into the living room." She took two steps and stopped. "Oh, you guys want anything? I have beer and beer. If you're hungry, there's lasagna I can heat up."

Rees surprised Morgan by requesting one of those beers. Morgan declined. Danni grabbed one for herself and led them to the living room.

Morgan removed her coat and sat on the couch next to Rees. Danni took the easy chair across from them.

The living room looked exactly the same as when Morgan had last been here. African tribal art decorated the walls, along with some hanging knit sculptures by a Cornell math professor friend that accurately represented hyperbolic space. Beautiful and eclectic. Like Danni.

Danni was eying Morgan's service piece. "I thought I felt the hardware. You're on the job, right? What's the deal?"

"It's about Edward Fischer." Morgan said matter-of-factly. The last thing she needed was to get Danni upset. Or worse, excited.

Danni shook her head. "Oh, yeah. Man, that's horrible. They don't call it high energy physics for nothing. It's surprising something like this didn't happen sooner."

"Yes," Rees said, "except something like that *still* might not have happened."

"All riiiight," Danni set down her beer. "Well, that sounds all dark and mysterious like. So, there's more to the story?"

Morgan gave Rees a hard stare and regretted not instructing him to let her handle all the disclosure here. "Yes, there's more. But I don't want to drag you into this deeper than we have to. Just tell me, was Fischer using the quantum computer at Livermore and if so, what for?"

Danni sat up like someone just ran electricity through her spine. "Hold on. Somebody murdered Edward Fischer? That's what this is about? It wasn't an accident?"

Don't get all worked up about this. Please, Danni. "Honestly, the less you know the better," Morgan said.

"Hey, don't go all Colonel Jessup on me here." Danni dropped her voice a couple registers. "You want the truth? You want the truth? You can't *handle* the truth!"

"That's a terrible Jack Nicholson and I'm serious about this, Danni." Morgan saw her struggling with it. She had a scientist's natural curiosity. Plus she was damn stubborn.

Danni dropped her head. When she looked up, she appeared more collected. "Okay. You want to know if Edward Fischer worked with my lab." She paused. "Because someone freakin' killed the greatest scientist of our time. But we're not gonna talk about that part."

Morgan shot her a warning look. "Danni."

"All right, all right. I'm going with it. Just give me a little to work with, okay?"

"We have reason to think Fischer used the quantum computer at Livermore," Morgan explained. "And that he might have been planning to do so again."

Danni nodded. "Okay. Well, I can tell you that if he did, it wasn't connected to anything I had access to."

Rees set his beer down and leaned forward. "There was work going on with the quantum computer even *you* didn't have access to?"

"Just once, yeah. A thing in partnership with DARPA. We weren't even told the name of the project, but I'm pretty sure I overheard it a couple times. Project Coffer, or something like that."

"Could that be Kafir?" Morgan tried over-enunciating. "Kaa-feer. Sound like that?"

Danni tilted her head and seemed to think back. "Yeah. I suppose it coulda been."

Rees had scooted so far forward, Morgan feared he would slip off the front of the couch. "What does that mean, kafir?"

"It's Arabic," Morgan said. "It means unbeliever. I saw that word on a notepad in Fischer's office when I interviewed him once. I didn't understand how it could be connected to his work. I still don't. But clearly it is somehow."

Rees looked elated. "Well, that has to be it then. The same DARPA project from Fermilab was ongoing at Livermore. Fischer *was* here." He turned to Danni. "Are there records? Can we find out what he was doing?"

Rees's excitement had infected Danni. Her eyes sparkled with it now. "Well, yeah. Yeah. At the lab. But that stuff would be on contained infrastructure. Air-gapped. No lines in or out."

"So that no one can access it via the internet," Morgan explained.

Danni nodded. "We'd have to physically go there to look at the records. But the thing is, I never did get clearance for that project. I wouldn't be able to access it even locally."

An idea flashed into Morgan's mind along with a ray of hope. She leaned in toward Danni. "What we did, you and I. Is it still there?"

Danni smiled. "I did it. You just thought of it. But, yeah. It's still there. I kinda liked knowing I had it."

Even without an internet connection, hacker programs like the one called Flame could be piggybacked in on flash drives to attack or steal data from an isolated computer. So as part of Morgan's work plugging leaks at Lawrence Livermore, sophisticated anti-spyware had been installed.

And something else.

A backdoor in.

Morgan had Danni write one into a subprogram, so she could access the system clandestinely, and spy on their data thief. In the end, that's how they found him. And now it might come in very handy again.

At that moment, a sound came from the direction of the kitchen.

CHAPTER 14

SABEL SCOUTED THE house and yard, and quickly determined where the targets were sitting. He quietly broke into the garage, and entered the home itself through an unlocked door that led right into the kitchen.

Intel on the house's only resident didn't rule her out as one of the conspirators, but three hostages just wasn't practical in this situation. She'd been classified as expendable and so she was.

After Sabel eliminated her, he'd get Rees and the mystery woman back to the car as quickly and quietly as possible. Hopefully before any nosy neighbors stuck their heads out for a look-see.

Sabel began his final approach through the kitchen, gun ready.

Something cracked under his left shoe.

He stopped.

He tried to remember if he'd seen carpeting when he looked in from the backyard. Or was it a wood floor in there? He wasn't sure. That made it difficult to assess how well that sound might have carried.

He kept still, and listened.

Stone quiet in there now. The conversation had halted.

They heard.

Sabel calculated the new scenario.

Enough time had already passed for someone in there to arm themselves from a holster.

It wouldn't be Rees, not based on his background. He'd probably never touched a gun in his life. But one or both of the women could be deadly now.

Narrow doorway from the kitchen to the living room. The enemy's shot would be perfectly framed by the space he came in through.

He, on the other hand, would have to sweep his gun through as many as forty-five degrees one way or the other, while he tried to pick out any armed targets from three people and keep Rees, at the very least, alive.

Sabel figured with his skills that put the odds for who got off the first shot at about even.

Not good enough.

He backed up toward the door he just entered by. Whatever the hell he stepped on, a piece of it must've got stuck in the sole of his shoe. It *crunched* again when he set his left foot down.

He had reached the door, though, and didn't need to go any further. He opened it behind him to provide a retreat into the garage if necessary. Then he crouched low and aimed his SIG Sauer up at the narrow entrance to the kitchen.

Let 'em come.

Effectively he'd reversed the tactical factors to work in his favor. Before his opponent could swing her weapon left and right and drop her sights down this low, Sabel would get a clean head shot in.

Come on in, ladies. The water's fine.

MORGAN KNEW THEY weren't alone in the house. She held her breath and waited.

Another crunching sound.

"That came from the kitchen," Danni whispered.

Morgan drew her weapon and spoke softly. "Get down on the floor. Both of you."

Rees was off the couch and on the rug about as fast as he could fall.

"What's happening?" Danni was still sitting on the couch, eyes locked on Morgan's gun.

Rees reached up and pulled her down.

Danni fell on top of him on the floor. "What the hell?"

As she moved toward the kitchen, Morgan could hear Rees telling Danni to stay put.

Please, for Christ's sake listen to him, Danni.

Closer to the kitchen now, she could see the entrance.

Classic keyhole set up here. Without something like a flash-bang grenade, she might as well walk in with a bull's-eye painted on her forehead.

If she stayed put, she could hold the living room against entry from the kitchen. And whoever was in the kitchen could hold any entrance into there from the living room.

Stalemate.

The one advantage Morgan might gain would be situational intelligence. Right now she knew that other person's precise location and they probably knew hers. She had to tip that balance.

A voice rang out from the kitchen.

"Put the gun down and slide it away. Where I can see it."

What the hell?

"You even turn, you're dead."

After a moment's confusion, Morgan recognized the voice.

A heavy *thunk*. A scraping noise. Then the voice came again. "Kerry. I got a bead on him. Get in the kitchen before he does something stupid and I have to actually shoot the bastard."

Danni. That's Danni.

Morgan stepped close beside the kitchen door, prepared herself, then jumped into the door frame, weapon at the ready.

A blond-haired man was crouched down there on the kitchen floor.

About five feet in front of him lay a SIG Sauer 9mm.

Behind him, Danni stood in the open garage door. She held the .22 target pistol Morgan had bought for her, pointed at the man's head.

Rees ran up behind Danni holding a golf club. "I couldn't stop her."

"Yeah, I know," Morgan said. "I never could either."

CHAPTER 15

REES STEPPED INTO Danni's kitchen and shut the garage door behind him. He walked over to stand beside Morgan, giving the blond man squatting down there wide berth.

Danni stayed back by the door and kept her gun pointed at the man's head.

Morgan had him covered from another angle.

And yet somehow with two guns aimed right at this guy ... Rees still felt like they were at some kind of disadvantage here.

Get on your knees," Morgan said to him. "Hands behind your head."

The blond man did exactly as instructed, shifting efficiently to his knees and lacing both hands behind his head.

Morgan wasn't taking her eyes off him for an instant. "Rees, pick up his gun."

Rees dropped the golf club he'd grabbed in the garage and retrieved the man's gun from the floor. He marveled at the weighty compactness of the thing. A marvelous piece of mechanical engineering, really. He recognized the big pipe on the end as some kind of noise suppressor.

Danni's gaze kept ping-ponging back and forth from the man to Morgan. "Who the hell is this guy, Kerry?"

Morgan glanced at Rees. "Take a good look at him. Is this the shooter from the pier today? Take your time."

Rees studied the blond man's face. "It *could* be him. I'm not sure. It looks like the same gun."

The man on the floor here was wearing a gray suit. The shooter at the pier had been dressed more casually. Also he'd been a good hundred feet or so away and he'd had sunglasses on.

"That was me," the blond man offered in a relaxed tone. "I was wearing a Jimmy Buffett T-shirt. Remember?"

"Yes, that's right," Rees said. "He was."

"Sorry I didn't finish this back there. Coulda saved you all a lot of trouble." He looked up at Rees. "You in particular, pal. It's most likely gonna go a lot worse for *you* now."

Rees felt disoriented. The man's tone was so wildly at odds with the situation. That wasn't even a threat just then. No bravado or bluff in it. It sounded like someone apologizing for missing a lunch date.

"Look at me," Morgan ordered the blond man. "Who are you working for and why are you trying to kill this man?" She indicated Rees with a sideways toss of her head.

The blond man gazed calmly back at Morgan. "Hey, listen, I'll cooperate. All right? But I can't tell you who I'm working for, 'cause I honestly don't know. As far as the mission itself, that was to eliminate Dr. Rees here and two of the other conspirators. When it turned out Fischer was still alive? Well ... that little oversight was corrected."

After a brief pause, Morgan said, "Keep talking."

"I was also supposed to recover some stuff." He turned to Rees again. "Looks like you and your friends caught a little break there. Herodotus and Anaximander, I mean."

As Rees watched the man, he noted that he was being watched right back. Though not overtly.

The blond man continued. "Guess you don't know who they are. But you know how to get in touch. Might wanna give them a little heads up."

He hasn't told us anything we didn't already know. He's just interviewing us. Rees turned to Morgan. "He confessed to killing Fischer. You heard it. We have three witnesses here. We can call the police now, right? They're sure as hell going to believe me this time."

Danni turned to Morgan then. "*He* killed Edward Fischer? This is the actual guy who did it?" She was breathing in shallow gasps now and her hands began to shake.

She took a step toward the blond man.

"Danni, no," Morgan said. "Stay away from him."

Danni took another step then stopped. She lowered her gun, and leaned forward. Then she spit in the man's face. "You piece of shit. Do you have any idea what you did? You took the life of a great man."

The blond man didn't react. Not at first. Then Rees saw his eyes drift. They seemed to lose focus. His jaw muscles twitched strangely.

Something drew Rees's attention lower. A dark stain had appeared on the man's suit pants, at the crotch. It spread out as Rees watched.

He was pissing himself.

Danni didn't appear to have seen it. Too close to have a good angle maybe.

Rees glanced at Morgan. The look on her face—she'd definitely caught it.

"Danni, get back." Morgan said. "Get back, now."

The blond man's eyes rolled up into his head, leaving nothing visible but the whites. He made a choking sound, then coughed. A wet spray erupted. Red droplets appeared on the white floor tiles.

Blood. And now blood began to run from the man's mouth.

He toppled onto his side and started to convulse violently.

Danni stepped back. "Oh my God. What's happening to him?"

"He's having some kind of seizure," Rees said.

The man curled up into a fetal position. The convulsions abruptly ceased. He didn't appear to be breathing.

Rees leaned in to see if the man's shirt was moving, looking for any sign of respiration.

The blond man exploded in a blur of motion.

Rees gasped and fell backwards into Morgan. As they both tumbled, he caught a glimpse of the blond man all over Danni.

Rees and Morgan hit the floor with an incredibly loud *bang*. Then Rees realized that wasn't them at all.

That was a gunshot.

He saw Danni on the floor now too. Behind her, the door to the garage was opened again.

The blond man was gone. But there was more blood on the floor.

A lot more blood.

CHAPTER 16

Six months earlier—Busra

ADNAN TOTAH CHECKED his watch. He stubbed out his cigarette. Just past two a.m. and that meant his current boss, Joshua Amsel, had been up in his room for almost three hours.

Time to get on with it.

Totah rose from his chair outside the closed café and started walking back to the hotel.

The warm night air offered scant relief from the day's withering heat. Not a problem for Amsel, of course. A block away, he and his men relaxed in the air-conditioned comfort of Cham Palace, Busra's only first class hotel. Money equaled privilege, as it always had.

Totah had money on his mind tonight, more so even than usual.

He had spent half the evening sitting in a dark corner of the hotel's bar, keeping watch on the old archaeologist until he finally staggered out. After the day's whisky-fueled celebrations, Amsel would be deeply asleep by now.

The whole operation pulled up stakes tomorrow. Amsel and his men would soon be gone. And with them would go the mystery of this whole strange affair.

The impossibly charmed dig. The weird, high-tech surveying tools.

And the codex.

Which was apparently the target of the entire effort. All that work, all those resources for one ancient document. How could it possibly be worth it?

One of Totah's men had proffered an explanation at dinner earlier that night. "Magik is at the heart of this thing," he said in a low voice. "We know he uses a jinni, maybe many. What if this is an ancient book of spells and incantations? Dark knowledge lost to the ages. Such a thing could bring power and fortune to one who knows how to wield it!"

Nods and agreeing grunts greeted the sensational conjecture.

Totah had a slightly more prosaic explanation, which he did not share with the table.

The Romans, Byzantines, and Ottomans—who had all been here at various times—used writing mainly for the purpose of record keeping. What kind of records would be worth the expense and risk of coming into the middle of a civil war to retrieve?

Records of hoarded gold. Of secret vaults, of taxes collected and diverted, perhaps by a dishonest Roman governor or Ottoman Bey.

What if the codex was a kind of treasure map?

That would explain much. Yes, it would.

Totah slipped into the hotel through a side door. He'd duct-taped the door's latch open before he left earlier in the evening. If Amsel had security people posted back in the lobby, Totah was already past them now.

He made his way up to Amsel's floor via the fire exit stairs, and stood outside the archaeologist's door listening. He smiled at what he heard there.

The old man had some extra kilos on him. Like many heavy men, he snored.

The room key duplicate had cost Totah two month's wages. It would be well worth it. If it worked.

He carefully slid the plastic rectangle in and out of the lock slot. The light on the mechanism flashed red. The door remained firmly locked.

No, no, no.

He tried the key again. Again the red light.

His heart, which had already been beating quickly, thumped against his ribs now.

He tried again, a bit faster.

A green light and a soft *click*. He was in.

Totah closed the door quietly behind him. The room had a stale cigarette smell. And it was wonderfully cool. The snoring continued from what appeared to be the separate bedroom of a small suite.

Totah stood still, breathing quietly through opened mouth, and waited for his eyes to adjust to the near darkness.

When he could see well enough, he crept over to the bedroom door and carefully closed it. It made a tight fit, and the door was heavy and felt quite solid. He could barely detect Amsel's snoring now, which meant that Amsel surely could not hear Totah's quiet movements in the next room.

When he turned around, the codex was sitting directly in his line of sight. It lay there on the dining table, resting on a folded piece of clean linen.

It had been opened.

A pair of cotton gloves lay beside it, along with several textbooks bearing German titles. Also a leather-bound notebook, which he had seen Amsel carrying many times.

Totah took out his smartphone. He'd made sure it was fully charged and that the camera's simulated shutter noise was disabled. The closed bedroom door behind him already eliminated what had been one of his bigger worries. The flash. That would not matter now.

He approached the table, thinking whatever page of the codex Amsel had been examining was already likely to be important. A piece of luck there.

As he stood over the ancient book, Totah couldn't quite make out the writing in the darkened room. Then he remembered the phone's flashlight function. With the bedroom door closed, it had become a viable option.

More good luck. Fate was smiling on him.

He shone his light down on the page, and soon thrilled to realize he could read the words there. Some of them at least.

There were no lines or dots above or below the words— marks that indicated vowels and helped distinguish certain letters from each other. Early Arabic lacked them. That meant this writing was surely very old.

And then, as he continued to decipher the text, a familiar pattern began to emerge. A kind of rhythm.

Totah's heart sank. Yes, he could read quite a few of these words. And he already had. Many, many times. Not a treasure map here.

This was the holy Qur'an.

It seemed that Amsel had found an ancient copy. While surely valuable, there were other ancient Qur'an manuscripts. Hundreds. Maybe thousands of them.

Still, there had to be something quite special about this one. Perhaps it was one of the five Uthman Qur'ans. One manuscript only *suspected* of being an Uthman Qur'an was held in a museum in Tashkent. It was considered priceless.

Totah carefully turned one of the stiff, brown pages of this Qur'an ... and found himself surprised, and a bit perplexed. Slowly he turned back again. Then forward. This simply could not be right.

In the name of Allah, what is this strange book?

Amsel's notebook on the table caught Totah's eye. Perhaps he would find an explanation there.

Totah possessed enough English to follow Amsel's general thoughts. As he flipped the pages of the old man's journal, his mind began to race along with his pulse. Soon came a low roaring in his ears. Then the bile began to rise, hot and bitter, in his throat.

Jinn? Amsel was playing with something much worse than jinn here. Satan himself had set his hand to this disgusting plot.

"Dogs," he muttered. "And you will die like dogs."

He turned off the flashlight function on his phone and put it away. Totah carried only a pocket knife, but it would do to cut the throat of the old man. Then he would take this abomination and commit it to the same flames into which its author had been cast.

He pulled out his pocket knife and opened it, then grabbed the codex roughly off the table.

"Put that down, Adnan."

Totah turned to see Amsel standing in his robe in the opened bedroom doorway. Something dark there in his hand.

"I didn't pay you well enough?" Amsel asked. "You have to steal from me too? I'm deeply disappointed."

Totah shook the codex at him. "This is a lie," he growled.

Amsel's eyebrows shot up. "Oh. So, you've read my notes. Well, this is very interesting. Very interesting, indeed." He paused a moment. "Tell me then—what were your first thoughts?"

Totah spit on the rusted copper cover of the evil thing. "It is a fraud."

"Hmm. And yet you saw it come out of the earth with your own eyes. Your hand-picked men excavated the site." Amsel took a step closer.

"You knew where it was because you planted it there. That is why this dig was so productive. You always knew exactly where everything was to be found."

"Yes, I knew it was there. But not for the reason you think." Amsel held a hand out, palm up. "Give that to me. Despite what you might wish to believe, it's quite real. That's precisely why it is exceedingly valuable."

A glint of light from the barrel confirmed the gun in Amsel's other hand. The old man took another step. He stumbled in the darkness.

Totah leapt forward.

The explosion of pain followed an instant after the muzzle flash. Totah's legs crumpled beneath him.

As he lay on the floor, feeling the hot blood spread across his chest and run down his side, Totah thought of the Paradise he would soon find.

He was dying a martyr, after all.

CHAPTER 17

THE GUY WHO killed Edward Fischer had leapt up onto Danni like one of those goddamn facehugger things from Alien. As she fell to the kitchen floor, she felt and heard her target pistol go off.

And then he was gone.

And then she saw the blood. On and all around her.

"Am I shot? I think I might be shot." She started to sit up, and then thought maybe she shouldn't.

Morgan appeared an instant later and knelt down beside her.

She took the pistol out of Danni's hand. "Hey, just breathe. Okay? I'm gonna check you out here. Just breathe."

Danni closed her eyes, afraid of what she might see. She felt Morgan's hands run over her head and neck first. Then gently roll her onto her side and examine her torso and legs.

"It's all right," Morgan said at last.

Danni opened her eyes.

Morgan brought her face down close. "The good news is that's not your blood. The better news is it's that asshole's blood."

Danni could feel her whole body vibrating. "I gotta get up."

"I don't know." Rees was looking down at her with concern. "You look kind of gray. You might want to just sit there a minute."

She picked herself up off the floor. "Yeah, I just, I gotta move."

Morgan offered a hand. Danni grabbed it and stood all the way up. No dizziness, but a cold flush washed over her. She felt the blood draining from her face. She flung her arms out and pushed Rees aside.

And just managed to get to the sink before she threw up.

Danni waited until she thought she puked up everything she ate in the last month. Then took Morgan with her to the master bedroom.

Rees stayed behind with the blond guy's gun, keeping a look out. Although no one expected that dude to come back any time soon.

In the bathroom, Morgan turned on the water in the tub. She directed it to the shower extension then unhooked that.

Danni pulled off her blood splattered T-shirt, and knelt with her head over the tub. Morgan ran warm water over her scalp and neck. Danni splashed some on her face. She watched the red water swirling down the drain. After a couple of minutes, the water ran clear and clean again.

"Feel a little better?" Morgan asked.

"Yeah. I'm okay. I think."

Morgan turned off the water and rehung the shower extension.

Danni stood up. She let the warm water from her hair run down her bare chest and back. She stared at the bloodied T-shirt down at her feet. It didn't look real.

Morgan handed her a towel. Danni towel dried her hair and patted beads of water off her chest and belly.

"Here..." Morgan took the towel and dried Danni's back for her.

Danni closed her eyes. It felt so nice. It felt so ... right. Yeah. It felt really right. *Why'd you let her go? Why didn't you fight harder to keep her?*

She wanted to say something. About how they'd made a mistake back then. How she still missed Morgan. But she couldn't think straight. Her head was swimming.

She ended up by saying, "So, this isn't like a regular day for you now, is it?"

Morgan hung the towel around Danni's shoulders. "Well, I'm definitely going to ask for a raise if this is the new normal."

Danni turned and looked into Morgan's eyes. She felt her own eyes begin to tear up.

Morgan embraced her then. They stood like that a long time. Silently. Holding each other as they had before, not so very long ago.

"Do you think I killed him?" Danni asked in a whisper. "Maybe he went off somewhere and died. I wasn't trying to kill him, Kerry."

Morgan's voice came softly in her ear. "It's okay, hon. You didn't do anything wrong. You might have saved all our lives."

Danni pulled back just far enough to see Morgan's face. "Whoever hired that guy, they're really worried about whatever Fischer was doing."

Morgan nodded. "Yes, they want to make sure nothing gets out."

"So that guy in my kitchen, even if he's dead now ... this isn't over, is it?"

Morgan hesitated, like maybe she wouldn't answer that one. "No. I don't think it is. These are serious people with serious resources behind them. But I won't let anything happen to you, Danni."

Danni nodded then hugged Morgan again. She wanted to stay there forever. But she could tell she was going to start crying bigtime if it lasted any longer, so she let go. "I guess I should put on something warm. Come on." She turned and walked out of the bathroom.

Morgan followed her. "Do you feel chilled? You could be a little shocky still."

Danni stepped into the walk-in closet. She kicked the clothes on the floor there out of her way. "No, it's just the lab is pretty cold. There's cryogenics."

"The lab?"

"Yeah." She turned to face Morgan. "We're going to Lawrence Livermore. We need to find out what this Kafir Project is all about."

"Danni."

"Screw those people, Kerry. I'm not gonna let the last work that Edward Fischer did disappear off the face of the earth. Not if it's in my goddamn lab."

Morgan folded her arms over her chest. "Listen, you can't just—"

"Kerry, I *work* in that lab. You think you're gonna stop me from poking around, trying to find Fischer's stuff? Also, it's safer doing it with you there and after hours. So now's the perfect time."

Morgan still had her arms folded, but she didn't look mad. "I'm not going to be able to talk you out of this."

"Duh." Danni grabbed a yellow cable knit sweater off a shelf along with an old pair of jeans. She dropped her sweat pants to the floor and stepped out of them.

"I want you to carry the gun we just got off that man," Morgan told her. "The nine millimeter. Not your target pistol."

"No problem." Danni walked out of the closet in just her panties, carrying the fresh clothes. She liked the way Morgan was looking at her.

And then the words seemed to just tumble out. "I missed you, Kerry. I really did. I still think about you. A lot. I think about us."

Morgan said nothing. The silence was awful.

Danni felt a rush of embarrassment and tried to backpedal. "And ... you don't have to say 'I missed you, too,' okay? I wasn't fishing or anything."

Morgan nodded. "Okay." Then she stood there quietly as the agonizing seconds stretched on. Finally the corners of her lips turned up. "It would be better if I said it, though, right?"

Danni smiled. "Eh, it wouldn't kill ya."

Morgan smiled back. "I missed you too."

Danni pulled on her jeans, feeling shaky and excited at the same time. "By the way, next time? Call first. You know, before you show up with Gevin frickin' Rees, and a trained assassin on your ass."

Morgan was still grinning. "Sure thing."

CHAPTER 18

AS SOON AS Sabel realized he missed his grab at the weapon, retreat became the only real option.

Even if he hadn't just been shot.

There were two other guns in that kitchen pointed his way, including his own SIG, loaded with custom, high-powered, hollow point rounds. That had left him no time to wrestle around with the woman who lived there over her .22 popgun.

He'd flown out the door into the garage then out to the yard, and continued trucking as fast as he could into the street.

Then he headed back to where he'd parked the stolen Toyota—tongue still bleeding from where he'd bitten it as part of the diversion. He swallowed the blood rather than spit it out and leave a visible trail.

Sabel stopped when he could be relatively certain no one had followed.

He examined the bullet wound in his leg. Small entrance wound in the anterior, upper, right thigh. Bleeding profusely. Might involve the femoral artery.

He palpated the back of the same leg. No exit wound.

He pressed hard and felt the nerve signal light up his brain like a pinball machine. He didn't resist the signal. That wouldn't work. But Sabel possessed a rare gift. He could reimagine that same signal as a sensation of intense cold. An ability he discovered quite by accident in the mountains of Afghanistan.

Sabel located the flattened .22 bullet in the meat of his hamstring. He began to formulate a plan for dealing with it as he continued on to the car.

After driving a short distance away to ensure no incoming police units would cut off his escape route, he stopped briefly and grabbed a sock out of his bag.

He wadded it up and pressed it against the femoral artery, right at the bend between leg and hip. Then he stripped off his necktie and used it to bind the sock into place. That would slow the bleeding, at least until he got himself to a hospital.

He located the nearest one on his smartphone and clicked the link to navigate there.

Less than ten minutes later, about a block or two away from the ER, Sabel pulled into a parking lot behind a closed auto parts store.

He stopped the car and texted the Office he was going offline for six hours. Then he grabbed the little squeeze bottle of hand sanitizer from his toiletries and got out.

Rummaging around in the stolen Toyota's trunk, he found a tool box there. He just wanted a set of needle nosed pliers and a Philips head screwdriver, and he found them both. Good start there.

With the Phillips, Sabel punched a small hole in the back of his right pant leg over the spot where the bullet had lodged. He removed one dress shoe and placed it on the hood of the car. He'd be needing that in a minute.

He turned to face the light from a nearby streetlamp. Then shifted his pant leg around until the hole in it overlaid the entry wound. He could spot that pretty easy, even with his leg badly bloodied.

Fresh blood continued to pulse out of it despite the compression bandage he'd improvised.

Sabel slathered hand sanitizer over the shaft of the screwdriver and all around the outside of the wound. Then he slowly inserted the screwdriver tip into the gory hole in his leg.

Cold. Freezing cold.

He pushed deeper into the leg muscle, deeper, feeling for the angle of the bullet's path through his quadriceps.

An icicle, freezing everything it touches.

He felt resistance and tested it. Yes. The bullet's path ended right there.

Sabel picked up the shoe. He grabbed it firmly around the instep with the heel down.

Using his left hand, he held the screwdriver steady. With his right, he raised the shoe up about even with the top of his head.

He swung down, hard and true.

The shoe's heel smacked the end of the screwdriver's handle. It drove the tip through the remaining muscle, through the skin on the back of his leg and out the back of his pants.

Sabel's concentration slipped. Pain leaked into his mind.

He cut loose with a howl that turned into a barking laugh. Finally, he brought that under control.

"Alright. Alright, now. Cold. It's so cold."

He returned to imagining his leg encased in ice. The blood flowing along the back of his thigh and calf—just melting ice water, running down, dripping into his sock.

From the hole he'd made in the back of his pants, a jagged bit of the bullet stuck out, along with the screwdriver's bloody tip.

"Yeah. There you go."

He grabbed the pliers, clamped down on the deformed bullet and tugged. It came out easily and all in one piece. Another nice bit of luck.

He dropped it there in the parking lot.

Driving with the screwdriver impaling his right leg like this would be a challenge. But when he got to the emergency room, no one would question for a moment that some kind of terrible accident had occurred.

Can you believe it? Putting in a light fixture and fell off the damn step ladder. Musta landed on the screwdriver 'cause, well, there it is.

Bullet wounds brought mandatory police response. Stupid household accidents brought a couple of wisecracks at worst, and top flight medical care.

Better than he'd get from an off-the-books medicine man, even if there was one handy to him right around here. And there wasn't.

So Sabel had done what he had to do. As he always did. Cashing in once more on his special talent.

CHAPTER 19

New York City

ONE LAST, BRIEF errand and Doubleman could call it a night. He just needed to see a man about a murder. Wouldn't take long.

And thank God for that. It felt good to be out of the snow and the bone chilling winter air, but the taxi smelled like a warm, wet dog. Make that a warm, wet dog doused in whatever cheap cologne this particular Middle Eastern taxi driver favored.

It had been a difficult day. To be sure, Doubleman had certainly seen worse. Yes, Gevin Rees—the TV science guy, as Carl Truby had called him—had proven to be more of a challenge than they anticipated.

On the other hand, the meeting with Truby had gone well. He okayed the back-up plan, which entailed a fair amount of wetwork. Unfortunate, because that was quite expensive. But it would still leave the Office with an acceptable profit when all was said and done.

Doubleman didn't know who stood behind Truby in all this, but the man represented the power elite across a number of nations. Worst case scenario here? Even if this particular job turned into a loss-leader, it would open a lot of very lucrative doors.

The driver pulled over and stopped at the corner of Fifth Avenue and East 28th Street, as he had been previously directed.

The man that Doubleman needed stood there in a camel hair trench coat, patiently waiting. Dependable as always.

Maher Faraj. The one they called the Specialist whenever another operative needed to know that he was in the loop.

Faraj lowered his large frame into the taxi just as the light changed. The driver eased them back into the flow of traffic.

"Thank you for making yourself available on short notice," Doubleman said.

Faraj nodded with eyes closed, a miniature bow. "Always."

"The details are here." Doubleman took an envelope from his coat and offered it to him.

Faraj accepted it, opened it. He removed the note and read.

Doubleman watched his eyes. They were a startling shade of green. A drawback in his profession. Too noticeable. Too easily remembered. Obviously the man had skills that outweighed that handicap.

When he finished reading, Faraj refolded the note and inserted it back into the envelope. "To confirm. The information you want includes the location of stored data and artifacts, yes?"

"Correct."

"You will bring Rees to me for interrogation in San Francisco?"

"Yes. A contact number for our man out there is in your envelope. We'll have Rees in hand very soon, if we don't already."

Faraj pursed his lips and nodded back. "Mmm. And so the data in question, this is from a Defense Department project. Codename Kafir."

Thick Plexiglas separated them from the driver, but Doubleman dropped his voice anyway and leaned in close. "That's correct. And not just the original project. Fischer and some others went rogue, it appears. We're just as interested in their phase II, if you like. It's all in your briefing there." Doubleman gestured to the envelope. "We think we already have one of them identified. The one they're calling Herodotus.

We need confirmation there and the names of any other surviving collaborators. We want anything Rees knows that might lead us forward."

"Very good." Faraj tucked the envelope into his jacket.

"Payment will be delivered as per the usual protocols." Doubleman leaned forward, and raised his voice to penetrate the Plexiglas barrier. "Driver, stop at this corner."

The driver continued through the green light and up Fifth Avenue.

"Driver, I said—"

Doubleman felt a sharp pain in his right ear.

FARAJ INSERTED THE ice pick cleanly and swiveled the handle to tear up the maximum amount of brain tissue.

He could never perform this procedure, technically neurolysis, without thinking of the odd English word for it.

Pithing.

A funny little word. Hard to say it without smiling.

Doubleman twitched briefly and then slumped. Faraj removed the ice pick and wiped the shaft with a handkerchief. Then he held that to Doubleman's ear, to keep things neat and clean.

They didn't always die quickly this way. And in fact Doubleman was still breathing. Probably he could not feel pain, though. All opportunities in that respect were lost.

Faraj felt genuinely sorry for that. He never took a life needlessly. Life was precious. A death must never be wasted. Unfortunately there had been little prep time for this contract, and he'd needed more or less to improvise here.

The driver glanced at him in the rear-view mirror. He reached back and slid open the Plexiglas divider between them. "There will be cameras at the toll plaza. Is there blood?"

"No. Nothing to see."

The driver nodded and slid the divider closed.

Faraj understood how the data and artifacts from the Kafir Project could be indescribably valuable to the right party. For very different reasons. And of course Doubleman's client wasn't alone in wanting to possess them. An Islamic group had already hired Faraj for exactly the same purpose.

So when Doubleman contacted Faraj with useful information just a few hours later? Well, the poor man had unwittingly signed his own death warrant right there and then.

Practically speaking, Faraj could not have gained these important leads from Doubleman tonight and also allowed him to live. Doubleman would eventually have figured out he'd been betrayed. And you did not double-cross the group that called itself the Office.

At least not without making sure that no one still breathing knew it.

That meant the Office operative who handed Rees over in San Francisco would have to die now as well. At least Faraj would have time to prepare for that.

He would not let that man down as he had Doubleman.

Faraj had no idea what the Kafir Project's output would eventually reveal. It interested him, of course. Not nearly as much as it interested his clients. They most certainly had, as they say, a dog in that fight.

Would it affect his life?

Quite possibly. But it could not alter his purpose. Nothing science could reveal would change the fundamental truth of existence.

Life is fleeting.

Outrageously so when compared to eternity.

Long life or short, it made no difference. The largest grain of sand is still but a grain of sand, lost on an infinite beach. So to long for *more* life, as most did—that was pure foolishness.

What mattered was the *depth* of feeling one reached while alive.

And no other feeling approached the enormity of pain.

The greatest joy imaginable could never come anywhere close. Those who knew the depths of pain had felt life as completely as it ever could be felt.

They alone knew its full value.

Faraj gave this gift to his charges, whenever he could. *That* was his purpose. What piece of scientific data could ever change that?

CHAPTER 20

REES DIDN'T THINK Danni would mind him using the computer in her spare bedroom and he had an idea he wanted to check out. He held Fischer's little flash drive in a hand that was still shaking, and read the brand name and model number.

An internet search quickly turned up a description of the drive in Google Shopping.

Rees pumped a fist in the air. "Yes. It *is* waterproof. All right then. Let's see what the hell we've got here."

He plugged the flash drive into one of the USB ports. An external drive icon popped up on the desktop. The title read: *Assembled sets A-20*. He double-clicked the icon.

Files, three of them. The file names just strings of digits.

Rees clicked on the top file. It had been created fairly recently. A media application opened, but not the file itself. Rees clicked the file name again. This time the application crashed. The file seemed to be corrupted.

And maybe not so much waterproof.

He clicked the next file. This one a little less than a year old.

The same media application reopened. But this time a video played.

"That's better."

An image appeared in a circular frame, the edges blurry. Within the frame a man with a full beard was speaking a foreign language. Something Middle Eastern, Rees thought. The man was more or less in focus, but not much else. Very little depth of field on this lens, apparently.

An indoor setting. Not large. Natural lighting from a skylight or windows.

The bearded man stood before an audience seated on benches. Their clothing looked rough, coarse. The man intoned to them in a mellifluent voice, rhythmic, rising and falling. At intervals, they responded to him in unison.

This was a religious ceremony.

The bearded man read from a book. A codex, to be more precise. Shining metal covers of copper or brass. In fact, the codex seemed to be the focal point of the shot. It certainly was the sharpest object in view.

The bearded man lifted something. Held it high. It was ... bread. And next, an unmistakable gesture. One that had been reenacted innumerable times down through the ages. He broke it.

A celebration of the Eucharist here. Holy Communion.

The image began to pixelate in an odd way. Then it faded to black. The recording had ended.

Fascinated, Rees clicked on the next file. This one closer to two years old.

A forest scene this time. Again the circular frame.

Difficult to gauge the scale in this one. There was nothing in the shot but vegetation. Ferns mostly, and some trees that could be magnolias. As before, the edges of the frame and the background were out of focus.

Rees heard footsteps coming up behind him and remembered that he'd set the gun down on the desk. Out of reach.

He jumped up, knocking his chair over and grabbed for the gun.

"Whoa. Easy, easy."

He recognized Morgan's voice, and nearly collapsed in relief.

When he turned around, Morgan and Danni were both there in the room with him. Danni had changed clothes, and her dark skin didn't have that grayish tone it had taken on back there in the kitchen.

Morgan held out a hand. "Why don't you give me that, Rees?"

Rees noticed the gun was pointed right at Morgan. "Sorry, sorry." He grabbed it by the barrel and gave it to her. "I guess I'm a little jumpy still."

Danni was staring at the computer monitor. "What is that?"

Rees righted the overturned chair. "Oh, I have a flash drive from Fischer. There's some video."

"No, I mean, that. What is *that*?" She pointed at the screen.

Rees turned back to the video. At first, he couldn't quite put together what he saw there. Familiar somehow, though.

"Is that a bird?" Morgan leaned forward. "It looks too big."

And then Rees remembered. Where he'd seen this creature, recently too. The colors were different. No way to guess the colors. "Is it a bird? Technically, no."

The animal onscreen had brilliant blue and red feathers arranged in a striking pattern. It stepped slowly across the shot with a bipedal gait. Head down. Hunting maybe. Either it moved silently or this recording lacked a soundtrack.

As they watched, the animal seemed to spot something in the vegetation. Its crested head whipped down, then came up with a wriggling lizard in its bite.

Rees heard the strike. So there was sound here too.

Danni stepped closer to the screen. "That's ... a dinosaur."

Rees smiled. "It certainly is."

Morgan crowded in too. "So, what is this? CGI?"

"Well, that's what I would have thought," Rees answered, "if this file wasn't about two years old. And if that wasn't a species of oviraptorosaur called *Anzu wyliei*. The first composite skeleton of that species was assembled, oh, maybe two months ago. So no, it's not animation."

Danni kept edging in closer, as if the screen had a gravitational pull. "But if that's not computer animation ... I'm a little confused. What are we watching here?"

"Well, based on the animal," Rees said, "I'd guess we're looking at what became the Hell's Creek rock formation. A little more than sixty-six million years ago."

As they watched, the dinosaur strutted off screen, rustling through the foliage, its lizard lunch still wriggling in its beak.

The image pixelated out. The video ended.

Wide-eyed, Danni shook her head. "What the hell was Fischer doing at Fermilab?"

Rees just couldn't stop smiling. "Bending spacetime."

Danni's jaw literally dropped. "He built a goddamn time machine? Like, for real?"

Rees knew how incredible it sounded, but could imagine no likelier explanation. "I suppose you could call it a time machine, from what I can make of his notes and now this video. Maybe what we just saw is, they sent a camera back to the Cretaceous somehow."

Danni looked as stunned as Rees had felt when he first grasped the direction of Fischer's work. She paced back and forth along a short stretch of the bedroom carpet. "But it's not possible. You can't actually do that."

Morgan shrugged. "Why not? If you had a multi-billion dollar facility like Fermilab, and DARPA funding, and a mind like Edward Fischer's..."

Danni stopped. "Okay, I'm no Edward Fischer, and neither is anyone else. But there's paradoxes. You go back in time and you're gonna change history. Maybe just a teeny bit. But over a long period that little deviation turns huge. Eventually you get a whole different universe. One where there's no Edward Fischer around to build a time machine. So then you can't go back and change things, right? And so then there *is* an Edward Fischer. And so you *do* go back ... and on and on."

It was Rees's turn to shake his head. "Okay, yes, but there's the Novikov self-consistency principle. Closed time-like loops might, in a self-governing way, reduce the probability of any paradoxical action to zero. All other actions are permitted. And there's also the multiverse scenario in which—"

"Hey, guys." Morgan raised her voice just enough to cut them off. "I have a question."

"Yes?" Rees and Danni both answered at once.

"If the Kafir Project is about time travel, why would DARPA fund it? How would you weaponize this research?"

"That's a damn good question," Rees said. "And the first thing that comes to my mind is, you could assassinate any enemy. Before they even came to power."

"Yes, but the past is the past," Danni countered. "If someone travelled back in time, then that already happened. Right? Along with whatever changes occurred. You can't go back and kill Hitler, 'cause if you did, that *already* happened in like 1939, or whenever. We'd all know about it. And then you wouldn't have gone back to kill him. Even if you'd still been born in that new timeline you made, which isn't very likely."

Rees didn't see any way around the paradox either. "She's right. The only backwards time travel that's remotely thinkable would have to be a scenario where you didn't change the timeline at all. Not in the universe you left from, anyway. Hard to see the military use in that."

Danni walked to the door of the spare bedroom, stopped and looked back. "C'mon, let's go."

"Go where?" Rees asked.

"To Livermore, to get on the secure computers. The data could still be there. Or we can just sit here till whoever wants this all to go away finds us again." Without waiting for a reply, Danni left the room.

"She made up her mind before we saw the video," Morgan said. "And I think she's right. This is the best way forward."

Rees agreed, and in minutes they were all in Danni's car and headed to Livermore.

Fischer had said that Herodotus would have a copy of the project data. Getting their hands on that would be wonderful. But right now they weren't even sure where Herodotus might be.

All that would cease to be a problem, if they could find another copy of the data on the computer at Livermore.

And Rees had another motivation for finding that data.

Even if getting it all in the open wasn't the surest way out of trouble, he would still need to understand all this.

He would need to for the same reason he needed to understand how the universe, and this galaxy, and all the stars and planets in it came to be exactly the way they were.

Because he was curious. Rees was intensely and profoundly curious. It's what drove him today as it always had.

CHAPTER 21

IN HER THREE years at Lawrence Livermore National Laboratory, Danni had been subjected to a random vehicle inspection exactly once. As she pulled up to the campus gate with two uncleared visitors hiding in her trunk, she hoped this would not be the night to make it twice.

"You're working late, Dr. Harris." The guard swiped Danni's ID and pass card, logging in her presence at a secured Defense Department site.

Danni smiled as she took back the ID. "Up against a deadline."

"That's a lot of real bull."

Danni felt her breath hitch. *Jesus Christ, I'm caught already?*

The guard was looking into her car. "What is that there, sixteen ounces?"

She followed his eyes to the giant can of energy drink resting in her cup holder. *He said a lot of Red Bull, you idiot. Red Bull.*

Danni smiled again. "Yeah. Yeah, gonna be a long night."

"Well, better get to it then."

"Right, 'cause it's gonna be a long night." *You already said that, Harris. Shut up and drive.*

The gate lifted and Danni drove onto the LLNL campus with her heart beating in her mouth. *Note to self—forget about becoming an international drug smuggler.*

REES COULDN'T MAKE out the conversation through the trunk lid. He assumed it was Danni talking with a guard. Moments after it ended the car lurched forward.

He lay curled up with Morgan curled up in front of him. Spooning, essentially. Regardless of her sexual orientation and the surreal circumstances, he had to admit to himself ... it really felt kind of nice.

There were drawbacks to *not doing close*. He had to admit that fact too.

It didn't surprise Rees, how easily he and Morgan had just been smuggled onto a US Defense Department secure facility. To settle his anxiety, Morgan had explained earlier how it was the University of California that managed the Livermore facility. The security services here were essentially campus cops.

A couple minutes later the trunk lid popped opened and Danni stood there waving them out. "C'mon. Coast is clear."

Rees crawled out after Morgan, then reached back in and grabbed Fischer's leather pouch. They might want to cross-reference something they found here with the notebook. He threw the pouch's strap over his shoulder and gently closed the trunk. The *click* sound of the latch catching still made him wince.

Rees and Morgan followed Danni to the door of an unmarked and unremarkable looking structure.

Danni pulled out her pass key. "So, this is the quantum computing building."

A camera over the door reminded Rees of something else Morgan told him. Their presence here would not remain a secret if anyone had a reason to look. Video images of all of them would be available until the recordings were overwritten. Seventy-two hours.

Danni slid her pass key. An electronic lock clicked.

She opened the door, and turned back to Rees and Morgan. "Remember if anyone's working a late shift, they're just gonna assume you were cleared through security at the gate. Everybody's kind of isolated in this building anyway, because we had to block out all external radiation."

"To shield the quantum effects from interference?" Rees asked.

"Yeah. So no phone or radio signals in there. Now, technically all visitors should be wearing pass badges, but people do take them off. If someone asks, you left it in the car."

Rees desperately hoped they didn't run into anyone. He suspected he'd start sweating like a sumo in a sauna. James Bond he was not.

Danni walked in first with Morgan behind her. Rees entered last, letting the door close after him with a too final sounding *thunk*.

The empty lobby was brightly lit with recessed fluorescents. Except for the lack of a poster or two on the walls, it looked like some very unpopular dentist's office. Magazines scattered across a coffee table. Old magazines at that. A faux leather couch. Bottled water dispenser.

The only thing unusual here was the climate. It was a cool night out to begin with. Inside, the temperature had dropped a good ten more degrees.

Goose bumps prickled Rees's arms. "You weren't kidding about this place being cold."

Danni led them over to the only door the room had, other than the one they came in. "You're lucky we're just after records in the mainframe." She positioned herself in front of what looked like a retinal scanner. "It's a lot worse when you're near the Core, working with Alan."

Rees heard the soft whir of machinery. Danni opened the door and held it for them as they walked through.

"Who's Alan?" Rees asked Danni as she slipped by him to take the lead again.

"Oh, the quantum computer. You know, after Turing."

They walked down a long white hallway. Nearly every door they passed had an additional security lock.

"It didn't have a name when I was here the last time," Morgan commented from behind Rees.

Danni spoke over her shoulder. "Yeah. That was before we brought it up to full capacity. Then it started generating its own code. Kind of talking to itself. We joked how it was becoming self-aware. Like Skynet in the Terminator movies. So we named him."

They reached a T-intersection. Danni led them to the right.

Rees had done a show segment not long before on artificial intelligence and recalling it sparked a question. "You think Alan could really be self-aware on some level? You know, there's a theory that human consciousness arises from quantum effects in microtubules in the brain."

Danni laughed. "I seriously doubt it. About Alan, I mean. It would be cool, though, wouldn't it?"

After the AI episode aired, a few hyper-religious viewers wrote indignant posts in the comments section of the show's webpage. Man overstepping his natural limits, etc. Your basic Dr. Frankenstein stuff.

"That would make you rather godlike, wouldn't it?" Rees said. "If you actually *created* consciousness."

Danni shrugged. "I suppose."

"You could start your own religion," Morgan suggested.

Danni slowed as they approached the end of the hall. "Eh, it's been done. My parents were Scientologists, so..."

"Really?" Rees said. "I never met one. I don't think."

"Well, you still haven't. I didn't follow them."

"You mind if I ask why?" It wasn't really the time or place, but Rees's own history pushed him to inquire.

Danni pulled her pass key again and stopped in front of another security door. "Basically, I found out a nutbag alcoholic sci-fi writer made it all up. Not like it's some big secret. Google it."

She swiped her card. The lock mechanism issued the same soft whir as the door from the lobby.

And in they went.

THE MAN KNOWN to others in the Office command structure as Mr. Singleton took the secure call over Ohio at forty thousand feet.

"Dr. Harris has just logged in at Lawrence Livermore," the analyst told him. "No information on whether Rees is with her. The probability is high."

"All right. Doubleman hasn't checked in. I'm officially taking charge of this account. All decisions come through me from here on forward."

"Understood."

Singleton disconnected. He looked out the window of the private jet. Probably Fort Wayne, those lights down there. He'd be in D.C. in less than an hour. He planned to have the new strategy up and running before they landed.

Doubleman, in New York, was almost certainly dead.

He would never go incommunicado in the middle of an operation. Massive reprisals would be required for the sake of both the Office's status and its security.

That would have to wait.

Sabel out in San Francisco had called in an address in Pleasanton that Gevin Rees sought out. The house was rented to a Dr. Danielle Harris, computer scientist at Livermore.

You didn't have to be a data analyst to see the connection to Fischer. The Kafir Project had processing components at Livermore Labs. When Sabel lost Rees after action at that house in Pleasanton, Singleton ordered electronic feelers set out for anything connected to Danielle Harris that popped up on the grid.

And something just had.

Unfortunately, Sabel was temporarily out of commission. A wound that required medical attention. For *that* man to take himself offline, it must be a damned serious injury. Rees's new bodyguard or whatever the hell she was—the woman was either very, very good, or the luckiest woman on the face of the earth. Still no name on her.

It all meant that Singleton would have to get creative, and bring more resources to bear here.

Rees and Harris would be there at Livermore in connection with Fisher's DARPA work. That was pretty much a given. And in that case, a very doable option had just opened up.

All that would be required was some highly classified information and the services of a good hacker.

The sorts of things Singleton always had right at his fingertips. Even at forty-thousand feet.

CHAPTER 22

"I DON'T KNOW if Fischer's name will be included as the lead scientist, but—" Danni stopped abruptly as she entered the computer terminal bay.

They were not alone here.

As he followed Danni and Morgan into the room, Rees saw a young man seated at a terminal. He had just swiveled his chair toward them and he greeted them with a look of happy surprise.

"Hey, Danni. What's up?"

He had to be one of the computer scientists here. But with his long, black hair and soul patch—the young man looked more like a DJ for an indie rock radio station.

"Hey, Louis," Danni answered. "I just need to take a look at some results from the last laser ignition fusion simulation."

Louis nodded. "Ah, and that data is all offline."

"Yeah, because foreign governments wanna steal technology for fusion reactors that eat more energy than they make."

Louis laughed. "Well, we're gonna achieve ignition eventually, if you look at the trend lines. So, who are your friends here?"

Danni turned back. "Oh, I'm so sorry. Guys, Dr. Louis Tyminski."

Morgan gave Louis a pleasant smile. "Special Agent Kerry Morgan, DCIS. Unofficial visit."

They'd agreed not to make up aliases if they had to talk to anyone here. For one thing Rees was likely to be recognized. Besides, he and Morgan both had plausible reasons to be here as their real selves.

Rees waved at Louis. "Gevin Rees. I'm researching an article on advanced energy sources." That little improvisation interleaved nicely with Danni's story about the fusion data, and Rees gave himself a mental pat on the back.

"Oh, wow. I thought it was you." Louis stood up. "But I wasn't sure. I used to watch your specials all the time when I was in middle school."

Feeling decidedly old, Rees accepted Louis's handshake.

There were four terminals in the bay, all with privacy dividers. Rees assumed each one connected to the mainframe Danni wanted to access. If Louis went back to his own work, Danni should still be able to dig around for the Kafir Project data they needed.

Louis turned to Danni. "So anyway, by a funky little coincidence, I just happen to be crunching that data right now. From the ignition simulation. I'd love to get your take."

And so much for that scenario, Rees thought.

"Ah, that would be excellent," Danni said with convincing enthusiasm. "I need to do a couple things first. But hey, I promised Gevin he could see Alan and we're running a little short on time."

"You want me to take him on the tour?" Louis asked.

Danni made pleading eyes. "Would you? While I pull up the data and get ready here?"

"Yeah. Totally cool. I mean cold," Louis chuckled. "But that's not a problem, Dr. Rees. We got heavy jackets for you. Does ... I'm sorry, I forget your name." He was looking at Morgan now.

"Kerry."

"Did you want to see Alan too, Kerry?"

"I'd love to."

Rees wasn't sure, but he thought he saw Morgan hold eye contact with Louis for an extra beat. Well, she was an attractive woman. She probably knew how to work that asset when she needed to. Why not?

Louis led them out of the terminal bay and back into the hallway. And Rees began to feel truly optimistic for the first time today. Danni had a portable terabyte drive hidden in her bag. If the Kafir project data was here, then they were already halfway home.

"YES, DR. HARRIS is on campus right now," Matthew Neery told the caller.

As the head security guard at Livermore Labs, Neery had responded to numerous complaints of cars parked in someone else's marked space. Once he even had to escort out an irate visitor who objected to being told he couldn't take cell phone photos in a Defense Department facility. *It's a free country!* the man kept yelling, along with threats of legal action and the repeated assertion that he was *a veteran damnit!* As if that were somehow relevant.

But Neery had never before received an emergency call from the Defense Criminal Investigative Service.

"Dr. Danielle Harris is wanted for questioning in connection with the sale of classified materials," the DCIS agent on the line said.

Neery sat up straighter in his chair. "Right. Okay. So then, what do you want us to do here?"

"First of all, is Harris alone or was she accompanied by anyone?"

"Let me check." Neery pulled up the log on his computer, scanned the page and found Harris. "Uh, no indication that she had guests tonight. I can double check with the gate. But it would be here if she did."

"Did your people inspect the vehicle?"

"Well, they wouldn't have done a *full* inspection, no. We don't do that here. Not regularly." *Someone's gonna try to pin some crap on us now. Just wait and see.*

"Then assume that she has one or two persons with her. The man's name is Gevin Rees. The woman's identity is unknown."

Neery knew that name. "Gevin Rees, the astronomer guy?"

"Yes. He may be involved in the leak. The unknown woman accompanying Harris is armed and extremely dangerous."

Armed. This just keeps getting better and better. Neery felt the phone go slippery in his palm. "Yeah, all right. So what do you need from us? You want us to hold her, or them?"

He prayed that was not the case. Please. He'd competed in fast draw competitions as a hobby back in college. Even won a few. But that was just a game. He never once fired his weapon in the field. Never even aimed at a live target.

He didn't get paid enough for that kind of shit.

"No," the voice said. "Put the whole campus on lockdown. Quietly though. Don't make any announcements. Don't let Harris or any of her companions depart the facility. If she tries to leave, then you detain her. We have agents on the way."

Thank Christ for that. "Yeah, okay. What's the ETA on them?"

"Coming in from the Oakland field office, so it should be about thirty minutes give or take."

Moments later Neery hung up, suspecting that was going to be the longest thirty minutes of his life.

CHAPTER 23

REES SET DOWN Fischer's pouch and selected one of the parka-like jackets off a rack.

Heavy Plexiglas, like the kind that protected bank tellers from bullets, comprised three of the walls here. This space apparently served as an anteroom of sorts just outside the Core.

Morgan and their computer scientist turned tour guide, Louis, each grabbed a parka as well.

"Of course, most of the work is done at terminals," Louis was saying, "no one really spends much time in the Core itself. You can't. Not anywhere near the heart of it, not while Alan's running. But I figure you want to see the actual hardware. So we'll just nip in and out real quick."

"Yes." Rees clapped his hands and rubbed his palms together. "Dying to see it."

He *was* genuinely interested in seeing the quantum computer. But more importantly, this was buying time for Danni to find and download Fischer's data.

Louis pulled on his parka. "Okay, so we're going into a zone where the hardware temperature is nowhere higher than a hundred picokelvins above absolute zero. Much colder than interstellar space. The coldest place in the known universe is on the other side of this door."

Morgan selected a thick pair of gloves from a bin on the floor. "I don't understand why you keep the whole facility so cold. The computer itself is insulated, right?"

"Well, you know this is a government funded deal here," Louis said, grabbing a pair of gloves himself. "Basically, it's a money thing. They don't want to spend what it would cost to run our heating system at full blast year round."

"No, she's talking about your cooling system," Rees said. "Why you run it at such high levels outside the Core."

Louis smiled. "Yeah, I know she is. We don't. We don't use the AC at all here. We'd freeze to death. It's all we can do to keep the place *this* warm. Do you know about negative Kelvin temperatures, Dr. Rees? Below absolute zero?"

"I thought nothing could be colder than absolute zero," Morgan said. "That's why they call it *absolute*, right?"

Rees zipped up his parka. "Well, it depends on how you define temperature. The temperature scale can also be considered as a cycle that comes back around to zero through negative numbers. It has to do with the ratio of high energy to low energy particles. Boltzmann distribution."

"Exactly." Louis entered a key code into a huge door that looked like the entrance to a high tech fortress. "And matter at negative Kelvin temperatures has got some bizzaro properties. It might even be a model for dark matter and dark energy. Anyway, we can't fully insulate against its effects on the surrounding space."

A green light came on above the big door.

"So it's sucking the heat energy out of the whole building," Rees said. "That's amazing."

Louis checked some gauges beside the massive door. "Yeah, negative Kelvin—like I said, bizzaro world in there, man. Plus the qubits are incredibly stable in that environment."

Straightaway Rees intuitively saw why. And he felt that sense of awe and wonder that always came when a natural principle manifested itself in a physical pattern. He thought of these moments as his version of a religious experience.

"Yes, yes," Rees said excitedly, "because you have a kind of negative entropy in there too. That's how you beat the decoherence problem."

He and Louis seemed to remember Morgan at the same time and turned to her together.

Morgan gave an apologetic little shrug. "You lost me on Q-bricks."

"*Qubits* are the quantum equivalent of computer bits," Rees said. "Superposition is the multiple states at once property of quantum particles. It's what would make—or I guess I should say it's what *does* make quantum computing possible. Ordinarily, the particles would collapse too quickly back into a normal state. That's decoherence."

Louis nodded along. "Yep. But here in the center of the Core it's like a pyramid wants to balance on its point and it can't fall over. Like Dr. Rees said there, it's a reverse entropy thing."

Louis grabbed a latch on the colossal door then stopped. "Before we go in, can I just ask both of you one question?"

Rees and Morgan both nodded, smiling.

Rees said, "Go ahead. Shoot, Louis."

Louis smiled back at them. "What are you guys really doing here?"

CHAPTER 24

Three months earlier—Jerusalem

BENJAMIN ZAKEN HAD a headache. Two actually.

The Director of the Israel Antiquities Authority hoped the double espresso he'd just ordered would help with one of them.

He also prayed that the man sitting across from him in this upscale café wouldn't be the worse headache of the two. Joshua Amsel was famously determined. The aging archaeologist would not be inclined to take the bad news well.

"Ben, you must let me dig here," Amsel said. "You've read of the results, from my recent sites. My new methods are groundbreaking."

For privacy's sake Zaken had asked for this little back section of the café they now had to themselves. Amsel, for reasons unexplained, did not want to see Zaken in his office.

The place was nearly empty anyway. The recent missile strikes out of the Gaza had a lot of people hunkering down. The possibility of another major conflict loomed large.

In a very real sense, Zaken and Amsel were lounging right now in the middle of a war zone. Zaken doubted that many people outside of Israel could comprehend how naturally one might do such a thing.

"It's amazing what you're doing, no question of it," Zaken said to Amsel. "You've always been a good scientist, Josh. But I'm not sure that you're aware of the political implications in your work."

Amsel literally waved that away. "I'm just trying to get at the truth, Ben, as any archaeologist should. I'm not interested in the politics. You know this."

Zaken's espresso arrived along with Amsel's ice tea and mint. He added two sugars and sipped it. He inhaled the rich smell of coffee and tried to imagine the capillaries in his brain dilating, the throbbing pain in his temples easing.

"In Israel," Zaken said, "and particularly here in Jerusalem, there is no divorcing archaeology and politics. That's just how it's always been."

Amsel took a sip of his mint tea. "I know the stories about Yadin."

Israel's first Prime Minister, David Ben-Gurion, had tasked the eminent Jewish archaeologist Yigael Yadin to go out and *find me the title deeds.* Archaeological validation of the new Jewish nation's historical right to reclaim these lands.

That's what Yadin started digging for. And, perhaps unsurprisingly, it's what he believed he'd found. More modern, some would say more *accurate*, archaeological work by men like Israel Finkelstein (out of Tel Aviv University no less) had called some of Yadin's conclusions into question. They made Zaken's job a lot more perilous in some ways. The wrong interpretation of Israel's history could have something very much like *legal* ramifications. It could spell disaster.

A wonder Zaken didn't have more headaches like this one.

Amsel glanced at something on the floor near his chair. "I don't try to steer the evidence. I go where the find leads me. But on a practical note, I can promise you the excavation will be focused and run on a tight schedule. We're talking weeks here, not months or years."

Zaken took another sip of his espresso. He'd made up his mind, but he didn't want to appear perfunctory about it. "First, I don't see how you could possibly promise such a thing. I don't care what new methods you're using, you don't know what you may or may not find. You can't say how long it would take to safely remove it. And second, this is the Muslim Quarter you're talking about digging up. You're asking me to displace families, possibly tear down homes and businesses. Have you any idea what the potential repercussions would be?"

Amsel sat back. "Let's not waste time. Is that a firm *no* then?"

Perhaps this would be easier than Zaken had feared. "I'm sorry, Josh. This is just practically and politically not possible. Not now. In the future perhaps."

Amsel lifted a briefcase that sat beside his chair, opened it, and removed a laptop computer. "Let me show you something."

As Amsel booted up the computer, Zaken felt his headache surge and his patience wane. He could see the screen from an angle and it appeared to be running a video now. "Unless that's a recorded message from the Prime Minister, I'm afraid you're just wasting your time."

Amsel turned the screen so Zaken could view it fully.

A handheld camera shot moved down a hallway in what looked like a private residence. The camera held for a moment on a landscape painting of the Jezreel Valley.

Zaken felt as if he'd just woken up naked in public. "That's, that's my home. What the hell is this? You broke into my home?"

Amsel looked pained. "It's very important, Ben, that you watch this and understand. For the sake of your career and your very freedom."

The camera had moved into the master bedroom, and then on into the master bath. Gloved hands grasped the medicine cabinet, and pulled it out from the wall.

Behind the cabinet—a hidden, recessed space. And in the space, inside a ziplocked bag, it looked like ... some kind of scroll.

"What did you do? What is that? I've never seen that."

Amsel reached over and paused the video. "It's the Book of Isaiah, or most of it anyway." He tapped the image on the screen. "That's the oldest biblical manuscript ever discovered, right there. Older even then the fragments from Qumran. Its existence is not documented in any museum or scientific collection. And so it will naturally be assumed that you acquired it illicitly on the black market."

Zaken's whole world reeled. He gripped the edge of the table. "But it's just a forgery. A forensic examination will—"

"Demonstrate its authenticity, I'm afraid. No, that's no forgery. I know, because I recovered it myself. It's genuine. As are a number of other equally rare artifacts, which have been cached in a half-dozen storage places both here and abroad. And this next part is critical. All of these caches can—with some effort, and perhaps a little help—be traced directly back to you, Ben."

Zaken's vision blurred for a second. The headache was a wild animal now, clawing its way out of his skull through his eye sockets. "If this is some kind of sick joke..."

Amsel continued, "Again, all these pieces are unique and undocumented. They could only have come to you via the black market. Highly illegal, of course. Not to mention an unforgivable breach of the responsibilities for the Director of the Israeli Antiquities Authority."

"How could you even have all these undocumented pieces?"

"Not relevant to your problem. You'll learn in time. If all goes well."

Zaken took a deep breath and blew it out slowly. "No one will believe this. No one."

Amsel pursed his lips and shrugged. "What other choice will they have, Ben? All these stashes can be traced by a discreet money trail back to you and to no one else. What are you going to say? That Joshua Amsel personally gave up historical artifacts worth, oh, let's say conservatively tens of millions of dollars? Any single one of which would represent the shining capstone of a man's whole career? No, no, it's ridiculous. You bought them illegally over the years. Or acquired them in trade, in return for overlooking antique smuggling probably. Yes, that seems more likely."

Zaken could hardly breathe. It felt like the air had been sucked out of the room, replaced with toxic slush. "Why? Why are you doing this?"

"Just approve the dig, Ben. Sign the permits. Deal with the backlash however you must. The Isaiah scroll, by the way, that's yours to keep. You can never show it to anyone, but you will know what it is. That's something anyway. Yes?"

Amsel actually extended his hand.

For a moment Zaken thought of grabbing a piece of cutlery and stabbing it. And what would be the use of that?

After a time, he reached out and bitterly shook the hand of his blackmailer.

Zaken had wondered once why anyone would actually make a deal with the Devil, as in so many old folk stories. Now he thought he knew.

Perhaps they simply had no other choice.

CHAPTER 25

DANNI KEPT GLANCING over her shoulder at the terminal bay's security door, imagining she heard the lock mechanism.

She'd penetrated deep into the offline computer's central directory, but had found nothing on the Kafir Project or Edward Fischer yet. She located partitions that she couldn't access even with her high security clearance.

Those looked promising.

Time to use the backdoor.

Danni didn't know how long Morgan and Rees could keep Louis occupied with their little tour, so she tried to work quickly. She wouldn't be really vulnerable until she was downloading data onto her personal drive. That procedure ran so far out of bounds, she couldn't easily explain it away.

What, this? Oh, just a little classified data theft from the US Defense Department. Keep it on the down low, okay? Wink, wink.

With a few keystrokes she launched the hidden subprogram that had helped put one of her own co-workers behind bars. Now, ironically, it threatened to do the exact same thing to her.

Within moments she had access to the forbidden partitions. She executed a search for the Kafir Project. "C'mon, baby. Be there. Be there."

Nothing.

She tried again with Fischer's name.

Zip. Zilch.

"Gotta be something here. Even if they scrubbed it. Some little crumb they left behind."

She kept at it, typing in any technical terms that seemed like they could be relevant.

Tachyons.
No.
Closed time-like loops.
Nope.
Grandfather paradox.
Nada.
Feeling pretty foolish, Danni typed in *H.G. Wells.*
She got a hit.

MORGAN WATCHED REES explaining to Louis how they really were here to research fusion energy for a magazine article. Nothing nefarious going on at all. *Hey, I'm just the science man from TV. You know me. I'm harmless.*

She thought he might almost have pulled it off, if it weren't for the obvious sweat beading on his upper lip and forehead. In a freezing cold room.

When Rees finally wound down, Louis said, "Yeah, I'm not buying that." He turned to Morgan. "Are you gonna try too?"

"No, I'm not." She gave him her best hardass cop look. "Why do *you* think we're here, Louis?" It was just a stall, but that was all they needed for now.

Louis shrunk back. "Uh, honestly, I don't know. I thought first it was some kind of test. To see if we'd follow proper security procedures or whatever. But Danni, Dr. Harris, wouldn't set me up like that. That's a weasel thing to do and she's never been a company man. So to speak."

"But now?" Morgan asked.

"Well, I heard you guys talking about Edward Fischer when you came in. Is this about the explosion at Fermilab?"

Silence.

Then Rees said, "Yes. That's right."

"Okay. So it *is* about Fermilab." Louis looked visibly relieved to have an answer to the mystery.

Morgan waited for Rees to spin out whatever fiction he'd just come up with to explain how it all connected.

Rees turned to her. "Special Agent Morgan, do you want to fill Louis in on the details?"

Oh, so I'm supposed to make that story work. Well, thank you so much, Dr. Rees. "Defective parts manufacturing at Fermilab," Morgan said. "And we think here too. Contractor fraud."

Part of Morgan's job at DCIS involved investigating malfeasance in defense contracts. That included machinery and parts that didn't meet the agreed upon specs. Usually because it saved the manufacturer money, which might then be siphoned away into a private account.

"So, what's with the charade?" Louis asked. "You think someone here is letting substandard parts slip by? Getting a kickback or something?"

Good. Keep answering your own questions, Morgan thought.

"Exactly." Rees pressed his lips thin and nodded. "And I'm writing an article, because we want to shame the people who did this. Stop this sort of thing from happening every day."

Louis made a wide-eyed blink. "Wow. Every day? How are they getting away with it?"

Rees turned back to Morgan. "Agent Morgan? You want to take that question?"

"No."

Louis continued looking at Rees. Waiting.

Rees cleared his throat. "That's actually—the exact rate of fraud is not public knowledge. Not yet. And ... I'm going to write about that too. I don't want to throw out too many spoilers right now."

Morgan suppressed a smile. Rees was a terrible liar. Most of the time that wasn't a bad thing in a person. Out of the corner of her eye, through one of the thick, Plexiglas walls, she saw Danni approaching.

Danni opened the door and stepped in wearing an apologetic smile. "Hey guys, we have to cut the tour short. I'm so sorry."

She was playing it cool, but Morgan could see the distress there just beneath the surface.

"I know what's going on," Louis announced.

Danni looked from Morgan to Rees, shocked. "He knows? Okay then. So here's the deal—"

"He knows about the defective parts," Rees said. "The contractor, who caused the accident at Fermilab."

"What?" Danni was staring at Rees like he had two heads and one of them was eating the other.

Morgan jumped in. "Louis knows we're looking for that same contractor's substandard parts here at Livermore. The fraud case you're helping us with."

Morgan could see Danni flip gears. Always fast, that girl.

Danni nodded. "Yeah. That's what I wanted to tell you. The guy just called and he wants to meet tonight. So if you want me to record him for you, we have to get going. Right now."

"Okay," Morgan said. "Let's get you fixed up with a wire."

They removed the heavy jackets and gloves and Rees grabbed Fischer's pouch. Morgan instructed Louis not to repeat what he heard tonight to any coworkers, and thanked him for his cooperation.

Louis then escorted them all to the building's lobby. On the way he casually asked Morgan if she lived in the Bay Area, and then looked crestfallen when she said she didn't.

OUTSIDE, THE NIGHT air felt like a heat wave compared to the frigid quantum computing building.

Danni looked around them quickly then said, "They know we're here."

Rees looked like someone just punched him in the gut.

"How do you know?" Morgan asked.

"On the way to meet you guys, I ran into a researcher coming back in. He couldn't go home. The whole campus is on lockdown."

"Does that happen often?" Rees asked.

Danni shook her head. "Never. Not while I've worked here."

Morgan instantly ruled out coincidence. "Someone tipped off security. Someone outside the campus. Because they had no reason to be suspicious of us here."

She began working on the options. Security here at Livermore Labs didn't represent anything like an unstoppable force. But the guards were armed, and she wasn't prepared to sacrifice innocent lives just to avoid being taken into custody.

Running the gate in the car would get them out. But it would probably turn into a chase that had a low chance of success and a high risk of people getting hurt again. Including them.

"Is there some way maybe we could hide the car and lay low?" Rees suggested. "Let them think we already got off the campus. They can't keep the place locked down forever."

Danni shook her head. Then suddenly she grabbed Morgan's arm. "The new particle accelerator. It's not functional yet, but the facility connects to the quantum computing building. The accelerator's huge. It extends way beyond the campus. We could get out underground, through the tunnels."

It sounded worth a try to Morgan and certainly preferable to any other option they'd considered. "All right, let's do it."

They waked back over to the door they'd just come out of. Danni pulled out her pass key again.

"Wait a minute." Rees vibrated with some new excitement. "Danni, you said you were coming to get us *before* you heard about the lockdown. So why did you leave the terminal bay? Did you find something?"

In the rush to get the hell out of there Morgan had nearly forgotten the whole reason they came out to Livermore in the first place.

"Yeah, I did. Hang on." Danni went to swipe her pass key, fumbled and dropped it. "Damnit." She bent down to retrieve the pass key. Then dropped it again as she stood up. "Shit."

Rees looked about to explode. "So what did you find?"

Morgan could see Danni's hands shaking. "Stay calm, Danni. We need to keep our heads."

Danni nodded, swiped the key properly and opened the door.

She led them quickly back through the outer lobby. "Okay, so they scrubbed all the data. But I found the original proposal. From before they even named the project. Probably why they missed it." Danni rushed over to the biometric lock.

Rees followed so close behind he bumped into Danni when she stopped. "Is it really time travel? Did they do it?"

Danni positioned her eye in front of the sensor. "It's funny, there was actually an H.G. Wells reference. The Time Machine. But it's not time travel. It's time *viewing*." The lock made its little whirring sound and Danni opened the door. "And I know why it was a DARPA project now. *Kafir*, unbeliever. It was right there the whole time."

Danni held the door open, but Rees didn't move. He just stood there blocking the way, lost in thought.

"Rees, we gotta go," Morgan said.

He snapped out of it and stepped through. "Unbeliever. I get it. It's crazy, but I get it."

Morgan felt like she'd walked in on the middle of someone else's conversation. "So are either of you going to tell me what the deal is here, or would that spoil the ending?"

Danni strode off down the long, white hallway. She spoke without looking back. "Islamic radicals. DARPA was going after them."

Morgan hustled after her. "How?"

Rees answered her from behind. "By undermining their entire religion."

CHAPTER 26

DCIS SPECIAL AGENT Shawn Gibson took the exit off Interstate 580 to Livermore faster than prudence would have suggested. He couldn't help it. The excitement pulsed through his whole body and right out his foot to the gas pedal.

Gibson would make his bones tonight. His first big arrest and an espionage-related case to boot. Not bad for the youngest guy on the squad.

An anonymous tip had come in. A computer scientist, Dr. Danielle Harris, was selling state secrets.

Based on that, some NSA guys identified a couple of chat room posters as Harris and a known Russian intelligence agent.

They forwarded the correspondence to DCIS.

ROZY: have copy HellCat trade for 16gigs RAM.
bBoy: Fair trade. Can do!

It looked like they were just discussing video game swapping. But *HellCat* was really Predator drone technology that Harris had illegally downloaded. *16gigs* was sixteen million euros.

Payment for the stolen specs.

As the car flew around the curling off-ramp, Gibson's partner, Charlie Swain, tensed himself against the extra g's. "Take it easy, Gibson. You don't get there in one piece, you don't get your guy. Or gal in this case."

Swain had been acting all blasé about it. Gibson thought he looked pretty jazzed, though. They were going after as many as three people, at least one of them armed. And one of 'em was a TV celebrity too.

High profile collar here for sure.

Swain could play it cool all he wanted. He was kind of a jock, and that Clint Eastwood act was just his style. But this was a big ass deal, and they both knew it.

When they pulled up, the guard at Lawrence Livermore waved them through.

Another guy in uniform waited for them just on the other side of the gate. Probably the head of security, Neery. They spoke with him on the way over.

Gibson parked and jumped out. Swain followed.

The other DCIS car with agents Phelps and Merriweather in it pulled up, and they got out too.

The uniformed guy walked over to the four of them. "Matt Neery. I run security here at LLNL."

Neery looked unsure whether he wanted to offer a handshake. Not surprising. Security guards usually went one of two directions. Either they acted like you were invading their turf, or they were just glad to let you handle everything and stay the hell out of harm's way.

Swain got right down to business. "You have eyes on Harris?"

"No," Neery said. "But we checked the security video on the building where she works. She's in there now with one man and another woman. We didn't go in. We were told to wait out here for you guys."

Phelps reassured Neery that was the right move, and they all took a short walk together over to the building.

Swain, who had been assigned lead on this thing, decided that Phelps and Merriweather would watch the two fire exits. He and Gibson were going in the front door together, weapons ready.

No warning. No chance for hostage taking or some kind of standoff situation.

At this point those three suspects were coming out of that building. Either in cuffs or in body bags.

It was up to them now.

REES FOLLOWED DANNI and Morgan along the hallway, past the entrance to the Core's anteroom, and on to another secured door. This one led to the new accelerator complex and down to tunnels that would take them well outside the Livermore campus and its security.

Danni swiped her pass key in the lock.

Nothing happened.

Rees felt his stomach drop. "Maybe it's not activated yet. Because it's still under construction?"

Danni swiped the key again. Still nothing. "I don't get it. I've been through here a couple times already. To look at the work they're doing."

Morgan leaned in and checked out the indicator lights on the lock. "I think they shut down your pass key, Danni. They're individually coded now. It was one of the changes I instituted when I was here."

Danni looked ill with tension. "Shit, you're probably right."

Rees wondered for a moment if she might actually get sick again. She'd wrung herself out pretty good back there in her kitchen. If she threw up now, it would have to be something like a major organ. Fortunately, the human body wasn't piped that way.

Rees suddenly had a thought. "Does the Core itself connect anywhere with the new accelerator facility?"

Danni's eyes darted back and forth as she accessed some memory. "Yeah, it does. Both facilities share the same super-cooling system. There's a common crawlspace for service and maintenance."

"That's what I was hoping," Rees said. "And the Core has a numerical lock. I saw Louis use it earlier. We don't need your pass key to get in there."

"But?" Morgan asked. She'd apparently spotted something on Danni's face that Rees didn't know her well enough to read.

"*But,*" Danni said, "the crawlspace access is right at the heart of the Core. Did Louis tell you guys about the conditions in there?"

Rees nodded. "The negative Kelvin environment. He said it drained energy from the space around it. A field effect."

"Yeah, typical inverse square field." Danni sounded defeated.

Before Rees could explain to Morgan what the implications were, she surprised him by putting it out there herself.

"We get ten times closer, the field gets a hundred times stronger." She looked at Rees, as if she'd just read his mind. "I'm not innumerate." She turned back to Danni. "So how cold is it where we have to go? To get to that access plate?"

Danni rolled in her lips and shook her head. "Somewhere below *it'll kill you.* How far below doesn't really matter."

Rees tried to tease apart the factors here. They were, in a sense, fighting two kinds of cold. The low temperatures that would leach heat from their bodies through the air, and the field effect that would steal heat energy directly.

Those phenomena were independent of each other.

"What if we shut the whole system down?" Rees asked. "I know there isn't time to let the environment warm up in there, but at least we wouldn't be fighting that field sapping our body heat."

Danni scrunched up her face. "It's still gonna be wicked cold."

"Yes, but is it higher than *it'll kill you*? That's all it has to be."

Danni didn't answer, she just hung her head. Rees couldn't tell if she was hammering out the numbers or didn't even want to consider it.

"If it won't work," Morgan said to her, "then that's just how it is. We'll take our chances out here."

Danni finally looked up. "Getting to the crawlspace and maneuvering through it—that's going to take more time than anyone would ordinarily spend in there. But with the system shut down ... it *could* work. We gotta move fast, but I think it's doable. Good chance we get a little frostbitten."

Rees became keenly aware of how cold it felt where they stood right now. Tropical compared to where they were headed. An environment that Louis had quite accurately represented as the coldest place in the known universe.

He'd heard it described as a painless, almost pleasant way to go—freezing to death.

At the moment, Rees didn't find that very comforting.

CHAPTER 27

Washington, D.C.

CARL TRUBY COULDN'T sleep.

It wasn't the helicopter flight back from New York. These little jaunts had become mundane for him years ago. Truth was, he hadn't had a good night's sleep since he learned what happened at Fermilab. How the whole goddamned thing got away from them.

Truby donned his robe, poured himself a scotch, and stepped out into his enclosed patio.

He stood on the deck watching the distant lights of D.C. illuminate the underside of a low cloud layer. A kind of false dawn. Too bad the real one was still hours away.

From the start, Truby knew he couldn't stand on the sidelines as this thing worked itself out. Not in his nature. The so-called hand of Fate or of God—that shit was a pathetic sop for weaker men. If he had a stake in the outcome, Truby never sat back and watched the trajectory of events.

He orchestrated it.

His extraordinary abilities had made him very rich and unspeakably well connected. Literally. The people behind the scenes whose interests he represented in this current action alone controlled more than half the globe. That was a conservative estimate.

The wealth that came his way, truth be told, he didn't care much about—although his current wife and all of his exes enjoyed it. Even the power per se didn't matter so much as what he could serve with it.

A marvelously stable social system.

One that worked. One that worked as well now as it had throughout history, regardless of whatever *appeared* to be happening in the public arena.

Truby was thinking about what might happen to that system if Fischer succeeded, when a shadow in the corner of the patio separated itself from a wicker chair and stood up.

"Don't be alarmed, Mr. Truby."

"A little late for that." Truby's heartbeat accelerated even as he got the words out.

The shadow stepped forward, into the patio light. A black man in a well cut suit, no tie, stood on Truby's back deck. Truby had never seen the man before in his life.

"My name is Singleton," he said. "I've taken charge of your account."

"Jesus. This couldn't wait for morning?"

"No. And it's too sensitive for anything but a face to face."

Truby stepped over to a nearby chair and sat down. A deliberate gesture of disrespect. Taking the power back. "What the hell happened to Doubleman? And how am I supposed to know you're really working with him?"

Singleton seemed prepared for that. He stepped forward and handed Truby a small piece of paper. "You'll find those numbers match the Cayman Island account through which you have paid for our services. I can wait while you check them."

Truby had by no means a photographic memory, but he'd always possessed a freakish ability to store names and numbers. These numbers were in fact correct.

He slipped the paper into his robe pocket. "That doesn't tell me what happened to your other man."

"He has become unavailable."

"You're not going to tell me are you?"

"A new decision point has developed. Gevin Rees will soon be in DCIS custody."

That didn't sound right to Truby. "Why are you involving them? I thought you had your own man on this?"

"The longer Rees is out there, the greater the risk that some party outside our reach apprehends and questions him. We have resources inside the DCIS. I recommend we use them to eliminate Rees now."

Truby's initial fear had turned to a more familiar emotion. Anger. "This is bullshit. *You* were supposed to grab Rees, not the feds. You come to my house in the dead of night to tell me you've screwed up. With Rees gone, how are we gonna locate the backup that Fischer made? What about the artifacts? The other conspirators?"

"We have a lead on the one called Herodotus. I believe you knew that already. And we have a contingency plan to eliminate the other collaborators. With them gone, the data and artifacts are effectively lost anyway."

Truby felt the knot in his gut returning. "Doubleman told me about your 'contingency plan.' You're going to kill more than a dozen people who worked on the project."

"Not necessarily. We'll interrogate each of them as we go. Odds are we'll find the two other scientists involved well before we get through the whole list."

Truby gave Singleton a hard stare. "What the hell do you need from me then?"

"I thought you would want to make this call personally. Was I wrong?"

No. You're sure as shit not wrong. "Do it. Shut Rees up."

Singleton started to turn away. He stopped. "One other thing..."

Truby shuddered to think what fresh hell this man might throw at him tonight. "What?"

"Your home security is woefully inadequate. Get yourself a new company."

CHAPTER 28

DANNI LOOKED UP from the keyboard she'd been typing away on. "I'll need about eight minutes or so to finish the shutdown sequence."

Rees stood beside Morgan in the Core's control room, wondering if following the proper protocol here really represented an effective use of time. "I'm sure it isn't the best thing for the quantum computer, Danni, but ... can't we just yank the plug?"

"It's not about the computer," Danni explained. "It's the cryogenics. We use massive amounts of liquid helium. When that warms, you have an expansion ratio of about one to eight hundred."

"Yikes." Rees recalled nitroglycerin had approximately the same expansion ratio and decided to stop making helpful suggestions.

"Yep," Danni said. "You don't want to be anywhere near here if this warms up too fast." She threw a nod to the anteroom. "You guys should go in there and get your coats and stuff on. I'll join you when I'm done."

"We'll see you in there," Morgan said.

Rees watched them share a look. Whatever they once had, it definitely hadn't gone away. Even in the middle of all this craziness, he felt himself hoping they both knew that.

And that they'd live long enough to do something about it.

Rees left the control room with Morgan and they walked next door.

He noticed for the first time an external safety lock on the Core's anteroom door. A red lever operated it. The thick Plexiglas here probably served as a safeguard against precisely the danger Danni just described. An explosive liquid helium leak. Unfortunately, they'd all be on the wrong side of that particular safety measure. So now it only served as a reminder of how badly it all could go.

Inside the anteroom, Rees again donned one of the heavy parkas, then slung the strap of Fischer's leather pouch over that like a sash. He pulled on a pair of insulated gloves, and watched Morgan grab a knit cap. He needed to say something, and he might not have many more chances to do it.

"Special Agent Morgan."

Morgan pulled her cap on and looked over at him. "Yes?"

"I don't know you very well, but I wanted to say, what you've done for me tonight ... I want to take a second and say thank you. That's all."

Morgan nodded. "You're welcome, Dr. Rees." She picked up a pair of the gloves. As she pulled them on, a grave look came over her face. "My agency is involved in this. Responsible. People I work with. Maybe even people I know. I just can't stomach that. I'm doing this for me too. I think you should know that."

Her own people had let her down, and Rees understood her pain. *People ultimately disappoint.* "I get it." He grabbed a knit cap off the shelf, hesitated a moment, then laughed.

"What's funny?" Morgan asked.

"Oh, I just flashed on, of all things, head lice. And then I thought, why worry? They'll probably freeze to death in there too."

Morgan nodded, straight-faced. "Good thinking."

"You know, you and Danni make a good team." Rees hadn't planned on saying that. It just bubbled out.

Morgan didn't reply. She nodded, though. And Rees thought he saw the hint of a smile.

Rees snapped the cuffs closed on his parka, and wondered if he and Morgan and Danni might all end up close friends one day. He knew people could tear your heart out without even meaning to. His own sister had done it. And he still believed that letting people in would always be a huge risk.

Maybe you just had to find people who made the risk worth taking. He'd heard something like that once, and tried to remember where.

"Rees." Morgan was looking toward the Plexiglas wall that separated them from the control room.

Rees looked over too.

Danni was still in there. She wasn't alone.

CHAPTER 29

"DON'T MOVE AND keep your hands where I can see them," Gibson ordered.

He had Dr. Danielle Harris at gunpoint and the other two suspects in sight. They were behind some kind of thick glass. They'd both spotted him, but neither had made a move to run or fight.

He keyed his shoulder mike. "Agent Gibson, inside the computer building. I have one suspect in custody, and eyes on the other two. There's a ... like a glass wall between us. Requesting backup. Over."

He waited. No response.

"Agent Gibson here. Repeat, I have Dr. Harris in custody. Requesting backup. Get the hell in here. Over."

Nothing.

He didn't seem to be getting through. Great.

Gibson had taken the lower levels of the building while his partner Swain cleared the upper floors. He hadn't figured on finding the suspects split up like this.

He sure as shit didn't expect to be cut off from any help.

And on top of everything else, it was goddamn *freezing* in this place.

"Can they hear us through that?" Gibson asked Harris, pointing toward the glass wall between them and the next room.

"There's an intercom." She was staying calm. That much was good.

"All right then. Turn that on. Keep both hands where I can see them."

She pushed a button on the console. "Okay. I'm holding the microphone open. They can hear us now."

Gibson cleared his throat. Took a deep breath. He couldn't see a microphone, but he bent down toward where he guessed it would be. "This building is surrounded by agents of the US Defense Department. You are all under arrest. Put your hands on top of your heads and keep them there."

And what are you gonna do if they don't, Special Agent Gibson? Shoot 'em through the damn glass?

The man he recognized as Gevin Rees quickly did as Gibson ordered. The woman too. Thank God for small favors.

That woman in there was armed, the report said. If Swain were here, one of them would cover the suspects while the other one confiscated weapons, cuffed them, and patted them all down. But like this? Alone, looking through a glass wall?

It sure as hell wasn't a scenario they simulated back in training.

Getting everyone in the same space where he could keep them all covered seemed like the thing to do. Swain would finish his sweep and double back to find him eventually.

That was the plan then.

Gibson kept his weapon pointed up, but ready. To Harris he said, "Turn off that microphone."

She released the switch.

"Now get up slowly. You and me are going into that other room."

Harris shook her head. "I have to finish this shutdown sequence."

Jesus, she's gonna resist. That's just great.

This was the last thing he needed. No back up and an uncooperative detainee. He glanced through the glass again. The other two still had their hands on their heads, at least.

"I have to finish running the sequence," Harris repeated.

Gibson raised his voice. "Hey! You have to do what I tell you to do, is what you goddam have to do. Okay? I am instructing you for the second time now to get up and walk ahead of me. Out to the hall and over into that other room. Now!"

She *still* wasn't moving. Goddamnit. At what point did he actually aim his weapon at her? And what then?

Harris pointed down at the console. "Listen to me. These dials are pushing the red zone already. See right there? If I don't finish the shutdown sequence, there's a very real chance of an explosive event. You been watching the news? What just happened back east at Fermilab, that's what I'm talking about. That's gonna happen right here, if you don't let me do this right."

Gibson didn't know if this was some bullshit stall or what. He sure didn't want to make the call alone.

C'mon Swain, c'mon. Get the hell down here.

Was it worth taking the risk, making her get up and screw the damn shutoff procedure?

He flashed on news images of that explosion back in Illinois. Smoke pouring out of a collapsed building. People in Chicago panicking, because some asshole tweeted about a radiation leak. Huge goddamn mess.

"How long is this gonna take?" he asked.

"Maybe four or five more minutes."

He nodded. "Key the intercom. Keep the hands where I can see them."

She reached down and did it.

Gibson looked at the suspects over in the next room there. He licked his lips. His mouth had gone as dry as week old toast. "Okay, this is what we're gonna do here people. You're—"

The door flew open behind him. He spun and levelled his gun.

"Hey, hey! Lower that weapon." Merriweather was standing there with his gun out, scowling at him.

Jesus. Thank God he didn't fire.

Merriweather had a kind of hard ass, old guy face ordinarily. Right now he looked pissed enough to shoot Gibson just for taking aim at him.

Gibson raised his gun to a safety position. "Sorry about that."

Merriweather eyeballed the other suspects through the glass wall. "What the hell's goin' on here? Are they secured over there?"

"Turn the mike off," Gibson told Harris. "Let go of the thing." He waited till she did it. "No. They're not secured. I haven't patted them down or anything. I just got here a minute ago."

"Where's your partner, Swain?"

"Clearing the upstairs areas. Look, we got a situation here."

"Yeah, I can see that."

"No, no, it's a safety deal." Gibson indicated Harris. "She's got to shut this all down by some kind of procedure. Otherwise there could be an explosive event."

"A what?"

"The goddamn thing can blow up. So she's gotta stay here a few more minutes to do this thing. I'm thinking we let her finish."

Merriweather looked back and forth between Harris and the other two suspects. He shook his head. "She's playing us. She's trying to give her buddies in there a chance to pull something."

A red light flashed on the console.

Harris jabbed a finger at it. "There. This is *exactly* what I was talking about. The liquid helium's starting to boil. I have to stop the shutdown process, and start re-cooling. Right now while there's still time." She reached for some controls.

Merriweather pointed his weapon at her. "Don't move. Don't touch *anything* unless you're told. You're under arrest, you understand?"

She didn't flinch. "Hey, you're putting us all in serious danger. You understand *that*? There's gonna be an explosion here in a few minutes, if you don't chill out and let me do this the right way."

Merriweather looked like maybe he'd change his mind. He kept glancing back and forth between the two rooms. "Screw it. We're moving her in there with them." He nodded toward the other room. "Let's go."

"You're making a big mistake," Harris said.

"You, shut up. And you, Junior," he turned to Gibson. "Cuff her."

CHAPTER 30

HANDS ON HEAD, Rees watched through the Plexiglas as two men—one considerably older than the other—handcuffed Danni in the Core's control room next door, and then led her out into the hallway.

Rees turned his head slightly toward Morgan. "Who the hell are those guys?"

Morgan had her cop face on. "Stay calm, Rees. See the blue jackets and the badges? They're federal agents. They're here to arrest us for whatever laws they think we broke. Understand? These are not the bad guys. Just cooperate. We'll be all right for now."

"Okay. Okay, just cooperate." Rees knew he was talking as much to himself as to Morgan. "But whoever's behind killing Fischer set this up. We're being framed or something."

"Probably. And we'll deal with that later. Not here. Not now. We're not trying to shoot our way out of this. We don't want to hurt them, and they don't want to hurt us."

Rees hoped like hell she was right about that second part. "Okay. I'm with you. Stay calm. Cooperate."

The two agents and Danni had reached the anteroom's thick, Plexiglas door. The older one said something to Danni, and pointed at the locking mechanism with the red lever. She said something back to him. He opened the door.

As they all came in, Morgan spoke up. "I'm DCIS Special Agent Kerry Morgan. I *am* armed. My service weapon is in a shoulder holster. ID is in my jacket."

That announcement seemed to throw the men off. The younger agent looked to the older one, like he was waiting for direction.

The senior agent quickly regained his composure. "Both of you, down on your knees. Keep your hands on your head." He pushed Danni out toward them. "You. On your knees, next to them."

Rees felt a little awkward sinking down without his arms for balance, but he managed. So did Morgan and Danni.

The older agent gestured at Morgan and spoke to his partner. "Get her weapon."

"What are we being charged with?" Rees glanced over at Morgan. She shook her head very slightly at him. "I mean, we're cooperating here. Fully. I just want to know."

"The sale of classified materials," the older agent replied. "You have the right to be silent, and if you have any sense at all you'll use it."

He kept his gun on Morgan and recited their Miranda rights. His partner carefully reached into Morgan's parka and removed her gun from its holster, then fished through her pockets and got her ID.

The older agent reached out a hand. "Give me that weapon."

His partner handed over the gun.

Morgan spoke up again. "That weapon is cocked and locked. There's a round chambered."

"I know what cocked and locked is agent Morgan." The older agent glanced at the ID. He checked something on the gun.

Then he turned and fired point blank into the other agent's face.

CHAPTER 31

Two months earlier—Jerusalem

THE SUN WAS up but the air still cool as Joshua Amsel walked the narrow cobblestone street that formed part of the Via Delarosa, the traditional route of Christ's journey to Golgotha.

Amsel's regular two-man security detail walked close by, in front and behind. Their job was simple.

Prevent the most hated man in the Muslim Quarter from being killed today.

The next phase of the project was well underway. Amsel wouldn't be able to keep its true aims from his top man for very much longer. That put them at a critical juncture that in fact worried him more than the actual threats against his life.

A young Muslim boy, perhaps on his way to one of the nearby madrassas, passed Amsel and his escorts coming the other way.

Amsel offered a smile. "*Sabahul khayr.*" Good morning.

The boy continued in silence, without so much as looking up.

Amsel had caused a number of families here to be displaced from homes and businesses. With the help of the Israeli government and military, of course.

The locals despised him and for good reason. Fortunately, they had no idea what he was *really* doing.

If they did, they would literally tear him limb from limb.

AMSEL PASSED THROUGH the dig site's perimeter checkpoint and headed into the temporary structure erected to store and protect the raw, unsorted materials.

His lead research technician looked up from a four meter long table covered with thousands of dun-colored material fragments. "Hello, Josh," he said.

"Good morning, Randy."

Though still in his forties, Randolph Osborn was a fragile man who hobbled when he walked. A three-inch platform on his left shoe made up for a congenital difference in leg length. The result of a genetic anomaly that also rendered him slight of build. To look at him, one wouldn't naturally consider that the weight of the entire world might one day rest on his narrow shoulders.

Amsel knew otherwise. He also knew that the day was not so far off.

The material on the table there looked like so many worthless bits of dirt and stone. Osborn was transporting one tiny piece at a time into an isolation chamber. Then scanning the material. Then moving on to the next piece. A laborious, painstaking process.

Amsel crossed over to Osborn's side. "How are we doing, Randy?"

Osborn selected a fragment of material from the table with a pair of long tweezers. He dropped it into the isolation chamber. The chamber itself looked rather like an incubator for preemies. "Oh, I'd say we're about fifteen percent through the samples we have sorted. Very different matrix here than in Bosra. Dense and heterogeneous."

Osborn initiated a scan. Together the two men watched a computer screen that displayed the results. They waited. After about thirty seconds, the reading came back negative. No relation to the target signature.

Osborn tossed the fragment into a collection bin at his feet. He picked up a new sample, and loaded it into the chamber.

"Not quite like lifting a three kilogram codex out of a small target area," Amsel commented.

Osborn made a scoffing sound and initiated another scan. "Not hardly."

They watched and waited again for the results. And again negative. This sample had also failed to show the proper signature. Osborn tossed it in the waste with hundreds of other bits.

As Osborn continued his work, Amsel let his eyes wander over the thousands of gray and brown fragments spread out on the table. Somewhere in there lay an historical artifact of unprecedented importance. Without the additional technology that Fischer had created here to identify it, it would be impossible to sort it from the worthless rubble.

The target zone represented quite a large space to investigate this time. The material they were after had been broken up and scattered throughout the geological matrix.

Outside this temporary building, Amsel's men continued to extract more raw material from that same zone. About twenty meters down brought them to the time period they were after. The centuries had laid layer upon layer of dust and soil upon their target. Though originally it would have lain less than a meter from ground level.

Shallow by any estimation.

Another scanning sequence completed. Again negative. Osborn patiently repeated the procedure and launched yet another scan.

"Well, I'll leave you to your work then." Amsel turned to go.

"Have you got a minute, Josh?"

Something in Osborn's voice immediately told Amsel that he would make the time. "Nothing pressing at the moment. What's on your mind?"

Osborn turned and faced him directly. "I don't have your level of clearance on this project. And that's probably just as well. But I was briefed on our objective. I understand what we're doing here. And I have no problem with it. In fact, I'm proud to be a part."

"I am as well. But this is not what you needed to tell me."

Osborn paused. "That objective, as I was briefed on it ... has it changed?"

Amsel liked Osborn. He was a good scientist, and beyond that he always appreciated the bigger picture. In fact, he was displaying that ability right now. Sooner or later a man like him would look up from the ship to the stars and see that the course had been altered.

"No, Randy," Amsel said. "The objective hasn't changed."

"Then what's going on here. Because *something* has changed."

"Yes."

"But not the objective?"

Amsel inhaled slowly and shook his head. It was time. "Not our real objective, Randy." Amsel paused.

"Go on."

"Unofficially, what we're doing right now, here, was planned from the start. It was Fischer's idea and I agreed to make it happen. Fischer's agenda is his own, not the Defense Department's."

"And your agenda?"

"My own objective is simply to learn as much as is possible in our field by using this technology while we still have access to it. There was never a good reason to look at nothing but the sixth and seventh centuries."

"So then the other materials we recovered back in Tel El Dab'a, those weren't really test runs. That was part of your ... what, wider investigation?"

"I'm sorry about the dishonesty, Randy. It was done to protect you."

Osborn showed Amsel a cold smile. "Very thoughtful. Who else is aware of what you're doing?"

"Apart from Fischer and myself, just one of our historians. There are three of us engaged in the expanded project. Or four now. That's up to you."

Osborn's face hardened. "And what if I don't want to be involved? I can just walk away from all of this? And then what happens?"

"What do you mean?"

"I mean, will it be a car accident? A suicide? Maybe a mugging gone bad. *That* always looks pretty random."

Amsel waited a moment to make clear that his reply was a considered one. "Randy, all I can do is to give you my word. Nothing like what you're suggesting would happen if you choose not to join in this work."

"That's another thing. What exactly is *this work*? What are we trying to accomplish, beyond our mandate? Obviously I can't continue in the dark like this."

Amsel shook his head. "No, of course not. But are you certain you want to know?"

Osborn didn't blink. "I think you want me to know. You had to figure I would suspect something eventually. So please, Josh, let's stop pretending you didn't plan for this very moment. Probably a long time ago."

Amsel noticed something behind Osborn. The latest scan had finished. The results were up on the computer screen.

This fragment's signature matched their target. They had their first piece of the artifact.

Osborn must have seen it on Amsel's face. He turned around and looked at the screen.

His eyes lit up. He shook his fist. "We got you."

As cool a customer as he could be when he wanted to, Osborn could not contain his joy of discovery. Exactly what Amsel had been counting on. Like himself, Osborn had a passion for history that approached an obsession.

And he had just shown his hand. He was all in.

CHAPTER 32

REES INSTINCTIVELY SCRAMBLED backwards, away from the deafening explosion of the gunshot.

The younger DCIS agent fell onto his back there in the Core's anteroom. He sputtered a couple of times and stopped breathing.

The older agent turned the gun on Morgan. "You just stay where you are." And then said to Danni, "Were you bullshitting about that explosion?"

Danni's face had gone about four shades paler. "No."

He nodded. "I didn't think you were."

The older agent backed away, keeping the gun trained on them. He opened the Plexiglas door and stepped outside. Then he closed it and pulled that red locking lever.

Moments later he was gone down the hall.

Morgan ran over to the younger agent and checked his neck for a pulse. "He's gone."

"Kerry," Danni said, "get his key. Get his handcuff key." Her voice was just a couple decibels shy of a scream.

Rees looked down at the man's face. The bullet had entered under his left eye. It made a surprisingly clean, circular hole. "Shouldn't we do CPR?"

Morgan was hunting through the agent's coat now. "Even if we got his heart restarted—and that's about a ten percent chance—we can't call for help in here. He would just bleed out on us."

Rees raced to the Plexiglas door and turned the handle. It wouldn't open. The locking mechanism on the outside apparently overrode the inside handle.

Meanwhile, Danni had struggled to her feet. "Just get the damn key, Kerry, and get me outta this shit. We have to go. Now!"

Morgan pulled an ID folder from the man's coat and flipped it open. Rees could see it clearly enough from where he stood. The man was DCIS. Her own agency again.

Morgan pocketed that ID, and took her own ID wallet back from the dead man's hand. She grabbed a key off his belt, rushed over to Danni, and removed the handcuffs. Danni let them clatter to the floor.

Rees stood there shaking his head. "I don't get it. Why didn't that guy shoot us too? I'm not complaining. I'm just confused."

Danni rubbed her wrists. They were already ringed with red where the handcuffs had pinched her. "He's making it look like an accident. That's why he locked us in here. He interrupted the shutdown sequence."

Rees flashed back on the older agent's parting words. *Were you bullshitting about that explosion?* "Oh, shit. We have to get the hell out of here."

"That's what I've been saying!" Danni hurried over to the rack of parkas. "He asked me if there was another way out. I told him no, but we can still go through the Core. If there's enough time left."

Morgan pointed at the anteroom's Plexiglas door. "There's no way to get that open?"

Danni threw on a parka and shoved her arms through the fat sleeves. "Not now. The liquid helium's starting to boil. It's gonna rupture the cooling system, and the safety program knows that. We could override it from out there in the control room. Not from in here."

Morgan grabbed the dead man's gun. She slid it into her own shoulder holster, and zipped up her parka. Then she looked at Danni. "Time. What do we have?"

"I don't know," Danni pulled on a glove. "Less than ten minutes. That's a rough guess."

Rees ran over to the huge door that led to the Core. "What's the key code?"

Danni pulled on her other glove. "Twenty-six, twelve, seventeen, ninety-one."

Rees punched it in. A moment later he could hear the mechanics inside clicking and humming. An indicator light over the door changed from red to green.

Danni and Morgan joined Rees there at the door. Danni pushed a button. The heavy door swung open silently under its own power.

A blast of super-cooled air spilled out from the Core and splashed into Rees like an invisible liquid. The cold soaked through his parka and gloves like they weren't even there. He shuddered. "Hoo, man! That's ... pretty damn intense."

"It gets worse." Danni's breath hung in the air in front of her, a white cloud of condensation. When the door had opened wide enough, she stepped through the swirling fog into the Core.

Rees followed her in. Morgan came right behind.

Rees felt all his muscles clench in response to the icy air. His body trying to generate heat by burning extra calories. Against this intense cold, that was like putting your hands out to stop a freight train.

Stacks of modular electronics and hundreds of lighted read-out displays packed the tight space. Like the cockpit of some advanced aircraft, but stretched out into a long tunnel. The engineers had laid out the tunnel itself in a spiral that they were following inward.

Some of the machinery they rushed past looked familiar to Rees, but all out of scale. He noted part of a standard H_3/H_4 dilution type cooling system, but something like fifty times larger than anything he'd ever seen.

On any other day he would have a million questions for Danni. Today all he wanted to know was whether or not they were going to make it out of there alive.

He raced along behind Danni as she led them through a narrow space between stacks of gold foil wrapped machinery. This section of the Core looked like it had been assembled out of spare satellite parts.

"Someday," Rees announced through chattering teeth, "I want a real tour of this place. It's amazing."

Puffs of condensation floated back over Danni's shoulder. "Sure. Someday. If it hasn't blown up, and we're not all locked down in a black site in Romania."

Rees and the others moved at a near run. It had only been a couple of minutes since they entered, but the vicious cold inside the Core was like a hungry animal. Biting at every little gap in his clothing, trying to drink the precious heat from his body.

Danni stopped at an inner wall that had a metal hatch in it. It looked like something you'd see on a military vessel. She yanked on a latch. Air hissed around the seal as the pressure equalized.

Danni looked back over her shoulder at Rees and Morgan, the white clouds of her breath puffing out more rapidly from the exertion. "It's gonna get pretty bad now."

Morgan was shivering visibly. "Yeah, 'cause it's ... so nice and toasty right here."

Rees felt himself shivering too, as badly as when they hauled him from the bay. Until just now, *that* was as cold as he'd ever been in his entire life.

The old records were falling fast today.

Danni climbed carefully through the hatchway. Dark in there, but Rees could see her waiting for him on the other side.

He placed his hands on the rim of the hatchway for balance and started through. "Ow! What the..." He reflexively let go of the rim. His palms felt like they were on fire beneath the gloves.

"Sorry, sorry," Danni said. "Shoulda warned you. Don't touch any metal in here for more than a second. Even with the gloves. Here, take my hand."

Rees did, feeling like an idiot. He should have known that. He needed to concentrate better. But the cold was sapping his energy. Mental energy too, it seemed.

He reached the other side of the hatchway and turned back, offering a hand to Morgan and passing along Danni's warning.

As Morgan's faced brushed by his, Rees could see her eyes watering from the bitter cold. The tears didn't fall, though. They just frosted up in her eyelashes.

After Morgan passed through safely, Rees stood up and looked around the strange space they were in.

They had entered a spherical room, maybe fifteen meters in diameter with a flat floor. Difficult to gauge the dimensions. The walls were coated with some matte black material. Dials and indicators on the machinery emitted the only eerie illumination.

Rees's ears and nose had stung painfully for the last minute or so. But seconds after they entered here that sensation stopped abruptly.

They'd gone numb.

A pity, really. He kind of liked his ears and nose. It would be a shame to lose them.

"Say hello ... and good-b-bye to Alan." Danni gestured toward the center of the spherical space.

A dark cube, about a meter along each edge, hung suspended on gossamer wires that looked like a spider's web made out of ruby-red, laser light.

Even with his life hanging in the balance, Rees couldn't help but marvel at it. That little box up there contained more computing power than all the world's normal CPU's running together in massive parallel. Much more. Great episode for the show there.

Danni led them to an area just underneath the cube. Rees felt his limbs growing slow and heavy. The shivering had stopped. Probably bad news there too.

"Sh-shit." Danni was looking down at the floor near her feet.

Several vertical pipes penetrated it right there. Probably for the helium pre-coolant. Next to them lay what appeared to be a kind of access plate.

It was bolted shut.

"C-c-crawlspace?" Rees barely managed to get out the word. He wondered how much longer he'd be able to speak at all.

Danni nodded.

So that was it. Their only way out lay under a bolted plate.

Morgan started searching the nearby area. Hunting for a wrench, Rees assumed. With any luck, the techs kept one handy.

Danni, with the least body mass of all of them, looked terrible. Even from what little Rees could see in this low light. She looked as though she might fall over any second.

That would be a disaster. Heat conduction. If she fell, her whole body would be in contact with a surface that sucked energy away much faster than this air did.

She wouldn't last two minutes like that.

"C-crouch." Rees told her. He demonstrated by getting down in a crouch himself, hugging his shins.

Danni nodded and did it. She seemed to understand that the position would reduce her exposed surface area. She'd lose heat more slowly, at least.

But her eyelids were already drooping.

Instinctively Rees wanted to go to her. Huddle together, try to warm her up. But with time running out, buying Danni a couple more minutes wouldn't help anyone. He'd just lose any opportunity to do something genuinely constructive.

Whatever he tried, it would have to be soon. Because Rees was beginning to feel quite comfortable.

And very sleepy.

CHAPTER 33

LIFE IS STRANGE, Agent Thom Merriweather thought. He took the stairs two at a time, eager to get out of the computer building ahead of the explosion he had set into motion. Plus he wasn't any spring chicken anymore, and the freakish cold in here was aggravating his damned arthritis.

Merriweather's DCIS counterpart back east had just cooked DNA evidence to fake that a scientist died in a lab explosion. Now here he was on the West Coast making sure another scientist really *would* die in a lab explosion.

Was that irony? He wasn't sure.

When he returned to this building with a CSI team, he would plant Special Agent Morgan's gun in whatever remained of that room down there. Ballistics would show it had been used to kill Agent Gibson. The other three deaths? Accidental. Caught in the explosion. And nothing would come back to Merriweather. Except another big payday from the Office.

He reached the ground floor and exited the stairwell into a hallway. And immediately spotted Gibson's meaty partner, Swain, coming his way.

"What the hell?" Swain frowned at him. "You're supposed to be on the fire exit."

Merriweather just kept walking. "I was. Then one of the guys who works here came out a minute ago. Said we all had to leave the area immediately. Some kinda leak. I'm just passing on the word."

"Where's Gibson?"

"Ran into him downstairs. He's right behind us. So c'mon, let's go."

Swain strode right past Merriweather toward the stairwell door.

Merriweather called after him. "Hey, Gibson's on his way up. We'll meet him outside."

"I'm not leaving the building without my partner." Swain opened the door into the stairwell. "What floor was he on?"

"I don't know. Anyway I told you, he's headed up now. C'mon, they want us outta here."

"What did I just say? I'm not going without Gibson. Now how many floors down when you last saw him?"

"All right. Okay."

Merriweather had Morgan's gun tucked in his waistband, in the small of his back under his coat. He reached behind, pulled it, and in one motion brought it up and fired.

But he must have squeezed off the round before his arm got all the way up. He was going for a solid head shot. Instead the bullet caught Swain in the chin with an explosion of blood, teeth, and bone.

Swain fell back into the opened stairwell doorway, spinning as he dropped. He hit the floor on his hands and knees and scrambled down the stairs out of sight.

Still very much alive, at least for the time being. And he was armed.

Well, that's a big aw, shit. Merriweather had to press the attack now. He couldn't take a chance on Swain ultimately surviving that shot.

He looked around for something he could throw in the doorway ahead of him. A distraction before following it down into the stairwell.

"Agent Merriweather."

Merriweather whirled around to face the voice.

The head Livermore security guard, Neery, was standing there with his weapon holstered. "I radioed when we saw you weren't at the fire exit anymore. But ... oh, Jesus."

Neery was looking past Merriweather, toward the stairwell door. Merriweather glanced back.

Bright red blood spatter on the doorframe. The security guard must've spotted it.

Merriweather pointed toward the doorway. "I wounded one of the suspects. The armed woman. She's a DCIS agent named Morgan. Bitch is a goddamn traitor. She took off down the stairwell."

Neery looked like he was gonna shit his pants. "What do we do?"

Merriweather's mind leaped ahead through the possibilities. The body count was rising. The story was getting too complicated. He didn't want to add this security bozo to the list of deaths he'd have to maintain he had nothing to do with.

Neery's expression suddenly changed, from worry to confusion. "Wait, whose gun is that?"

"What?"

He was looking at the gun Merriweather held in his hand. Morgan's gun. Merriweather realized he'd accidentally flashed his shoulder holster, a second ago when he raised his arm to point. His service piece was still in there.

Neery had seen both weapons.

"You know, you have a surprisingly good eye, my man." Merriweather raised his gun to kill Neery, and heard a shot go off behind him. He ducked as he turned.

Swain stood there in the stairwell doorway, bracing himself on the frame. Tough sonofabitch. Looked like something from a goddamn zombie movie. Lower half of his face blown off. Shredded gore hanging where his mouth and jaw should have been, dripping blood and spit.

But Swain had missed his shot, and Merriweather wasted no time in pumping three quick rounds into the center of his chest. Tough guy or not, Swain dropped for good this time.

Merriweather turned back around to take care of Neery.

Neery drew his weapon and fired. Unbelievably fast.

Merriweather felt the thump of the bullet and took a halting step backwards. No pain, not yet. But all the strength drained out of his body. He couldn't even raise his arm to return fire.

He didn't want to do it, but he just had to look down.

A hole in his jacket. Right over his heart.

He looked again at Neery, frozen there. Smoke curling up from his gun. Looked like something out of an old Western.

"What are you ... a goddamn cowboy?"

Everything felt light, even as it all turned dark.

Life is strange, was Thom Merriweather's very last thought.

CHAPTER 34

STANDING THERE AT the center of the Core, Rees had only one overwhelming desire. He just wanted to lie down. A little rest and he could think more clearly. If he could just close his eyes for a moment. Only a moment.

And he knew if he did, it would be the last mistake he ever made.

Danni was nodding off down there in her crouch. The hypothermia getting to her too. She couldn't have much time left.

Morgan was still searching for a wrench. She wasn't having any luck there.

That meant it was all up to Rees.

He struggled to think under the drug-like torpor induced by the penetrating cold. There was no safety in backtracking. No way out there. He had to figure some way, any way, they could open that access plate and go forward, get out of there through the crawlspace.

And if they couldn't?

Then when the cooling system blew up, dousing them all with liquid helium—it would actually be a *coup de grace*. At least it would all end quickly.

First thing, he needed to stop imagining the cold as an enemy. Too romantic to be useful right now. The cold was simply a fact. Facts were never the enemy. *Nature to be commanded must be obeyed,* as Francis Bacon had more or less put it.

What did nature say about cold?

Lack of heat is basically reduced atomic motion. Which affects...?

A nebulous idea struggled to take form in Rees's head. So damned tired and bleary.

His eyes landed on a valve there in the cooling pipes, just above where they penetrated the floor. Near the access plate. The *metal* access plate.

An image came into his mind then. A ship. A huge, passenger liner.

The Titanic.

Yes. Yes, there were possibilities there.

He wanted to ask Danni if that valve was what he thought it was. He sucked in a lungful of the super-cooled air, preparing to speak. That set off a dry coughing fit. White spots danced in his field of vision.

No. Don't you pass out, goddamn you. Can't pass out.

Rees clamped his mouth shut and breathed through his nose. He managed to get the cough under control.

He would just have to open that valve and see if he was right. In any case, he didn't have any time or any other ideas.

He squatted and grabbed the valve's handle with a gloved hand. No burning sensation now. The cold had numbed his hands so badly he couldn't feel anything. In fact, he could only confirm that he gripped the handle because his eyes were telling him so.

He pushed. His fingers slid right off. No real grip left. The signal from his brain couldn't reach the muscles in his half-frozen hand.

He tried again with both hands this time. He leaned down too, so that his chest crushed his fingers hard against the valve handle.

Something moved. But had he only just slipped again?

He pulled back to look. No, he hadn't slipped. The valve handle really had moved.

Just then Morgan came over to his side.

"W-wrench?" Rees asked.

She shook her head. She had a length of heavy pipe. About two feet of it. She was shifting it from hand to hand. That made sense. It would probably freeze her fingers solid if she held it firmly for too long.

She gestured Rees away, then bent down and wound up to swing the pipe at one of the bolts. She was lining up almost parallel to the side of the bolt, but at a slight angle. Rees saw what she was trying to do. Loosen the bolt with a glancing blow. A trick Rees had used once or twice with a hammer on a stuck nut.

Morgan swung the pipe. When it struck its target, it spun right out of her grip and clanked to the floor. She was having the same problems with her numb extremities.

Her idea wasn't going to work. He would have to follow through with his own plan.

He pushed Morgan to get her attention, then pointed to Danni crouched on the floor near the access plate. "M-m-move her."

Morgan apparently understood what he was asking for and didn't seem to care why. She was probably out of ideas too. She slid her arms under Danni's armpits and dragged her up and away.

Rees grabbed the valve handle again with both hands. And again he pinned his fingers down with the weight of his torso. After a moment's resistance the valve snapped down into the open position.

He fell back, putting some distance between himself and the valve. Clear liquid began to flow out.

Helium, liquid helium. It *was* a release valve. Just as he'd hoped.

The helium hissed and boiled as it began to pool up on the floor. Like water being poured onto a hot griddle.

The puddle of helium spread out from under the release valve, and soon reached the access plate. In a few more moments it had covered the plate entirely.

The helium boiled so furiously that the puddle stopped growing. It had reached a stasis between liquid coming in from the valve and gas going up into the air. Good. Evaporative cooling was sucking all the heat energy from the metal plate. The first step in his plan.

Now Rees had to guess how long to wait. Too soon and there would be no effect. Too long and the whole cooling system might blow before the next step of the plan.

Morgan watched. It wasn't clear that she understood what his aim was here. Rees didn't have the capacity now to explain.

Brittle fracture. Metals under extreme cold lose their ductility.

The Titanic sank in part because the hull didn't deform when it struck the iceberg. It shattered. The iron in the Titanic's hull plates had unusually high sulfur content. At about five degrees below zero Celsius, the temperature of the seawater she sailed through, the high-sulfur hull plates had become extremely brittle. Better iron wouldn't have done so, not at those temps. But nearly all metals did when the temperature got low enough.

That access plate down there would be a cadmium alloy, to resist the extreme cold. But it wasn't designed to be exposed to the evaporative cooling effects of liquid helium phase-shifting into a gas.

That's what Rees was counting on.

He judged that it had been long enough. The pipe Morgan dropped still lay nearby. He retrieved it and whacked the valve handle up and shut, cutting off the flow of liquid helium. In moments the pooled helium had all boiled away.

Rees shifted the pipe to his other hand, and knelt next to the access plate. He raised the pipe over his head and slammed it down with all his strength, square on the center of the plate.

It made a loud *clang*. The pipe flew from his hand and clattered to rest nearby.

Rees inspected the access plate again.

Not even cracked.

Not a scratch on it. If the metal had been rendered brittle by the liquid helium, then the impact of the pipe just didn't generate enough force to shatter it.

It had been his best shot, and he'd failed.

Oddly, Rees felt no fear. Perhaps because there was no uncertainty to be anxious about. There was no way out now. And soon it would all be over.

He felt Morgan pushing him away. She gestured at him, to pull Danni back further. She zipped down her parka. Then she removed her gloves.

At first Rees thought she was hastening the end. Sure. Why wait? Why not just let the cold in and fall asleep?

Then he saw her fumbling for the gun in her shoulder holster.

She understood Rees's basic plan. And she had an impact generator much more powerful than that length of pipe. In his mental fog, Rees forgot all about the gun Morgan took off the dead man in the anteroom.

He helped Danni shuffle backwards with him, away from Morgan and the access plate. Nothing in there provided any real cover, so he coached her to crouch down with him, and turn away.

Then he positioned himself between her and Morgan. They would just have to hope that any flying fragments or ricochet wouldn't wound them too badly.

Rees nodded to Morgan, then turned away and waited to hear the gunshot that would either save them or signal the end.

When it came, the report wasn't as loud as he'd expected. Maybe the material lining the walls here dampened the sound.

He turned around to look.

The bullet had split the access plate into three pieces. But the bolts still held it fast to the floor. It continued to block their exit.

Morgan raised the gun to fire again. She turned around to check with Rees first, and he waved her off. They might not have to risk the ricochet.

The length of pipe lay between Rees and the access plate now. He picked it up on his way over, then stooped down to look more closely at the plate. One of the cracks there looked like it might be wide enough to...

Yes. He was just able to jam the end of the pipe into the crack. He wedged it into place and stood back up. Then he stomped down on the pipe as hard as he could.

The effort threw him off balance. He fell onto his back. When he lifted his head and looked forward through his knees, he saw three of the four bolts had snapped right off.

Brittle fracture again.

Morgan re-holstered the gun. She rotated one remaining piece of metal plate out of the way.

Their escape route was open.

Rees stood back up, and felt his legs shaking underneath him. Was he losing control of them? Now that they finally had a way out, would he be unable to walk through it?

He looked at Danni and Morgan. Both of them were wobbling too.

It wasn't Rees's legs. It was the floor, vibrating wildly.

The cooling system. It had begun to rupture.

CHAPTER 35

MORGAN HAD JUST felt warmer air rushing up through the crawlspace hatchway. And then the floor started to shake.

She glanced at Rees and Danni. Danni was still out of it, but the fear on Rees's face told her what she needed to know. He was feeling these vibrations too, and he'd come to the same conclusion.

This whole place was about to blow.

Together Morgan and Rees managed to lower Danni into the access space. They followed her down as quickly as their numbed limbs would allow.

The crawlspace only travelled in one direction from where they'd entered. Deciding which way to go wasn't an issue, at least.

Thick, multi-colored power cables snaked horizontally along the gray cement walls. The fat pipes that carried the liquid helium hung from the roof. They were banging against the braces that anchored them, like a wild animal caught in a trap.

Not quite room to stand up, but not literally a crawlspace either. They could sort of duck walk, humped over. Just wide enough for them to move three abreast.

A string of red work lights in wire cages ran along the roof of the tunnel, alongside the pipes. These tracked straight ahead twenty yards or so and either stopped at a dead end or made a sharp turn. She couldn't tell from where they were standing.

Morgan and Rees positioned themselves on opposite sides of Danni and each took an arm. She was conscious, but Morgan couldn't tell how lucid she was.

The liquid helium pipes continued to clatter above them, shaking bits of dust and cement down as they shuffled forward.

Soon they were at the end of the chain of red lights. Morgan saw that where they'd appeared before to stop was in reality a T-intersection.

Morgan took Danni's face into her hands. "W-which way out, Danni? Which way?"

Danni didn't seem able to speak quite yet. She looked off in both directions. Closed her eyes. Then opened them and nodded to her left.

"Th-this way?" Morgan said, pointing.

Danni nodded again.

Together they all turned to the left and began to scuttle forward. They hadn't gone very far when Danni started shaking her head. They all stopped.

"What is it?" Morgan asked. "You want to g-go back? Is it that way? Is the exit back that way?"

Danni nodded once.

Morgan checked in visually with Rees. He shook his head. Leaving it up to her. She knew Danni much better than he did. And Danni wasn't the kind to second guess herself. If she wanted to change directions, she must have seen or remembered something.

Morgan and Rees got Danni turned around. They all headed back through the T-intersection and continued on their new course.

Danni's right. Morgan thought. *She's right. Please, let her be right.*

The liquid helium pipes rattled more violently with every passing moment. The creaks and groans of metal warping under pressure grew louder. They might be instants away from the whole tunnel flooding with liquid helium.

The three of them plodded on. Nothing else to do. They were racing against an unseen clock.

As they continued down the tunnel, the red work lights overhead began to curve gently out of sight. Morgan saw Rees looking up too. Probably asking himself the same question. Were they under the new accelerator construction yet? Was that the curve of the giant, circular machine they were seeing now?

She hoped to God it was. Because that meant they were going the right way.

The moments crept past like an ultra-slow motion film. They should have been sprinting for their lives. But they could only manage this half-stooped shuffle. It was pure torture. But it was also the best they could do without abandoning Danni. And that had never for one second been an option.

From somewhere behind them the crippled cooling system started to emit popping sounds. Were those rivets tearing loose?

"Door." Danni lifted her chin. She was looking ahead and a little to the right.

Morgan followed her gaze and spotted it. There *was* a door up there.

Rees seemed see it too. He tried to pull them ahead faster, but Danni was already topped out.

The seconds dragged by.

They were only a few feet from the exit when a deep boom rumbled down the tunnel. A breeze followed right after. The explosive rush of liquid helium expanding, displacing the air ahead of it.

"That's a b-breach," Rees said.

Goddamnit. We're so close. Morgan guessed they had only seconds before the super-cooled helium caught up to them and froze them solid where they stood.

In two more steps they had reached the exit—a massive, metal door on giant hinges.

The door had a wheel-type latch that wouldn't have looked out of place on a submarine. Morgan tried to spin it, but her hands slid around the smooth wheel.

Rees reached over to help.

It sounded like a freight train was bearing down on them in the crawlspace now. Morgan remembered hearing that a tornado passing close by was supposed to sound just like this.

The breeze had ramped up to a howling wind. The killing helium was filling the tunnel. Rushing toward them.

Rees grabbed the wheel mechanism with one hand, and with the other he drew a circle in the air. Counter-clockwise.

Yes, good, they ought to be trying the same direction. And intuitively that way seemed right. She nodded at him.

Rees grabbed ahold with both hands. Together they cranked on the wheel. For a terrifying moment nothing happened. Then it came loose and started spinning.

They both lost their balance and fell over.

The wheel stopped.

Morgan scrambled to her knees and gave the door a push. It didn't budge an inch. She tried pulling. No good either.

Rees reached up and torqued the wheel again. Morgan heard a *chunk*.

She pulled again, and this time the door slowly swung open.

Rees rushed through, dragging Danni behind him by her hands. Morgan took her feet, but she tripped and fell halfway through the doorway.

"Close it! Close it!" Rees yelled.

She could barely hear him over the roar of the approaching blast. She crawled the rest of the way through the doorway, turned back and grabbed the inside handle, then began pulling the heavy door toward her.

Before it had come halfway a giant hand swatted it from the other side. The pressure of the exploding gas.

The metal door clobbered Morgan as it slammed shut.
She felt herself falling.
Silence.
Then blackness.

CHAPTER 36

Two weeks earlier—Jerusalem

HIS FRIENDS CONSIDERED Mazhar Mashhad trustworthy and loyal. A hardworking day laborer and a devoutly religious Muslim, who occasionally took work out of town for weeks or months at a time.

All in all, a man well-liked by people who—if they knew his true purpose—would most certainly want him dead.

Mashhad set down his shovel and left the archaeological dig around sunset with the other workers. A cool, moist breeze picked up. Rainclouds, dark and succulent, crowded in from the east. It had been a dry winter and a good rainstorm would be welcomed gladly.

Taking his habitual route toward home, he cut through the Suq al-Qattanin, the Cotton Merchant's Market. Here incense perfumed the evening air, as tourists haggled for Holy Land souvenirs, a fair number of which had been manufactured in China or India.

Mashhad nodded and smiled at the familiar merchants he passed. Many residents of the Muslim Quarter had known him since his arrival here five years ago.

Mashhad had recently presented himself for work at the new archaeological dig, despite a local call to boycott the project. He had two good reasons for ignoring that plea.

The first he offered publicly. "If I don't take the job," he told people, "some foreign worker will. This way at least the money stays here."

The second he kept to himself.

He was not there for the job.

Mashhad succeeded in getting himself hired. He spent the first week observing and querying his fellow laborers.

"So, what wonderful history are we digging up here, that's worth tossing whole families into the street over?" he asked of them.

And he received various answers.

"An extension of Zedekiah's Cave," one man offered.

"Looking for more of the little Kotel and I hope we don't find it. Just more Yahood coming into the neighborhood to pray," another told him.

"I have not the slightest idea and I care even less," said a third.

There had been an official application for permits, of course, with details about the dig's archaeological aims. Mashhad had seen it.

All that was a lie.

He had sneaked into all the trailers on site, to examine plans for the operation. What he found there was incoherent. A puzzle with key pieces quite obviously missing.

One set of records, though, he felt confident would provide the answers. The lead archaeologist, Joshua Amsel, carried it with him nearly everywhere. A weathered notebook bound in black leather.

The old man left the site with it in his possession again today, and returned to the Arthur Hotel still carrying it. He and the other members of his team were staying there along with their security detail.

Mashhad veered away from his regular route home to head for the hotel. There he waited outside for several hours, until he saw Amsel leave for dinner with a visiting researcher.

He slipped inside the hotel and made his way upstairs.

The cardkey he inserted into the door lock connected it via thin black wires to a small box of electronics in his pocket. It broke the lock's code in a matter of seconds.

Mashhad entered Amsel's room.

Working by flashlight he made a fast survey of the place. First checking common concealment areas.

Under drawers, mattress, inside the toilet tank, behind paintings, etc.

No notebook.

Amsel was not carrying it when he left for dinner, which strongly suggested it was still here. Probably in the room safe.

The safe itself was not concealed. It sat visible in the closet, as in most hotel rooms.

Mashhad recognized the model.

As with virtually all multi-user safes of this type the combination reset button was located inside. A new combination could only be entered with the safe unlocked and wide open.

Mashhad removed a thin, flat piece of metal from his kit, much like a slim jim for breaking into cars. He bent it into a Z shape. Then he slid it through the tiny gap between the top of the door and the body of the safe.

He angled the metal strip so the inside end pressed against the inner wall of the safe door.

Right where the safe's designers had placed the reset button.

It took perhaps a minute to find and depress the button. That allowed him to enter a new combination, which in turn opened the safe.

Inside, along with a UK passport and a large amount of cash, he found the leather bound notebook.

A quick skim confirmed what Mashhad had hoped. The story of the dig's hidden purpose seemed to lay there inside.

Also there was a list of storage lockers, some in Israel, others not. These might be for hiding smuggled, black market artifacts. This was information that would no doubt be useful to his employer.

Amsel would know his safe had been breached when it failed to open with his passcode—which Mashhad had never known and could not re-enter. There was, therefore, no reason not just to take the notebook. Which presently he did, along with the money and rest of the safe's contents. It would look like an ordinary hotel robbery.

He left, letting the hotel room door snick closed and started down the hall. He heard a shout behind him. He turned toward it slowly.

An Israeli soldier assigned to Amsel's security team drew his handgun and took aim. Even if Mashhad had been armed, he'd be dead before he could bring his weapon to bear.

Very slowly, he raised his hands. Then he sank to his knees.

IT TOOK ALMOST twenty minutes before he was again on his way, refusing the apology that had been offered by the soldier and his commander.

It wasn't necessary. How could the man have known?

Mashhad's very life depended on his great skill at projecting a false identity. On his being perceived wrongly, and not as the Israeli spy he truly was.

He had already notified his employer that he would have something for him tonight. They'd agreed to rendezvous where they had once before. The garden at the Ticho House, not very far from the Arthur Hotel.

He made his way there without further incident.

This job lay outside Mashhad's professional purview and amounted, more or less, to a favor for an old friend. One who had saved his ass some years before. For that reason, their meetings had all been clandestine.

The grounds at the historic Ticho House were lovely even in winter, with terraced shrubs alongside olive and cypress trees. Up above, the dark and starless skies held the promise of long overdue rains.

And in fact, generous drops began to fall just as Mashhad and his employer spotted each other, across the garden.

Mashhad couldn't tell if it was the arrival of the blessed rains—as they called the season's first real downpour—or the present that he carried under his arm that brought the smile to the lips of the director of the Israeli Antiquities Authority.

In any case, Benjamin Zaken looked very pleased indeed.

CHAPTER 37

MORGAN HAD BEEN unconscious for over eight hours now. Rees counted each additional minute she didn't wake up as bad news. It increased the likelihood they were looking at severe brain trauma here. He was already worried and steadily growing more so.

No, not worried. More like scared to death.

And all over a woman he hardly knew. That was something he really needed to revisit at a later time. If he lived that long.

After the helium explosion, Rees scouted the empty accelerator building, and looked for someplace they could hunker down a while.

Eventually he chose a kind of electronics utility closet. It was located close to where Morgan had collapsed. They'd be hidden away if anyone actually *did* come by. And their body heat should warm the small space up a bit.

He carried Morgan in and laid her down on top of his parka. He and Danni huddled up against her. Even unconscious, Morgan shivered badly. So did Rees and Danni. At one point he could hear the *clickety-click* of three sets of chattering teeth.

The minutes dragged by. Morgan still didn't wake. At some point Rees and Danni resolved to take turns sleeping.

When the end of Rees's watch rolled around, he decided to wake up Danni. They had a momentous choice to wrestle with. "Danni. Danni."

She lifted her head and looked up at him through bleary eyes. Then she craned her neck to check out Morgan. "Is she awake?"

"Still unconscious."

"How long have I been asleep?"

"Around two hours. Basically no change. I'm worried about brain swelling, or even a hemorrhage. We may have to chance it and turn ourselves in. So we can get Kerry to a hospital."

Danni nodded. "If she doesn't wake up in another ... like, fifteen minutes, I say we go for it. Surrender to whoever's out there."

"Agreed. And what do we do if she does wake up?" Rees had been trying to think of a logical next step, and he'd come up with exactly squat.

Danni grimaced and shook her head. "I dunno. We still have one gun. From the guy who got shot back there, outside the Core. The other one Kerry gave me is back in the control room."

"Yeah, I don't think a weapon does us much good, really."

Danni's eyes played back and forth as she appeared to consider something silently. When they settled on Rees again, there was new life in them. "Maybe we don't have to turn ourselves in. We could force someone to drive us to a hospital. You know, at gunpoint."

Rees felt the urge to laugh and squelched it. "Ahhh, yeah. I suppose we could. But assuming that worked, what then? There's still the little problem of someone out there trying to kill us all."

Danni slid over closer to Morgan, and looked down at her tenderly. "You still have no idea who sent you that note? The Herodotus guy?"

"No. Just that he or she wants to meet down at JPL ... well, it would be today now. This afternoon. At this point, we couldn't even make it there in time."

"So we'll just have to figure out the next step when we get to it."

Rees wasn't thrilled with the idea of improvising, but he thought she was probably right about that. "Let's say we do make it to a hospital. We could leave Kerry to get the medical attention she needs, then run for it. Head for Mexico. Go off the grid."

Danni shook her head. "I don't think I could do that. Just leave her there on her own."

"Leave me where?"

Rees and Danni turned together. Morgan lay on her back, staring up at them.

Rees felt the relief hit him like a tranquilizing drug. "We're not leaving you anywhere, Kerry. Don't worry."

Danni looked into Morgan's eyes. "How do you feel?"

Morgan glanced around the utility closet, obviously confused. "What is ... where the hell *are* we?" She tried to sit up. Her face contorted in pain. "Ahhh. Ow, ow. Shit, my head."

Danni reached over and supported Morgan's head, lowering it gently back down to the coat beneath her. "Take it easy. You got knocked out. We think you have a concussion."

An unfamiliar spark of fear flashed in Morgan's eyes. "Knocked out? How long?"

"About eight hours," Rees said. "What's the very last thing you remember?"

Morgan stared up at the closet ceiling, eyes searching. "I remember ... we were going to Lawrence Livermore, to try and find Fischer. Fischer's work, I mean. And ... are we still there?"

"Yes, we're still there." Rees could see the alarm on Danni's face and tried to reassure her. "She has some retrograde amnesia. It's normal from what I understand."

Danni didn't look very reassured. "Kerry, you remember the men that came here looking for us? You said they were DCIS agents. Remember that? And one of them, the older guy, he shot the other one. You remember?"

Morgan frowned. "No. No. I don't."

"It's all right," Rees said. "We'll take you through what happened."

For the next few minutes, he and Danni helped Morgan piece together the missing hours. How Danni had found the original proposal for the Kafir Project in the offline computer. The two DCIS agents showing up. The shooting. All of them escaping through the Core.

Eventually they walked her up mentally to where they were now. In the lower reaches of Livermore's new accelerator complex, hiding in an electronics storage closet.

"So, are we outside of the security perimeter?" Morgan asked.

Danni shook her head. "Not yet. But the accelerator tunnel will take us way beyond the main campus. Then we should be in good shape."

"Yes, but we still have the *what then* problem," Rees said. "Our goal in coming here was to find the data from the Kafir Project. We get that out publically, they have no reason to keep coming after us. Boom, game over."

"We hope," Danni added.

"Right. We hope," Rees agreed. "But we don't have the data. We don't even have the project proposal now. That's on a hard drive back in the control room outside the Core. If it wasn't destroyed in the explosion. Anyway we can't get there. Not now."

Morgan touched her fingers lightly to her head, just above the front hair line. "Man, that's a hell of a lump." She looked up at Rees. "Kafir Project. I do remember that much. Time-viewing. So why was DARPA funding Fischer's work? Did we find that out?"

"Yeah," Danni said. "The Kafir Project was supposed to counter violent Islamic extremism. On a sort of foundational level. By attacking the historicity of their beliefs."

"Historicity. Basically, whether it's all true," Morgan said.

Danni nodded. "Yep, whether it really happened. Islam is a historical religion. If the story's bogus, the whole religion is trashed. It's a psy-op, basically. Could be a knockout one too."

Morgan looked doubtful about that. "They wouldn't believe it, the Muslim world. What were we going to do anyway? Show them movies of Mohammed drinking wine and eating bacon? They'd just say it was actors. Christ, there are idiots out there who still think the moon landings were staged."

"There were two parts to the proposed program," Danni explained. "The time-recordings were just for starters. They could also sort of lock onto physical objects from the past. Important historical artifacts. And trace them through time. Rees gets this part better than I do."

Using Fischer's notebook and what Danni had told him from the proposal, Rees had worked out how the technology probably functioned.

"Time viewing—or spacetime viewing we should really say—involves capturing information at an atomic level," he said. "That's partly why they needed the quantum computer. Insane amounts of data. You can trace your target forward through time too, to get a kind of arrow pointing at where it might be now. Then, when you dig up the artifact, you can test it, show that it *exactly* matches the time recording, virtually atom for atom."

"Provenance," Morgan said.

Rees nodded. "Exactly. Irrefutable proof of authenticity. But you need both the recordings and the artifacts to do that. They corroborate and reinforce each other."

Morgan massaged her temples. "Yeah, I still think they wouldn't buy it. They'd say you doctored the evidence somehow."

Danni jumped back in. "Fischer thought so too. That's why he wanted to make the technology open source. Give it all away. Let the Islamists confirm everything for themselves. It all was part of the proposal."

Morgan laughed, then winced. "Ow. I'll bet that went over great with the Pentagon. If you can look anywhere in space and time, you keep the technology secret. Use it to spy on your enemies making battle plans."

Rees had worked that bit out too. "Except that's not possible. It's all about power. I mean literally, physical energy. I'm just inferring this from Fischer's notes, but I think they were using the high energy proton-antiproton beam collisions at Fermilab to disturb the Higgs field. In a way that wasn't previously imaginable before Fischer's breakthrough, I mean."

Morgan had her hand raised, like a student in class. "Um, let's pretend that I don't have a degree in advanced physics, and that you're a nice TV science man who can explain it all anyway."

As exhausted as he felt, Rees still smiled at that. "Right. Okay, they were bending spacetime. That's the stuff history is made of. They were bending it back to touch itself. Making closed loops. That's how this all works. A particular place and time in the past actually comes into *physical contact...*" he pantomimed bending two ends of an elongated object around to touch each other, "...direct physical contact with detectors. Right here in the present. But spacetime is actually pretty stiff stuff."

"Ah, so it's not easy to bend," Morgan said. "See, I'm getting all this."

Rees made a little bow. "That's because I'm very good at this. It's my job. So, imagine a length of plastic tubing, like six inch diameter PVC pipe. It's stiff stuff too. But if you lay out two miles of it, you could bend it, very gently, just with your hands even. Eventually you could make a loop. A very big loop, but a loop."

Morgan nodded. "Still with you. Keep going."

"Now try that with two *feet* of six inch diameter PVC pipe. Try to bend that into a loop with your bare hands. No one's that strong. It turns out you can bend spacetime into a closed loop and actually touch the past, *if* the extension along the time axis is long enough."

"So how much time elapsed do you need? How far back?" Morgan asked.

Rees shrugged. "I'm not sure, but I roughed it out. I think you'd want to have at least a thousand years or more to work with, given the energies they could generate with the Tevatron. The longer the better."

"So the dinosaur stuff was probably the first thing they recorded," Danni suggested.

Rees had entertained the same thought. "Yep. Easier to capture. You'd have to convert the entire mass of Jupiter into pure energy to record something like the Kennedy Assassination. And forget about anything that happened yesterday, or a week or a month ago."

They sat quietly a moment. Rees became aware again of the faint background hum of the facility's electronics.

Morgan broke the silence. "So, what is it?"

"What is what?" Danni asked.

"What is it they're looking for?" Morgan replied. "You said they needed the time-recording *and* a historical artifact of some kind. To prove it was all real. So what artifact was going to totally undermine Islam? Did Mohammad write a tell-all book? 'How I Just Made Up the Qur'an?'"

A recorded image flashed into Rees's mind. An image of a book and a Christian ceremony. It had been coming back to him throughout the morning. But he couldn't work out any connection to the Kafir Project's purpose. Until that moment.

The revelation must have shown on his face.

"You just figured something out," Danni said. "I know that look. I've seen researchers get that look. It's always good."

Rees felt the excitement driving out his fatigue. "It's just that I think Kerry isn't far off. I think it *is* a book. And I've seen it. In one of the videos on Fischer's flash drive."

Morgan squinted at him. "With the dinosaur? You sure *you* didn't hit your head, Rees?"

"No, there was another video file on there. I didn't play it back for you, because it didn't seem to mean anything at the time. But it does now. I think it means something huge."

Danni looked like she would reach out and start shaking him in a second. "Well for Chrissake, Rees, what does it mean?"

"It means I know who Herodotus is. And where to find him."

CHAPTER 38

IT AMAZED THE surgeon they didn't have to put Sabel under to remove the screwdriver, clean the wound, and sew it all back up. He told them he had allergies, that he'd experienced terrible reactions to general anesthesia in the past.

"Could you guys try it first with a local?" he asked the doctors.

They were skeptical, but they did it. That was good. He wouldn't have to lose time while recovering from a general anesthetic.

He'd only asked for the local because they would have freaked the hell out if they'd seen what he could really tolerate. They'd want to write a goddamn paper on him.

He didn't need the attention.

When it was all over, Sabel told them this was bound to happen one day. "'Cause people are always telling me to go screw myself."

Everyone had a good laugh over that. Har, har.

The surgery took less than thirty minutes. They told him he could be discharged in about forty-eight hours if everything looked good by then.

He slipped out less than an hour after he got his final unit of blood. On the way out, he stole a new pair of pants. Also a week's worth of antibiotics from the hospital's dispensary.

As he hiked out to the stolen Toyota, Sabel thought his limp must look pretty damn obvious. Could make him stand out. He practiced walking without it, in case he needed to later.

Not a problem. Just a shitload more pain.

When he reached the car, Sabel dialed the Office. After a coded exchange with the operator, they redirected the call through a scrambler, and then on to an untraceable relay set-up that bounced it all around creation.

A minute later he was talking to Singleton. Bit of a surprise there. Sabel didn't ask why Doubleman wasn't on the job. He didn't really give a shit which one of them chose to run this op. He got paid just the same. And Singleton wouldn't have told him dick anyway.

"I'm back online," Sabel said.

"Understood. Gevin Rees may be dead."

"*May* be? Okay. I thought we wanted intel from him. I just went through a teeny bit of trouble there trying to take him in alive, you know."

"He was going to wind someplace where he might have had the opportunity to go public," Singleton said. "Per my recommendation, the client opted to eliminate that possibility."

"So, that's it then?"

"No. The operative assigned to terminate Rees may have failed to complete his mission."

And that probably means one of your boys got taken out. See, the TV guy's not so damn easy is he? "Okay. What now?" Sabel asked.

"First, we need to confirm that Rees truly is out of the picture. There was an explosion. We need a visual on the body."

Sabel laughed at that. "Another explosion? You guys running out of ideas over there?"

"Your current cover will get you close enough for verification."

"That ID's only meant to fool civilians." It had been a bit of a rush job, and Sabel didn't think the Office's people had hacked the online records that would back it up.

"It's a chaotic scene there. No one's going to be doing checks."

"So where am I going then?"

"Lawrence Livermore National Laboratory. You're not too far from it now, I believe."

"What about Danielle Harris and the other chick? The one who met Rees at the hotel?" Sabel asked.

"Also killed in the explosion. Again, that's only as far as we know. We need confirmation there too. And we have tentative ID on the other woman now. The chatter we're picking up is that her name is Kerry Morgan. A DCIS agent."

DCIS? Doesn't sound like your ordinary type bodyguard there. Something going on you guys aren't telling me? "Okay then," Sabel said. "Let's recap. You want confirmation of death on Gevin Rees, Danielle Harris, and Kerry Morgan."

"Yes."

"And if any of them survived the explosion?"

"Then you finish the job," Singleton said. "Continue on the assumption that we're right about Herodotus. He should be at least as useful as Rees would have been. Take him alive and contact us for further directions."

And that was the end of it.

Singleton signed off without asking how badly Sabel had been injured, or how he was doing. Typical. The Office didn't do employee picnics or company Christmas cards either.

Sabel's feelings weren't hurt. They couldn't be. He didn't really have any in the normal sense.

Part of his special gift.

He set his smartphone navigator for Lawrence Livermore National Laboratory and drove out of the parking lot. Rees and his companions weren't going to be hard to find now.

They're either dead, or they're about to be dead.

Sabel smiled at the thought. When it came right down to it, that description fairly covered most of the folks he'd ever worked with.

CHAPTER 39

THE QUEST TO reach the mysterious Herodotus was underway. Danni noted that in this little drama she'd somehow gotten herself cast in the role of Dante's Virgil.

She wasn't leading Morgan and Rees down into hell, but she was taking them back underground, through the new particle accelerator's tunnel. And the collision temps here would be hotter than any inferno the Florentine poet could ever have imagined.

Their game plan hinged now on the hopes they wouldn't get shot or arrested the second they poked their heads up on the far end of the accelerator complex. No one had ventured a guess what the odds there were.

There was no point. They had no other option.

The three of them trudged along the tunnel's cement floor by the beams of two LED emergency flashlights they found in the utility closet. The liquid helium had long since evaporated. Rees and Danni walked together in front. Morgan kept an eye on the rear.

Rees was explaining his theory on Herodotus's real identity. "When I saw the breaking of the bread, I realized it had to be a Christian ceremony. The Eucharist."

"But the Kafir Project was supposed to be about the history of Islam," Morgan countered. "Or the non-history. Why record a Christian church service? Do we even know what time period it was?"

Rees answered over his shoulder. "Well, it would have to be from before the seventh century. It would need to predate Islam, if they're doing what I think they're doing."

"Which is?" Danni asked.

"Okay, based on what you read in the original proposal, we have a good idea about the Kafir Project's agenda."

"Obtain historical evidence to refute key elements of Islamic belief," Danni recited. "I think that's verbatim."

"And that included real, historical artifacts." Rees's voice sounded ragged from fatigue, but edged with excitement too. "When Kerry joked about a tell-all book, it came to me. The liturgical book the priest read from, in the time recording—that was literally the focal point. Why would a book of Christian writings be so important to Islamic history? And as soon as I asked that question, I knew the answer. Because it's a Syriac Christian lectionary."

"Rees, can we slow down some?" Morgan sounded exhausted.

Rees glanced back at her. "Of course. I guess I should explain what a lectionary is."

"No, I mean physically. Walking. Can we slow it down? Every step is like somebody's whacking my head with a hammer."

Rees slacked his pace. "I'm sorry. Is this better?"

"Yes it is. Thanks. And yeah, please explain about the lectionary thing. I'm not exactly at the top of my game right now."

Rees nodded. "All right. So a lectionary is a kind of calendar for what the priest reads to the congregation. Which verses on what days. The one in the time-recording would've contained passages from the *Tanakh*, the Jewish scriptures. And of course there'd be some version of the gospel story in there too."

"How do you know all this stuff?" Danni asked. "Aren't you an astrophysicist?"

Rees gave a modest shrug. "I started investigating the history of my childhood religion. And then I just got curious, I suppose. I still keep up with biblical archaeology and textual criticism."

Morgan played her flashlight beam over some unopened crates of equipment they were passing. Shadows marched backwards across the tunnel wall. "You said it was a *Syriac Christian* lectionary, Rees. Why is that important?"

"Well, a few years ago a certain Aramaic scholar noticed something interesting about the Qur'an. There are a number of words and verses that are virtually incomprehensible—even to educated Qur'anic scholars. But they make perfect sense if you strip away the diacritical marks and assume the text was written in Syro-Aramaic, not Arabic."

Morgan chimed in again. "You're losing me, Rees. Did I mention I just got my clock cleaned pretty good?"

"Okay, in the seventh century," Rees said, "the Arabic language was written without vowels, like Hebrew. And a number of the consonants looked exactly alike. The same four characters could spell eight or ten different words."

A dim memory struggled to surface in Danni's mind, but didn't quite make it. Something to do with martyrs.

Rees continued. "Marks were added, dots and dashes, above, below and beside these consonants, or what's called the rasm. But the early scribes who had to decide what possible word each clump of ambiguous letters represented in the Qur'an were all working under the assumption it was written entirely in Arabic. And it might not have been."

Danni remembered now. "White grapes."

Rees turned his flashlight on Danni's face. "Yes! You've heard about this."

Danni raised a hand to block out the glare. Rees quickly lowered the beam away from her eyes.

She dropped her hand. "Yeah, it made the rounds in the press a few years back. The Seventy-two virgins that Islamic martyrs are supposed to get in heaven. It was really a bunch of white grapes."

"Well, that's gonna be a bit of a letdown," Morgan said dryly.

Rees agreed with a little laugh. "That alternate *white grapes* translation was based on a radical idea. At least some of the Qur'an was originally selected readings from the bible for use in a Syriac Christian church service. Based on a lectionary written in Syro-Aramaic. The theory's hugely controversial. Or I should say it was."

Danni understood why it wouldn't be anymore. Not if someone had the frickin' book now, and you could compare passages word for word. She also understood why it would devastate fundamentalist Muslims.

"The Qur'an is supposed to have been dictated to Mohammad," Danni said. "Directly from God."

"Well, through the angel Gabriel, actually. But in God's own words." In his excitement, Rees was gesturing with the hand that held the flashlight. The swinging beam made shadows leap and dance around the accelerator tunnel. "To Muslims, the Qur'an isn't like the gospels are to Christians. It's more like, well, Jesus. The book itself is considered miraculous, an object worthy of worship. It's where you turn to understand what's right and true. To settle disputes. It's the *literal* word of God—who revealed it in Arabic, because that's the 'purest language.' And if whole passages of the holy and miraculous Qur'an were just cribbed from a Christian prayer book? One that was written before Mohammad was born? A book not even composed in Arabic..."

"Totally undermines the extremists," Morgan said. "It really could be the ultimate psy-op."

A thought came to Danni that raised tough questions. "So is that who's coming after us? Islamic radicals trying to stop the Kafir Project? But think about that. They have agents in the

Defense Department? And at Fermilab too? I mean, that doesn't even seem possible. Is it, Kerry?"

"Well, someone got inside, that's for sure." Morgan frowned. "But no, I can't believe it's Islamic radicals either."

Rees had gained a few steps on them again. He seemed to notice, and slowed down. "I agree. There's something we don't have yet, some bigger piece of the puzzle. Which is why we absolutely have to talk to Herodotus."

"So who is he, already? Danni asked.

"An historian," Rees said, "like the original Herodotus. The Kafir Project needed someone with the best theories on where and when to point the time recording technology. And I think it's the man who proposed the whole lectionary idea. He's a tenured professor of religious history at San Francisco State University. Professor Burhan Kazemi. I actually have a couple of his books at home."

"San Francisco State is like a half hour from here," Danni said.

Rees nodded. "I think Professor Kazemi is Herodotus. In fact, I'd bet money on it. Fischer said that he'd have the data, the full time-recordings. We get our hands on that and we're halfway home."

"Halfway," Morgan said, "because we need the lectionary too. If we want to stop all this. *We* have to prove what *they're* trying to bury, whoever they are. And that takes both parts, right?"

In his excitement, Rees had moved ahead again. He spoke back over his shoulder. "Yes, definitely. We need the lectionary too. The historical evidence here stands on two legs or it falls down. The person Fischer called Anaximander is supposed to have the lectionary. And if anyone knows who that is, it's going to be Burhan Kazemi."

They'd finally reached the far end of the accelerator ring and Danni pointed out the exit coming up on their right.

"That's the way up and out guys. That door there. So, assuming we can get past whatever police and security are up there, do we know where we're going now?"

"San Francisco State University," Rees said without hesitation. "That's what the note was telling us. Where to find Kazemi at work, and..." He stopped, seeming to catch himself. "But, uh, I leave it to Special Agent Morgan to make the final decision here."

Morgan went silent for a few beats. "I hate to say it, but this has moved way beyond just being my case. We all have to agree on this. But I'm with Rees. We get ourselves over to SF State and look up Professor Kazemi. Collect the time-recordings and find out how to get our hands on this book."

"It's a codex, actually," Rees corrected. Then added quickly, "Doesn't matter."

"Well, all right then." Danni strode ahead of them and opened the exit door. She stopped there in the doorway and turned back. "But if anyone else tries to shoot me, or freeze me to death, or otherwise kill me..." she paused, then continued in a snooty English accent, "I shall be *very* put out."

Rees gave her a funny look.

Morgan smiled at her.

The Princess Bride. She and Morgan had watched it together in bed one night, lying side by side. It was one of her favorite films.

Someday, Danni hoped, they would watch it together again.

CHAPTER 40

MORGAN'S LINGERING HEADACHE had Rees worried. But she seemed to be doing better as time passed. Now they only had to get to San Francisco State University and find Professor Kazemi without being arrested or killed.

What could be simpler? Rees thought, and the dark humor there buoyed his spirits a little at least.

Danni had just led them into the unfinished lobby of what she informed them would eventually be the main building for the accelerator complex. Livermore Labs had apparently ordered the construction crews away. The place was empty.

They crossed the plywood floor, and stopped inside the front doors.

Through the glass wall, Rees surveyed the scene outside. The rains had passed. The sun was shining on the muddy site, a handful of bright yellow, heavy construction vehicles, and a couple of temporary buildings that had been wired into the grid.

"We're going to need a vehicle," Morgan announced.

Public transportation was right out. TV astronomer Dr. Gevin Rees would be quickly recognized.

"What if we hot-wired that dump truck out there?" Rees suggested. "It's counterintuitive. Two of us get down on the floor of the cab. No one's going to imagine we're making our getaway in that thing."

Danni looked less than impressed by the idea. "That's like trying to sneak away in a ten thousand pound, diesel banana."

"Do either of you have any cash?" Morgan asked.

Rees shook his head.

"Not enough for cab fare, if that's what you're thinking," Danni said.

They all agreed using a credit card could trip an electronic feeler. Also that they should avoid Morgan's cellphone. The enemy, whoever they were, had her name now. Morgan removed the battery so the phone couldn't be pinged for their location.

"You know what?" Danni suddenly looked excited. "We don't have to *pay* the taxi driver. We have a gun. Kerry could make 'em take us over to SF State. What do you guys think?"

"I think that's the second time you've suggested carjacking with a lot of enthusiasm," Rees said. "This life suits you a little too well."

Danni's eyes flashed. "We're not gonna hurt 'em. Course we don't tell *them* that. You know, we make up a story. Like we're bank robbers or something, so they'll cooperate."

"And when the taxi driver calls the police to report where he dropped us off?" Rees asked. "Then what?"

Morgan kept on nodding, as if she were actually considering this. Finally she said, "Maybe that's not such a terrible idea."

Rees laughed. He stopped when Morgan kept the straight face. "Wait, are you serious? I think the diesel banana idea still rates better."

Morgan smirked. "I don't mean carjacking, Rees. I mean making up a story. Didn't you guys say we gave some cover story to one of the programmers last night? Who was that?"

Rees reminded himself there were still gaps in Morgan's memory. "Louis ... whatever his last name is. Timothy."

"Tyminski," Danni said.

"Tyminski," Rees echoed. "He thinks we're running a secret contractor fraud sting." And then it hit him, what Morgan was getting at. "Oh. Oh, I get it."

Morgan nodded. "We tell him *that's* why we need his help. Because he's already in on the operation."

"You want to get Louis to drive us to San Francisco?" Danni didn't sound too thrilled with the idea.

"Does he have a car?" Morgan asked. "Does he live nearby?"

"Well, yes to both, but..." Danni scrunched up her face.

"No, it really works, Danni." Rees found himself in full agreement with Morgan now. "We can even explain whatever he might have heard about us. It's all a frame up, we tell him. We'll say the corruption goes all the way to the Pentagon. Someone in power is trying to take us out. That's not even very far from the truth."

"Is he into conspiracy theories?" Morgan asked.

Danni sighed. "Actually, yes he is."

Morgan shrugged. "Well, there you go."

They all went silent for a time. Rees assumed that like him, Morgan and Danni were trying to work out if this was the right thing to do. They would be putting Louis's life at risk. Even if they didn't tell him about the Kafir Project.

But what other choices did they have? They needed more resources to get to Kazemi. And while he was keeping watch the night before, Rees had thought deeply about the Kafir Project. Why it was created and what it had aimed to do.

Was it really that insane?

What if the data and historical artifacts did strike a blow? Against groups like ISIS, and Boko Haram. Against the fanatics who flew planes into the Twin Towers, and England's 7/7 attackers. What if all this threw cold water on the people right now training to be human bombs? How many young Islamic men would line up to die for a partly plagiarized book, and the promise of white grapes?

Tangible evidence had been uncovered here, evidence that might in time change the world. But it could all disappear forever if they didn't do something to stop the men who killed Edward Fischer.

They had to find a way forward.

Danni spoke up. "Okay, two things. First, there's probably a land line in one of those trailers. We can call Louis from in there. I don't have my contact list anymore, but he's got the coolest phone number in the universe. It's area code nine, two, five and then *phi*."

"That *is* cool," Rees agreed. He turned to Morgan, "Phi is the irrational number that—"

"I'll take a rain check," Morgan interrupted. "Okay, Danni, what else? You said there were two things."

"Second ... he's gotta pick up a pizza or something. I'm frickin' starving."

"And we need coffee," Rees added. "Even if we have to hold up a Starbucks. I'm all right with using the gun for that."

LOUIS HAD BEEN in the terminal bay working on analysis of the fusion ignition data when the cooling system ruptured. It sounded like a squadron of fighter jets taking off inside the building. Shook the whole place. The secondary containment walls outside the Core probably saved his life.

That it happened less than an hour after he heard all about the contractor fraud seemed like a wild ass coincidence. At first.

Then he ran past the bodies.

Louis had never seen a dead body before, not in person. Never even been to an open casket funeral. So much blood. It looked kinda fake. But the smell, like piss and copper. Something about that smell triggered ancient instincts. They were real dead bodies, all right.

And even that didn't shock him like what he heard next.

Dr. Danielle Harris was a spy.

She stole classified data and sold it to the Russians. They told him that she came in that night to download more.

The Feds also told him how the hot DCIS agent with Danni, Kerry Morgan, had started all the shooting. In an attempt to escape a Defense Department sting, they said. How Gevin Rees got caught up in all of it no one had a clear angle on. Not yet, anyway.

Louis knew he'd have a hard time unwinding, so he popped an Ambien when he got home. He crashed out and slept until his cell phone ringing woke him up late the next morning.

The caller ID said local call, but he didn't recognize the number.

He answered. "Yeah, Louis here."

"Louis, it's Danni."

Danni's familiar voice instantly sandblasted the cobwebs from his head. The silence that followed wasn't from having nothing to say. It was from too many thoughts blurring by too fast. Danni spoke again before he could focus on just one.

"Louis, what did they tell you?"

His mind continued to race, but one word repeated itself over and over in his thoughts. He finally managed to spit it out. "Bullshit."

"We weren't trying to bullshit you, we just—"

"Not you, Danni. Those Defense Department suits. Bunch a spooks. Talking about how you're a Russian spy. And Special Agent Morgan is a desperate criminal. Shooting up the place like a, a Mexican bandito."

"You know that's crap."

"Course it's crap. They were shooting each other! What the hell, man. And even our security guy Neery—harmless little dude—even he had to put one of 'em down. So like, what? Those are the *good guys*? Yeah, I don't think so."

"Good. That's good. Because we need your help, Louis. We really need it bad here."

He probably should have taken more time to think about it, but he was impulsive. Always had been. And anyhow he counted Danni as a friend. "Sure. Only one thing..."

"Okay."

"One more time, what the hell is really going on here?"

"Louis."

"Look, someone's seriously pissed at you guys. And it's not some defense contractor skimming money. It's more like some kind of, I don't know, Bourne Identity shit. With black helicopters and the whole deal. Right? I'm right, aren't I? So tell me the truth, Danni. Just tell me the truth and I'm in. Okay?"

The sound got all muffled then. It sounded to Louis like she had her hand over the mouthpiece, maybe checking with someone standing nearby. Probably Morgan and Rees were there.

Then she came back and gave him the truth. All of it.

It had to be the truth.

Because if you were making up a story that you really, really needed someone to believe? The line—

DARPA was trying to fight terrorism with a time machine...

That line would most definitely *not* be in there.

CHAPTER 41

SABEL ALLOWED HIMSELF a limp on the injured leg. He knew from experience that infirmities made normies a little uncomfortable. Which rendered them easier to manipulate.

And he was just about to do a *lot* of that.

Sure enough, in less than an hour at Livermore Labs he managed to schmooze his way to the spearhead of the rescue effort. In part by claiming a working relationship with one of the trapped agents. And then by looking a little scared, but goddamned determined to help his friend and partner.

They ate it up.

As he suited up in protective gear and breathing mask, Sabel thought again about how funny life was.

He knew what he and his kind were called.

Sociopaths.

People said it was horrible, despicable. Then they struggled to achieve exactly what he could manage with ease. Influencing people to do what you want. Get what you want, when you want it. Maybe all the hating at folks like Sabel just came down to fear of having to compete with something like a superior race.

He'd read an article once on how some psychologist found out sociopaths more or less ran everything. Captains of industry, political leaders, that kinda stuff—pretty much all sociopaths.

Didn't surprise Sabel one little bit.

HE ENTERED THE computer building with the first of the rescuers. Right off they found two guys shot dead on the ground floor.

One of those would be the Office man sent in while Sabel was out of commission. Popped by one of the security guards there. Sabel would've loved to see how *that* went down. An Office man taken out by the equivalent of a mall cop. Had to be an interesting story there.

Over the next few hours, they worked their way through the rest of the building. And something called the Core.

But no Gevin Rees.

No Kerry Morgan or Danielle Harris either. One more dead DCIS agent downstairs. Why that guy had been taken out, Sabel had a hard time figuring. Probably he just saw too much.

He combed the building and the connected facilities with the rescue crews through most of the night and morning to confirm what he already suspected. They all got out.

Rees and the other two had managed to move on.

He returned the rescue gear and beat it. While he was hiking back to his stolen car, his burner phone rang.

He answered it. "Yeah."

"Yes, hello. I need to pick up a package for the office."

"You do, uh?" The Specialist. So they'd decided to bring him in. Sabel only worked with the Specialist twice before, but he recognized the voice. The man was being discreet, so he assumed the call wasn't getting scrambled through the Office's normal coms channels for some reason.

"Yes," the Specialist said, "I saw on the news there was an accident? I'm nearby. Looks like a real mess. Has the package been damaged?"

"As a matter of fact it's intact, but that delivery to you has been cancelled."

"Really?"

Yes, 'really,' dickwad. And how the hell do you not know that? "Yeah, sorry about that, sir. You should check back with the office, in case there's been a mistake."

"Yes, absolutely. Thank you."

Sabel disconnected the call with red flags flying.

The Office didn't make this kind of error. Which meant the Specialist was working for someone else. Well then, he just had to get to Rees first. Better for Rees too, if he did.

Sabel didn't feel deeply for anyone, of course, but he didn't have any special desire to see a man go through pure hell either. He was a *live and let die* kind of guy, like the song said. After all, death wasn't any big deal. You either moved on, or you weren't around to miss anything.

Drawn out, unbearable pain and horror on the other hand— that was a whole other thing.

That shit was just sick.

When Sabel reached his car, he popped a couple of Provigil pills. He leaned back, closed his eyes ... and twenty minutes later felt like he'd slept for twelve hours.

He drove out of Livermore and headed for the City.

The current objective was to reacquire Rees and avoid the Specialist while he was at it. And the only real lead he had now was this Herodotus guy. Who happened to be next on the list to round up anyway.

The Office's research division said there was a high probability that the man taught at San Francisco State. One of five historians on the Kafir Project. Rees would have to hook up with him sooner or later.

So that would be the most effective line of action. Use Herodotus to relocate Rees.

Sabel merged onto the 280, then dialed the Mark Hopkins Hotel.

He assumed Rees's choice of accommodations hadn't been random. Fischer and his conspirators would want a hub out here. The hotel could be it. Worth making a quick call to see if any messages came in for Rees overnight.

"Thank you for calling the International Mark Hopkins, how may I assist you?" a bright, female voice said.

"Yes, this is Dr. Gevin Rees. I stayed with you last night. I was expecting a message that never came, and I'm a little worried now. My friend who was supposed to call, well, I can't reach him." He injected the sound of fear into his voice, but with some control. "No one knows where he is. Are there any messages I might have missed?"

"One moment, Dr. Rees." Soft music came on for about ten seconds. "No, sir. The only message I have, it shows here you picked that up last night. Nothing else after that."

"Yes, which message is that again? Can you reread it to me?"

"Certainly. Just one name here. Last name, maybe? Hero-doh-tus. I don't know if I'm saying that right. It says, 'If you know my history, you know where to find me at work. Look for me in the JPL library tomorrow afternoon.' And that's it."

"Yes, I did get that one." Sabel kept the worried tone alive in his voice. "And you're absolutely sure there's nothing else?"

"No, sir. That's the only message we have. I'm sorry."

He thanked her, disconnected and made a quick call to the Office. They'd want to know about the Specialist freelancing on this job. Plus they might be able to nail down Herodotus's identity now. He was betting on Herodotus being a smart scientist. And a lousy field agent.

The bet paid off.

In less than ten minutes the Office's SIGINT department called back. Someone had placed a payphone call to the Mark Hopkins hotel switchboard yesterday.

Who calls a luxury hotel from a payphone?

An amateur who thinks that's playing it safe, that's who. The call came from a street corner near San Francisco State University.

So the Office had it right all along. Herodotus was that historian at SFSU. Professor Burhan Kazemi.

Look for me in the JPL library tomorrow afternoon.

He would run with the whole amateur angle there and guess Kazemi had no chance to arrange a code with Rees. So, this was literally a library they were talking about.

And the JPL, Jet Propulsion Laboratory thing? Probably a red herring. Might throw off someone who intercepted the message. Send them down to SoCal.

Not a bad little trick for an amateur.

Off to the SFSU library then. But which one? The campus would have several, probably.

Assuming Rees didn't know that either, it would just be the most natural choice. Otherwise Kazemi would've been more specific. So maybe this is the library he usually hung out at. Which, of course, Sabel still had no clue about.

No big deal there either.

One of Kazemi's students or colleagues would know that. Your friendly neighborhood sociopath could pick up that kind of info for the price of a smile.

And Sabel had smiles to spare.

CHAPTER 42

A HALF HOUR after they called Danni's co-worker Louis Tyminski from one of the trailers, Rees watched the man drive up to the construction site in their new getaway car. A little, sky blue Fiat 500.

Rees eyed the subcompact skeptically. "Are we all going to fit in there?"

Louis spoke to him through the rolled down driver's window. "Actually, it seats four adults quite comfortably."

Morgan peered in the back. "Yeah, if two of them are hobbits."

Rees and Morgan took the rear seats, which appeared to be designed specifically to induce deep vein thrombosis. Rees had to set Fischer's pouch on his lap. No room on the floor for even a small bag.

After they'd cruised far enough out of Livermore to feel safe doing so, they hit a drive-thru. Louis bought everyone breakfast. Rees kept his face turned away from the cashier the whole time. A precaution against being recognized.

Using Louis's phone, they had confirmed that Rees's picture now flooded the internet. Presumably it was all over the TV news as well. Out there in connection with the "disaster" at Livermore, as they were calling it. And with the dead DCIS agents.

Agents, plural. Three of them now.

Morgan and Danni were also identified by name in the stories. Their faces wouldn't be familiar to the general public, though. Not for a while at least.

So, all in all, they were in pretty good shape. Fortified with coffee and breakfast burritos, they were on their way to meet

Professor Burhan Kazemi, the man Fischer had called Herodotus. From that point on, they should be more less back in line with Fischer's original plan. Rees didn't know exactly what that was, but it had to be better than the scratching around in the dark they'd been doing so far.

Louis, for his part, had taken in the whole bizarre story with what Rees judged to be an amazing amount of *sangfroid*. He didn't even ask a lot of questions. What had him most intrigued, as it turned out, was Morgan's and Danni's relationship.

He came right out with it too. Which Rees was beginning to see was just Louis's style.

"So, are you two an item or what?" he asked Danni.

Danni laughed. "Uh, we dated and, you know, we did the long distance thing for a while..." She looked back at Morgan.

Awkward silence then.

"It's a moot point, Louis," Morgan finally said. "I don't play for both teams."

Louis nodded. "Too bad. I was hoping you were bi and available."

Danni laughed again. "Well, so much for tact."

"Yeah, it's overrated." Louis took the freeway fork toward the Bay Bridge. "Hey, I have a question for you Dr. Rees."

Rees saw Louis's eyes focused on him in the rear view. "I'm neither bi nor available, Louis. Sorry."

Morgan and Danni both laughed at that.

"That's funny," Louis said. "No, it is. You should bring more of that to your shows. But no, seriously, my question is why did anyone think this whole thing would work? Muslim fanatics will just deny it all. They'll say the lectionary and the recordings are fakes. Even if you give 'em the technology to validate it, you can't make them pursue it."

"Probably yes, the radicals will deny the evidence," Rees agreed. "But what about mainstream Islam? There's a long tradition of rationality there. Islam kept Aristotle's works alive through the Dark Ages. Imagine if all of this new evidence ushered in something like the Enlightenment for them. If you change the median here, you just might change the extremes as a consequence."

Morgan was eying Rees. "And what if you're just projecting? Because of your own experience with Mormonism. People are not all scientists out there."

Louis glanced back at Rees in the mirror. "You're a Mormon?"

Rees had to smile. "It sounds like you're asking me if I'm a Martian, Louis. Yes, I *was* a Mormon. Past tense. I examined the history. It didn't stand up. End of story. It's a lot like what Fischer's trying to do with Islam. So maybe I *am* biased." He turned to Morgan. "I do realize not everyone will react to historical evidence the way I did. But a lot of them might."

Rees let it go at that, and thankfully no one pressed him.

In truth there was a *lot* more to his Mormon apostasy than just encountering the historical evidence. It had taken a big push to initiate Rees's explorations in the first place. A push that came in the form of a terrible personal loss.

Almost thirty years ago now. Hard for him to believe.

IT HAD BEEN an unusually hot summer in the suburbs of Salt Lake City. A seventeen year old Gevin Rees arrived home to an empty house and the light on the phone machine flashing. He pressed the button and listened to the desperate message from his sister, Anna.

He immediately dialed her apartment. She didn't answer.

They hadn't spoken since her excommunication from the Mormon Church. Shunning wasn't official Mormon practice, but when Anna came out as a lesbian the Rees family chose the most extreme response. They disowned her, and forbade any further communication.

That didn't stop him thinking about her all the time. Outside of the immediate family, Rees preferred to remain in his own shell. A loner and fine with it. In part because Anna had always been his best friend anyway. Then suddenly she was gone. And he knew what it meant to be truly lonely.

But he couldn't bring himself to defy his parents.

The phone machine message she left was difficult to decipher. Anna had sobbed through it, and she sounded drunk or drugged.

Rees called 911 then grabbed the keys to the Olds Cutlass off the hook in the kitchen.

Two minutes later he rocketed onto the freeway to the blast of someone's car horn. Driving way too fast and he knew it. Twelve more minutes and he was flying down the freeway exit for the neighborhood Anna had moved to.

So close. She had stayed so close.

He skidded to a stop outside her apartment building.

The lobby's glass doors burst open before he'd even gotten out of the car. Two paramedics and a stretcher. Anna had a clear mask pressed over her face. One of the paramedics squeezed a large bulb connected to it.

They wouldn't let him ride in the ambulance with her. It would've saved everyone a lot of trouble. He crashed while driving to the hospital.

Rees only knew from being told later that he'd hit a tree on the roadside. He never even saw it coming. Everything just went away.

And then he was sitting very still.

He smelled antifreeze and gasoline mixed with fresh air. The front windshield had vanished. Clouds of steam hissed from the exposed engine. Rees kept blinking, over and over, but his vision remained blurry. Something wet and hot running into his eyes.

He drifted in and out. A Good Samaritan stopped and pulled him from the car.

He eventually woke up in ICU. The doctor explained about the emergency lobectomy. To stop the hemorrhaging in his lung.

Rees was on a ventilator, but he managed to communicate that he needed a pad and pen. He wrote down the question. It didn't take long to get an answer.

Anna was gone.

He wept silently through that first night, and many other nights down through the years. He lay awake in the ICU listening to the medical devices beep and chime, and wishing hopelessly that he'd gotten home earlier. Taken her call. He was sure that he could have saved her.

He was furious with himself. And even more troubling ... he was furious with Anna.

Mad at himself for not defying his parents' authority. In the future he would serve no authority except the truth.

Mad at Anna for killing his best friend in the world. At the time, he couldn't see how he would ever forgive her for that.

And in fact he never really did.

LOUIS MADE A right onto Valencia from Cesar Chavez Street. Maybe ten minutes from SFSU now.

"Where'd you go?" Morgan was watching Rees again.

He gave her a dismissive shrug and smiled. "Just absent minded. You know us academic types."

"Hey, I got another question, Dr. Rees," Louis announced from the front seat.

Morgan continued to eyeball Rees, like she wasn't buying the absent minded professor line.

Rees gladly transitioned away from the whole subject. "Yes, Louis?"

"Who do you think's behind this? Trying to keep it all quiet?"

Danni spoke over her shoulder. "Are we still going on the assumption that it's *not* the Islamists? Because they really do have the clearest motivation here."

Morgan squinted and shook her head. "I just can't believe some terrorist group achieved that kind of penetration. All the way into the DCIS, and beyond. Someone knew we were at Livermore Labs. Probably from when Danni passed through security. But if a terror organization had cracked the Defense Department's servers, they'd be doing a lot more with it than that. No, this is an inside job."

Rees agreed, but that presented its own problems. "If it's something like a rogue group within the Defense Department, then why fight one of your own projects?"

Louis jumped in. "Three words. Military, industrial, complex."

Rees's usual anti-conspiracy skepticism began to rise, and just as quickly sat down and shut up. *That's not an entirely ridiculous idea.*

The quiet in the car suggested Morgan and Danni were thinking along the same lines.

Louis apparently read the silence as a cue to keep going. "Think about the trillions spent in the war on terror. Trillions, man. I mean, in addition to the *actual* wars in Afghanistan and Iraq. That money doesn't just get spent, it gets made too. Lockheed Martin, General Dynamics, Kellogg Brown and Root."

"Fifty percent of the annual defense budget goes directly to contractors," Danni added. "I know that from researching our own budget requests at LLNL. And most of the time they're kinda their own government oversight committee, believe it or not."

"Exactamundo," Louis said. "So what happens to all that money if radical Islam really does get kicked in the nuts by all this? That hurts some powerful pocketbooks, man. There's your motivation."

As much as it sounded like the paranoid plotline for a Hollywood movie, Rees had to admit it made sense.

Louis, meanwhile, had just executed a left on Twenty-Sixth and was now quickly making another left. This time onto an alley behind a row of businesses. He was doubling back.

Morgan leaned forward. "Louis, what are you doing?"

"Testing a theory. What are the odds that a silver BMW X3 got onto the freeway a few cars behind us in Livermore and a *different* one just followed us into an alley in San Francisco?"

Rees and Morgan both turned to look through the rear window.

A big BMW X3 was cruising back there. No cars between it and the Fiat. If the X3's driver was tailing them, then no attempt was being made to conceal the fact. That couldn't be good.

Morgan turned forward again. "Louis, get us back to a street with some traffic." She pointed up ahead. "Cut up between those buildings there."

Louis slowed down to make the turn.

Rees kept his eye on the X3. It didn't slow down. It accelerated. He managed to get out, "Hang on!" just before the impact.

CHAPTER 43

One day earlier—Jerusalem

AMSEL WOKE EARLY to the sound of his cell phone chiming a text.

Outside the hotel room window, a band of light pinked the rim of the blue-black sky. The sun hadn't quite risen.

Normally the chime wouldn't have woken him, but Amsel had been sleeping fitfully ever since the room safe had been robbed. The money and passports hadn't been hard to replace. The journal was the greater loss. But the suspicion that it had been more than just an ordinary robbery disturbed him most of all.

The text had come from a professor of paleontology back at Oxford.

> Do you know anyone at Fermilab? Big explosion
> there. BTW still waiting to hear about your carbon 14
> work.

When he'd flown out to be briefed on the Kafir Project, Amsel didn't apprise his colleagues of the details, of course. But he didn't try to hide that his destination was Fermilab either. He'd be seen there. Word gets around the academic world. So, he casually put it out that the trip had to do with new carbon dating technology.

That simple act might have changed everything. By triggering this text. Otherwise he would not have heard the news for hours yet.

The internet soon provided more details. The blast involved the Tevatron. Numerous injuries and probably deaths. And the lead story still developing: the world's most famous scientist, Edward Fischer, may have been killed in the accident.

Amsel immediately called Randy Osborn.

Osborn's groggy voice croaked out of the receiver. "Yes, hello?"

"Meet me in the lobby, quickly as you're able. And bring Robert."

Those last words had been agreed upon much earlier. A coded message. It told Osborn to collect what the military people called a B.O.B., a bug-out-bag, and be prepared to leave in an instant.

After the call, Amsel gathered up his own go-bag from the closet. He doubted he'd need it now, though.

He rode the elevator to the lobby. As he waited there, he thought back to the beginning of all this. His first face to face meeting with Edward Fischer at Fermilab.

Three military men and two gentlemen in dark suits who did not introduce themselves briefed Amsel in a boardroom in Wilson Hall.

Fischer sat in the corner, reading a novel—Dickens, Amsel recalled—and remained silent throughout the briefing. He didn't even look up.

Amsel listened intently without saying a word himself.

No one read from or handed out any materials. No PowerPoint images were used. Amsel was not allowed to take notes.

When it ended, the military men and the two Amsel assumed were US intelligence officers asked him if he had any questions.

He had one. For Fischer. He turned to the great scientist and looked him squarely in the eye. "Are you as crazy as they say you are, sir?"

Fischer answered without pause. "Easily. But the boldest ideas always seem crazy. *Exempli gratia*: everything is made of bits so small that twenty million, million, millions of them make up a single grain of sand. Clocks slow down as we speed up. Stars can swallow themselves whole. It takes something like a lunatic to imagine such things. The trick lies in distinguishing the useful madness from the genuinely insane ideas. And that I can do quite well."

Amsel came onboard from that moment forward.

Later that day, the two men walked the grounds of Fermilab together. They were strolling by the bison field when Fischer revealed his ideas for what he called *extending the project*.

Amsel had just gestured to the grazing animals. "Is it true, Dr. Fischer, that the bison are meant as canaries in a coal mine? In case something goes terribly wrong here one day?"

Fischer gazed out at the small herd. Two bison calves played a game of chase across a carpet of green grass. "Oh, I think they're far too robust for that. We frail, hairless apes should start dropping long before they would. No, they have no hidden purpose."

"But you do." Amsel didn't look at Fischer when he said it, giving him the option to ignore the comment. Pretend it never happened, if he so chose.

Fischer responded by laying everything out in great detail.

When he finished, Amsel gave his reply. "I'm an old man, Dr. Fischer. I have no family. I've given my life to illuminating the past. Trying to answer the question of how history has shaped our collective identity. You want to know if I'm willing to seek answers to questions not asked. Answers our government benefactors might not like to hear."

Fischer placed a hand gently on Amsel's shoulder. "We won't be living in the same world afterwards. And some very powerful people like things just as they are. They won't be at all pleased. So, I'm really asking ... are you willing to die for those answers?"

Amsel's answer took the form of a question. "Well, let me ask *you* something. Say an advanced alien race abducted you, and told you they could explain the mathematical structure of the universe. In comprehensible terms. But there's a catch. Immediately afterwards they *might* kill you. Wouldn't you want to know anyway?"

Fischer smiled.

AMSEL EMERGED FROM his reverie to see Osborn step out of the elevator carrying a small valise. The bug-out-bag and its precious cargo.

Osborn walked across the lobby with his usual uneven gait and a cheery smile. "Good morning, Josh." He glanced down at the valise. "Thought I might need to bring some documents back tonight, so—"

"If we're being watched at this moment, it's too late to put on a show," Amsel interrupted. "It's time to execute the exit strategy. I received a text, this morning, just before I called you." Amsel fed Osborn the news about Fermilab and the so-called accident, and added, "I'm afraid Fischer may be dead. Most likely it's all a cover for his assassination, and a way to destroy the time-recordings in the same stroke. Which means we've been compromised."

Osborn nodded. "I agree."

"They're going to assume I was involved. But they won't know who else if anyone on the team assisted me. Between Fischer and myself, you and Professor Kazemi were only ever referred to by your aliases."

Osborn's nostrils flared and he lifted his chin. He looked like he was bracing himself. "Did we lose the time recordings?"

"I don't think so. Fischer created a backup. If Kazemi doesn't have it yet, he will soon. The goal now is to bring the recordings together with our artifacts." Amsel glanced at the valise. "You have it all there?"

"Yes. Except for the materials already in storage, of course."

It flashed again through Amsel's mind that—depending on who had stolen his journal—those artifacts might already be gone. The storage locations were all recorded in there. No need to bring that up now.

He set down his bag and unzipped the main compartment, removed a fat roll of hundred dollar bills and handed that to Osborn. "You'll need this."

Osborn quickly tucked the money in a pants pocket where it made a conspicuous bulge. "Why give all this to me? You're coming too."

Amsel shook his head. "No, not yet. You know where to go and what to say. If I'm not there in an hour, leave without me. I'll see you in San Francisco."

Amsel checked that Osborn remembered how and where to contact Kazemi. They said their brief good-byes, and Amsel watched the other man walk away. A fragile figure, carrying the world's future gripped in one hand. When Osborn was out of sight, Amsel promptly turned back and took the elevator up to the top floor.

He exited the elevator alone. Then, taking great care that no one saw him, he walked to the stairwell at the end of the hall.

AMSEL SAT ON the roof of the Arthur Hotel, in the shade of a taller building, and smoked.

A little over a half hour later, the door to the roof opened. Three men dressed in street clothes and dark sunglasses came out.

This much was good. No one had witnessed him coming up to the roof. Assuming they looked elsewhere for him first, these three had burned up precious time and manpower. All of which improved Osborn's odds of getting out with the artifacts.

And that was the modified plan in a nutshell.

Amsel believed his own chance to leave Israel alive had long since passed. Probably even before they killed Fischer.

He stood up, and began to walk toward the roof's edge as he spoke to the men. "I know who you are and why you're here."

They advanced across the rooftop on a course to intercept him.

He tried to judge the point where he and they would intersect if neither changed speed. Just about at the roof's limit, it seemed.

But he would get there first.

Amsel continued walking toward the roof's edge. "Of course, I don't know who you gentlemen work for. Not exactly. But then neither do you, would be my guess."

The lead man drew a handgun from under a light jacket. "We need you to come with us." He kept the weapon pointed upward, not at Amsel.

So, they weren't here to kill him. He'd suspected as much. He continued walking. He had already cut the distance to the roof's edge in half. "Do you know why you're supposed to bring me in alive?"

The men didn't answer.

The lead man's features—dark hair and eyes, olive complexion—suggested he might be an Israeli. Not that it mattered. What was happening here far exceeded the realm of governments and nations, whether these men knew it or not.

"Are you armed?" the lead man asked him.

Amsel needed maybe twenty more steps to reach the edge of the roof. "In a sense, yes. And I *am* dangerous. I might be the most dangerous man in the world at this moment. I asked you, do you know why you're supposed to bring me in alive?"

"Keep your hands where we can see them." The lead man had stopped now.

The other two were fanning out. Trying to flank Amsel.

Amsel watched them in his peripheral vision, and kept walking. "You see, the people you work for want something. They want me to tell them where they can find it. They will torture me, drug me, cut pieces from me as I watch. Until they have what they need. I don't suppose that matters to you."

The lead man didn't respond. His companions continued to move in on both sides.

Amsel had reached the edge of the rooftop. He stopped and turned around. "I wonder. If I said you're jeopardizing the world's best chance to end thousands of years of bloodshed, how could you know I was telling you the truth?"

The two men on his flanks broke for Amsel at the exact same moment. He was ready for them. He'd positioned himself just inches from the edge.

Amsel stepped back off the roof, out into space. He felt his foot keep going down, down. He began to fall.

A hand caught his shirtfront.

Another snagged his belt.

Amsel felt his momentum stop, then reverse. They were pulling him back in. They had him.

No! No, I can't let them take me. They would make him give up the information. He had no doubt of that. Everything would have been for naught. All ruined. All lost forever.

Both of the men who grabbed him had their full attention focused on preventing Amsel's fall, on trying to pull him back in. It's not the first thing that crosses your mind, after all, that a man trying to jump off a building might still be a lethal threat.

Amsel saw the holstered gun inches from his face. He grabbed it.

The man who held Amsel's belt must have felt that. Instinctively he released the belt and lunged forward for his gun. The other man continued pulling back on Amsel's shirtfront.

Time stopped.

The three of them hung there on the lip of the hotel's roof, frozen. All the forces at work against each other, cancelling out.

To nothing.

In the next moment, the symmetry broke.

And time began.

Like a door opening downward, the three men slowly swung out and away from the roof. It seemed to take minutes, but could only have been a second or less.

Someone screamed.

They began to accelerate. All of them together.

From Amsel's perspective, the top of the hotel flew up and away from him. Soaring off into the cool blue morning sky of Jerusalem.

A strange and lovely sight on which to end a life.

CHAPTER 44

DISORIENTED, BUT THE sound and smells, footsteps on shattered safety glass, spilled gasoline and oil. They were so familiar to Rees. Wasn't he just here a moment ago?

But where was *here*?

And then he understood.

Fischer's work. Time travel.

He must have travelled backwards in time. Of course. That was it. He'd travelled back to...

That horrible day in his youth.

But why? Why this day, of all the important or even forgotten days of his past?

Once again he was being hauled from the wreckage. Alive.

Once again his sister lay dying. Without him.

"Do you believe in fate?"

Someone speaking to him then. The Good Samaritan. The man who had stopped and pulled him out of the twisted and smoking metal.

Rees tried to focus. He couldn't. Nearby someone moaned.

"Naturally, I concluded the explosion at Livermore last night was related to the one at Fermilab. That meant *you* were there. Or nearby. I needed a safe place from which to surveil the Livermore facility." The voice was accented. Unfamiliar.

Rees couldn't make any sense of it. But he had to get to the hospital. He had to find Anna.

"A construction site is always handy for a stakeout. Strange cars coming and going that the locals don't recognize, but don't concern themselves with. Yes, always a good spot."

Rees sensed himself being dragged backwards now. He could feel the heel of one shoe pulling loose.

Receding in his vision ... a woman. Lying still against a small blue car. Sleeping? Dead? Who was that?

Morgan.

He almost had it. Then it slipped away.

"I was preparing to go in there searching for you," the Good Samaritan was saying now. "But instead, out you walked from an empty building that no one had any business being in. I must say, you rather stood out. And of course, I knew your face."

Rees felt himself being lifted into another car. But that wasn't right either. It didn't happen like that. An ambulance had taken him to the hospital.

"What would you call that, Dr. Rees?" the voice asked. "Chance? I call it fate. We were fated to meet. And I will not let you down. After you give me what I require, I will repay you with a gift few have ever known."

The fog in Rees's vision lifted a bit. He could see the Good Samaritan now. Except ... this wasn't him. Complexion too dark. And the bright green eyes. Not right.

He felt a strong hand take his arm, push up his sleeve. A sting. Then someone turned down the lights.

Am I time travelling again?

Back. He had to go back further. Back before the phone call. He would defy his parents this time. Go to see Anna. Tell her she was all right. Tell her he would always be there. That he would never leave her alone again.

He could reach her now. Reach her in time. He felt such gratitude for Fischer's work, for making this possible, that he wanted to cry.

He was lying down now.

A wonderful warmth flowed through him. A tear pooled in the corner of his eye.

He was drifting. Drifting back, back farther through time.

Anna, I'm coming. I'm sorry it took so long.

CHAPTER 45

MORGAN OPENED HER eyes. She was sitting on the ground on some little back street in the City. Leaned up against the rear tire of the blue Fiat ... or what remained of it.

Danni crouched in front of her. Blood and tears streaked her face. "Are you all right, Kerry? Are you hurt?"

She squinted up at Danni. Shook her head *no*. She shouldn't have done that. It hurt something awful. Morgan felt jangled up, but her clarity was creeping back.

Louis's car had been hit. Slammed. A big-ass BMW. She'd climbed out of the wreckage. She remembered going for her gun. Seeing the Taser...

The goddamn bastard zapped me. That's why her body ached and tingled like this. She looked around. "Rees. Where's Dr. Rees?"

"He took Rees." Louis was standing behind Danni. "The guy in the Beamer. He had a gun."

Morgan tried to stand and immediately slipped back down, painfully bumping her tailbone. "Shit." She tried it again, pushing off the car this time, and managed to get to her feet. But a new pain shot up from her right knee then. She looked over at Danni. "Your face. You're bleeding."

Danni touched a spot on the top of her head and inspected her finger. "It's just a cut. I'm okay. *You're* hurt, though."

"My knee. It's all right, just banged up."

"I'm fine, by the way," Louis said. "Or I think I am." He explored his face, tentatively. "Is my nose broken? The airbag really smashed it."

Morgan retested the injured leg, gently settling more weight on it. It held, but she wouldn't win any foot races anytime soon. "I didn't get a good look at him. But it wasn't the man from your house, Danni. At least I don't think it was."

Danni shook her head. "Definitely not. I saw him clearly. This guy wasn't blond. He was dark. Like, Mediterranean maybe. And much taller."

"He had a gun and he didn't shoot you." Louis looked bewildered. "Why didn't he shoot you?"

"You don't sound too thrilled about it," Morgan said.

Louis threw up his hands. "No. Jesus, no. It's just, how weird is that? One second it's *pow, pow, pow*. All those dead guys at Livermore. The next second it's like, 'Hey, I don't want to really hurt you guys, sorry.'"

Morgan didn't know what to make of that either. It *was* weird. No time to think about it right now though.

She limped over and pulled Fischer's leather pouch out of the car. Fischer's notebook and the flash drive were in there. All of it evidence that they needed to hang on to.

She limped back over to Danni and Louis. "We have to get out of here." She held both arms out. "Get on either side of me. I think I can go faster if you help."

They did, and she could.

Louis pointed off to their right. "We passed a park, a block or so back there. There'll be bathrooms and water. We can clean up. Figure out what to do."

Morgan nodded. "Sounds good. Let's go."

TWO POLICE CRUISERS with lights flashing passed them as they walked to the park.

Morgan knew SFPD would run Louis's license plate. With an abandoned car at the scene of an accident, they might figure it as being stolen. They'd try to reach Louis. In the end, though, the heat on the three of them wouldn't really be any higher. Not as a result of this crash.

Rees was the one in real trouble here. Morgan had already turned his situation over ten ways in her head and didn't see a whole lot of options.

The walk to the park had been mercifully short. After she and Danni washed up, they sat down at a wooden table near the bathrooms. Louis came out of the men's room a minute later. His nose was red and swollen, otherwise he looked fine.

Louis sat down on the bench next to Danni, and scoped out the park in a quick 360. Then he said, "Well, what the hell do we do now?"

"The same thing we were already doing," Danni offered. "Right, Kerry? We find Kazemi and the time-recordings. He leads us to the other guy and the lectionary. Then we make it all public as fast as possible. And screw these bastards."

"And then what? They just cut Rees loose?" Louis wore a humorless smile. "Nah, I don't think so. He's seen people, you know. They can't just let him go."

"No they can't," Morgan agreed. "So we're going to have to take him back."

Louis held his palms up toward Morgan. "Whoa, hey, slow down there. I respect the guy, but like, I'm not a commando. Anyway how would we even find him now?"

"Remember," Morgan said, "whoever grabbed Rees wants to get Herodotus too. And Rees knows where that man is."

Danni put a hand to her mouth and spoke through it. "Oh my god, they're going to torture him."

"They might," Morgan agreed. "But they won't *kill* him. Not yet. They have to confirm whatever Rees tells them." A new idea suggested itself to her right then. "The man who rammed us—was anybody with him, or was he by himself?"

Danni and Louis looked at each other.

"He was driving," Danni said. "There wasn't anyone else. Was there?"

"No, he was alone," Louis answered.

That's what Morgan had hoped. "Good. If he's on his own, he'll probably tuck Rees away someplace safe while he confirms that Professor Kazemi really is Herodotus."

Danni's eyes blazed with determination. "So he'll be coming to the university for Kazemi. Right! That's where we'll get him."

"Right," Morgan said. "We get that man, we get Rees back." She turned to Louis, to check his reaction to all this. He didn't look like he was exactly on fire about it.

"Yeah," he said. "It's scaring the shit out of me, but yeah. Let's do it. But, you know, carefully."

Morgan didn't know if what she was feeling at that moment was genuine optimism or just excitement. In truth, she looked forward to the next confrontation. This time she wouldn't be watching helplessly through a Plexiglas wall, or limping stunned from a car wreck.

This time she would be armed and ready. And filled with a cool and calculating fury.

She'd been betrayed by agents in her own department. People she cared deeply about had been threatened, attacked, and injured.

They wanted Kazemi and all the rest of it? Fine. That would be the bait. Let them come. She was going on the offensive now.

And they were all going down.

CHAPTER 46

REES FELT SICK. Every time he opened his eyes, the room spun crazily. Closing them didn't help much either.

He had been abducted. That much was clear. Sometime after their car was rammed.

He was seated, bound and gagged. Something like a washcloth or handkerchief wadded up and stuffed into his mouth. He felt his gorge rise at one point and had the terrifying thought that if he vomited now, he would probably choke to death.

A cheap motel room. His best guess at the location. Small. Grubby. It had a smell like scented cleaning products and old socks.

He'd been duct-taped to a sturdy, wooden chair. He could see a set of flocked, olive and brown drapes in front of him. Closed right now, but bright rays of sunlight cracked in around the edges.

He couldn't turn his head far enough to see behind him at all. But he could hear someone moving back there. It sounded like just one person. It had been quiet for a while.

Then, whoever was back there started moving again.

He walked into view.

It was the man who crashed the BMW into Louis's car. A big man. Six foot three or four. He had a broad face, the nose slightly hooked. Brown skin. Dark, thick brows and extraordinary eyes. Emerald green.

He smiled in a way that made Rees think of a doctor or dentist greeting a client. "Ah, you are awake already. Feeling dizzy, though. Mmm, fuzzy. Correct?"

Rees nodded carefully. The man's accent sounded Middle Eastern.

"We can take care of that," he continued. "We want you clear-headed."

The green-eyed man turned away and bent down over a low coffee table. Rees couldn't see what he was doing. His body, broad like his face, blocked the view. There was a toiletry kit on the table down there. Next to that a gun. And another weapon. Maybe a Taser. Rees had never seen one up close.

The man turned back around holding a hypodermic syringe.

Rees cried out involuntarily. The sound leaked through the gag as a muffled, high-pitched note.

The man smiled warmly. "No need to worry, Dr. Rees. This is not dangerous. Not dangerous at all. I have here only a cocktail of stimulants and certain cognitive enhancers. As I said, we want your head clear. In any case, I think you will find this quite pleasant."

The man approached Rees, holding the syringe daintily, pointing it upward.

Panicked, Rees tried to rock in the chair. He felt the windings of duct tape pull against his ankles, arms and neck. He could shake the chair, but couldn't turn it away from the needle.

"You don't want to make this difficult." A note of concern now in the man's voice. "Here is why. If you won't be still and let me inject you there, in the metacarpal vein," he dipped the needle toward Rees's wrist, "then I will instead inject you in the eye. You understand? One or the other. It is your choice. A free choice."

He hadn't said it with any malice. More like someone offering you the option of Coke or Pepsi.

He continued, saying, "I am making you this choice not because the eye is such a good candidate for an injection site. It is in fact a very poor one, as I'm sure you know. I do this because I'm very confident of your selection. So, which shall it be, hmm? The wrist, yes?"

Rees tried to nod with enough amplitude so that the man could distinguish it from all the fear-shakes he had going on.

"Yes, I thought so. Good. Very good."

Rees watched the injection process. Not painful. But the green-eyed man didn't disinfect the site first, and Rees counted that as a bad sign. Something perversely meticulous about this guy. If infection didn't concern him at all, Rees thought he knew why.

He began to feel it, whatever it was, in a matter of seconds. Rees had never touched recreational drugs, afraid of what they might cost him cognitively. But now he knew what they meant by a *rush*.

He had a sense of motion, of hurtling through space. He sucked in a deep breath through his nose. It felt like strength flowed in rather than air. As if pure energy were filling his lungs.

Moments later, transported via millions of alveoli, the power began singing through his capillaries, engorging every cell in his body, turning them all into glowing corpuscles of light.

A clean, cold wind swept through his head at a thousand miles an hour, blowing away the grit and dust of confusion, scouring and honing the leading edge of his mind, until it was keen enough to cut bones.

You've made a mistake here, Rees thought with some satisfaction. *You're supercharging my best weapon. You didn't want to do that.*

The green-eyed man watched Rees closely and smiled again. "Yes. You see? As I predicted, you enjoy this part. And now, I am going to remove the gag. You may wish to shout or call out for help. I will tell you I have purchased the adjoining rooms. But still the sound might carry. And so again I give you a choice."

From his shirt pocket, Rees's captor produced a silver pen and removed the black cap. Not a pen at all. An X-Acto knife, with a razor sharp blade. Rees's vision felt so heightened by the drugs, he imagined he could see the shining razor's stainless steel edge straight on. The neat rows of iron and carbon atoms vibrating and dancing.

"If you cooperate and keep quiet until you're asked to speak," the man replaced the cap on the razor tip of the little hobby knife, "this shall live here in my pocket. Are we agreed? Hmmm?"

Rees's shaking and quavering had stopped. His body was composed of some high-tech material now, like billions of layers of graphene. He gave a single and very precise nod.

Fine, we're agreed. And I'm going to get that knife too. Don't know how, but you can throw that into the bargain.

"Very good." The man returned the hobby knife to his shirt pocket and stepped behind Rees.

Rees felt hands unwinding the duct tape from over his lips and pulling it painfully away from his hair. He tried to work the stuffed piece of cloth out of his mouth with his tongue.

The green-eyed man came back around in front of Rees and pulled it free.

"There you are."

He opened the wet and crumpled washcloth, folded it neatly, then laid it on the table next to the gun.

"Who are...," Rees had to stop to clear his throat. "Who are you and what do you want?"

"My name is Faraj. You have information that I have been paid to extract. There are various ways of doing this. Torture, as you may know, is not the most reliable."

"If I don't have whatever you're asking for, I'll say anything to make you stop. So how do you tell the good data from the bad?"

"Yes, precisely. You are an intelligent man. I know your work."

"Really? Maybe we could have you on the show. There's plenty of science behind what you do, I'm sure. By the way, what exactly did you give me there?"

"Since you're interested, something a bit like MDMA— which is rightly called ecstasy—but with a much shorter half-life. And also some nootropics. Tianeptine and a few others."

"You could make a lot of money selling that on the street, I bet. What are they paying you, anyway? Maybe I can outbid them."

Faraj frowned. "I'm afraid not. That is a matter of honor for me."

"Ah. So you're a man of principles."

Faraj's green eyes flashed. "I am aware you're jesting, but yes. Very much so. More than you can imagine. And as much as I would enjoy discussing this with you, I'm afraid we must now proceed to business."

"One quick question."

Faraj showed him a tolerant smile, like you might for a child transparently stalling to delay his bedtime. "All right. One."

"You're going to kill me, Faraj. And I bet that's your real name too. Anyway, I promise I won't believe anything you tell me to the contrary. About killing me, I mean."

"That is very forthright of you."

"Yes, well, like they say *in ... medicamentum veritas*. I think that's right. My Latin is terrible. And you've already explained why torture is not your best option."

"Yes, quite so."

"So if it isn't to save my life and it isn't to make the pain stop, why exactly am I going to cooperate here? You must have some excellent reason to expect that I will."

"Just so. You have already said it yourself, hmmm? In your little wordplay just then. *In drugs there is truth.* You have been given something that allows you to think clearly and to remember well. That is important. But the drug combination is also disinhibiting."

"A truth serum? Really? See, this stuff would be wonderful for the show. I have to be honest with you here—and this may just be the drugs talking—but I'm pretty sure I can still lie to you." Rees grinned. "Wow, how's that for a paradox, eh?"

"Yes, with some subjects this is true. But this is also only the beginning. In part to assess your tolerance. Everyone is different. We don't want you dying on us just yet."

"Oh, well thank you for that."

"Also we are establishing a platform from which to begin the real work. There is one more drug to add to the cocktail. In small doses it is extremely short-acting."

"Interesting. And what does this drug do?"

Faraj had turned away again. When he turned back he had another syringe. He was loading this one with a red fluid from a small glass vial. He drew up a tiny amount.

"That, I have found, is quite difficult to describe. Have you ever experienced DMT?"

"Ah, no. Heard of it. Hallucinogen, right?"

"Yes. A psychedelic. You will please be still again or..."

"Or the eye, yes. I remember."

Once again Faraj injected Rees. This time it stung a bit. Seconds passed. He felt ... nothing.

No change at all.

Perhaps he was immune to this drug's effects. Or maybe the dose was too small. There might be some advantage to be gained here. If he knew what the drug was supposed to do, he could pretend—

Without warning the floor in front of him split in two.

A dark and bottomless cavern yawned open, and a horrible stench spewed out, making him gag.

The chair tipped forward.

Rees fell in, screaming.

CHAPTER 47

DESPITE KNOWING THAT he might be minutes from his own death, Randolph Osborn felt strangely calm.

He was armed and that certainly helped. At the very least, the gun would prevent them taking him alive. Though he'd be happy to avoid it, the prospect of dying didn't terrify Osborn.

What these people might do to him if he were captured did.

Given his uneven legs, he was walking as well as he could across the soft, damp grass of an open field. Below the Conservatory of Flowers in Golden Gate Park. The gracefully arching, white-framed, glass structure up ahead looked like God's own greenhouse. Not a bad spot for the road to end, if that's how it all went down today. Not bad at all.

As he approached the location he'd been given for the dead drop, Osborn had the gun in hand and ready, concealed within a wadded up green windbreaker.

He picked his way past a group of youths playing hacky-sack. Nearby them a father held his son's feet as the boy giggled and attempted a handstand.

He mused on how starkly indifferent life was to death. The world turns blithely on and on. Just without you.

Amsel had fallen off a rooftop while attempting to escape arrest by the Israeli authorities. So the official story went. Black market antiquities smuggling, they said. At least he took two of the bastards with him.

Behind Osborn, the hacky-sackers burst into laughter and applause over an exceptional run. He didn't look back.

He approached a side exit to the Conservatory of Flowers. An orientation point for the dead drop. Perhaps two hundred feet to go now.

Close, very close to the end of all of it. One way or the other.

He had stashed the leather valise that he brought from Jerusalem within a grove of eucalyptus trees several blocks away. Covered it up with leaves.

He wasn't sure why. If he failed here, neither Kazemi nor anyone else would know where to find it.

Perhaps he just didn't want the wrong people to have it. The contents were too important and too ... wonderful for evil men to possess. Better that what it held should be once again lost to the ages.

Only steps away now from that exit door.

Osborn looked around for anything that might tip him off to a stakeout. The thing was, he didn't know what that would be.

A gardener with a suspicious bulge under his jacket?

A homeless man with one of those curly, clear cords dangling from a radio earpiece?

A new mother with a big green, military walkie-talkie in her stroller?

He laughed out loud, and quickly stifled it. It wouldn't do to draw attention.

Osborn reached the conservatory exit door, fairly sure he had the right one. From here, the dead drop would be approximately fifty feet west, behind a sprinkler control box.

Finding the box presented no trouble at all. He looked around. Still no sign of anyone watching him. He knelt down on the wet grass, felt the water soak cool through his pants to his knees. A patch of dark brown soil behind the box looked freshly turned.

Setting aside the windbreaker and gun, he dug in with both hands. The smell of rich, moist earth drifted up. Before long his fingertips brushed something hard. He found the edges and pried it up.

It was a small, Tupperware container—muddy, but still well-sealed. Inside, a piece of paper, folded up square. It would have details for the rendezvous with Kazemi, and any important new developments.

He resisted the impulse to open it right there. Instead, he quickly brushed the container off and thrust it into one of the windbreaker's pockets. He picked up the gun, and concealed that within the windbreaker as before.

As he stood back up, Osborn half expected to see a dozen federal agents rushing in on him.

What he saw was one man walking toward him. Middle-aged, white. Soft in body. Tall.

Osborn began to walk toward the tall man. He needed to go in that direction, and anyway he didn't want the man out of sight behind him.

He judged that the tall man would pass him maybe six feet away. There would be time to shoot if he made a sudden move. Osborn gripped the gun tighter under the windbreaker.

He tried to keep his breath calm and even. If it was just this one man, he might have a chance. They could be underestimating him. Writing him off as a crippled academic. That would be their mistake.

Osborn and the tall man made eye contact. Just a few steps away now.

The tall man smiled. "Beautiful day for the park."

Osborn returned the smile. "Yes."

They passed each other.

The tall man kept going.

Osborn glanced back over his shoulder. The other man didn't turn around. Osborn walked steadily on.

And that was that.

No sign of anyone else nearby following or approaching. He felt his eyes begin to tear up. The stress, no doubt.

He turned his mind to the long walk back to the eucalyptus grove, and the valise waiting there for him. In privacy, he could stop and read the note.

He glanced behind one last time.

The tall man had turned around. He was walking quickly toward Osborn, taking long strides.

Beneath the windbreaker, Osborn cocked back the gun's hammer. He felt his heartbeat in his throat. He waited until he thought the man would be about ten feet behind him.

With the gun still hidden from view, he spun around. *I'll shoot him through the jacket, that way he won't try to dodge.*

The tall man must have seen something in Osborn's face. He froze where he stood.

"I ... you dropped your wallet." He pointed behind himself. "Back there."

Osborn kept his finger on the trigger. He tried to read the tall man's face.

"I saw it on the grass," the man went on. "I recognized you from your driver's license photo. Maybe it fell from your jacket?" He held out a worn, black leather wallet toward Osborn.

That *was* his wallet. He'd dropped it.

Osborn accepted the wallet and apologized for appearing rude.

The tall man understood he'd startled Osborn. He graciously offered that you really do have to be careful walking alone in a park these days, even in broad daylight.

They both went on their separate ways.

AS HIS HEARTBEAT settled down to normal, Osborn made the trek back to the eucalyptus grove. He arrived about ten minutes later.

The valise was gone.

His first thought was that he'd picked the wrong grove. There were a lot of them around here. He quickly backtracked out to get an overlook of the whole area.

Across a grassy field maybe forty yards away, a man with bushy, gray hair was walking into another stand of trees.

He was carrying the valise.

It wouldn't help to shout. That would only give him time to run.

Osborn couldn't think of anything to do but follow in the faint hope that the man ahead of him would stop somewhere soon.

He started across the field, and to his great surprise the other man had already stopped. He was standing within a copse of trees on the far side of the grass, still in view.

The man's clothes were ragged and muddy. His hair and beard unkempt. Homeless. He probably lived in or around the park somewhere.

Osborn had the gun tucked into the waistband of his pants under the windbreaker, which he was wearing now. He took it out and let the weapon drop by his side, out of view to the nearest street.

Osborn had nearly finished crossing the field, and the homeless man still hadn't spotted him. He was close enough now to shoot him easily.

He stopped, about twenty feet away, and quietly raised the gun in a two-handed grip.

He had only been given brief instruction, but he knew how to properly aim the weapon. The homeless man's head was perched atop the front sight now, and centered in the rear sight notch.

If he didn't shoot this man, he would almost certainly lose what Amsel and others had already given their lives for.

Just one homeless man that no one would miss and the future of the world very possibly hanging in the balance.

Osborn tightened his finger on the trigger. He thought about the valise.

About what it contained.

And stopped.

He couldn't. He couldn't do it.

"Hey! Hey, you there!" Osborn kept the gun aimed at the homeless man. He knew he was taking a huge chance here, but hoped he could win with just a bluff.

The man wheeled toward Osborn, wide-eyed. Then immediately bolted with the valise. Running with surprising speed, disappearing like a deer through the trees.

Shaking now, Osborn lowered the gun.

He plodded up to where the man had been standing just a moment before.

A large zip-lock bag lay there on the fallen eucalyptus leaves. Next to it ... the lectionary codex with its badly oxidized copper covers.

Rocks and rusted metal.

To the untrained eye it must have looked like so much trash.

The homeless man had dumped the worthless weight and kept the nice-looking, leather valise.

He would pawn it, most probably. For a few dollars to buy drugs, or a bottle of booze.

Osborn picked up the codex and the zip-lock bag, whose real worth was incalculable, and began walking back toward the street to hail a cab.

CHAPTER 48

ANNA REES LEFT a short message and hung up. No one had answered. No one there. She was alone.

She would always be alone.

Because you're twisted.

And so she decided to get on with it.

She held her hands out before her, palms up, and looked at the delicate veins there in the wrists. Little blue wires under the thin, translucent skin, carrying the hot current of life through her body.

She picked up the X-Acto knife. She knew better than to make horizontal cuts, attacking those superficial veins. Deep, vertical slashes. That's what you wanted. Deep enough to reach the larger blood vessels down there.

She was standing in her bathroom, naked in front of the sink. If she looked up, she would see herself in the mirror there.

She did not look up.

With her right hand, she lightly touched the tip of the razor to the skin of her left wrist. She pressed down. The pain made her gasp and back off.

A droplet of bright red blood beaded up where she'd pricked herself. It blurred as tears welled up.

She blinked away the tears, grit her teeth, and tried again in the exact same spot.

The pointed tip of the razor disappeared into the blood droplet. She pressed harder this time.

The pain made her cry out, but she kept on pressing. This was nothing compared to the agony she felt inside now. She would endure any physical pain to be free from the terrible soul suffering.

Besides, *this* pain would stop soon.

Encouraged by that thought, she pushed the blade in halfway to the shaft, biting her lower lip to stifle the scream.

She dragged it down toward her elbow. One inch. Two. Three.

The searing pain made her whole frame spasm. She nearly lost her grip on the pen-like body of the little hobby knife.

Dark red blood ran down the inside of her left wrist. It dripped, spattering, into the sink.

She felt something deep inside her wrist squirm.

She stopped cutting.

As she watched, something emerged from the slash. Blood-smeared, tubular and ivory white.

A tendon.

No, not a tendon. It wriggled. It was slithering out of the bloody gash, like a worm weaving up out of the ground into a rain puddle.

Then another bloody worm-thing followed and intertwined with the first. Then a third one, much larger, the size of a small garden snake. On this last one she could see a head without eyes.

But it had a mouth. The mouth gaped open revealing multiple rows of tiny, needle teeth.

Anna screamed.

Something awoke within her. Some *things*. She tried to scream again, but no sound came out this time.

The skin on her stomach rippled with undulating waves, like an elastic membrane over a writhing ball of eels.

Something was rising deep in her throat too. It pushed up toward her mouth, pressing against the back of her tongue.

She looked down at her belly and saw in her skin the outline of an arm. Inside pushing outward. And a hand with fingers splayed. The hand began to inch down. Down below her abdomen. Down between her thighs.

Whatever the thing was, it wanted to be born.

Something was tearing now deep in her gut. The pain. White hot, unbearable pain.

God, please. Oh, God, please make it stop.

She looked up and straight ahead, into the mirror.

And Gevin Rees saw himself standing there.

Bloody and nude. Teenaged again. The wounds from the car accident still fresh. A jagged, white tip of shattered rib bone tearing out through his side. It pumped up and down with each ragged breath.

At his feet lay his sister, Anna. Dead. Decaying. The gray skin liquefying and sloughing off her skull.

The putrid smell made him wretch. That jangled the shards of broken rib bones and sent new shocks of searing pain through his body.

She was dead, yes, but still aware somehow. Her eyes wide open, looked up at him, pleading. Piercing him with a sadness so horrible it would be better that the world itself had never been.

Rees wept. He wept with an agony too large for time to contain. An agony that only eternity could encompass.

Anna, Anna. I'm so sorry. Please, forgive me.

Then, as he watched, his sister began to change down there. She was becoming translucent. The floor beneath her as well. The walls, ceiling, everything was turning insubstantial.

He could see something through them now. The motel room.

He had returned. He sat, still duct taped into the chair, his face wet with tears.

Faraj stood before him, green eyes sparkling. "So you see, Dr. Rees, this would be very difficult to describe in words."

"Goddamn you." Rees's voice cracked with emotion. And the physical torment that he had been ... what, hallucinating? The echoes of it still bounced around inside his body. It might have all been a hallucination.

But the pain, the pain had been very real.

Faraj picked up the syringe and red vial off the coffee table. Holding them in front of his face, he again drew up a tiny amount of the drug. "As I explained, in small amounts the effects are quite short-lived." He paused, then filled the syringe entirely with the drug. Perhaps ten or fifteen times as much as before. "But with a dose of *this* size, the psychosis is permanent."

Good God, no. Oh, no.

Faraj withdrew the needle from the vial, held the syringe upright, and tapped it twice with the nail of his forefinger. He squirted a brief red stream into the air, like an arterial spurt. "There is no outer physical manifestation. To the world you would seem to be in a vegetative state. You are well off, insured I assume? You would be taken care of. You might live perhaps forty years. Maybe more."

"No. No, please. No, I couldn't..." The horror that filled Rees's mind drove every other thought out. To experience *that*. For the remainder of a lifetime?

The fear that gripped him surpassed anything he'd ever felt or even imagined possible.

"What do you want to know?"

CHAPTER 49

AS THEY DESCENDED toward San Francisco, Singleton gazed out the window and listened to the hum of the Learjet's engines pulsing. *Louder, deeper, softer, higher.*

The pattern repeated every few seconds. Harmonic oscillation. All complex mechanisms had their own rhythms.

That was the first sign the current operation had gone sideways. No rhythm. In part the result of far too many on-the-fly adjustments.

Then there was the client, Carl Truby. To say he was getting a bit difficult was like saying that a bullet to the brain—

"Trying to figure out how to get rid of me, are you?" Truby said.

Excellent timing, Mr. Truby. Singleton turned toward the only other passenger on the plane.

Truby sat opposite Singleton, staring at him over a plate of thousand dollar an ounce Caspian Sea caviar that neither of them had touched.

"What makes you think that?" Singleton asked.

A smile dimpled Truby's fat cheeks. "I can see the gears turning." He shifted in his seat. Truby was a soft and pudgy man. His suits, though no doubt tailored, never fit quite right. Singleton suspected it was intentional. A camouflage of normalcy for one of the most powerful elites on the planet.

Singleton found Truby's answer amusing, but kept his face a mask. "If I were that readable, I'd have been dead a long time ago."

"I need to stay hands on." Truby had dropped the smile.

"Your best move would be to remain on the jet when we land. Let me fly you straight back to D.C. You're risking unnecessary exposure."

"Oh, I'll keep a low profile in San Francisco. But I am staying in the goddamn loop from now on. You know my record, so you know what kind of skills I have. Face it, you need me there."

"You put a moron into the White House once, a very long time ago. That was quite a trick, sure. But I don't see it coming in handy at the present moment."

Truby smiled amiably at that last jab. "In fact it *was* quite a trick. A bigger trick than taking out one half-deranged scientist and a goddam TV show host. Which you and your people still haven't managed to pull off."

"That's why I'm wrapping this thing up personally."

"And I'm supposed to assume you'll do a better job than Special Agent Merriweather?"

Singleton didn't react to that.

Truby cracked a wide grin. "Oh, ho, you do have one hell of a poker face. I will give you that. But you have to be wondering how the hell I knew Merriweather was your guy."

Singleton had already worked that out. "You have your own resources in the Defense Department. I assume they told you—as my people told me—that a witness saw Merriweather fatally shoot a fellow DCIS agent before he tried to kill that witness as well."

"Sloppy work there, wouldn't you say?"

"So, Carl, am I supposed to be surprised that you could put two and two together?"

"No, asshole, you're supposed to be thinking—if he can work that out, then there's a trail out there someone else can follow."

"Thank you for your concern. We can take care of it."

"Can you? What if someone already documented that trail, including large sums of money making their way to your man Merriweather? What if that same someone is perfectly willing to screw you up the ass with it all?"

Singleton literally couldn't believe what he was hearing now. And *that*, apparently, did show on his face.

Truby laughed. "Ah, finally. A reaction. I was starting to think you were a goddamn android or something."

"Are you threating my organization, Mr. Truby? Be very careful with your next answer."

Truby looked quite comfortable. He spooned some caviar onto a cracker. "I'm trying to help you see why it's in both of our best interests for me to be directly in charge from this point on."

"I want to be sure I understand you. You intend to take over tactical command of this operation, with my organization as your resources. Order us around?"

"You're a little slow on the uptake for a private spook, or whatever you consider yourself, but you catch on." Truby popped the cracker into his mouth. "Mmm. This really is excellent stuff."

"And blackmailing me with the threat of exposing an operation that *you* paid for—that's your best play?" Singleton allowed himself a smile. "You have some idea what I do, in the course of my regular work?"

"Yeah. And I also know what's at stake. If you screw this thing up, my world goes away. I have nothing to lose here, so I could give a shit. You understand? I'll burn you and your people to the ground. So you just step back now and do as you're told, and that won't need to happen."

"I'm intrigued. How is it you see your whole world going away?"

Truby loaded up another cracker with caviar. "Well to be clear, it's your world we're talking about too, smartass. You know what Fischer was trying to pull off? Beyond the crazy shit he was supposed to be after?"

"I do. And so, what? Are you afraid the world will descend into anarchy without the promise of heaven or the threat of hell?"

Truby was chewing loudly and seemed to be savoring the flavor of the caviar, unconcerned about making Singleton wait. He cracked open a bottle of mineral water and poured himself a glass. Sipped it. Set the glass back down.

Finally he looked across the table at Singleton. "You really think it's heaven and hell that keeps folks in line?" Truby laughed. "You know, for a sharp guy you're pretty stupid."

"We've got time. Educate me."

Truby's eyes narrowed and he cocked his head contemplatively. "What do you think religions are *really* for, Mr. Singleton? Huh? To teach us right from wrong with stories about blindly following an order to slit your kid's throat? Or how you shouldn't raise your hand against evil, but go ahead and beat your wife into obedience? No. That's not what it's for. It's *us and them*. That's what it's for. That's the whole point. It's us and them that makes it all work. *Come out from among them, and be ye separate.* You familiar with scripture?"

Singleton was not in the mood. "Truly fascinating, Carl, but I fail to see—"

"Then shut up and I'll explain it." Truby's voice took on an almost giddy tone now as he continued. "All religions create an *us*, Mr. Singleton. That's the believers. But the genius of monotheism is that it created both an us and a dirty, blasphemous them in one stroke. Right and wrong, baby! No more my god's bigger than your god. There's only my God. We're good, and you're not just different. You're *evil*. Now there's a reason to fight. Hell, it's a better tool for manipulation than nationalism. Better even than race, and that's saying something, my *brothuh*." He hit the last word with a parody of urban black diction.

"All right. I see your point."

But Truby was on a roll. "Shit, racism looks like sibling rivalry by comparison. He raised his voice. "Listen to me, the people I work for need there to be a true religion. Two at the very least! Without that, there's no goddamn leverage. You see me getting a man into the White House without those buttons to push? Let alone keep him in there for two terms?" He leaned across the table, and slammed his meaty fist down on it. "No! It's unworkable, goddamnit! And we won't let it happen. Do you get it now? Do you understand this yet, Mr. Baxter?"

In the silence that followed, Singleton heard the jet's engines humming. *Louder, deeper, softer, higher.*

He felt his face growing hot. He had believed until this very moment that no one still alive could connect him with his birth name, Richard Baxter. He sat there too shocked even to be impressed.

Acting intuitively, he picked up a cracker. Grasped the small spoon. Dipped it in the caviar and deposited some on the cracker. Took a bite.

And breathed. He just breathed.

Truby leaned back in his seat. "That's right. You play it cool, Richard. I need you cool and calm if we're gonna finish this thing."

He's made his move. Just chill out. It'll be your turn soon enough.

Truby was watching him with cold, fish eyes. "I didn't appreciate that late night scare you gave me. I did some looking. You think you know how deep my connections go? The favors I'm owed? You don't know the half of it. You have a storied past, my friend. Lots of people out there who would love to find out where you are now."

Singleton looked at the clump of black, shiny eggs on the cracker in his hand. Workers harvested them from a living fish. Three days before it spawned. They stunned the fish with a blow to the head, then slit its guts open.

He looked at Carl Truby's bulging belly. A knife sat within reach.

Truby had that face on again. The one he wore when he said he could see the wheels turning in Singleton's head. "Yeah, you could take me out," he said now. "Make it look like one of a thousand different accidents. But you know I know that. You know I'm prepared for that. The bomb, so to speak, is armed. And it's on a dead man's switch. Everything blows up if I'm not around to stop it. Everything I've got on you goes public. And then they come for you, Richard."

In his mind, Singleton heard the grinding of gears and screeching of metal. The machinery of this operation tearing itself to pieces.

No rhythm to it. No rhythm at all.

The landing gear made a whirring sound as it extended, followed by a clunk that Singleton could feel through the cabin floor.

He finished the cracker and caviar. Truby was right. It really was excellent stuff.

Money didn't buy happiness, but it did buy all the pleasures that Singleton cared for most. He truly enjoyed his life, and the role he played in the world that men like Carl Truby kept spinning.

And Singleton was a realist.

"It's your show," he said.

CHAPTER 50

LOUIS THOUGHT HE might enjoy a stroll on the SFSU campus a little more if he weren't worried any second now someone was going to jump out from behind a bush and blow his head off.

And that was an actual possibility, if the man who grabbed Rees was here already looking for this Herodotus guy. So given the gravity of the situation, it struck him as odd when he heard Morgan start laughing.

She pointed up at the main library building, dead ahead of them. "The J. Paul Leonard Library. JPL. You know, we could've just looked that up."

Danni did a comic palm smack on her forehead.

Louis could see he wasn't in on some joke. "What? What am I missing?"

"The message from Professor Kazemi, our Herodotus. It said to meet him at the *JPL Library*," Danni said. "Rees thought it might mean—"

"The Jet Propulsion Laboratory," Louis cut in. "Down in Pasadena. You guys weren't even sure this was the right place?"

Morgan and Danni laughed it off, and Louis let it go. Privately, he thought it didn't exactly inspire warm confidence in his teammates.

MORE THAN A half-hour later, after they'd scoured all six floors of the library several times with no sign of Kazemi, Louis's confidence cooled by a couple more degrees.

They had pulled up the religious history professor's picture on Louis's phone. A male of Middle Eastern descent, mid to late forties, balding, heavyset, with a fringe of collar-length graying hair. He wouldn't have been very hard to spot.

He just wasn't there.

As the three of them walked off the staircase onto the library's ground floor, Louis asked, "What if Kazemi's a no-show? Maybe he got spooked after what happened at Livermore last night."

Morgan agreed it was possible. They decided to stop at the reference desk to check if anyone there had seen the history professor around.

The library assistant's arms were sleeved-out with tattoos, and a mouse could easily have crawled through the flesh tunnels in his ears. Louis was pretty sure the man was stoned too.

"Yeah, he was here," the library assistant said. "He had to go home. He wasn't feeling well. He left a message for, uh, you guys, I guess. He said to say, 'My history book is here.' Said you'd know what that was about. Oh, and I told your other friend too."

Morgan did an actual double take. "I'm sorry, who?"

"Oh, I didn't get a name. Blond hair, light blue eyes. He was here about, mmm ... an hour ago? Looking for the professor. And also for that astronomer guy."

"Gevin Rees?" Morgan asked.

"Uh huh. Hey, I thought he was in some kind of trouble."

Morgan flowed with that. "Yeah, no, they just wanted to interview him as a witness. So did anyone else come by for the professor? Or Gevin Rees?"

"Nah. Just you guys and your buddy there earlier."

Morgan gave the librarian an appreciative smile. "Okay. Well, thank you for the message."

Louis tried to force a nonchalant grin that probably looked like gas pain. Then he followed Morgan and Danni as they walked away from the reference desk.

When they were out of earshot, he erupted. "What the hell? What's the deal with the book? Why are they looking for Rees? They *have* Rees already."

Morgan started to answer, then waited as a couple of students walked close by. "All right. First, we might not be talking about just one group here."

"A multi-player game," Danni said in a conspiratorial whisper. "That could be why the man who slammed into us didn't shoot anyone. He's not even *with* the blond guy. He's got, like, different rules of engagement."

It made sense, and they quickly agreed on a couple of important strategic points. First, the guy who grabbed Rees probably hadn't beaten them to the library. He would have needed some time to question Rees before he set off to get here.

Second, the blond man was probably still lurking somewhere nearby. Somehow he had known that Rees was coming here. So he'd almost certainly be staking the place out. Which meant he must have seen them already.

Now he was probably just waiting for them to go someplace with fewer witnesses and security cameras.

Even though Louis's instincts told him to run away fast and far, he had to admit these were two very good reasons not to leave the library quite yet.

Then there was the whole question of the book. The one the librarian had mentioned.

Morgan was first to offer a theory there. "So Kazemi *was* here, but decided it wasn't safe to hang around. What if the history book thing is—he left us a message there?"

"Like, for a new, safer rendezvous point?" Danni suggested.

Morgan nodded. "I can't think what else it could be about."

They hiked back upstairs to look for a history book authored by Burhan Kazemi.

That quickly proved to be a bust. Kazemi's book, or rather books, were there all right, tucked far back in one of the history aisles.

But they were all opened and scattered on the floor.

They riffled through each book, and shook them all out one at a time. They found nothing.

"Well," Morgan said, "if there *was* a message stuck in one of these books, that blond guy got it."

"Did he?" Louis picked up one of the books. "Assume he stopped when he found something. Because you would, of course. There are, what," he looked around the floor, "nine books here. And no unopened books by Kazemi left on any shelf. The odds you'd have to pull out all nine of his books to find the right one on your very last try? That's eight to one against. Pretty unlikely."

"You know," Danni said, "Kazemi could've just left a note for Rees at the reference desk. With the rendezvous info in it. Time and place. So why the rigmarole about a book? Unless it's like a code. You know, to help protect the information. Like he did with the whole JPL thing."

Morgan recalled something then. "Rees said there was an ancient book called The Histories. Maybe *my history book* means—"

Danni finished her thought. "Herodotus's book. Yeah, it's the first great history book."

The book was only one aisle over. The Histories. Morgan pulled it off the shelf. As she opened the cover a piece of paper fell out.

It landed at Louis's feet. He picked it up and read it out loud. "Ferry Building plaza. Five PM. Come alone."

"This is good," Morgan said. "It's very good. But our top priority is finding Rees. And our best shot is still right here. We wait here until the man who abducted Rees comes here looking for Kazemi."

After another brief discussion, they all agreed on the plan. Morgan led them down to a first floor corner of the library, with a view of the entrance and the reference desk. Their stakeout spot.

As they waited for an armed killer to show up, actually *hoping* he'd show up, a lot of questions ran through Louis's mind. One of them on heavy rotation.

What the hell am I doing?

CHAPTER 51

REES'S CAPTOR HAD insisted that he take time to consider well, before the real questioning began. Then he stepped out of Rees's line of sight and busied himself in another area of the motel room.

But Rees *couldn't* think. His head just kept filling with nightmare images. Hellish scenes from his hallucinatory drug experience. The green-eyed bastard no doubt knew this. It might all be part of the softening up process.

He had no watch or clock to check. The drugs made guessing how much time had passed nearly impossible. It might be twenty minutes. It might be four or five hours.

Rees finally heard his captor approaching again.

The man who called himself Faraj stepped back into his field of view. He stood there looking relaxed, and spoke in a gentle voice. "Do you have the data, Dr. Rees?"

Rees still felt the sharpening effects of the first drugs. Quite possibly it had made the hallucinations more horrible. But for now, it helped him think fast. And that was a very good thing.

If a solution lay hidden somewhere here in this room, he would find it. He had to.

"If I tell you everything. Will you kill me, without...?" Rees looked down at the syringe still lying on the coffee table. He had no doubt it had been left within his view for a reason.

Faraj smiled. "Without putting you into a permanent state of psychosis? Yes. I give you my word I will kill you, Dr. Rees. It will not be quick. But you will understand the full height of human existence, which can only be appreciated from its nadir. It is a privilege."

Rees pretended to be considering whether to cooperate or not. He'd already decided he would talk. To buy time, if nothing else. *If there were a way out, even in a direction that seemed absurd ... what would it be?*

"No," Rees said, when he judged he'd stretched the pause as long as he could get away with. "I don't have a copy of the Kafir Project data. The time-recordings."

"Do you know who does? Or where it is kept?"

Rees thought the truth would likely sound more convincing. "No I don't. But I think a man named Kazemi may have it. Or he knows where to get it."

"And Kazemi, he is Herodotus? We are speaking of the religious history professor at San Francisco State University are we not?"

His captor clearly knew a lot already. Rees was glad he hadn't started off trying to make up phony details. "I think so. I'm not positive."

"And Anaximander? You know who this is?"

"No idea. My understanding is that he has the lectionary codex, though."

"And what about the time-viewing technology itself? My clients are very interested in reproducing it."

So he didn't get the pouch and Fischer's notebook. Morgan still has it. Rees tried to buy more time to think. "Why do they want the technology? It could only hurt their cause."

Faraj chuckled. "Oh, they don't believe that. They are certain the technology will validate their faith. They are very keen to show that the Prophet, peace be upon him, anointed Ali as his successor."

Rees had never imagined an Islamic group would be anything but afraid of the time-viewing technology. But he understood now. "The Shias. That's what they want out of this? To prove the Sunni's are wrong, and they're right?"

"No small thing, as I'm sure you know."

"Yeah, I do. It would realign the entire Islamic world. They're going to be sorely disappointed. Both sides, in fact. Because, here's the thing. I don't *have* the technology." He decided to risk a lie here. "No one ever had it apart from Fischer and DARPA. And I'm not sure anyone in DARPA fully understands it. It's lost now that Fischer is really dead."

"Hmmm. And what do you know about the second phase of the project? The work which was not condoned by your government."

Rees had no idea what his captor was talking about now, and that unsettled him. He didn't want to appear like he was holding out. "I'm sorry, but I don't know anything about any second phase. Unless you mean the time-tracing? Finding the buried, historical artifacts?"

Something flashed there behind Faraj's green eyes. "Interesting. So Fischer told you nothing about his extending the Kafir Project's mandate?"

"He didn't get to tell me much of anything. Your people killed him too fast."

"On the contrary. That was *your* people, by proxy. But no matter. I will explain on the chance you have heard more than you understood, and it jogs your memory. You are, I take it, aware of the Kafir Project's original purpose?"

"To attack the historical foundations of Islam. In order to undermine radical extremists. That's my understanding."

"Yes, and that is correct. It would seem, though, that Edward Fischer had also intended from the very start to expand the project."

Fischer's words came back to Rees. *And did you stop there?*

Fischer had asked him that in their very first phone conversation. After Rees explained how he'd examined the historicity of Mormon scriptures. Rees *hadn't* stopped digging there.

And neither had Fischer.

"They weren't stopping with Islam," Rees said.

Faraj shook his head. "No."

Rees could see now why the Kafir Project had been scrapped by its own sponsors. Why now those same people, with access to Defense Department computers and personnel, wanted Fischer and the data and all the principal players gone.

Phase II. The expanded project.

"Fischer searched back even further," Rees said. "To the beginning of the Common Era. Christianity. He investigated the historical origins of Christianity too."

"Yes. Judaism as well. It appears he was on something of a quest."

This all made sense. Of course Fischer would have looked back further, once he had his hands on the tools. He wasn't fighting Islamic radicalism. Not for its own sake.

He was waging his own personal war on religion.

There were plenty of people in the US government, or closely associated, who just wouldn't stand for that.

Rees's focus had turned inside. Now he looked up again. "I understand. But I wasn't told about any of that. Nothing about the ... additional targets."

Faraj tucked in his chin and drew a deep breath through his nose. He puckered his lips and nodded. "Yes. Yes, I think this is the truth." He turned and picked up the red syringe again.

"What? What are you doing?" Rees asked. "You just said you believed me."

Faraj approached Rees with the syringe. "I said I thought you were telling the truth. And soon, I will know for certain."

"No! No!" Rees began rocking the chair back and forth again.

Faraj stopped and shook his large head. "You will remember that you have only two choices here. The same two as before."

Rees could turn his head far enough to look to either side. To his left—couch, painting, light switch, stain on the wall. To his right, about five feet away—thermostat and ... the room's TV set. It sat on a cantilevered wooden shelf, mounted about shoulder height on the wall.

A strategy began to form.

Rees kept rocking the chair as violently as he could. "I don't care. I don't care! No. I won't let you do it!"

Faraj brought the needle up beside his own face, and tilted it toward one bright green eye. "It will be extremely unpleasant, Dr. Rees."

He's left-handed. He'll want to come around to my right side. "No! No! Get it away! No!" Rees found it quite easy to sound like he was unglued. But inside he'd become a machine. Cold and emotionless.

He had discovered that by alternately pushing off one foot and then the other, he could rock the chair from side to side as well as forward and back. And by jerking his head and trunk at the same time, he could rotate it too. And scoot it.

Toward that TV shelf.

Faraj huffed impatiently. "I take this to mean that you have made your choice. So be it. The eye then." He approached Rees with the needle in his left hand.

Rees had managed to turn the chair through about forty-five degrees clockwise. He halfway faced the TV now. It was about three feet away and to his right. He started to whip his head quickly from side to side.

Faraj frowned at him. "That won't help. In fact you may cause me to tear your cornea with the tip of the needle. Or worse."

Yes, but you'll try to steady me first with your right hand. You don't want to make a mess of it. You're neat and tidy aren't you?

Rees turned his head away from his captor, to the far right. He held it there.

Faraj still had the syringe in his left hand. He came around to Rees's right side. But to do so he had to duck down awkwardly, under the TV shelf.

That's it. That's right. Get over here asshole.

Faraj placed his right hand on Rees's left cheek, trying to hold him still. The big man had gotten himself wedged in tightly now. Between the chair, wall, and the TV shelf.

Rees craned his head further back and to the right as far as he could, until it felt like the cords in his neck would snap.

Faraj had to lean in even farther then, bend down a bit more awkwardly. Rees could feel his warm breath. It smelled of some kind of breath mint.

Lower, he's got to come lower.

And as if he just responded to the silent command, Faraj squatted down on his haunches. Getting more comfortable, taking the strain off his bent back.

Yes! There you go.

Rees pointed his toes, rocking the chair backwards. He bent his head straight back. Cocking it to fire. He held an image in his mind. A war machine dating back to the Dark Ages.

Faraj's grinning face was just two feet from Rees's own now.

Rees lifted his toes off the floor.

He allowed a half-second for the chair to start its drop. It rocked him forward. A moment later he whipped his head forward too.

In his mind's eye, Rees could see the forces and levers and axis points all at work in perfect mechanical harmony. The counterweight of his body dropping with the chair, the throw-arm of his spine, the sling-like motion of his neck. All together they functioned like the interlocking mechanisms of a medieval trebuchet. A particularly deadly kind of catapult.

He could see exactly where the thick, supraorbital ridge of his skull would connect with the fragile nasal bones of Faraj's face.

He closed his eyes.

In his imagination, he watched the impact drive shattered splinters of the other man's nasal bones up into his forebrain.

He felt his head still accelerating as it smashed home on its target.

The world exploded into colored sparks and streamers of light.

Rees felt and heard Faraj's nasal bones and eye socket cracking, crushing, caving in.

He opened his eyes and watched his enemy falling backwards.

Rees's chair continued rocking forward as his momentum carried him. Now he too was falling. Falling in slow motion.

He turned his head to keep from breaking his own nose on the floor.

His body thumped on the carpet, then bounced. He came to rest on his left side as the chair rolled to a stop.

Rees took a deep breath. He lifted his head.

Faraj lay on the carpet next to the coffee table. Flat on his back. Motionless.

Is he dead? He looks like he's dead.

Faraj groaned. His eyelids snapped open. The green eyes found Rees. They opened wider.

Oh, no. No, please...

Faraj began to sit up. Stunned perhaps, but very much alive.

Rees had failed. There would be no freeing himself from the duct tape, as he had hoped.

There would be only retribution.

Rees's tormentor had fully sat up now on the floor. Torrents of bright red blood gushed from his ruined nose and streamed down his chin, onto his white shirt.

Rage burned in his emerald eyes.

Then his expression changed. It softened. His eyes began to wander. He looked ... confused.

And then Rees saw it.

The hypodermic in Faraj's left side. He'd fallen on it. The plunger was fully depressed now. The syringe ... completely empty.

Slowly the life drained out of Faraj's face. All expression there vanished.

He sank, limp, back down to the carpet. He lay there on his back, eyes open. Completely still, except for his steady breathing.

His words came back to Rees. *To the world you would seem to be in a vegetative state.*

Hell. Faraj had gone to hell.

And Rees thought there could be no better place for him.

CHAPTER 52

TO MORGAN'S EXPERIENCED eye, Danni and Louis both looked like they were about to jump right out of their skins.

They'd all been watching the library's ground floor for about a half hour now, eyes peeled for the man who grabbed Rees. The man they hoped would come here looking for the history professor, Burhan Kazemi.

So far, nothing.

Danni and Louis were neither prepared nor trained for the painful combination of tension and boredom that comprised a typical stakeout. And this was worse. Because at the same time they all knew the blond man was watching them too, from somewhere not far away. It was taking a mental toll. Morgan had to admit even she was struggling, with nothing to distract her from a headache that seemed to grow worse by the hour.

A student stood up from a nearby library computer, collected her things, and left.

Morgan got an idea. She turned to Danni and Louis. "You want to take a look at that video Rees told us about?"

Danni's face brightened instantly. "Oh, yeah. The one with the book in it? The lectionary?"

"Yes." Morgan opened Fischer's pouch and dug out the flash drive.

Louis was watching her like a dog expecting a treat. "Is that from Fischer's project?"

Morgan held the flash drive out in her palm. "Yes. Videos. From the time-viewing they did."

Louis was practically salivating now. "Are you serious?"

With the mood already considerably better, Morgan led them all over to the opened up computer.

Danni sat down at the keyboard as Morgan plugged in the flash drive. Morgan and Louis stood behind her. Morgan kept one eye on the library entrance.

The first file Danni tried to open just wouldn't. She tried three times and only managed to crash the video program. She cussed the file and went on to the next one.

This one sprung open with video of a bearded man speaking to an assembled audience. He was leading a ceremony in some Middle Eastern language. From what Rees had told them, it must be Aramaic.

The familiar circular shot framed the book, the lectionary, dead center in sharp focus. Just as Rees had described.

"So when is this from?" Louis asked.

"Seventh century or earlier," Morgan replied. "That's what Rees said. Because it has to be from before there was ever a Qur'an."

Louis shook his head in disbelief. "It's incredible. It's ... wow, they really did it. Look at that."

The video played another half-minute and stopped.

Danni launched the next file.

The feathered dinosaur video ran then. As Morgan and Danni watched the animal hunting again, commenting on details they missed the first time, Louis stood there in silence. Literally speechless.

When that one finished, Danni returned to the first file. "This file might be corrupted. Let me see if I can do anything."

She opened a cascade of windows. The computer screen filled with lines of code. She scrolled down through page after page of it.

Morgan marveled that these strings of letters and numbers and words all actually meant something clear to Danni.

Louis stabbed a finger at the screen. "Hey, stop, there's something."

"Yeah, I see it too." Danni typed rapidly. She deleted some characters, typed something else in their place, and navigated back to the desktop. This time when Danni double-clicked the first file, it opened. "Yeah," she said. "Now that's what I'm talkin' about."

Moments later the file began to play. Again the same fuzzy, circular frame, just as in the other two recordings. Morgan suspected it was some artifact of the time-viewing technology.

A horrific scene suddenly appeared on the monitor in front of them.

Morgan quickly looked around to make sure no students were near enough to catch a glimpse of the screen.

Louis's mouth hung open almost comically. Danni's face had gone blank, except for a strange tautness.

Morgan's experience in law enforcement naturally turned what she was seeing into a crime scene. Out of habit, she began to analyze the evidence.

The man had been dead for at least twenty-four hours. Likely more than that. Closer to forty-eight if she had to guess.

Postmortem lividity in the lower extremities suggested he died in just that position, right there.

This would be the primary crime scene then.

The naked body, exposed to the elements, showed signs of scavenging by wild animals. Likely the work of carrion birds. Morgan didn't know if locally there would have been feral dogs or wolves, but they probably could not have reached the body.

Not hanging, as it was there, high up on a capital T-shaped wooden cross.

CHAPTER 53

IT DIDN'T TAKE long for Rees to free himself.

Once he'd worked one hand loose of the duct tape, he dragged himself and the chair over to his captor's side and located the X-Acto knife, still in the man's shirt pocket.

The rest went quickly.

He felt surprisingly steady on his feet, and thought it might be the stimulants, although they seemed to be waning. A quick body check revealed no serious injuries from the car crash.

When he finished that, he looked down again at the man on the floor there.

Faraj lay on the soiled motel room carpet with his green eyes open. His breathing was steady. His nose had mostly stopped bleeding. The spread of dark blood on his face and neck made the injury appear worse than it probably was. His peaceful expression revealed no trace of whatever nightmare roiled inside his head.

A nightmare from which he would never wake.

Rees wondered if holding a pillow over Faraj's face would be the more ethical thing to do. To end a living hell that could stretch on perhaps for decades.

He bounced the idea around in his head awhile, and in the end decided against it. He didn't need to add a mercy killing to the list of actions he would have to account for some day. So he wasn't leaving Faraj there in that horrible place just out of a desire for vengeance.

Not just.

On the coffee table along with the gun and Taser, Rees found a cheap cell phone. Also a set of rent-a-car keys. The phone's time and date display answered one question immediately. Only a couple of hours had elapsed since he'd been taken.

If the keys were to the BMW that hit Louis's car, he didn't need them. The Beemer must be drivable, but Rees thought it would probably stand out too much.

He peeked out the curtain. Sutro Tower sprouted up in the distance over a row of rooftops. He was still in the City.

Then he checked inside the toilet kit there for anything that might be useful. Pill containers and colorful vials. More hypos. A few recognizable surgical implements. And a handful of wicked-looking devices he didn't even want to guess about.

In the room's closet, he found a blue gym bag with clothes and actual toiletries in it. Multiple passports too, in a zippered compartment. All with different names. None of them Faraj.

And cash. Lots of it. He rifled through a stack of US currency in various denominations. Altogether there looked to be about thirty-five or forty thousand dollars there.

Well, it's not going to be hard to pay for a taxi now.

A knock came at the door. Faraj might have confederates.

Rees grabbed the gun off the coffee table. He remembered Morgan's remark about the safety. He searched desperately for the switch but he didn't see it. The damn thing might be useless unless—

"Housekeeping." A female voice out there.

Rees steadied his breath before he spoke. He tried to affect a light tone. "Yeah, can you come back later, please? Thank you."

"Yes, okay."

Rees listened to the retreating footsteps, then waited. After three minutes he was reasonably convinced it hadn't been some kind of ploy.

He dumped the clothes and toiletries out of the gym bag, and dropped the money back in it, along with the gun. The Taser he left. He had no idea how to use the thing anyway.

After drinking what felt like a gallon of cool water straight from the bathroom tap, Rees splashed his face and the back of his neck.

He began to look up into the mirror, and froze.

Images from the hellish drug hallucination flashed back into his mind. Blood-smeared snakes. Something stinking and horrible with eyes of green fire, lurking in a deep pit.

He shuddered. "You're all right. You're all right," he said to himself in as soothing a tone as he could muster. He sucked in a couple of deep breaths, then raised his eyes to the mirror. And he saw...

Himself.

A frightened, middle-aged man with disheveled, brown hair, graying at the temples. Dark rings under his eyes. A red splotch, low on his forehead that was beginning to swell. He touched it with his fingertips and winced.

He managed a weak smile. "Welcome back, buddy."

As he dried his face with a musty smelling hand towel, Rees's mind ached with thoughts and images of his sister, Anna.

In the depths to which the drug had plunged him, he had felt her pain as his own. Felt all her loneliness. The self-hatred. The hopelessness.

Suddenly, Rees became aware that something had changed within him. Changed profoundly.

I forgive you, Anna. I understand now. I understand.

Volcanic emotions erupted within him. He gripped the bathroom counter, closed his eyes, and let them come.

Twice the tears and sobs appeared to subside. Twice they came back even stronger. When his emotions had finally settled, Rees found himself sitting on the floor of the bathroom, thinking not of Anna, but of Morgan.

He had felt a bond with the DCIS agent. Deep and personal, almost from the very beginning. It seemed foolish now that he hadn't immediately recognized where it came from.

The hole in his heart. The one he had refused to let anyone fill over all these years.

Serve only the truth. That's what he told himself. That was the deep commitment that had emerged out of the tragedy with Anna. He would serve no authority but the truth of things from then on.

But the truth was that the human heart, like nature itself, abhors a vacuum. He knew that. And he'd been trying to pretend otherwise.

That was dishonest. Which meant he'd been violating his own credo. Well, he was through with doing that.

But now Morgan was probably dead. Along with Danni and Louis. There was a way to find out. Louis had a cell phone. Rees should be able to reach them on it.

If they were alive.

Rees had Faraj's phone now, but didn't have Louis's cell number. And then he recalled what Danni said when they decided to reach out to him. *Louis has the coolest phone number in the universe.*

Yes he does, Rees thought. It was just the area code plus the first seven digits of the irrational number *phi*. Using a mnemonic system that turned digits into linked words, Rees had long ago memorized the number out to a hundred decimals. Nerd party trick.

He just couldn't remember the damn three digit local area code for the East Bay.

A quick call to 411 took care of that. He punched in the number, afraid that some police officer investigating Louis's death would answer.

After four rings Rees heard...

"Hello?"

It sounded like Louis's voice. "Louis?" Rees asked.

"Who is this?"

"It's Gevin Rees. Is everyone all right there?"

Louis gasped. "Holy shit, Dr. Rees?"

"Yeah. Are you guys okay? Are Kerry and Danni with you?"

"Yes, yes we're all, we're fine. Are *you* okay? Where are you?"

"I'm all right. And actually, I don't know where I am. Still in San Francisco somewhere. Where are you guys?"

Rees could hear Morgan and Danni talking. Then a rustling sound.

Morgan's voice. "Rees, listen to me carefully. Theresa and I are fine. We haven't found Professor Keating. We don't know where Keating is."

What the hell is she talking about? Theresa? Keating?

"What?" Rees asked.

"Professor Keating. Herodotus's partner," Morgan explained. "Theresa is working on locating him. She's gone back to the ranch."

The ranch? For a moment, Rees thought he'd lost his mind. The drugs flashing back on him. Then he realized what Morgan was doing. "I'm alone, Kerry. No one's forcing me to make this call. I got free and I'm all right."

A whoosh of breath in the receiver. "Okay. Thank God. I couldn't rule out them using you to find us. Torturing you. Or threatening something awful."

"I get it. It's okay."

If Rees had played along with the charade, Morgan could have inferred that someone outside their circle was listening in. Someone who wouldn't notice her using fake names and places. In fact, if he had thrown a couple of phony names right back at her, Morgan could have been dead certain he was speaking under duress.

"Are you someplace safe, Rees? Is anyone pursuing you?" Morgan asked.

"No. No, I'm all right. I was afraid the man who hit us with the car might have killed you. Wait, why *didn't* he shoot you?"

"I'm glad you're okay too, Rees."

"No, it's just—"

"Don't worry. Louis said almost the exact same line. Must be a scientist thing. We're at the library at San Francisco State. Professor Kazemi isn't here. But he's our man all right."

"He's not there?"

"He *was* here. He left a message, a new meeting place—the Ferry Building plaza, at five o'clock. He wants you to come alone."

"Can't blame him for that," Rees said. "That's in the Embarcadero, right?"

"Mm-hmm. Pier One."

"Okay. I'll find it. Give me a half hour with him alone. Then let's all reassemble there and figure out our next move."

"We'll try to meet you there around five-thirty. But there's a problem, Rees. The blond man knew we were coming to the library. He was here earlier asking around, looking for Kazemi and for you."

"How the hell did he know we were coming there?"

"I don't know."

Rees took a moment to think about what this might mean. "Okay, obviously he didn't know I'd already been grabbed. So that confirms it. At least two groups are after the results from the Kafir Project."

"Yeah, we think so too. And there's one other thing."

Because I don't have enough to deal with right now. "Okay, go ahead."

"I have Fischer's pouch, and the flash drive," Morgan said. "We plugged the drive into a computer in the library. There was a third video on there."

"I know. It's corrupted or something."

"Danni got it open. I think we know why they shut the whole project down now."

"I've been ... filled in on that part too. They weren't stopping with Islam." Rees felt a strange flutter in his chest. "What was on that video, Kerry?"

"A crucifixion. Or the aftermath, I guess you would say. The ... victim had been dead for at least two days."

Rees felt dizzy. He had a terrible premonition of the floor splitting open beneath him again. He closed his eyes and tried to clear his mind. "All right, I get the picture. Where does this leave us now?"

"We think the blond man is probably still around here somewhere, waiting for us to leave. I'm armed, but he has a big advantage."

"Because he knows where you guys are."

"Right," Morgan said. "I was thinking we could phone in a bomb threat. Then we leave with the crowd."

An image came to Rees's mind. People running and screaming as shots rang out. "I don't think you want to do that. He could use it for cover. Shoot everybody between you and him, then shoot you. It would look like a killing spree on a campus. With a threat already called in—you'd actually just be making it even easier for him."

"You're right. I'm ... not thinking well. I've got that damn awful headache again."

An idea came to Rees then like a hilltop vista. Stretched out and visible in a single glance. "What if *you* didn't call in the threat? I think I have something. And you've got just the right skill set there to pull it off."

"Let's hear it," Morgan said.

CHAPTER 54

THE FEMALE DCIS agent and the chick from Lawrence Livermore were doing something at a computer terminal on the library's first floor. A new guy with long black hair was hanging with them now.

Sabel had eyes on all of them, but only intermittently. It wasn't easy to spy on someone from close range. With so many exits on all sides of this building, though, he didn't really have a choice here. At least there were enough bookshelves and moving bodies to cover him pretty well.

As for Gevin Rees? Nowhere to be seen. Ditto the historian Burhan Kazemi. Herodotus.

Sabel just couldn't catch a break on this mission.

He'd tail these three when they left the library. Reacquire Rees through them if he had to. It seemed like his best shot now.

Sabel got a weird vibe all of a sudden. Nothing specific. Just more *energy* in the air.

Then he noticed something odd about how people were interacting. They were ... clumping more. And people were moving kinda quick between the clumps.

Something was definitely up.

A student with a dark brown complexion and straight hair, Indian maybe, came around the corner. He went all bug-eyed looking at Sabel, then turned and walked away real quick.

Okay, what the hell is going on here?

IT TOOK ONLY a few minutes for Danni to set up the Facebook account for *Nowisthetime Triplesix*, and a Twitter account for *nowisthetime666*.

It was Rees's idea, and she thought it was brilliant.

The blond-haired guy really did look a lot like a young Gary Busey.

She grabbed a picture of the well-known actor off the internet. A couple minutes in Photoshop and she'd tweaked Busey's face to look even more like the image she had in her mind.

That freaky blond guy looking up at her in her kitchen.

It was pretty well burned in.

Then Danni spammed the message and picture to every Facebook account that "liked" the SFSU Facebook page. Also tweeted it through the nowisthetime666 account.

> justice needs a killing hand today on the #SFSU campus I AM THAT HAND!!! die good and the master will welcome U!

Not five minutes passed before Danni thought she saw a reaction.

Morgan was looking around too. "They've all got their phones out," she said. "They're talking about it. I see the fear on their faces. I think it's working."

Louis looked unconvinced. "Yeah, I don't know. It doesn't mean—"

Danni cut him off. "Guys, look." She pointed to the library doors. "Over by the entrance."

Two Campus police in the doorway. Three students talking to them, making animated gestures. One of the students pointed into the library.

Louis jumped. "Did you just see that? Did you see that? She pointed right in here. He's in here. Holy shit, he's *in here!*"

"Keep it down, Louis." Morgan pulled her gun. She held it out of sight behind her back. "Get down, both of you. Behind the table. If he's in here, he's got to make a decision now."

Louis squatted on the floor as directed.

Danni didn't even consider it. "I'll help you spot him, Kerry. If he comes for us, *then* I'll duck."

Morgan seemed to know better than to argue with her right now. She just nodded and kept her eyes forward.

A moment later Danni heard a loud voice not far off. It came from around a corner, though. She couldn't make out the words. Then she heard a full shout.

"Hey! Hey! That's him!"

Heads turned.

A student was running around the corner, heading toward the library entrance.

He looked like he'd just witnessed a plane crash. "The guy is back there!" Pointing behind him now. "He's back there!"

Some students looked confused. Like they were just hearing about the threat. Others rushed right out of the library.

In moments, nearly everyone was up and moving en masse toward the exit.

The two campus cops raced inside, weapons drawn. They pushed through the stream of students, shouting for everyone to stay calm and leave the library.

Louis was still squatting at Danni's feet, behind the table. "What's going on up there?"

Morgan holstered her gun. "We're getting out of here. Now."

SABEL DIDN'T KNOW how the hell they did it, but they must have got his picture out there somehow.

He'd been burned.

He hit the nearest library exit at something between a walk and a run. A neat trick on his injured leg. The damn thing felt like it was gonna buckle on him any second now.

Once he got outside he slowed down some, and headed straight for a narrow band of trees that bordered the rear of the university grounds.

The first couple of students Sabel passed didn't react to him.

The next one he encountered looked up from his cell phone and stopped dead. "Don't. Don't, please." He took off running.

Jesus, someone really did a number on him.

Glancing over his shoulder, he spotted a pair of campus cops racing after him. About forty yards back and closing.

When he reached the tree line, he side-stepped behind a tree trunk and pulled the .38 S&W snub-nose. Only firearm he had left in his travelling armory. The gun had shit accuracy.

He'd have to aim for center of mass.

He waited for the two cops to cover a little more ground. Then he stepped out and fired.

He shot without aiming. Something he'd trained at for thousands of hours. One round a piece. Took about half a second.

They both dropped.

He thought he got one of them in the shoulder. The other one fell down holding his leg. Nicked them both. Distance just too great for accurate aiming with the .38's little nub of a barrel.

Whatever. They weren't chasing him anymore.

Students were running everywhere now. Freaked out by the gunfire.

It reminded Sabel of when he was a kid, and poured lighter fluid into an ant mound.

They had boiled out in a frenzied cloud. Thousands of them. He had some matches, and he was gonna light up the mound.

He just didn't.

On a whim, he walked away.

Curious about how it'd be later, after sparing so many little lives. Would it give him a zing, being a sort of benevolent ant god? Would he feel some of these magical emotions that other people were always talking about?

No. He didn't feel a damn thing.

The next day he returned and burnt out the mound.

As he climbed the fence on the far side of the trees, Sabel thought about those ants again. What if they were just too small and insignificant? Maybe he'd get a charge out of sparing a *human* life.

He doubted it, though. He doubted it very much.

CHAPTER 55

THEY WEREN'T FAR outside the university library when Morgan heard two gunshots in rapid succession.

People around them dropped to the ground or started running in random directions. Morgan, Danni, and Louis reflexively crouched down in the walkway they were on.

It had just turned into an active shooter situation.

Morgan had a tough call to make now. She wanted to get them all the hell out of there. But they were responsible, at least in part, for what was going down.

It didn't take long for her to decide.

Morgan pulled her badge, which had a chain tucked in the leather holder. She hung it around her neck. Good chance she'd have a gun in hand soon and she didn't want to be mistaken for a threat.

"All right, guys," she said, "It sounds like they found him. They're going to evacuate the university campus now. Stay deep inside a group whenever you can, and head back for where the bus dropped us off. I'll meet you out there." She stood up and started to leave.

Danni grabbed Morgan's sleeve and pulled her back down. "No. What are you doing?"

"I have to go help the campus police."

"Then I'm coming."

"You're not armed, Danni. If I'm watching out for you, I'm taking my attention off the threat. That makes it more dangerous for me out there."

Morgan could see Danni trying to fight the argument. But she was too smart not to agree.

She released Morgan's sleeve. "Okay. The bus stop then. I'll see you there." Danni voiced the last part like it was an order. And knowing Danni, it probably was.

Morgan nodded and stood up.

Louis tugged at her pants leg like an insistent child. "Hey, be careful out there, all right?"

"I'll see you both at the bus stop," Morgan said. Then she headed out at a trot.

A minute later, in the grassy area behind the library, Morgan saw six or seven students lying down. She couldn't tell if any of them had been shot, or if they were all just lying low.

Keeping low herself, she worked her way out onto the grass. She had an eye on the trees up ahead of her. That seemed like the best route out. Also a good spot to shoot from while you covered your retreat.

Morgan heard someone moaning nearby. She spotted a campus cop down. Another one next to him.

She scuttled over. Held up her badge. "I'm a federal officer. Where's the shooter?"

One of the men was holding his leg with both hands. Blood seeped out between his fingers. He jerked his chin toward the tree line. "The trees. At your twelve."

Morgan drew her weapon and scanned the trees. If the shooter was still in there, she was a wide open target. But she couldn't run for cover and leave two wounded officers out here.

She turned to the other campus cop. He'd taken one in the upper chest or shoulder. Lot of blood. He looked pretty shocky. Pale. Sweating.

"You're going to be all right," she told him. "We're gonna get you medical attention."

He managed a tight nod, but didn't try to speak.

Morgan scanned the tree line again. "Is anyone else out here injured?"

The cop with the leg wound answered her. "I don't think so. But it's possible. Sorry."

She sensed motion in the corner of her eye.

She turned quickly to see a man hurrying toward them, bent over at the waist. Not the blond man. Too well dressed for a student. Probably a teacher.

As the man got closer, he saw her gun and pulled up short, showing her his hands. "I teach physiology here. I know emergency medicine."

"We've got two injured here," Morgan told him.

The man came forward and steadied himself with a hand on Morgan's shoulder, then dropped down to one knee. He glanced back and forth between the two injured men. Seemed to be triaging them.

He started with the upper body wound. Morgan would have too. Copious blood flow there. The bullet might have hit the brachial artery.

"Keep your head down, if you can," Morgan told him.

The teacher nodded and sunk down a little more. "Yeah. Okay."

Morgan turned to the cop with the leg wound. "Can you point to exactly where the shooter entered the trees?"

"I think ..." he pointed a bloody, shaking finger, "see the two taller trees, close together?"

"Yes."

"Just left of that. There's a gap."

"I see it." She stood up. Multiple sirens now in the distance. She back turned to the two cops. "Hear that? Help's on the way guys."

If the blond man had taken off through those trees, he probably didn't look back. She could still ensure that the area was safe and clear now. She thought she owed them that much at least.

Morgan started toward the tree line, zig-zagging her way forward. Impossibly, given the situation, a line of dialog popped into her mind from an old comedy movie.

Serpentine, serpentine.

That had to be Danni's influence. Always quoting her own favorite lines. The thought almost made Morgan smile even then.

SINGLETON THOUGHT THE only bad thing about what just went down here was that Carl Truby had been right. Coming to the SFSU campus and backing up Sabel *just in case?* Not a move he ever would've made on his own.

But Truby didn't trust Sabel.

Understandable, since his only prior experience with this operative had been two failures in a row. Once on Fisherman's Wharf and again out in Pleasanton. Nothing like that had ever happened before with this rather extraordinary asset. In fact he had *never* failed them before this op. Not once.

But Carl Truby was calling all the shots now and he wanted Singleton to act as back up.

And he'd been right. The fat sonofabitch had been right.

He'd saved their asses with that move. These people they were after here were sharp. Really damn sharp. The trick they'd just pulled with the internet and Twitter? It was brilliant, really. He'd underestimated them.

He wouldn't do that again.

"I've got a medical kit," Singleton told the two campus cops. "I'm going to run and get it and I'll be right back."

He stood up and hustled toward the university's entrance.

About twenty steps away from the injured cops he pulled out the pocket-sized receiver. Turned it on. It registered a strong signal coming from the tracking bug he just planted on DCIS Special Agent Kerry Morgan's coat.

Singleton knew from experience the range would be sufficient to tail her from an unseen distance.

At least part of the plan was going very well. Finally.

Now he had that business with Truby to deal with.

Singleton would not walk away from all this with the goddamn sword of Damocles hanging over him. He'd made some calls the second he and Truby parted company at the airport.

So Truby had a dead man's switch and he couldn't be taken out? Fine. Now Singleton had one too. If anything happened to him, everything about the Kafir Project and Truby's involvement would wind up in the offices of ten different Senators and four large media outlets.

Two can play that game, Mr. Truby.

Nothing left to do now but to inform Truby about what had been done. Then watch the look on his chubby face when Singleton took control of the operation back.

As he neared the main entrance to the university grounds, the thought of all that made him smile. Despite the dark clouds moving in, the day seemed brighter already.

CHAPTER 56

REES EXITED THE cab in the Embarcadero a few blocks short of the Ferry Building.

He wanted to approach on foot and scout the area before meeting up with Kazemi, but first he had to address the potential problem of someone here recognizing him.

He ducked into one of the dozens of souvenir shops that dotted the waterfront. Only one hat in there big enough for him. Not particularly stylish. Robin's egg blue with a grinning cartoon crustacean above the words—*I got crabs at Fisherman's Wharf!* At least it had a wide brim he could pull down low.

He bought the hat along with some dark sunglasses, and walked out grateful that the shopkeeper didn't seem to recognize him.

Rees donned the hat and glasses as he started up the waterfront. Not much in the way of a disguise, but he hoped it would get the job done.

And just as that thought went through his head, he passed a row of newspaper vending machines. Three different papers, one of them national, had his smiling face splashed all over the front page.

Okay. So, that's not going to help.

It was funny, really. Rees's talent agent constantly pushed him to increase his exposure. Do more radio talk shows, TV game shows, even commercials. Well, he'd definitely increased his exposure this time. His agent was probably working on a book deal already.

At least dusk had arrived early. Cloud cover was blowing in from what looked like another storm front. The growing gloom would further hide his features. That was good.

He wondered if he should have the gun tucked into his waistband under his jacket, instead of zipped up in the gym bag. He'd tried it back in the motel room. It just felt like the gun wanted to fall out every time he took a step. So into the bag it went.

Rees stopped just short of the Ferry Building to reconnoiter. Vaillancourt fountain was just across the street. Rees didn't see anyone hanging around there. The clock tower on Pier One showed four-thirty on the dot. Still a half-hour before the meet. If the blond man was here—

"Don't turn around."

The voice had come from behind him.

The gun.

Rees tore at the zipper on the gym bag. It didn't budge.

Screw it.

He whirled around and swung the bag at his attacker. It struck the man in the side of his head with a loud *thonk*, knocking off his hat and sending him sprawling to the sidewalk.

Rees drew back his foot to deliver a swift kick to his face.

The man brought his arms up. He said something behind his hands that Rees couldn't make out. But he thought it might be...

Rees set his foot back down. "What did you say?"

The man lowered his hands. He pulled down a scarf that half-covered his face. "Herodotus. I said Herodotus."

Rees got his first good look. He immediately recognized Kazemi's round face and fringe of graying hair from a dust jacket on his bookshelf in New York. He reached down and offered his hand. "I'm so sorry, Professor Kazemi. Are you all right?"

Kazemi scooped up his hat. He grasped Rees's hand and labored up to his feet. Then threw his arms around Rees in a huge bear hug. He spoke into Rees's ear. "For the folks over there watching us."

Rees saw them now too. A handful of people walking nearby had stopped to observe the fracas he'd just made.

Kazemi released Rees from the hug and let out a raucous laugh. Then he hooked an arm around Rees's shoulder and started them walking. "Smile, Dr. Rees, smile. We're just a couple of feisty drunks who had a fight and made up."

Rees forced a smile as they continued to walk up the waterfront. Two old friends who maybe had a little too much to drink, that's all. Kazemi even staggered a bit for effect.

The people watching them turned and continued along their way.

"I'm so sorry," Rees said. "I wasn't expecting to meet you before I got to the Ferry Building."

Kazemi rubbed the side of his head. "Yes, well I thought it would be wise to lurk out around the perimeter. See who else might show up. Then I spotted your hat."

"My hat?"

"Even tourists don't wear that awful stuff. They buy them for souvenirs. And the sunglasses, with it being so dark out? I assumed it was supposed to be a disguise. So of course it *had* to be you. I was going to ask you to follow me quietly, but..."

"I'm an idiot, sorry." Rees took off the hat and tossed it onto a bench they were passing.

"No, you're just understandably a little edgy. Here..." Kazemi removed his scarf. "You can cover up a lot of your face with this. No one will think anything of it. And take my hat too. It's not quite as humorous as yours, but it will attract a little less attention, I think."

Rees donned Kazemi's Tilley hat and wrapped the wool scarf around his lower face. All the while apologizing profusely.

"I'm sorry as well," Kazemi said in return. "That I wasn't at the library for you. I waited a while and ... it just seemed too risky. What with everything last night." A worried expression pulled down the bulbs of his heavy cheeks. "Have you met with Fischer yet? Yesterday he instructed me to contact you at the Mark Hopkins, in the evening time. That's the latest communication we had. He and I were to meet last night at the Exploratorium, but he never showed up."

"I ... have bad news there," Rees said.

As they continued along the waterfront, Rees recounted the events of the past two days. Kazemi nearly broke down on hearing of Fischer's violent death.

His eyes were glassy and his voice cracked when he could speak again. "I told him. And then I thought he'd actually beat them. When he got out of Fermilab alive. Did he..." Kazemi choked up again. He blotted his eyes with a coat sleeve. "Did he have a chance to tell you how you inspired all of this?"

"What?" Rees thought he must have misunderstood the man. "No, that's not correct."

"Well there's my answer. Yes, it was some years ago, you did an interview with Skeptic Magazine."

Rees vaguely remembered the interview. "Yeah, but I'm pretty sure we didn't talk about time-viewing."

"No, but you did discuss how you were no longer a Mormon, in part because of what you learned about the history. And also because archaeology didn't support the Mormon scriptures. Jewish tribes in the ancient Americas, and other such nonsense."

Something from the interview came back to Rees. "I said the Abrahamic religions were fortunate in that *their* origins were lost in the distant past."

"Yes. Fischer was well into the theoretical work by then. He told me you got him thinking. What might happen if they weren't? Lost, I mean. The origins of those religions."

The revelation stunned Rees. He had trouble refocusing quickly. Kazemi had just asked him a question he didn't entirely catch. "I'm sorry, Professor, what was that again?"

"Your new companions," Kazemi said, "are they all right now? I've been reading about you three in the news. Livermore Labs."

"It's four of us now, actually. And I'm not sure how they're doing. Not at the moment. But if everything works out, they'll be meeting us at the Ferry Building plaza around five-thirty."

"I look forward to that." Kazemi steered them left at the corner, up Clay Street away from the waterfront. "But first we have a little errand to run."

As they walked, Rees tried to prioritize the million questions he had waiting. Finally he decided just to start throwing them out. "Dr. Fischer said *you* had the data. That's the time-recordings, right?"

"Yes. And the artifacts' molecular signatures. You know about all that?"

"I understand the principle. Fischer also said someone he was calling Anaximander had the recovered historical artifacts. The lectionary codex."

"Among other things, yes. His real name is Randolph Osborn. He was one of the project archaeologists. He's coming in from Jerusalem today. We're set to meet at the observation area on the south side of the Golden Gate Bridge. Six o'clock. I didn't want to risk bringing us all coming together at one time and place. Not yet."

"I guess that makes sense."

"But the thing is, I don't have the time-recordings."

"What?" It came out about twice as loud as Rees had intended. Thankfully no one was passing anywhere nearby.

Kazemi gave Rees's shoulder a reassuring pat. "I know where they are, Dr. Rees."

Rees ventured a guess. "In the cloud? Distributed storage? It must be massive."

"Oh my, no. Edward was adamant about that. He was afraid they could be traced and deleted. No, it's up there." He pointed up the street ahead of them.

Rees looked to the tall buildings ahead and on the left. "The Embarcadero Center?"

"A few blocks further there's a UPS store. That's where we're going. That's our little errand."

Once again Rees thought he must have misunderstood. "Fischer *mailed* the data to you? But ... isn't it something like five hundred exabytes?"

Kazemi nodded. "Something like that, yes. Anyway I have a rented mailbox. That's how we communicated secretly. Everything by mail. *Ink and paper*, he would say. That's how we'll beat them. Ink and paper. You have a gun, you said. In your bag?"

The change of subject had come so abruptly, it took Rees a beat to realize he'd been asked another question. "Oh, yes. It's in here."

"Right. You stand watch then, while I pick up the time-recordings."

That sounded like a spectacularly bad idea to Rees. "I've never fired a gun in my life."

Kazemi gave him another reassuring pat and smiled. "I'm sure the people you'll be shooting at won't know that."

"That's hilarious, Professor," Rees said, in a tone of voice he generally reserved for funerals.

CHAPTER 57

AS HE HURRIED up Clay Street, Kazemi glanced over at Dr. Gevin Rees, walking beside him. The man didn't look happy about his new job as an armed bodyguard.

Kazemi understood completely. It didn't particularly thrill him that his only defense against trained assassins was a middle aged TV astronomer.

Rees burned with questions, of course. Kazemi listened attentively as the man served up another one.

"Dr. Fischer had a flash drive with him when he and I met. My friends have it now. It had some video recordings on it."

"Ah, yes," Kazemi said. "We abstracted sounds and images from the full data sets. They don't prove anything by themselves, of course. They're like an impression made in clay, revealing only the surface. The full data sets record down to the molecular level in four dimensions."

Rees nodded along excitedly. "That's why you can trace the artifacts forward along the time axis, and locate them now."

"Or backwards to their origins. It's like digging for an underground power line. It might be hard to find at first, but once you do? It's quite easy to follow."

"I saw two of the videos," Rees said. "One of them looked to be from the Cretaceous Period."

"One of the first test runs."

"I thought so. I also saw a celebration of the Eucharist."

Kazemi remembered the first time Fischer had played that clip for him at SF State. How emotional it had all been. "That would be the lectionary sequence. I take it you understand the significance."

"Only because I've read your work on the subject, but yes. I do." Rees paused. He seemed to be steeling himself for something. "There was another video I didn't see, because it wouldn't open. The people who are helping us have seen it, though. It showed a ... crucified man."

They stopped together at the corner to wait for the light to change.

Kazemi turned and looked very directly at Rees. "You know we expanded the range of the project, beyond the original design."

"Yes, I know about that."

Kazemi spoke slowly, giving the words the weight they deserved. "Then you already understand, Dr. Rees, exactly what is in that recording."

Rees looked down at the sidewalk for a moment. When he looked back up, Kazemi saw pity on his face, and deep sadness in his eyes.

"They just left him like that," Rees said. "I never imagined. Never. Of course, tradition has it he was taken down before sunset. Because of the Sabbath."

Kazemi took a moment to consider how best to come at it all. Rees was a scientist. What he'd want were the unvarnished facts, plain and straightforward. "The Romans were brutal overlords, Dr. Rees. They were well aware of Jewish sensibilities regarding burial rituals and the Sabbath. How delicate an issue it was. Far from being accommodating, though, the Romans used it to their advantage."

Rees frowned. "How do you mean?"

"They found they had an even more powerful deterrent. Better than the execution itself. They let the bodies remain until—I'm sorry, there's just no delicate way to say this—until they rotted off. I don't know if you've read Crossan, but essentially he was right there."

"That's ... it's horrible."

"Yes. And yet the practice made sense from the Roman point of view. The thought of his body ending up like that would've given serious pause to even the most zealous Jew. To be denied a decent burial. To be left for crows and dogs. It would have been, for a devout Jew, literally a fate worse than death."

The crosswalk light changed to *walk*. The two men continued up Clay Street.

"Okay. So then what you really have is a recording of a Roman crucifixion," Rees said. "How did you know that it's..."

"Him? A multiplicity of factors. Including the correct time range. It was thirty-three C.E., by the way. And we have the location of the execution, on a rock formation near the walls of Jerusalem. A formation that does in fact resemble a cranium. But what fairly sewed it up was tracing his origins back to Nazareth. Which was a tiny, tiny little village, by the way. Although I was more or less certain even before that."

"Because of those other factors?"

"Yes, and because two days before his crucifixion, this man and his followers caused a major disturbance in the Temple. Which is why he was arrested. We also have a time-recording of him addressing a small gathering. He recites a parable about a mustard seed. I have to tell you, I damn near fainted. Further research with the same technology will only, I believe, confirm that who you saw there in that video—that is in fact Rabbi Yeshua, the Nazarene. The man who came to be known as Jesus Christ."

Rees went silent for a while. Kazemi assumed he was either digesting what he'd heard or deciding what to ask next. They stopped again at the last intersection before the UPS store and waited for the *walk* signal.

Rees turned to Kazemi. "You needed some relevant historical artifact too, though. It's the nature of the technology.

You have to recover something material to prove that a specific time-recording is genuine."

"That's right. And we did. The obvious one. Not much survived until the present. But the signatures verify what we do have."

The light changed. Rees was either ignoring it or hadn't noticed. "Bones then," he said. "The bones of Jesus Christ."

Kazemi nodded. "Fragments of bone. And some dentition. But you're wrong in an important way." He pointed up at the traffic light. "Let's go."

"Wait, how am I wrong?"

Kazemi stepped into the street and Rees followed right on his heels. "They aren't the bones of Jesus Christ. Jesus Christ is a quasi-mythical figure. What we recovered are the mortal remains of Rabbi Yeshua. A spiritual revolutionary. A brave and wise man, who died opposing repression by the Roman state and the Temple authorities as well."

They reached the other curb just as the light changed to red. Rees looked like an older version of one of Osborn's religious history students now. Eyes wide with wonder and filled with questions.

"And the empty tomb?" Rees asked.

"What do you think?"

He didn't hesitate. "There was no tomb."

"Of course not," Kazemi said. "Which is why Paul never mentions it. That was later legend. Yeshua was a penniless, itinerant faith-healer from a backwater village. He had no family or friends in Jerusalem. If a homeless man from Appalachia died in New York City, what are the chances his remains end up over in Woodlawn, in a three hundred thousand dollar, marble mausoleum? It would've been the equivalent of that kind of money we're talking about."

"And the Joseph of Arimathea story?"

"Well, first of all there never was a place called Arimathea, not then. The name itself is a kind of pun."

"A pun?"

"A pun or a play on *aristos mathetes*."

"Best disciple."

Kazemi smiled. "Ah, you have some Greek. And the word ending there, *ea*—that's a suffix that indicates a town name, like *ville* or *burg* would in English."

"So Arimathea would be read as ... Bestdescipleville?"

"That's exactly right. Joseph of Bestdescipleville. A fictitious name for a fictitious character. A literary invention to make credible a story that involved physical reanimation. Which is not even how Yeshua's early followers understood the idea of resurrection!"

"Yes, I've often wondered about that."

"Well, read Paul carefully. A seed goes into the ground, he says. And what comes out of the ground in *no way* resembles the seed. What dies is the natural, the corruptible. What rises is the *spiritual*. Flesh and blood cannot inherit the kingdom of God, he wrote. Now, does that sound like a corpse with holes in its hands?"

"Something happened to galvanize those men," Rees said. "That much is inarguable."

"Oh, certainly. Their leader, the man they believed to be the Messiah, who would restore Israel's independence from Rome and so much more, was executed by his enemies. Can you imagine the cognitive dissonance? Intolerable. Absolutely intolerable. It had to be resolved somehow. And abandoning everything they cherished and believed wasn't the way to do it. You know about Rebbe Schneerson, don't you, in Brooklyn?"

"I've heard of him. But my interest in Judaism has always been historical."

"Well, many of his followers hailed him as the true Messiah too. When Schneerson died of complications from a stroke, the idea that he would resurrect spread through the Lubavitcher community like a viral video. Sure enough, a number of his followers, including a prominent French Rabbi, believed they had seen him again. So he's not *really* dead, you see."

"They found a way out of the mental conflict, the Messiah's work being unfinished—which isn't possible if he's really the Messiah."

"Exactly. Just as Yeshua's followers did." Kazemi gestured to the UPS store coming up on the right. "And here we are."

Rees had not run out of questions by any means, and Kazemi promised him a more complete review of the project's results as soon as it became practical.

When they both were ready, Kazemi stepped inside the UPS store, and left Rees to guard the entrance.

REES HELD THE gun inside the gym bag, and tried not to look like he was about to have a heart attack every time someone passed by.

A middle-aged woman in a long winter coat sauntered past, walking some kind of toy breed dog.

A few minutes later a teenaged boy in tight orange pants rolled down the far side of the street on a skateboard, wheeling toward the waterfront.

Less than a minute later, a couple of young men exited the UPS store together, laughing loudly.

Each time someone appeared, Rees tightened his grip on the gun inside the gym bag a little more. Despite the growing cold, a trickle of sweat ran down his spine.

The minutes continued to creep agonizingly by.

Rees became convinced Kazemi had been in there much too long. Something must have gone wrong. Should he go in? Should he wait maybe just a little longer?

He started toward the door, and was reaching for the handle when it opened.

Kazemi burst through the doorway with an intense look on his face. He passed Rees without slowing. "Let's go. Go."

Rees trotted after him until he caught up. Kazemi was holding a padded mailing envelope in one hand. It had been torn open.

"What the hell happened in there?" Rees asked.

Kazemi pulled a book out of the mailing envelope and held it out to Rees. "Here."

Rees took it. The book was clothbound. He opened it as they both continued down Clay Street.

Handwriting inside. Dates and entries. Not a book, a diary. Rees felt his heart beating faster as he flipped through page after page of the now familiar, cursive script.

He looked over at Kazemi. "I don't understand. What the hell is this?"

Kazemi glanced back at him, then looked forward again and shook his head. "I haven't the faintest idea."

CHAPTER 58

REES THOUGHT DANNI Harris would never stop hugging him. And he didn't mind it one bit.

It was drizzling intermittently and darkness had already fallen by the time Morgan showed up at the Ferry Building plaza with the rest of them. Danni was so excited to see him, Rees worried that she was going to inadvertently shout out his name as she ran across the plaza.

When she finally released him, Rees introduced Professor Burhan Kazemi to her and the others. Naturally, everyone had a thousand questions. Rees asked them to set all that aside for the moment.

"First things first," Rees said. "We're meeting the man that Fischer called Anaximander over by the Golden Gate Bridge at six o'clock."

"Does he have the artifacts?" Morgan asked.

"We think so. We don't have much time so..." Rees turned to Kazemi. "Professor, would you please show them."

Kazemi brought out the food diary that they'd picked up at the UPS store and held it up.

"That's it," Rees said. "The diary I told you about on the phone. That's all we found in the mailbox Fischer directed the professor to."

"I think I recognize that." Morgan reached for the diary. "May I take a look?"

Kazemi handed it over. Morgan cracked the diary open, and squinted at the pages in the weak light out there on the plaza.

Rees could see it on Morgan's face—the same confusion and disbelief he'd felt himself. "So," he said to her, "what do you think?"

Morgan closed the cover and flipped the diary over, checking out the front and back. "Well, this looks a lot like what I saw Fischer writing in back at Fermilab. Saw it a few times. He said it was for posterity." She looked at Rees, her eyes hard now. "And it's all just food?"

"Every page," Rees replied. "What he ate, where he ate it, and when. And detailed notes about each meal. I notice he's not particularly fond of steamed carrots. I'm sure that's very important."

"Are we certain Edward Fischer really wrote that weird thing?" Danni asked.

"That's a good question." Morgan was wearing Fischer's leather pouch. She reached inside and pulled out the green spiral science notebook along with some loose papers. The notebook had warped and expanded now that it had dried out some. She opened it, and held it up alongside the food diary.

Rees stepped closer to get a better angle.

Except that the food diary appeared to have been written with a different pen—the letters more scratchy-looking, less smooth—the handwriting matched perfectly.

"It's definitely Fischer's writing," Rees said.

Kazemi rubbed his fleshy face and growled. "This is ridiculous ... I knew the man. Yes, he had his eccentricities. No more so than many exceptional minds do. But the whole mad scientist business—that was just something the press enjoyed playing up. Like Einstein's forgetfulness." He shook his finger at the diary. "I will tell you this. Whatever that is, it's not insanity. That much I know."

"Well, it's not the time-recordings either," Rees said. He noticed Morgan wincing, her eyes squeezed shut. "Are you okay?"

Morgan gave him a smile that seemed forced. "Just tired." An odd look came over her. "Could you take these for me, please?" She held out the diary along with the science journal and loose papers.

Rees grabbed it all and dropped it into the gym bag he took from the motel room, keeping a worried eye on Morgan while he did.

Morgan looked as if she were about to say something. She brought a hand up, then stretched out both arms ... and began to sway.

Danni quickly stepped in. "Kerry, are you all right?"

Morgan grabbed Danni's shoulder to steady herself. "My head is..."

Rees rushed to Morgan's other side. He couldn't see well in the low light, but her face looked extremely pale. "Let's get her somewhere she can sit down."

Rees and Danni helped Morgan into the Ferry Building. Louis and Kazemi followed close behind. They sat her down on the nearest open bench. She slumped forward, head in hands.

Rees noticed they were drawing some looks from ferry passengers who walked past. Not much could be done about that right now.

He crouched down in front of Morgan and gently lifted her chin. "Look up at me, Kerry."

She did. Rees could see her face clearly now under the Ferry Building's halogen lights. And that raised a frightening question.

It's bright in here. Why the hell are her pupils still dilated?

And then, looking back and forth again, he saw it was worse.

Only *one* pupil was dilated.

CHAPTER 59

SOMEONE HAD SECRETLY jammed an air hose into the base of Morgan's skull and was inflating it to a thousand pounds per square inch. Nothing less could explain the insane pressure and pain inside her head.

Rees got up out of the way as a very worried-looking Danni crouched down in front of her to take his place.

Danni took her hand. "Kerry, you don't look so hot."

"Well, it's been a long day and I haven't touched up my makeup."

Danni didn't even grin. "I'm glad you can still joke, but this is serious."

Morgan looked up at Rees, Louis, and the history professor, Kazemi. They were all staring down at her on the bench. By their expressions, you'd think they were keeping vigil beside her death bed.

I must look as bad as I feel.

"Kerry, you've got one pupil dilated." Rees didn't bother explaining. He seemed to assume she'd understand. She did. They were talking brain injury here.

"Yeah," she said. "My vision is going in and out." Even as she said it, Rees's face started to blur.

"When did the headache come back?" a fuzzy Rees asked her.

Morgan tried to remember. It was getting harder to think. "Not long after the car crash. The second impact must've compounded the injury, when I got slammed at Livermore."

"That's what I was thinking." Rees and the surroundings were coming back into focus again.

The concern on Danni's face had been replaced by a deceptive calm. Morgan knew that look. Danni had just made a decision that all the forces of heaven and hell couldn't change. Morgan could only hope it was a good one.

"We're getting you to a hospital now," Danni said.

Morgan looked up past Danni. "Louis, please call 911 for me."

Danni's jaw actually dropped.

"Hey," Morgan said to her, "I'm not thrilled about it. But if I've got a bleed or a blood clot in my brain, there aren't a lot of options here. Plus I think you all can make it to the finish line without me at this point."

Rees grasped Kazemi's shoulder. "Actually, Professor Kazemi and I can finish this without any of you. And we probably should. The man we're meeting by the bridge isn't expecting a crowd. We could spook him." He looked down at Morgan. "As soon as we have the artifacts, I'm calling the press. That should make things a little safer for you, Kerry. At least for the short term."

"Right," Morgan said. "I almost forgot, I'm going to be arrested now. And you guys too, pretty soon." She looked up at Louis. "*You* don't need to be here. They might not connect you to all this."

Louis glanced up and took a deep breath. When he looked down again he was nodding. "Yeah. Yeah, I do. I'm in this for the whole ride."

Danni smiled at him as he pulled his phone to make the 911 call.

Moments later it was all done. The ambulance would arrive in minutes.

Morgan tried to give her gun to Rees. But, to her great surprise, he already had one with him. *Long story*, he told her.

There wasn't even time for appropriate goodbyes, just quick assurances that they'd all see each other again soon. They hoped.

Rees and Kazemi raced off to get a taxi. Morgan's eye caught on one of the other passengers leaving the Ferry Building. She wasn't sure why, though. Just something about him.

"How are you feeling now, Kerry?" Danni squeezed Morgan's hand.

"Kind of stupid, really."

"You're having trouble thinking?"

"Yeah, but that's not what I mean. I mean stupid for what I did to you. And us. Back then."

Morgan looked up at Louis, standing behind Danni and listening to their conversation. It wasn't until Danni also turned back and stared at him that he got the hint and stepped away.

Danni turned back to Morgan. "It wasn't stupid, Kerry. I just got a little ahead of ... well, of us I guess."

"You're right, it wasn't stupid. That's just a copout. It was something much worse than that." Morgan tried to think of how to say it. That she'd really just been afraid. Afraid to be a part of something she couldn't completely control or protect.

A couple. Or even a family.

She wanted to explain to Danni, to this incredible woman in front of her, how absolutely idiotic that seemed now.

But her vision started fading again. Not blurry like before. Going dark now. She looked up at the halogen lights. It was as if someone was dimming them slowly. She looked straight out ahead again at the indistinct shapes of people walking past.

And then everything turned to shadows. Just shadows.

With nothing visual out there to distract her, she noticed that a part of her mind was still working on identifying that man. The one she'd seen leaving the Ferry Building just after Rees and Kazemi.

His face was familiar. *That's* why she noticed him. But familiar from where?

And then she had it.

The teacher from the university. The one who said he knew emergency medicine. That was him.

"Kerry? What's happening?" Danni's voice, coming from directly in front of her.

Morgan spoke to the shadow that was all she could make out of Danni now. "I can't see anything. It's just dark shapes."

"It's okay. The ambulance is on the way."

The fear Danni was trying to hide was leaking into her voice. Morgan was afraid too. Terrified, really. But she stuffed all that. She had to focus on that teacher. She tried to think back in time, through the pain and fog in her head.

Out there on the lawn at the university, with the two downed officers, what had happened? She replayed it ... until a moment stuck out.

He put a hand on my shoulder. Morgan tried to reach back there with her fingers. She couldn't quite get to the spot he'd touched. "Danni, look on my coat. Back of my left shoulder."

A moment later Morgan felt a hand plucking something off the fabric back there.

Then Louis's voice, somewhere up behind Danni. "What is that thing?"

"Does it look electronic?" Morgan asked.

Danni's voice said, "Yeah. Yeah, it does."

Morgan held her palm up. "Set it in my hand." She felt Danni's fingers graze her palm. Then she closed her fist. Worked the thing down to her fingertips and rolled it between them. "It's a bug."

"No, no, no. What the hell? I mean, c'mon, what the hell? Who stuck that on you?" And that would be Louis, not keeping it together.

"Someone back at the college," Morgan answered. "He said he was a teacher. I just saw him again here in the Ferry Building."

Danni's voice said, "So they've been listening to us this whole time?"

To Morgan the device felt too large for just audio surveillance. Those were really tiny these days. "I'm not sure. But I think it may be a tracking bug. I think he used me to find Rees and Kazemi. And now he's going after them. He's following them to the man who has the artifacts."

"We have to call Rees right now." Danni's voice had gone high and shrill. "We have to warn him."

"I'm on it." Louis said.

"No, you're not."

The voice had come from somewhere behind Morgan. Male. Slight southern accent. Morgan recognized it instantly.

"Any of you move, or yell ... I'll kill all of you right here. Don't care who sees it either. Understand?"

The blond man. He was here.

CHAPTER 60

THE TAXI STOPPED in the parking lot below the Golden
Gate Bridge's southern observation area. Rees was fairly
confident he and Kazemi hadn't been followed here to the
rendezvous spot.

That didn't mean the man they were meeting up with
hadn't been either.

Just before he exited the cab, Rees slipped his hand into the
gym bag slung over his shoulder, and gripped the gun in there.
They were close to pulling this whole thing off now and he
wasn't about to let up his guard and blow it in the final stretch.

Together Rees and Kazemi crossed the parking lot as a
steady drizzle drifted down through the lights onto empty
parking spaces. The foul weather had chased all but a few
determined sight-seers away. Anyone coming for them
wouldn't have the luxury of hiding in a crowd, at least.

Downhill to the east of them, Fort Point guarded the
entrance to San Francisco Bay. Off to the north, the Golden
Gate Bridge arced across to the Marin headlands, its curving
road deck illuminated by a string of amber streetlamps. Rain
and mist erased the top halves of both towers.

They arrived at the Bridge Café, the arranged rendezvous
point, as Kazemi's watch read six o'clock straight up. Right on
time.

No one was waiting for them.

The place was closed. Unfortunate, because Rees really
could've used a large, hot coffee about then. He was wet and
very cold. Once again.

After a brief discussion Rees moved far enough off so that Osborn, when he arrived, wouldn't spot an unknown man standing with Kazemi and shy away.

And then they both waited.

A handful of people passed back and forth over the next half hour, heading to the stairs for the observation area or coming back down to the parking lot. None of them gave Kazemi a second look.

Though he wasn't squeezing the gun grip hard, Rees's hand was starting to ache. And it was beginning to look like their man wasn't going to show.

First no data cache, and now no artifacts. It was all falling apart right there in front of him.

To occupy his mind with less gloomy thoughts, Rees counted car headlights on the bridge and wondered what ordinary, run-of-the-mill business their drivers were engaged in. Whatever it was, he would happily trade places with any one of them right now.

He turned back to check on Kazemi again.

The door to the Bridge Café was open.

A man stood there in the darkened space, looking out. He said something to Kazemi, who turned around and waved Rees over.

Osborn. It had to be him. He was already here.

INSIDE THE CAFÉ, Osborn apologized profusely. He explained that he'd arrived about an hour early. He'd sat down to wait, and then the jet lag promptly dragged him right off to sleep.

He led Rees and Kazemi to a table by the service bar. Rees noticed Osborn had a pronounced limp. He thought the man might have been injured, until he saw the one platform shoe.

"So tell us, how did you arrange all ... this?" Kazemi gestured around the empty café.

Osborn sat down in a chair next to a white, plastic shopping bag, the heavy-duty, reusable kind. "Oh, well, Amsel sent me off with quite a roll of bills. You wouldn't believe the things strangers will do for you when the price is right. The owner of this fine establishment was very happy to rent it out for the night. Ten thousand dollars cash, and he suddenly lost all curiosity in what I wanted it for. The place is insured, I suppose."

Rees glanced around. A couple of neon beer brand signs provided the only dim lighting. He took a seat at the table across from Osborn, and Kazemi sat down next to him.

Osborn offered Rees a weary smile. "I'm sorry to be meeting you under these tense circumstances, Dr. Rees. So Edward Fischer recruited you too, did he?"

"I didn't really know what for at the time," Rees said.

Osborn laughed at that. "I can only imagine your surprise then when you learned."

Rees nodded more or less automatically. He was trying to listen, but he couldn't take his eyes off that plastic shopping bag on the floor beside Osborn's chair. "Is that it? The artifacts?"

Osborn glanced down at the bag. "Yes, not a very appropriate means of conveyance. Lost my valise in Golden Gate Park today."

Just seeing the bag and knowing its contents sent a thrill up Rees's spine.

When their authenticity was validated, and he believed it would be, the Jesus relics alone would become the most valuable material objects on earth. Not just historically, either. In all likelihood monetarily as well. Every shard of bone in there would make a Fabergé egg look like a Happy Meal prize. Throw in the lectionary codex, and the contents of that plastic shopping bag down there could be worth literally billions to the right collectors.

"I have an important question to ask you now," Kazemi fixed Osborn with a stern gaze.

Osborn swallowed and nodded. "Yes."

"Restrooms are which way?" Kazemi smiled. "I was going to head off to the bushes if we had to wait for you very much longer."

"I'm so sorry about that." Osborn said.

He directed Kazemi to the left of the service counter. Kazemi got up and carefully edged his way around the table in the low light, then walked off past the bar and around a corner.

As they waited for him to return, Rees quickly recapped the events of the last two days for Osborn. He concluded by showing him Fischer's food diary.

Osborn flipped through the pages with a bemused look on his face. "Well, that's just plain bizarre." He closed the diary and handed it back to Rees. "Do you think he lost his mind?"

Rees returned the diary to the gym bag and set that on the floor. He paused to seriously consider Osborn's question. "I don't know. I'm hoping maybe there's a code or a clue in there. Something that points to where the data cache really is."

"Without the complete time-recordings, we can't validate the historical artifacts. And vice versa. I take it you understand how all this works?"

"Basically, yes. Though as far as the artifacts go, I only know about the lectionary codex and the, uh, bone fragments. I was told you looked even further back."

"Yes. Fischer's aim was to search back as far as the birth of the Abrahamic religions, to Judaism. And that's what we did."

Rees was still sopping wet from standing out there in the drizzle for more than a half hour, but he didn't even feel the cold now. His excitement and curiosity had completely possessed him. "This may not be the time for it, but ... I'm very interested to know what you found out. Actually, strike that. I'm *dying* to know what you found out."

Despite his obvious exhaustion, a shared passion warmed Osborn's expression. "I should think you would be. It's really too much to go into briefly. But I will tell you we answered a long-standing question. Why no one had ever found any evidence of a large scale conquest of Canaan by the Israelites returning from Egypt after the Exodus."

"Because it was a peaceful infiltration?"

"Well, in a sense, I suppose." Osborn smiled. "You see, they never left."

"What?"

"The Israelites didn't conquer the Canaanites, Dr Rees. They *were* Canaanites. Just one particular tribe of Canaanites. Their patron god, Yahweh, was one of the seventy sons of El, the Canaanite father god. Only much later did Yahweh graduate from being a member of the Divine Council to being identified with El himself."

"That part sounds a lot like Theodore Mullen's theory."

"Yes, essentially. Except it's something more than a theory now. Mullen was only working from some Qumran Deuteronomy fragments and the Ugaritic texts. We have a lot more than that. We can establish as fact that the first Israelites were Canaanites, just as the first Christians were Jews, and the first Muslims were Christians. The pattern repeats itself down through history. A subgroup making itself into something else by means of a new religion."

"Something politically autonomous," Rees added. "Subject to new rulers."

Osborn nodded. "Yes. And arguably that was the whole point."

"And the Exodus? That was a total invention?"

"No, not entirely. The Exodus story was borrowed and reworked from the history of a people the Egyptians called the

Hyksos. Far from being slaves in Egypt, though, the *Hyksos* were Semitic rulers of the Nile Delta. Until they were expelled under Ahmose the 1st, that is."

"But the ramifications here ... if there was no Exodus, I mean *provably* no Exodus—then there was no Moses either," Rees said, trying to appreciate that this was now verifiable fact. "That's, that's just huge. More than huge. There isn't a word that big."

Osborn was nodding his head. "Yes. No Moses. And so of course no Ten Commandments. Not in the sense that God sent them down from a mountaintop. So there you have it. The whole historical foundation for Christianity and Islam crumbles."

Rees felt the enormity of it as a strange kind of numbness all over. It was hard to appreciate how significant this really was. How much it might change.

"And that's why," Osborn continued, "I'm not entirely sure we should make all of this public."

That caught Rees completely off guard. A moment passed before he asked, "Why not?"

Osborn rubbed his eyes. He looked bone tired now. "I'm a scientist like yourself, Dr. Rees. I couldn't say no to the chance to explore all this history. But I've had to ask myself too, do I want to destroy the faith that brings meaning and comfort to billions of people?"

"But would it?" Rees countered. "Whatever's wise and true in any of these religions—that has nothing to do with history. That part won't change. What changes now, at least for the fundamentalists, is how we *know* what's wise or true."

"You're talking about the epistemic authority of the texts."

"Yes, exactly that. Their authority as arbiters of truth." Something Fischer said came back to Rees just then.

It's all coming together. The end of their authority.

"The moral authority of these texts will take the big hit now," Rees said. "Right alongside their fictitious histories. And by extension—well, at least you'd hope—the *political* authority of the fanatics out there. Because that authority is essentially derived from those texts. I think that's what Fischer was aiming for all along."

Osborn's focus seemed to turn inward for a moment. Then he looked out at Rees again with renewed intensity. "And is that what *we're* aiming for, Dr. Rees? Fischer's gone. This is all our responsibility now."

Rees had considered that fact at great length already. "When I think of the beheadings, and the mass executions. Young girls shot in the face for ... just for promoting female literacy. Homophobia, and lunatics who justify poisoning the environment behind a single line in the book of Genesis. The possibility that we might undermine the authority of *those* people? Well, I think it's worth a shot. Don't you?"

At that moment it occurred to Rees that Kazemi had been in the restroom quite a while. And then, as if on cue, the history professor stepped into view around the service counter.

Rees knew something was wrong before he had any idea why he knew it.

Another man stepped into view following close behind Kazemi. A black man in a dark business suit. They both stopped.

Rees reached for the gun in the gym bag near his feet.

"Don't do that." The man displayed the gun he'd been pointing at Kazemi's back. "You want to keep your hands up where I can see them. Now both of you stand up slowly. Move away from the table."

Rees had learned enough of firearms in the last two days to recognize this one had a silencer on it. He did as he was directed and so did Osborn.

"Go stand with them," The man waved Kazemi over with the barrel of the gun.

Kazemi came and lined up beside Rees and Osborn.

Rees glanced furtively at the front windows of the café. The blinds were down so he couldn't gage the thickness of the panes. But if he could get a few steps in before the gunman noticed, he might make a dive through the glass. There was nothing he could do for Kazemi and Osborn here. Out there he could at least shout for help.

The gunman's eyes lasered in on Rees. "Dr. Rees, because you look like you're getting some kind of foolish idea, we're going to keep you busy. Those two bags down there. I want you to kick those over to me."

Bang, bang, bang.

Rees jumped at the sound. Pounding. It was coming from the back of the café. They probably had a rear service entrance to this place.

"Hey. I hafta use the bathroom." A voice shouting through the door. Male voice. Slurred.

The gunman kept his weapon pointed at them. He narrowed his eyes and held his forefinger to his lips.

Bang, bang, bang. The same voice again. "Hey! Hey, I know there are people in there."

The gunman turned his head, eyes still on Rees and the others, and shouted back at the door. "We're closed. Find a public restroom."

"They are all locked."

Bang, bang, bang.

Some quality of that voice sounded familiar to Rees. But he couldn't place it.

"This is an emergency!" the voice outside insisted more loudly. The pounding started up again and didn't stop this time.

Bang, bang, bang, bang, bang...

As the pounding continued, the gunman sidled over to the service door, keeping a wary eye on his three captives. He unlocked the door, then aimed his gun at it. He closed his other hand around the doorknob.

Rees was trying to decide if he should shout some kind of warning, when the door swung violently out and open, jerking the gunman along with it.

Rain blew in through the dark entryway. There was a loud and rapid clicking sound next.

The gunman stayed on his feet, but he dropped his weapon. His whole body stiffened, and he made a strange, vibratory groan. After a couple of seconds he fell backwards to the floor, jerking and twitching.

The clicking sound continued for a few more seconds and stopped abruptly.

A man in a tan trench coat stepped in through the open door, dripping wet. He was holding a Taser gun. He stooped down and retrieved the handgun from the floor.

The other man hadn't been knocked out by the Taser. He was clearly stunned, though. He struggled to sit up.

The man in the trench coat aimed and fired twice. There was that loud *pop, pop* sound of a suppressed firearm that Rees actually recognized.

The man on the floor fell back flat. He stopped moving.

His killer closed the door behind him. Then he turned and looked straight at Rees. Water dripped off the end of his dark, misshaped nose.

His eyes burned with the same rage Rees had seen back in the motel room. Even in the café's dim light the green in them sparkled.

Faraj. The man who had abducted Rees.

He was back from Hell.

CHAPTER 61

LOUIS EYED WHAT had to be the barrel of a gun.

It was being pointed at them from inside the pocket of the blond man's pea coat. Nothing for the ferry passengers going by to see here. Probably just looked like four people having a conversation by one of the benches.

In a relaxed voice the blond man told them all just to chill out. His people were only after the time-recordings and the artifacts, he said. They weren't going to hurt anyone.

Louis had to keep fighting against the impulse to hope it was true. He kept telling himself this was like being on a hijacked airliner post 9/11. Screw whatever they say to get your cooperation. You're not gonna land somewhere and negotiate.

You're going into the side of a building. Period.

Any plan of attack he could think of would improve their chances. Up from none at all.

The emergency rescue vehicle that Louis had called for would be showing up any time now. And when the blond man saw the paramedics arriving, and port security running over too—his best option would be to just kill the three of them and split.

The blond man was easing around now to the front of the bench that they'd sat Morgan down on. He raked his eyes across them. "Stay quiet, and take off your coats. All of you. Slowly."

He's checking to see if we're armed, Louis thought.

And Morgan was armed. But she was blind now. In a few seconds the blond man would have her gun. Then any chance they had of getting out of this situation alive would vanish.

Morgan stood up and started to take off her coat. At first it confused Louis—she didn't have to stand up to do that. She hadn't been sitting on the coat, it wasn't that long.

And then he understood.

Jesus, she's gonna go for her gun. She can't even see him. He'll kill her!

The blond man skipped back a step and pointed the gun in his pocket at Morgan. "Sit back down Special Agent Morgan. Or you're killing everybody. You understand?"

Morgan stopped. She had her jacket partway off. She shrugged it back on and sat down on the bench. Then she started to remove it again.

Louis glanced over at Danni. She didn't look scared at all. She looked ... angry. Really angry. She was taking her coat off now too.

Louis slid his own coat off one arm, then the other. He started to wad it up, thinking he could maybe throw it at the guy then dive into him. He would knock the man down, then shout at Danni to grab Morgan's gun.

A siren wailed in the distance. The first responders were almost here.

Louis had to do something really soon.

He glanced down at Morgan on the bench. She had one side of her jacket completely off and was beginning to remove the other side. The side where she kept her weapon holstered.

When he sees the gun, he'll be totally focused on that, Louis thought. *Then I can—*

Morgan's coat came off then revealing ... her empty holster.

Louis remembered Morgan trying to give the gun to Rees earlier. But Rees didn't take it. Or did he? Was he remembering this right?

Morgan folded up her coat, and just before she dropped it at Danni's feet she flashed something at them.

Her gun. It was in there.

Now Louis got the plan. *She's trying to get the gun to Danni.*

Morgan had used the extra motion of standing up and sitting back down for misdirection. She knew that *she* couldn't use the gun, so she stashed it in her coat and let them see it.

Louis watched the blond man's eyes go straight to Morgan's empty shoulder holster.

"He took her gun away," Danni volunteered. She'd been watching his eyes too. "Your guy back at Livermore. He took it. He shot the other DCIS agent with it."

"Shut up." The blond man scrutinized Morgan's face. "What's wrong with you, Kerry? Your eyes look funny."

"Concussion." Morgan's voice sounded weak. "From the explosion last night. I may have a brain bleed. It's screwing up my vision."

The emergency vehicle's siren had grown much louder. The blond man had to be hearing it too by now. In a few more seconds, he'd realize it was coming here.

For the moment he was still focused on Morgan. He made a sympathetic face. "Well, I hate to tell ya this, Special Agent Morgan, but you look pretty sketchy. You just might not make it."

In the corner of his eye, Louis saw flashing lights out through the Ferry Building's glass doors. The emergency vehicle was pulling up outside.

The blond man turned toward the doors. His face tightened. He saw the lights too. He knew.

Now. Throw the coat now. Louis cocked back his arm to throw.

Without warning Morgan's head slumped to her chest. She rolled forward and started to fall off the bench.

Danni reflexively dove to catch her.

"No!" The blond man barked the order at Danni.

She couldn't have followed it even if she wanted to. She was already in mid-flight.

She stretched out her arms, and Morgan fell right into them.

They tumbled together to the floor. Landing right on top of Morgan's coat. On top of the gun.

The blond man turned back to the windows of the Ferry Building again. Flashes of red and blue light played off his face.

He wasn't looking at Louis.

Now's my chance.

Louis raced at their assailant with desperate speed, legs churning.

The blond man wheeled and fired a shot through his coat pocket.

It was like a gorilla just punched him in the chest. Louis felt his cheeks puff out. He stumbled and hit the floor, sliding to a stop at the man's feet.

As he lay there, another shot rang out. Then five or six more. Then it all stopped.

Louis looked up.

Danni was up on her knees now with Morgan's gun in her hand. She was still pulling the trigger. The empty gun click-clicking, again and again.

The blond man stood right over Louis with his hand in his pocket. There was a scorched hole there in his coat now.

Through the ringing in his ears, Louis could make out the wail of the emergency vehicle's siren winding down.

The blond man swayed for a moment, then took a wider stance to steady himself. He looked down at Danni with an odd expression on his face. Confusion.

He pulled his gun from his pocket and looked at it strangely. Like he didn't recognize it. Then he pointed it forward.

Danni threw her body across Morgan.

The blond man just stood there with his gun pointed at Danni and Morgan. But he didn't fire. Seconds ticked by.

Louis heard shouting in the distance. Heavy footfalls echoed across the terminal. He turned his head to see paramedics jogging through the Ferry Building's glass doors.

When Louis looked back, the blond man was still gazing down at Danni and Morgan.

He lowered his gun.

Then he smiled. "I'm your God. I'm letting you live." He continued to stare at them. Bright red blood at the corners of his mouth now. He blinked several times and turned his face up toward the lights.

Slowly, his expression changed to consternation. And then something like ... disappointment.

He looked out straight ahead again, eyes unfocused. "Yeah," he said to no one in particular. "That's what I thought." Then he fell forward, body twisting, and landed on his side with a thud.

Louis tried to climb to his feet and to his great surprise pulled it off. The pain was coming, though, he could feel it. Burning its way through the shock. He couldn't tell exactly where he'd been shot, but it felt wet and sticky inside his shirt.

And he could hear a kind of sucking sound when he inhaled.

As Louis watched her, Danni rolled off of Morgan and rose up on her knees. She looked down into Morgan's face. "Kerry? C'mon, Kerry. Stay with me. You have to stay with me."

"The paramedics are here, Danni," Louis said. "It's gonna be all right. It's gonna be all right."

Danni pressed an ear to Morgan's mouth, then looked up at Louis with terror in her eyes. "She's not breathing."

CHAPTER 62

THIS ALL WASN'T happening. It couldn't be.

Rees's former captor wasn't *really* here inside this little café by the Golden Gate Bridge. He was just hallucinating all this. A drug flashback. That's what part of Rees's mind kept trying to tell him.

And he had no time for that shit.

He dropped to his knees there on the café floor, and reached inside the gym bag. His fingers quickly found the gun. As he pulled it out, a foot swung in and kicked it from his hand. It spun off into the darkness somewhere.

The foot drew back again and smashed into Rees's face.

He flew backwards. His head smacked something hard, and for a second he saw stars.

Rees tried twice to sit up, and managed it on the third effort.

Faraj stood there looming over him, holding the gun that he took from the man who now lay dead at his feet. He pointed it directly at Rees's forehead.

"You have caused me no small amount of trouble, Dr. Rees." Faraj flicked the gun toward where Kazemi and Osborn were still standing side by side in shock. "Get over there with them. Now."

Rees got up and did as instructed. Right then and again a moment later when they were all ordered down on their knees, hands behind their heads.

"We had an agreement, Dr. Rees." Faraj spoke with the restrained impatience of a schoolteacher explaining something to a slow student. "I consider such pacts sacrosanct. A matter of honor."

"Bullshit." Rees had an intuition that playing to the man's strange morality might win him some leverage. "You *lied* to me. You said the condition was permanent with a large dose."

"I never lie. And you assume far too much. For one thing, that I am naïve to the drug. I am not. I have taken it innumerable times."

Rees understood instantly. *He's developed a tolerance.* "My god, you do that to yourself?"

Faraj showed Rees a sad smile. "And still you do not see? Without tracing its heights *and* its depths, one cannot know life's full measure. I have lived my life more fully, with more amplitude, than perhaps any man alive."

Kazemi and Osborn had wisely opted to remain silent through this freak show. They couldn't have any idea what the hell was going on here anyway.

Faraj gestured to the gym bag on the floor between them. "I recognize my property. Is my cell phone in there? Foolish of you to keep that, you know."

That's how he found us, Rees realized. *He tracked his own cellphone. Stupid. Stupid.*

Faraj pointed the gun at Osborn's bag next. "The plastic bag there. What does it contain?"

"Historical artifacts," Osborn blurted out. "There are more. They're priceless. You'll never get the rest of them if you shoot us."

"I require only enough to prove out the technology. And by my understanding even a tiny fragment will do. Isn't that correct?" He turned to look directly at Rees. "I am still assuming the science was your purview. And though you have told me once this technology was lost, I am now less inclined to believe you."

"Yes, I lied to you before," Rees confessed. He needed to play a new angle. "I do have the technology. Fischer explained it to me in detail. It'll be a hundred years before anyone catches up to Fischer's vision. I can show your people the science that died with him. And in return," he nodded toward Osborn and Kazemi, "you let them go."

It was a bald-faced lie. With Fischer's detailed notes and math as a guide, any number of competent physicists could grasp the science. And those things all lay right there in the gym bag in front of them. Rees watched his enemy and waited.

Would he buy it?

Faraj's face softened. It took on a look of kind concern. "You do understand how this will end for you, Dr. Rees? You broke our agreement. My promise to spare you the full effects of the drug is rescinded. Once you have transmitted the technology to my employers, *and* we confirm that it works ... you will still have to settle up with me."

He bought it.

This play could save Osborn's and Kazemi's lives. But at what price? To suffer in delirious, hellish torment for decades.

Rees looked at the gun. When Osborn and Kazemi were safe, he could always rush his captor. The equivalent of suicide by cop. It still beat the alternative. Lousy as it was, it actually represented the best option here.

"All right," Rees said. "I accept your terms. Now let them go."

Faraj reached a hand into his coat pocket. It came out holding a syringe filled with the familiar red fluid. He flipped the safety cap off and nodded at Kazemi and Osborn. "I will need to render both of them temporarily ineffectual, for practical reasons."

Rees understood. If Faraj didn't kill Osborn and Kazemi, then at the very least he needed to incapacitate them for a while. There were police stationed not a minute away from here no doubt, over at the bridge's toll plaza. Faraj had to keep them quiet until he had Rees safely out of the area. And he could accomplish that quite well with a small, transient dose of the drug.

Just a little taste of hell.

Faraj approached Kazemi with the syringe, keeping the gun on him the entire time.

Kazemi raised his hands defensively. "No. No, what are you doing? What is that?"

"He's just going to knock you out." The calmness in his own voice surprised Rees. "So he can get me out of here without you calling for help. You'll be all right when it wears off." No point telling him about the horrors that were coming.

On Rees's other side, Osborn spoke up. "This is crazy. We don't know what's in there. Shoot me if you want. I'm not letting you stick that needle in me."

"In fact you are not." Faraj tossed the hypodermic on the café floor. "Dr. Rees here will inject you."

It took a moment, but Rees got that part too. If Faraj tried to give the injections himself, he'd be much too close. One of them might grab for his gun.

Faraj pointed down. "That is a filled, ten milliliter syringe. Inject two full millileters of the drug into each of your companions, Dr. Rees."

Rees picked up the syringe. He briefly imagined throwing it like a dart. Just a crazy fantasy. Even if he managed to stick the needle into Faraj somehow, the plunger wouldn't depress.

Kazemi turned his face toward Rees. The hopelessness in his expression came from some place far beyond fear. "I don't think I can do this. I just can't."

Rees tried to will strength into Kazemi with his eyes. "Listen to me. I've been injected with this drug. Okay? This very same drug. It won't kill you. But I promise you, this man will. Please. Let me do this."

Kazemi bit his lip and nodded gravely.

Rees injected Kazemi at the wrist, exactly as Faraj had injected him. He gently depressed the plunger, keeping a careful eye on the graduation marks.

One milliliter ... one point five ... two.

He pulled out the needle. A drop of blood beaded up on Kazemi's skin.

Kazemi must have sensed it was over. He turned back to Rees with the countenance of a man about to be hanged.

"It'll be all right," was all Rees could think to say.

Kazemi's face slackened. He rocked there on his knees a moment, then fell over backwards, his calves and feet bent awkwardly underneath him as he lay still on the café floor.

Sorry Professor. Wish I could say pleasant dreams. Rees looked back up at Faraj. "I don't suppose you have a clean needle? For him?" He indicated Osborn with a sideways jerk of his head.

"Sorry, no. We will just have to take our chances gentlemen."

Osborn was unbuttoning the cuff of his shirtsleeve as Rees turned to him. Then for some reason he started to rock back and forth.

A moment later Rees realized it wasn't Osborn who was rocking. It was *him*.

What the hell is happening?

A wave of dizziness had hit him. He suddenly felt on the verge of panic. He inhaled deeply through his nose, and tried to calm himself.

You've hardly eaten in forty-eight hours and you were drugged earlier today. You're just dizzy. That's all. Just dizzy.

Rees struggled to stay on his knees. There was no knowing what this lunatic would do to them all if he collapsed now. "I need ... I just need a second," he said.

He felt the syringe drop from his fingers. Then the floor rose up fast toward his face. He managed to get his hands beneath him in time to break the fall. The cool linoleum pressed against his cheek.

"Dr. Rees." Faraj's voice floated down from somewhere above him. "I will not tolerate games. If this is some kind of stratagem..."

It's not a stratagem you asshole. Rees silently gave himself a stern order. *Get up, get up! Right now, or you're gonna die down here.*

He brought his hands in close beneath his shoulders, to press himself upright. His fingers found Osborn's plastic shopping bag. Directly beneath him.

He could feel something through the plastic. A hard, rectangular outline.

The lectionary codex.

With vellum pages. Thick, leather pages. Hundreds of them stacked between two metal plates.

Rees felt for the edges of the codex through the plastic bag. Dug his fingers under them.

There. Got it.

He scooted his knees under him, and humped over the bag, keeping it hidden from view. "I'm all right," he said weakly. "I just got dizzy. Give me another second."

The gun would be trained on him. Rees hoped his first move would be inscrutable at least. No way to do all this in one, smooth motion.

He rose up, not so fast as to seem like a threat. And as he did, he pulled the bag and the codex up with him, close to his chest.

He looked across at Faraj's face. Confusion there.

That was the extra moment he needed.

Rees thrust his arms out and jammed the bag directly toward the gun.

He heard a loud *pop.* The codex jerked in his hands.

He pushed hard with his legs, using every atom of adrenaline-charged strength he had left. Driving himself straight toward the gun.

A second loud *pop*. Another shockwave ran up his arms.

He had his head tucked down behind the plastic bag. He couldn't see anything, but he felt it when the codex connected with his target.

Faraj had no time to brace himself. When Rees slammed into him, they both tumbled backward.

The two of them crash landed on something. Not the floor. Softer. The dead man.

They had fallen onto his body.

Faraj was still holding the gun, but Rees had ended up on top of him. He dropped the plastic bag and grabbed the weapon with both hands. Then he wracked Faraj's gun arm back and over his head, and smashed the gun against the floor. Once. Then again. Then again. Trying to knock it loose.

Rees's advantage lasted only a moment. His opponent was far more powerful. Faraj grabbed Rees's face and pushed hard. Rees's head arched back further and further, until it felt like his neck would break.

He desperately tried to find and pull the gun's trigger. He couldn't tell what direction the weapon was pointing, but it didn't matter. In this bizarre equation, he'd actually be better off regardless of which of them got killed here.

Rees was losing his grip on the gun. He squeezed his fingers over and over.

The gun *boomed* in his ear. He felt the heat flash on his face.

Rees rolled away and looked back.

Faraj lay there, still holding the gun. There was a lot of blood.

But he was moving.

Alive. The bastard was still alive.

Rees watched as Faraj sat up on the café floor. Blood gushed from his forehead. The bullet had grazed him there, tearing a deep horizontal gash. The white of his exposed skull was clearly visible.

Faraj swung the gun wildly, left and right, searching for his target, at the same time trying vainly to wipe the thick flowing blood out of his eyes.

Rees started to rush him, intending to kick the gun away.

Pop! Pop! Pop!

Faraj was firing blind now as he swept the gun back and forth across the room.

By pure chance he had missed both Rees and Osborn.

Rees decided to alter his plan.

He shouted to Osborn, "Get the hell out of here! Now!"

CHAPTER 63

DANNI CONTINUED ARTIFICIAL respiration on Morgan until the paramedics took over.

She'd established that Morgan still had a heartbeat. She had no experience checking pulses, but she could hardly find one even at Morgan's neck.

That had to be bad.

The paramedics stepped in without missing a beat. They rushed Morgan on a rolling stretcher to an emergency vehicle waiting outside.

Louis remained conscious throughout all of it. From what Danni could make of the paramedics' technical jargon, he'd taken a bullet in his right lung. Serious but survivable, is what they all seemed to think.

It didn't stop him from asking one of them to witness an oral last will and testament of some kind. Danni tuned out the details.

Outside, two of the paramedics loaded Morgan into the emergency vehicle as a second one pulled up.

Danni stood in the rain and watched as they climbed in there after her. "I need to go with her." She told a woman paramedic, who was closest to the opened rear doors.

The woman shook her head. "Sorry. Not on a siren run."

"We're married."

The woman locked part of the stretcher down with a lever that made a mechanical *clack*. She didn't even look up. "Sorry, can't do it."

Danni dug out her Lawrence Livermore ID and held it up. "Federal agent. Special Agent Morgan has information affecting national security. You're hindering my investigation. I'm gonna need your name."

The woman shifted around and locked down another point on the stretcher. *Clack.* Then she looked over at the ID.

"You're full of shit." She reached a hand down. "Get in."

ON THE WAY to the hospital, Morgan's heart went into V-fib. Ventricular fibrillation. Not stopped, just flailing uselessly.

Watching it all in the close space of the emergency vehicle's patient compartment, Danni felt like a ghost.

She was right there, but she could affect nothing. Nothing at all.

They intubated Morgan. One of the paramedics continued to squeeze oxygen into her with a flexible bag, while the other charged up an external defibrillator.

The high-pitched whine of the machine charging sounded like an electronic camera flash that Danni owned. She'd taken photos of Kerry using it. At the ruins of Sutro Baths on one foggy day in some other life.

Don't give up, Kerry. Don't you dare give up.

Danni remembered the dead DCIS agent back in Livermore. Outside the Core. Kerry had said the odds of restarting a heart were ten percent.

You have to make it, Kerry. You have to make it for both of us now.

After smearing some gel out of a tube onto Morgan's chest, the paramedic applied the paddles. "Clear!"

Morgan's body bucked off the stretcher.

The paramedics watched the lines on the green monitor. They didn't seem to like what they were seeing there.

One of them produced a horrifyingly long needle, and used it to inject adrenaline directly into Morgan's heart.

The other one charged up the defibrillator again.

They waited.

Danni the ghost watched. Watched and wished that time travel really was possible.

Because if it were, she would go back to that day at the beach, at Sutro Baths. She would bend the timelines of their two lives. Weave them together. Touching from that point forward, curled around each other like lovers limbs.

Then she would gently point their mutual course toward a safe, warm place. Far from crazy people and their insane ambitions.

"Clear!"

Morgan bucked again on the stretcher.

CHAPTER 64

REES HAD HIS arms full as he fled the café, hugging the gym bag he'd brought from the motel and the plastic bag with the artifacts. He shoved Osborn in the middle of the back with them, trying to rush him out the rear door.

There was nothing he could do for Kazemi lying unconscious back there. Plus, he had a strange sense that Faraj wouldn't bother with him. The man seemed to have some bizzaro morality about killing when he didn't deem it absolutely, positively necessary.

Just outside the door, Osborn stumbled and fell to his hands and knees in a puddle. Rees remembered the man's leg and the platform shoe.

Osborn wasn't going to run his way out of this.

Rees looked around through the dense rain, coming down in sheets now. He spotted a row of trash cans nearby—tucked into a dark corner behind the building, under the roadwork that formed the southern approach to the bridge.

Rees yanked Osborn to his feet and directed him toward the trash cans. "Get back behind there. I'll lead him away."

Osborn nodded once and headed for the cans without saying a word.

Rees threw the gym bag's strap over his head and across his chest like a sash, and tucked the plastic shopping bag under the other arm. Then he took off running.

As he hit the cement stairway to the observation area, something exploded in front of him. He pulled up in shock and confusion. Then he realized that must have been a bullet strike.

Rees didn't waste a second looking back. He leapt up the remaining stairs, taking them three at a time.

The observation area itself was empty. But not far off he could make out the lights of the toll plaza through the downpour. Bridge security over there. Probably California highway patrol too. Safety. If he could reach them.

Panting hard, Rees cut left on the sidewalk that bordered the roadway and sprinted toward those toll booths. His chest hurt so much now it felt like he was breathing in flames. And what started as a side stitch had turned to a knife in his ribs.

His lungs couldn't keep up with his body's oxygen demands. More evidence of that—his vision was starting to narrow. Myopia. He was probably going to black out soon.

He had to slow down or fall down, there wasn't any third choice. He dropped to a walk-trot and silently cursed himself for being so damn out of shape.

He dared a quick glance over his shoulder. No one back there. Just rain beating hard on the empty sidewalk. He might actually make it.

He was nearly within what he judged to be shouting distance of the toll plaza now. Maybe another thirty seconds to go.

Farther up the sidewalk ahead of him something was moving in the dense rain. He couldn't quite make it out. It was moving fast, though, and it seemed to be coming his way.

Rees stopped and watched as the figure resolved into the outline of a man. A man running.

Faraj. It had to be him.

He must have taken the roadway up from the parking lot instead of the footpath. And in doing that, he'd effectively blocked any approach by Rees to the toll plaza.

As Rees continued to watch, the running figure left the sidewalk and cut an acute angle eastward across the landscaping. Swinging out now to cover Rees's retreat back through the observation area.

Rees turned on his heels and jogged away. Miserably slowly, and still the best speed he could manage right now. He checked back over his shoulder every few steps.

Faraj was gaining on him quickly.

The 101 freeway ran just a few feet to his left. Even in this weather the cars were flying past him at fifty miles an hour or more. If he jumped the safety railing and tried to flag one down, he'd be flattened in seconds.

There was nowhere to go but straight ahead.

Onto the actual expanse of the Golden Gate Bridge.

It had to be a goddamn bridge.

Despite the growing fear, he pushed himself to jog faster. His legs felt like two tubes full of wet cement. Zero chance of outrunning his pursuer.

He was just going to have to think his way out of this.

Rees remembered hearing somewhere that the bridge was closed to pedestrians at night, to discourage suicides. *Like they need more discouragement*—was the bit of dark humor that had come to mind at the time.

It was still accessible to cyclists, though. He'd heard that too. So there had to be some kind of gate to buzz you through. And they'd need to have CCTV there to check you out. Probably there were cameras all over the bridge too.

Good, good, and good.

As soon as bridge security saw Rees on foot out here, they'd have to assume he was a jumper. They'd send the police out to stop him.

He just needed to stay alive till then.

Seconds later Rees did indeed spot a security gate up ahead.

Yes! I'm coming guys. A lonely jumper in the rain. You gotta save me now...

He pushed his legs until they felt on the verge of cramping. The he slid to a stop at the gate and slapped his hand on a button beside it.

A small camera peered down at him from above the gate's frame.

Rees waved his arms frantically at it. "Help! Help me! Help!" He had no idea if the camera was mic'd or not. It didn't matter. They'd get the message.

He glanced back behind him again. He could see Faraj more clearly now. And then he realized that he was trapped now. Shit. *Of course* they weren't going to buzz him through this gate.

He'd just have to climb it.

Rees threw the plastic bag over the gate. It landed on the other side and skittered to a stop. He started climbing after it. He had barely gotten off the walkway when a loud *clang* rang out. Sparks flew just inches to the left of his head.

The shot had barely missed him.

In a panic he scrambled to the top of the gate and slipped and fell down the other side, cracking his elbow hard on the walkway. An excruciating bolt of pain shot up his arm. Ignoring that, he scooped up the plastic bag lying next to him. Nothing seemed to have spilled out.

He leapt to his feet. As he began running again, Rees eyed the bridge's giant suspension cable. He could probably get to it, but he didn't know if he could force himself to walk on it. He might actually hyperventilate and pass out. Anyway, he'd be an easy target up there. No cover at all.

Upward wasn't the way out then, even if he could keep his fear in check.

Rees stopped running and brought the plastic bag up to his face, then clamped the top of it firmly in his teeth. He was going to need both hands for what he had in mind.

He threw a leg over the bridge's railing and straddled it. Looking down, he couldn't see past the raindrops that formed an illuminated curtain as they fell through the bridge's amber lights. For that, at least, he was immensely grateful. Strangely enough, it really helped.

He swung his other leg over the railing and lowered himself gently to a narrow steel perch about even with the bridge's deck. Four or five feet further below an enormous beam ran parallel to the roadway. Plenty wide enough to walk on. In theory. But so was that ledge outside the Mark Hopkins and he'd nearly bought the farm there.

It didn't matter. That's where he needed to get down to.

He was facing the center of the bridge, and to his left he spotted Faraj already over the pedestrian gate and barreling toward him through the rain. He must have seen Rees climbing out over the railing just now. Nothing could be done about that.

Rees began lowering himself down to that wider ledge. Halfway there.

Without warning, his fingers slipped off the wet rail.

He was falling.

A horrible weightless moment later his feet struck the lower beam and shot out from under him to the rear. His chest thumped metal. Hard. The plastic bag with the artifacts in it went flying.

Rees felt his legs swinging freely. Nothing beneath them, only his upper body lay on the ledge. And he was sliding backwards.

Sliding right off the bridge.

He swept his palms back and forth wildly on the wet metal, seeking any feature to grip. His fingers finally caught a groove, a seam of some kind. He dug in and halted the slide.

Pulling with all his strength, Rees hauled himself back onto the beam. As he lay there catching his breath, he saw the white plastic bag. Amazingly still on the ledge with him, a couple feet away. He grabbed it and pulled it in close.

From down here he could see all the way under the bridge. Another twenty or so feet below him, a series of crossbeams ran horizontally beneath the bridge deck. All the way to the west side of the span. If he traversed the underside of the bridge on one of those, then climbed back up ... he might be able to double back unseen to the toll plaza.

A slanting support beam provided the only route down there. Rees felt his guts go watery just thinking about it, but there was no other choice.

He'd need both arms again for this. He rolled the top of the bag up and chomped down on it once more and climbed out onto the steeply angled support beam. Hugging the iron like it was a long lost brother, Rees managed a terrifying shimmy.

Then the nausea hit. He was going to vomit.

And lose the bag in the bargain.

No. No, goddamnit no!

He made himself swallow his own gorge. Again and again. And he slid. Inches at a time. All the way down, down, down to the bridge's next level of construction.

He'd made it.

The raindrops scattered some of the amber roadway light under the deck. It was still very dark down here, but Rees could see well enough to find his way to one of those beams he'd seen running to the other side of the bridge.

The crossbeam itself looked to be a little more than two feet wide. Again, wide enough to walk it easily, if it you were talking about two lines painted on a sidewalk. But with a fall meaning certain death? Even without the risk of fainting, which was entirely real, he still wouldn't have chanced it.

Rees got down on his hands and knees and began to crawl. He inched his way out under the bridge deck and immediately discovered the cold metal was slick with the mist swirling under there. He slid his knees along the slippery surface rather than lift them.

He'd crawled maybe forty feet out onto the crossbeam when the now familiar voice came from behind him.

"I must compliment you on your determination, Dr. Rees."

He craned his neck to look back over his shoulder. Faraj was carefully walking the very beam Rees was on. In the low light the dark blood running down the man's face looked like black tar or motor oil.

Faraj could easily shoot Rees now. That he wasn't doing so revealed how badly he wanted Rees to pay for breaking their deal. Or how much he needed the artifacts. Or perhaps both.

One thing for sure, Rees couldn't outpace the man by crawling like this. He swallowed hard, sucked in a deep breath, blew it out.

And stood up.

The universe started to tilt. Rees made it stop with nothing but the force of his will. Fuel by his desire to live.

He had to live now. There was so much to live for...

"You have more grit than I gave you credit for, sir."

Without even looking back, Rees could tell Faraj was closer now than before.

Rees's hands were free, but he kept the white plastic bag gripped in his teeth, holding his arms out for balance. It wasn't like he needed to chat with this maniac anyway.

He moved by stepping forward with his right foot, then scooting the left foot up behind it. Doing this over and over. He didn't want to risk swinging one leg out past the other, not if he could avoid it.

As he progressed farther out under the bridge deck, Rees began to see some kind of vertical crisscross bracing blocking the way up ahead. When he got a little closer, he spotted a gap in the lattice. Maybe fifteen feet up from the beam he was on.

It looked like he could fit through it.

Behind him Faraj began to wax philosophical. "The fear you feel right now, the terror—it teaches you how wonderful are the dull everyday moments in life. Yes? We need the dark to appreciate the light, Dr. Rees. That's want I wanted to show you. You can see that now, I'm sure."

Rees had arrived at that crisscross bracing. He grasped two handholds over his head. With the plastic bag still in his teeth, he started up it like he was climbing a giant iron trellis. One that happened to be more than twenty stories up in the air.

Just like going up a ladder. That's all. Just one move at a time.

Step up, take new handholds.

There, see? Not so hard.

Step up again. Reach a little higher.

Step up again.

Almost to that gap now...

Rees felt a hand clamp onto his right ankle. The bolt of fear up his leg like he'd stepped on a felled power line.

He looked down.

Faraj's bloody face looked back up at him. "I don't wish to pull you off this bridge, Dr. Rees. So, please, come down now. Please."

Rees tried to shake his leg free, but Faraj had a grip like a bulldog's bite. It wasn't going to happen.

"Keep that up and you're going to fall, sir," Faraj warned with what sounded like genuine concern.

He really doesn't want me to die here, Rees thought. *It would spoil his party.*

Faraj had pulled Rees's right leg off its foothold and he continued to tug hard on it. Rees's weight rested almost entirely on his left foot now.

A bizarre thought went through his head. That this was why a lizard's tail evolved to snap free. In order to escape predators.

Caudal autonomy, it was called. Sadly, he couldn't just give Faraj his leg and race away.

No. But I can give him more of it than the bastard wants...

"All right. All right, I'm coming down." Rees took the plastic bag from his teeth. He needed a better grip on it, or he might lose it when he made his move. He stuck his right arm through the handle holes and slid the bag up to his elbow. Then he re-gripped the metal bracing.

"Carefully, Dr. Rees. Climb carefully." Faraj hadn't eased up the tension on Rees's right leg at all.

He was still reeling in his catch.

Good. You just keep on pulling hard down there.

Leaving his left foot just where it was, Rees lowered his handholds one at a time. And crouched down. Then he grabbed two lower handholds and crouched down even more.

He was in a deep squat now.

Coiled up.

All the weight still resting on that left foot.

Faraj continued to pull on Rees's cocked right leg.

Rees gripped his two handholds as tightly as he could.

You want that leg, huh? You want it? All right ... take it!

Rees popped his left foot off its toehold, explosively uncurled both legs, and let himself drop until he was hanging full length, straight-armed from the bracing.

With no tension to pull against, Faraj fell back and away. He flailed his arms for something higher up to grab.

And snagged the plastic bag hanging from Rees's elbow.

The force of the big man jerking to a halt tore Rees's right hand loose from the bracing.

He kept his right arm bent like a hook, to stop the bag from sliding off. Both feet hanging in space now. Nothing but his left hand's grip keeping them both from a fatal fall.

Down below Rees, Faraj was leaned way out over the bay. Thirty degrees or more from vertical, feet hinging on the sharp edge of the crossbeam.

Rees looked down at the white plastic bag dangling from the crook of his right elbow. Faraj's dark hand gripped the other end. It was the *only* thing stopping the big man from toppling off the beam.

Reese's mind flashed on the artifacts in that bag. What it had cost to have them. Everything that they could change.

But he could feel the fingers in his left hand starting to slip, and knew exactly what he had to do.

There was no other way.

Faraj was looking up at him now. He seemed to know what Rees had decided and his green eyes burned with hate.

"You go back to hell," Rees said.

He unbent his right arm and let the bag slip off past his hand.

Still clutching the precious bag, Faraj fell away from him like a tree chopped at the base.

He didn't scream.

From Rees's perspective, watching from directly above, Faraj seemed to fall in slow motion. His body growing smaller and smaller, spinning slowly and shrinking. Until the only thing still visible was the white dot of the plastic bag.

And then that vanished too.

Gone. Faraj was gone for good this time.

And the dearly won artifacts along with him. All of it gone forever.

Rees felt like he wanted to cry or maybe scream out in anger and frustration. But he couldn't. He was just too drained.

Inside there was nothing left.

CHAPTER 65

REES DIDN'T HAVE to wait long for bridge security and the police to show up. They had probably mobilized right after they saw him on the camera back by the pedestrian gate.

They insisted that he stay put down there, and he saw no reason to argue. He was too cold and shaking far too much. Probably couldn't manage the crawl back from the center of the bridge's underside on his own anyway.

The rescue squad from the Southern Marin Fire Protection District arrived next with climbing ropes and a safety harness.

While he waited for them to reach him, Rees took out his wallet and surreptitiously dropped it into the bay. He wanted to buy himself at least a little time before they figured out who he was. Who knows, it might come in handy.

Soon they had him back up on the bridge deck, where the rain had diminished to a light drizzle.

Strangely, his fear of the bridge was gone. He felt ... empty. That's all. He might as well have been standing in the middle of the Great Plains. Had he just been cured of his lifelong phobia? Well, how about that. He'd have to patent that little procedure. *Lose your fear of heights in one night!*

He managed a bitter smile at the thought.

Soaking wet and with his hair plastered down flat, Rees wasn't immediately recognized. The crazy grin probably helped there. Anyway *he* was the victim here, running for his life from a man with a gun. Bridge security would have seen that much on their monitors and told the police about it. That might be partly why they weren't scrutinizing him very closely.

Rees had decided it would be wise still to say nothing at all from this point forward. Not until he could contact a good lawyer. So he remained entirely silent as the police asked their questions. The paramedics soon stepped in to inform the officers that their man here was clearly in shock.

It wasn't very far from the truth.

He had no thoughts of making some kind of daring escape, going back on the run. He was far too tired and discouraged. This despite the fact they were probably going to lock him up for a very long time. Espionage, murder, treason. Who knows what else his enemies would frame him with?

We lost. No artifacts. No time-recordings. Nothing. No way to corroborate our side of the story at all. It's over.

REES FOUND HIMSELF lying on a stretcher in the back of an emergency rescue vehicle for the second time in as many days. Different police officer this time, though. It was a pity Officer Honeycutt wasn't there. Rees would've enjoyed seeing the look on his face.

An image of Kerry Morgan popped into his head. He hoped she was all right. San Francisco General seemed like an excellent hospital. She would be getting the best possible care there.

Rees noticed the blue gym bag lying nearby him in the back of the emergency vehicle, the one he'd taken with him from the motel room. One of the rescue workers must have tossed it in there with them.

The mystery of the food diary still ate at him, even now.

He wanted to see it one last time, before they confiscated everything. He decided to risk speaking. Curiosity, ever his defining trait, won out over fear that saying anything at all was still a bad idea.

Rees checked the nametag on the officer accompanying him to the hospital, and cleared his throat. "Officer Dover, can I have my diary, please? It's in that blue bag down there."

The police officer looked surprised and understandably puzzled. It probably seemed like an odd way for Rees to break his complete silence.

Dover tried asking Rees questions again, as he had back on the bridge.

Rees just kept repeating, over and over, but softly and politely: *Can I have my bag please?*

After a minute or so Officer Dover turned to the two EMTs. "Is that all right with you guys?"

They had no objections.

Dover started inspecting the bag—probably looking for weapons or anything dangerous. Seconds later his eyes went wide. He pulled out the thick stack of cash and showed it to Rees.

"This is yours, sir?"

"Yes," Rees answered calmly. It didn't even feel like lying. Faraj surely owed him that much. And *he* certainly wasn't going to need it anymore.

The officer put the money into an evidence bag, and explained to Rees that they would keep it for the time being. Then he handed the gym bag over.

Rees reached in and removed the food diary.

Whatever that is, it's not insanity. This much I know. Kazemi's words coming back to him.

He thumbed through the pages, flipping them back and forth, hoping some pattern would jump out at him.

Nothing did.

If he just had more time and the right resources, maybe he could crack whatever code or cipher Fischer had used here. Find the actual time-recordings. They were only half the picture, yes, but they would certainly be helpful in court.

He returned the food diary to the gym bag and noticed the one odd scientific paper in there again. He'd glanced at it briefly in his room at the Mark Hopkins. The only paper in Fischer's pouch that wasn't his own work.

Something to do with DNA synthesis.

He pulled that out again and read the title.

Next-Generation Digital Information Storage in DNA.

It was research from Harvard Medical School's Department of Genetics. Lead researcher, George M. Church.

And then he heard Fischer's voice. A moment from their short conversation on the wharf...

They think they've destroyed all my work, but it's still right here in my DNA. Oddly enough, we owe that one to church.

Suddenly it was so obvious. We owe that one to Church. Not church.

Fischer had been making a little joke.

Rees skimmed through the paper's opening abstract. Its authors had achieved petabyte-sized storage in a fraction of a gram of DNA, suspended in a liquid medium.

That meant the totality of the Kafir Project data—all five hundred exabytes—could easily be stored in a vial of...

Rees yanked the food diary back out of the bag. What was it Kazemi said, on the way to the UPS store? Something Fischer had told him repeatedly.

Ink and paper. That's how we'll beat them. Ink and paper.

And they had!

Rees opened the diary again.

There it was, staring him right in the face. The scratchy-looking handwriting. That was from an old-fashioned fountain pen nib. He'd owned one himself once. You filled them yourself, with your own choice of ink.

Fischer had filled his with a *very* special ink.

He'd employed a form of steganography here. Secret messages embedded in other documents. Hidden in plain sight for anyone with the skill to decode them.

Fischer had encoded all five hundred exabytes of the Kafir Project data into the base pairs of synthetic DNA strands, and then suspended them in ink.

Then he scratched that ink into the pages of the diary with an old fountain pen.

The time-recordings. The now lost artifacts' identifying atomic signatures. All that precious data.

All of it...

It was right here in his hand.

CHAPTER 66

Four months later—San Francisco

"THERE'S NO TIME, Rees." Danni sounded close to panicking.

To her half-naked back Rees said, "If you don't hold still, I'm going to stab you."

"All right, just hurry up."

Rees pulled the two panels of the dress together and held them with one hand while he whip-stitched the top closed. He knotted the thread and bit it off. "I think if I stitch it again in the middle here—"

"Shh, shh, quiet." Danni froze. Then she thumped her foot. "The music's started!"

Rees laughed. "That's just the welcome music. Jesus, Danni, you weren't this nervous when we found a gunman in your kitchen."

"Well, I was armed then. Hey, that's it. If I get Kerry's gun and shoot the organist, that'll buy us time till they find another one."

"Good thinking," Rees said.

Rees tried to work fast, but the dress needed two more stitch points at least to forestall a wardrobe malfunction going down the aisle.

He was tying off the last and lowest point—his face about level with Danni's rear end—when Morgan stepped into the vestibule.

"I knew it," Morgan said. "This started while I was still blind right?"

"Funny. Ha, ha. My damn zipper broke," Danni threw a backward nod to Rees, "and this guy is trying to sew me a whole new outfit. How much time do we have?"

Morgan casually folded her arms. "Well, since you and I are both out here, I really don't think we're going to miss the ceremony."

Rees stepped back to inspect the repair on Danni's wedding dress. "That works," he said.

To his eye, the garment just looked like it had hooks in the back now instead of a zipper. The dress itself was fun and a little daring. It suited Danni perfectly.

Danni turned to face Rees. "Is it gonna hold?"

He shrugged. "It's a little slipshod, but it should last at least as long as the marriage. I mean the ceremony."

Danni shot him a withering look. "Wow, you two are just hilarious today."

Morgan stepped over to the full length mirror.

Rees watched her turning around to check all the angles of her ensemble. She wore a flowing, cobalt blue dress that complimented her dark brown hair and light complexion. He'd always found her attractive, but dressed to the nines like this— she was really a knockout.

"You look ... stunning, Kerry," Rees said.

Morgan smiled. "Thanks. You don't have to sound so shocked." She turned to Danni. "Hey, before I forget, your father wanted to know if it's okay to take flash pictures. And to get up and move around during the ceremony. And to take some reaction shots of the guests. He'd also like to go over our vows and make suggestions for changes."

Danni laughed. "That wouldn't surprise me."

She came over to stand beside Morgan in front of the mirror. They looked in the glass at each other. Morgan took Danni's hand.

Danni burst into a huge grin. "It's really happening."

Morgan nodded. "If it's not, Gevin flew out from D.C. for nothing."

Rees huffed out a small laugh. "I'd have flown here for lunch at this point. I needed to get away. Senate hearings are not as fun and relaxing as everybody says they are."

"Yeah. I've been watching on C-SPAN," Danni said. "They're a bunch of idiots. Some of them, the questions they were asking—it's like they're suggesting you made all this up. You and Fischer."

No, it's not like that," Rees said. "It *is* that. It's exactly that. And on the one hand, they're entitled to their doubts. On the other hand ... they're idiots."

Danni's reflection smiled at Rees.

Morgan was studying her hair in the mirror now. It was still shorter than she usually kept it. It hadn't completely grown out since the last surgery.

"I heard a rumor they're extraditing Carl Truby from Hong Kong," she said.

Rees had heard it too. "Even the Chinese don't want him. It didn't help him that most of the non-extradition countries out there are Muslim theocracies."

"Gee, what rotten luck, huh?" Morgan didn't sound particularly disturbed by Truby's misfortune. "Maybe now we get to see farther up the food chain. Meet some of the mystery people he really works for."

The same idea had occurred to Rees. He thought the very possibility of that happening was probably a death sentence for Truby. So be it.

"Did they figure out who burned Truby?" Danni had her back to the mirror and she was peering over her shoulder at Rees's sewing job now.

Rees shook his head. "No. Except it's connected to the same shadow organization Truby hired to kill Fischer. And us.

They turned on him for some reason. We'll probably never know exactly why."

Danni smiled at the back of her dress in the mirror. "Hey, that doesn't look half bad, Gevin."

"Neither do you two." He started for the door. "Can't wait to see you both walking down the aisle, paving the way for humans to marry dogs. That's what comes next, right?"

Danni shot back. "So says the man who's trying to discredit the world's great religions."

"Hey, I just want to rebuild the time-viewing technology. That's all. You know, Pat Robertson says it's actually a gift from God. He says it will prove everything he believes."

"That gays cause hurricanes?" Danni asked.

Rees laughed. "Something like that, yeah."

As he left them to make their final preparations, Rees's thoughts turned unexpectedly to his sister.

Anna loved weddings. She would have loved this one in particular. It still hurt. It always would. That was the price of risking intimacy. It was a price Rees was again willing to pay.

Just the week before he'd finally located the quote he'd been trying to remember for months. Bob Marley:

The truth is, everyone is going to hurt you. You just got to find the ones worth suffering for.

Rees was pretty sure he'd found them.

CHAPTER 67

OUTSIDE THE CHURCH it was a surprisingly warm April day for San Francisco. There were still a few minutes left to enjoy the sunshine before the ceremony began, and Rees had never been as fond of warm weather as he was these days.

He stood basking in the sun with a few of the other wedding guests—who were chatting or grabbing a last cigarette—and took in the front of the old brown brick building.

The Episcopal Church of St. John the Evangelist didn't look particularly impressive from the outside. The architecture was rather understated. But inside the structure, the airy, vaulted nave and magnificent stained-glass windows gave it a sense of venerated tradition.

They conducted formal high mass there on Sundays, he'd been told. Swinging incense censers and ringing bells. The priest made calls and the congregation chanted responses. And anyone at all could get up and take communion.

Anyone.

Gay or straight. Christian or not. Believer or skeptic.

That last part said it all to Rees. Inclusivity. No lines drawn in the sand. No theological walls to stand on and hurl rocks down upon the unbelievers. It was the kind of church Rees hoped would someday be much more commonplace. Because of what Fischer had done.

Danni picked it out. Her mother, it seems, had always dreamed of a Catholic wedding for her only daughter. Of course this wasn't quite that. But when Rees had seen the woman just a few minutes before, her eyes looked moist and she was clearly over the moon with joy.

Rees's thoughts were interrupted by the sight of a man walking toward him up the sidewalk. Walking with a pronounced limp.

"Hello, Dr. Rees." Randy Osborn smiled warmly. "Don't you clean up nicely."

Rees smiled back. "Randy. What a great surprise."

The two men shook hands and regarded each other silently for a few moments.

"I didn't know you were coming," Rees said. "Are you sticking around for the reception? There are a few things I'd really like to discuss with you."

"Yes, I heard about CERN. Replicating Fischer's work with the Large Hadron Collider. An ambitious idea. Sorry they rejected your proposal."

"It's the artifacts. Or rather the lack of them. I need something that shows a signature match to the time-recordings we recovered. That's evidence that can't be faked."

"And you think it would tip things your way?"

"That's why I'm assembling an expedition to revisit some of Joshua Amsel's digs. We'll be looking for a needle in a haystack without the guidance technology Fischer developed for him. But I think it's worth a shot."

"You are as ever the optimist."

"People want to know, Randy. In the end they just want to know. Is this real? Is this all true? You can't suppress human curiosity."

"Maybe not. But you can sure try," Osborn added with a hard smile.

Rees understood. There had been resistance to his efforts from behind the scenes. From influential people who wanted the world to remain forever in ignorance of its true past. Most likely the same powers Carl Truby had once represented.

"I have some ideas there too," Rees said. "I'll tell you more at the reception."

"Sorry, I'm not staying for the wedding. I just came to see you. I'm off to meet Professor Kazemi now."

Rees nodded. "How's he doing these days?"

"Better. Still has some bad nights. But overall, better."

"Give him my best," Rees said.

"I will." Osborn reached into the pocket of his jacket and pulled out a little box wrapped in plain brown paper. "The other reason I came by." He held it out for Rees. "A gift."

Rees accepted it. Very light, whatever it was. "I'll put it with the other presents."

"That's for you, actually."

"For me?"

Osborn's expression grew serious. "Yes. For saving my life that night. I never really thanked you properly."

"Oh, well..." Rees felt his face flush and glanced away. He was surprised and strangely embarrassed too. He met the other man's eyes again and gave him a single nod.

"May I tell you a quick story before I go?" Osborn asked.

"Of course."

"The Apollo 11 astronauts undertook a goodwill tour back in 1969. Presenting moon rocks to foreign leaders. At the time these were the rarest stones on earth. Each one worth millions, at least. Well, a few years ago some geologist in Holland discovered the moon rock on display in the Rijksmuseum was just an ordinary piece of petrified wood."

"Stolen from the museum and replaced with a fake?"

Osborn shook his head. "No. The chunk of petrified wood precisely matched photos of the stone presented by the astronauts. It's the very same rock."

"Well that's ... odd, to say the least."

"The thing is," Osborn said, "all those moon rocks passed through the hands of dozens of NASA scientists. Men who were not at all times supervised. Men scraping by on government salaries." Osborn's serious expression melted away. He smiled and offered Rees his hand. "Good luck with your quest, Gevin. And give my best wishes to the new couple."

"I will do that." Rees said, as they shook hands good-bye.

REES HAD JUST seated himself back in the nave when Louis plopped down next to him. The ceremony would be starting any moment now.

Louis leaned in close. "Was that Randy Osborn I saw out there leaving?"

"Yes, he's in town to see Kazemi."

"Another present for the ladies?" Louis was looking down at the little box still in Rees's hand.

"Uh, no. Osborn gave it to me."

"Really. Well, what is it?"

"I have no idea, Louis. I haven't opened it yet."

Louis rolled his eyes. "Well open it already. I want to see what it is."

"Of course," Rees said apologetically. "How rude of me."

He peeled off the tape and pulled back the wrapping paper, revealing a white cardboard box. About the right size for a small piece of jewelry.

He lifted off the top.

Cotton packing inside there. Rees pulled that out. The little box was empty. Was this supposed to be a joke?

"At least he didn't spend too much," Louis said.

The organist switched tunes and began playing a march by Tchaikovsky. Heads turned toward the back of the church. Rees turned to look too.

Danni and her father entered the church first, followed by Morgan and her father.

Morgan was smiling, making eye-contact with friends and family.

Danni's eyes sparkled with tears. And her own smile could have ignited that fusion reactor back at Livermore.

Rees realized he was still holding the little gift box and its cotton packing. He started to reassemble it all, to tuck it into his coat pocket.

His fingers felt something hard there within the cotton. He looked more closely at it.

He must have accidentally taken two pieces of cotton packing out of the box together, with something solid sandwiched between them.

He peeled the two pieces of cotton apart.

There on the bottom layer sat a small, gray stone. Porous. It looked volcanic. Pumice maybe?

A crazy thought passed through Rees's head, that he was holding the missing moon rock from Osborn's story.

Then his breath caught. With a rush of excitement, he understood what Osborn had been telling him. The low-salaried scientists handling priceless materials. How one of them appeared to have stashed away a piece of the treasure for himself.

Rees looked up at the life-sized crucifix mounted on the wall up behind the altar, at the figure of the man suspended there in agony. Then he looked back down at the little gray shard nestled within the cotton batting.

That wasn't pumice.

It wasn't any kind of rock at all.

It was an ancient fragment of bone.

The Kafir Project is a work of speculative fiction. However, the history and science portrayed herein are all based on peer-reviewed, academic research. The most significant of these titles have been listed below.

SELECTED BIBLIOGRAPHY

Braun, S., J. P. Ronzheimer, M. Schreiber, S. S. Hodgman, T. Rom, I. Bloch, and U. Schneider. *"Negative Absolute Temperature for Motional Degrees of Freedom."* Science 339, no. 6115 (2013): 52-55.

Church, George M., Yuan Gao, and Sriram Kosuri. *Next-Generation Digital Information Storage in DNA.* Science 337, no. 6102, pg. 1628. August 16, 2012.

Coote, Robert B., and Mary P. Coote. *Power, Politics, and the Making of the Bible: An Introduction.* Minneapolis: Fortress Press, 1990.

Cross, Frank Moore. *Canaanite Myth and Hebrew Epic; Essays in the History of the Religion of Israel.* Cambridge, Mass.: Harvard University Press, 1973.

Crossan, John Dominic. *Who Killed Jesus?: Exposing the Roots of Anti-semitism in the Gospel Story of the Death of Jesus.* San Francisco: HarperSanFrancisco, 1995.

Dever, William G. *Who Were the Early Israelites, and Where Did They Come From?* Grand Rapids, Mich.: William B. Eerdmans Pub., 2003.

Ehrman, Bart D. *How Jesus Became God: The Exaltation of a Jewish Preacher from Galilee.* New York: HarperCollins, 2014.

Eissfeldt, Otto. *El And Yahweh.* Journal of Semitic Studies 1, no. 1 (1956): 25-37.

Finkelstein, Israel, and Neil Asher Silberman. *The Bible Unearthed: Archaeology's New Vision of Ancient Israel and the Origin of Its Sacred Texts.* New York: Free Press, 2001.

Festinger, Leon. *A Theory of Cognitive Dissonance.* Stanford, Calif.: Stanford University Press, 1962.

Komarnitsky, Kris D. *Doubting Jesus' Resurrection: What Happened in the Black Box?* Drapper, Utah: Stone Arrow Books, 2009.

Luxenberg, Christoph. *The Syro-Aramaic Reading of the Koran: A Contribution to the Decoding of the Language of the Koran.* Verlag Hans Schiler, 2007.

Lüling, Günter. *A Challenge to Islam for Reformation: The Rediscovery and Reliable Reconstruction of a Comprehensive Pre-Islamic Christian Hymnal Hidden in the Koran under Earliest Islamic Reinterpretations.* New Delhi: Motilal Banarsidass, 2003.

Mullen, E. Theodore. *The Divine Council in Canaanite and Early Hebrew Literature.* Chico, Calif.: Scholars Press, 1980.

Ohlig, Karl. *The Hidden Origins of Islam: New Research into Its Early History.* Amherst, N.Y.: Prometheus Books, 2010.

Price, Robert M. *The Empty Tomb: Jesus beyond the Grave.* Amherst, N.Y.: Prometheus Books, 2005.

Redford, Donald B. *Egypt, Canaan, and Israel in Ancient times.* Princeton, N.J.: Princeton University Press, 1992.

ADDENDUM

For updated research and news about the book or the author, and burnings of the book (or the author) go to:

kafirproject.com

or

https://www.facebook.com/thekafirproject

And if you enjoyed The Kafir Project, please take a minute to stop by Amazon.com and/or goodreads.com to put up an embarrassingly glowing review.

Many thanks,
Lee Burvine

Made in the USA
Middletown, DE
03 October 2016